Tropéano's Gun

Tropéano's Gun

An Aliette Nouvelle Mystery

John Brooke

Cover design by Terry Gallagher/Doowah Design.
Photograph of John Brooke by Anne Laudouar.

Printed and bound in Canada by Hignell Printing.

Author's Note: Many of the locations in this novel are fictional, although those familiar with the area may notice more than a passing resemblance to actual places.

We acknowledge the support of The Canada Council for the Arts and the Manitoba Arts Council for our publishing program.

Library and Archives Canada Cataloguing in Publication

Brooke, John, 1951 August 27-, author
    Tropéano's gun / John Brooke.

(An Aliette Nouvelle mystery)
Issued in print and electronic formats.
ISBN 978-1-927426-54-8 (pbk.).--ISBN 978-1-927426-55-5 (epub)

    I. Title. II. Series: Brooke, John, 1951 August 27- Aliette Nouvelle mystery.

PS8553.R6542T76 2014   C813'.54   C2014-905450-5
                                                C2014-905451-3

Signature Editions, P.O. Box 206, RPO Corydon
Winnipeg, Manitoba, R3M 3S7
www.signature-editions.com

to Annie
encore et toujours
for love and support

The saddest thing that can happen to a person is to find out their memories are lies.

— Juan Gabriel Vásquez
The Sound of Things Falling

PROLOGUE

'I am amazed and not a little dismayed, Inspector.' Divisional Commissaire Gael Doquès, Directeur du Service Régional de Police Judiciaire, was referring to the quaint Saint-Etienne Walther P38 dangling from his uncomprehending fingers. He meant *Chief* Inspector, formally speaking, but the Divisionnaire tended to speak down when he wasn't happy. And how could the boss be happy when embarrassed by a very avoidable professional lapse resulting in a tragedy? How could he not be slightly flabbergasted when presented with this clunky artifact? The thing was at least thirty years old, and could be fifty. Like a prop from some black-and-white film.

He wondered aloud whether it still fired.

Chief Inspector Aliette Nouvelle admitted that she hadn't oiled it recently.

Ever? She'd received it upon graduation from the police academy in Bordeaux close to twenty years before this uncomfortable day and had promptly stowed it in the back of her underwear drawer. And left it there. She didn't want it. Didn't need it. Which was the point.

Her point, at any rate.

She was not going to reveal where it had been stored, or how long. No, she would stand on her record. One does not progress to Chief Inspector on the strength of bad results.

Neither would she ever claim to be perfect.

Still and all, the fact was, Chief Inspector Nouvelle had arrived at this juncture without once having fired her gun. There were many guns involved in the course of her professional journey. Obviously and inevitably. She accepted that. Everyone has a role to play. She always considered her role to be more on the strategic level—even when face to face with the criminal element.

The Commissaire's point: 'So let's be clear. For the record, yes?
You were not carrying your sidearm on the occasion of the murder
of Agent Tessier.'

'No.'

'Not to mention, the fugitive remains at large.'

The inspector nodded. The Commissaire waited.

She mumbled, 'No.'

'Why not?'

Of course he was going to ask. For the record.

She had been rehearsing her reply for weeks, ever since receiving the
official directive ordering her presence here. She'd received it months ago,
actually. The incident had happened in July. They had dealt with Sergio
Reggari, who had served as Instructing Judge in the affair, way back in
August. Aliette herself had already made two trips here to Division to
say her bit, but they delayed her reprimand until the official enquiry
was completed, all search efforts exhausted. DST Agent Margot Tessier
had not been found. She could even be alive, travelling with a swarthy
Dutch-born ex-Israeli soldier who made beautiful omelettes—though
anyone who'd met him (and Tessier) would have to doubt it. That had
taken them through to mid-December. Yes, then the holidays, when
everything stops. The new year never starts quickly. Next week it would
be February. Chief Inspector Nouvelle had never been a priority.

On the two-hour drive from Saint-Brin to Montpellier she had
fine-tuned her response, honed it to essentials.

Now it fell apart. 'Because I have never ... I mean to say, I don't
believe in ... I mean to say, a gun has never really fit with ... with my
way of doing things. With all due respect, sir.'

'Well there's the rub, Inspector. You have no respect.'

For rules, for operational procedure. He rattled off the relevant
clauses from the code.

And what was with this antique gun? Clearly, she had ignored
the system-wide service arms recall and upgrade. Wilfully, or through
carelessness? The Commissaire frowned grimly.

Was this the end? Was she looking at a future in industrial security?

Gael Doquès pushed a button on his phone system, muttered
a command. He sighed in the way an exasperated commander will.
'Luckily—for you, I mean—*we* have respect, Inspector.'

He was still forgetting to add Chief. Deliberately? Aliette yearned to correct him.

She didn't dare.

He folded his hands on his desk. 'We respect what you've accomplished.' Were it otherwise, would she be sitting here today? 'We know you are a capable investigator. Though your leadership skills and judgement have been exposed as wanting, we have faith you can pick up the pieces and move forward...' Now he even smiled.

A knock on the door. '*Entrez*!' A techie entered. No uniform, sleeves rolled up, hands had just been washed but dark smudges were still apparent. His eyes bulged with honest astonishment when Gael Doquès proffered the old gun with a mordant shrug. 'Can we re-fit the inspector?'

The techie took the gun and exited.

Doquès continued. '...And we are prepared to help you make the transition.'

The inspector nodded, bowing slightly, trying to show him she was grateful.

There was a cool nod in return. Then an impasse: two professionals with nothing in common but a mistake. Doquès made a show of perusing his notes, Aliette looked out at cars passing in Rue du Comté-de-Melgueil till there was another brief rap on the door and the techie glided back in proffering a large zip-lock evidence bag. The Commissaire received it. The man left soundlessly. Turning to the inspector, handing the package across the table, the Commissaire instructed, 'Consider yourself upgraded.' Adding, 'Choose a holster that suits. Send a requisition.'

She sat with the package on her lap like a baby, staring through plastic at a brand new flat-black SIG Sauer SP2022. A detached silencer. Two complimentary cartridges.

'You will wear it on duty. And practice, Inspector. Regularly. Like everyone else. Yes?'

'Of course.'

'And there's a program we'd like you to attend. For support?' Doquès held out a business card. 'This woman has been working with us for several years now. She has helped some of our best people get back on track.' A patient smile. 'We know it's tough out there. You're not the only one. Are you?'

'No.' Impossible to be the only one. Surely, somewhere in France was another cop who thought like her.

'It's about fitting with the program, Inspector.' He meant: Guns are part of what we do.

She perused the card. PsychoDynamo … Catchy.

Gabrielle Gravel, Doctor in Psychology. Psychotherapist. World Technique Practitioner.

Her services included Analytical, Behavioural and Support Therapy, Family Systems Therapy and Life Coaching.

The inspector wondered which one of those she was. And World Technique Practitioner? What did that mean?

There was no chance to ask, and she sensed her Divisionnaire neither knew nor very much cared. The meeting was over. Gael Doquès stood, extended a hand. 'Good luck, Inspector.'

He meant, We'll be watching. Closely.

'*Merci.*'

Part 1

Question d'attitude

~ I ~

FRIDAY IN TOWN

The voice at PsychoDynamo informed her, somewhat brusquely, that Gabrielle Gravel conducted initial investigative consultations Fridays from eleven till one. It took half an hour.

'I'm actually calling from Saint-Brin. I have a very busy schedule. Is there not a—'

'That's not my problem. Your name?'

'Nouvelle ... Chief ...' No. 'Madame Nouvelle. Are you Gabrielle?'

'No!'

Sorry ... The inspector opened her agenda and flipped to Friday. She had three morning meetings in the city pencilled in. 'Half past twelve then?'

'Fine.' And the call was abruptly ended.

'You have a nice day too, madame ...' replacing the phone, already seriously dubious of the World Technique, not looking forward to this at all.

There was also the matter of hellish city traffic. Her now well-used city map put Rue Argence in an enclave not far from Place de la Madeleine, which was pleasantly walkable from either the courthouse or the police building, her regular stops when in town on business. She had done it from both, in search of something interesting for lunch. If she parked at the north end of Boulevard d'Angleterre, a relatively uncongested and direct route in and out of town, she could complete the day's circle on foot and make her getaway from there.

Bon: she would walk to her consultation and save herself the agony of a crawl through the medieval maze that was the clogged heart of Béziers.

On Friday morning Aliette found a spot on the boulevard near Cimetière Vieux, the old city burial ground. Positioning her police parking permit clearly on the dashboard, she walked twenty minutes through the morning crowds to Hôtel de Police. The city's central police station was a workaday three-storey box in Place du Général de Gaulle. The National Police services occupied the major part of the facility, with the Béziers detachment of the Police Judiciaire relegated to a corner of the third floor. It was not only guns that had been upgraded for improved efficiencies. Following the system-wide reorganization, Aliette's regional counterparts were now also headquartered here. Chief Inspector Nouvelle could have been too, if not for the emotion-burdened moment of her transfer from the north. Needing distance, she had been granted permission to keep her operations based at Saint-Brin.

Why not? The cost-efficiencies balanced out.

And there was always a spare office at HQ. Aliette took off her coat, set up her desk, fetched coffee and brioche from the canteen on the second floor, had another look at the notes supplied by her Inspector Magui Barthès, then called down to the holding cells in the basement. A young woman who worked at a goat cheese enterprise was accused of murdering her employer's wife. One Justine Péraud.

She was escorted up, haggard from lack of sleep, still in a state of shock from her action. A uniformed officer waited as the inspector conducted an initial interview. Difficult. Sad. On the face of it, a crime of passion. But perhaps not. A stubborn girl, defiant in her sense of righteous love.

The inspector was gathering her things back into her bag when Chief Inspector Nabil Zidane sloped by the partially open door, file folder under his arm, headed for his corner suite. He noticed her, nodded a weary *bonjour*.

'*Ça va*, Nabi?'

He stopped at the door, offered a shrug.

Nabil Zidane was Aliette Nouvelle's PJ equal in terms of rank, but as head of the city squad—twenty inspectors to her two—he was, in effect, the most powerful police officer in the region. But stress has no respect for power.

Nabi was fiftyish, with a wiry six-foot frame, slightly stooped as if on perpetual alert. The deep lines across his brow bespoke his years in a tough and dirty city. A narrowing widow's peak, but the better part of his lushly inky, swirly hair had survived the wars. A long, broad Moorish nose projected the strength he kept to himself. It also marked him as a man from the southern side of the Mediterranean. A soft thing always anchoring the gaze beaming from his perfectly round eyes hinted at a cop who would rather talk than shoot.

After all, with five children and a busy dentist wife, Nabi was a family man at heart.

That morning his normally copper skin had an almost grey tinge to it. He looked scared. 'Monty's not getting anywhere with this.'

Lieutenant Hugues Monty was the city's highest-ranking National Police investigator.

'Getting anywhere with what?'

'These street stabbings.'

'Ah.' They had been on the news, but not much up here on the third floor.

Two in the space of a week, brutal and apparently random, in that no links from one victim to the other could be established. Then again, many street people tended to be known by first names, and often not their given one, and neither victim's formal identification had yet been confirmed. One had been killed near a derelict house known to be a popular squat. The other was found behind a row of eateries on Place de la Madeleine, in an alley lined with bins filled with discarded food.

With two, the media were getting interested.

Madman hunting homeless!... They hadn't got to that point yet. But their clientele was seriously addicted to fear and they were always happy supply it.

As for Chief Inspector Zidane, two street knifings were not his problem and wouldn't be until the Procureur assigned the case to the Judicial Police. For that to happen, Hugues Monty had to bring the Proc evidence and workable context. Hugues and his guys were still working on it.

So... 'What is it, Nabi?'

Zidane's dark Kabyle eyes bounced once. Stepping into the room, he removed a sheet of paper from the file. Aliette looked at a photocopy showing two handwritten fragments. They had been scrawled in longhand on scraps of lined paper, as if torn from a student's workbook.

We must learn to live a better life This world is absurd, is falling apart People like us we are burdened by clarity Are we brothers? sisters? People like us we are not kind to people in our way We have no time to spare nor heart to wait People like us must step up must sacrifice must take steps we must show you who you are

How in the world did he get so far from where he should have been?

'And these are?'

'Notes found on or near the victims.'

'OK.' And no surprise that they had been withheld from the media gang. Notes equalled profile, or the beginnings of one. Public disclosure was a warning flag to the killer.

Zidane stepped closer. 'How do you read that?'

'Angry crazy person for sure.' Too many schizophrenics wandering around, unaccounted for.

But Aliette could sense Nabi's deep agitation as he replaced the sheet in the folder.

'Thanks,' he murmured, almost dreamily, backing out of the room.

Aliette knew Nabi was not giving her the whole story. Not that she had any right to expect him to. None at all. His case or not, it was a city matter. The problem was, she liked him. He was discreet, if a natural-born calculator. But a decent man, with a good heart. He'd quietly done what he could to help her during the previous summer's frustrating fight with the DST—the French answer to MI5 or the FBI. More than that: Sergio, privy to a higher level of gossip, hinted that Nabi Zidane had defended her when the Divisionnaire had called looking for a head to chop. She zipped her case, picked up her coat. And tried to be encouraging. 'Angry schizophrenics are not the most subtle people … Hugues will get him, I'm sure.'

Zidane did not look too convinced. He smiled wanly and left her.

A minute later, Aliette went on her way. Rounding the corner at the end of the hall en route to the lift, she met Mario Bédard and Liza Fratticelli, carrying coffee and brioche, shoulder to shoulder, thick as thieves. Aliette had been wondering the same thing about Mario and Liza that others had been wondering about herself and Sergio Regarri. '*Bonjour.*'

There were five regional chief inspectors. Aliette was coming to know and mostly like Julien Lesouple, who had the Faugères territory, north and east of hers, though the residual strain of his broken marriage was boring, and his fussy equivocation as they negotiated jurisdictional access to a suspected drug lab in an old barn which straddled the district line was starting to grate. She had been getting to know and *not* like Mario Bédard, a strutting bantam-sized alpha male who guarded 'my Capestang,' the territory south and west of hers, with an absurdly possessive eye. Liza Fratticelli had the area south and east of Julien, from Agde to Pézenas to Mèze. Their paths hadn't yet crossed professionally, though it was good to share the occasional lunch with another female Chief Inspector. And Nabi Zidane, of course, at the centre of it, here in the city. Not a boss, more a de facto leader by virtue of numbers.

Voilà: 'our group' — as Aliette was getting used to saying.

When he wasn't being an imperious jerk, Mario Bédard was friendly. '*Ça va*, Inspector?'

'*Ça va, ça va* ... But what's the matter with Nabi?'

'That would be the chickens coming home to roost.' He smirked.

Liza added a knowing nod. The lift arrived, Aliette got on, interested, but not in the mood for Mario. Smiling, looking at her watch. 'Got Martine in twenty ... '

'Have a nice day,' Mario saluted as the door drew shut.

The thought of Liza with Mario was disturbing.

Chief Inspector Nouvelle had two meetings at the Palais de Justice concerning ongoing cases. The offices of the court were in the lavishly renovated Bishop's Palace directly behind Saint-Nazaire Cathedral. She walked ten minutes, across Les Allées, through Place des Trois

Six, where City Hall and the Municipal Police were located, past the local DST group's unmarked digs in the elegant house in Rue Bonsai, offered a *bonjour* to the two armed gendarmes at the courtyard gate and glanced up at Sergio's window as she crossed the cobblestone quad to the grandiose doors.

Magistrate Martine Rogge, two doors along from Sergio, was instructing an investigation into the manufacture of so-called party drugs. A new strain of Pink Ecstasy was circulating, several kids had been delivered to the ICU at Centre Hospitalier, battling psychosis, livers sorely battered, but fortunate to be breathing. Simple numbers said a death was inevitable. The chemists had been traced to a farm off the single-lane road through Saint-Nazaire-de-Lazaret, in the hills along the line where Aliette's territory bordered the next. Almost exactly on the line: some of the dusty deeds and records had the property squarely on the Saint-Brin side of the hill. Others registered it in Faugères, where her counterpart Julien Lesouple ruled. This bureaucratic glitch caused gaps in the process. The suspects were either lucky or, more likely, especially cynical in that they knew perfectly well the barn housing the lab was on a stretch of land no one really wanted, making it problematic for territorial-minded police. Aliette got on well enough with Julien, but they both wanted the case and there would be no raid until ownership was clearly established. It would not affect the raid, but defence lawyers could and would make hay out of administrative technicalities. This morning's meeting with Magistrate Rogge had been quietly and expressly set without inviting Julien. Aliette was prepared to move. It looked like Martine was prepared to oblige. But ... but, but, but: Sorry, she would have to finesse it with Julien.

Everything moved apace, according to the rules. Of course. *Merci, madame le juge.*

Martine Rogge was also instructing the new file on the murder at the cheese producer's. But that was another matter, and it had barely begun. One case, one meeting.

Next up, the Children's Judge.

Four adolescent girls had been partying on the high, rocky banks of the River Orb in the park at Réals. Only three came home, their friend having somehow fallen into the river and drowned. The *somehow* was the issue. The three girls told three different stories. Chief Inspector Nouvelle, instructed by a frustratingly timid Magistrate Claire Houde, was guiding her Inspector Henri Dardé through a delicate investigation overburdened with earnest social workers and intrusive parents. She had an idea for Henri she needed to discuss with Claire.

... Who was cautiously supportive.

Merci. They would talk again next week.

Lastly, pretending business, she looked in on Magistrate Regarri to set up a weekend date.

Leaving the Palais de Justice, Aliette headed into a now mild late January day. She stopped in Les Halles for a slice of pizza on a paper plate, coffee in a paper cup, walked another five minutes and enjoyed it sitting on the edge of a garden box in front of Cathédrale de la Madeleine. The warm sun felt good. Could this be spring? Didn't look like it. The leaves on the small palms planted beside her were still lifeless, limp, brown... Then, unfolding her map like a weekend tourist, she found her way to Rue Argence, a brass shingle by a door: PsychoDynamo.

'*Bonjour?*'

A distressingly thin woman looked up to receive her. A stained orange wool sweater hung from her skeletal shoulders. Coffee? Tea? Or teardrops. She'd been crying. Pale, tired flesh accentuated the blotchy red streaks across her cheeks, a mouth that appeared to be clenched tight, constantly grinding. A halo of dull, wispy hair was going grey around a face that somehow twinned with the forsaken plant dying in its pot on the corner of her desk: Poor daisy. Poor lady. She nodded but forgot to say hello. Her resentful, teary eyes fell back to some task on a page in front of her... Source of the bitchy voice on the phone?

The waiting area was cramped and airless. Three chairs in a row five steps from the reception desk. A tired coat tree where two winter greatcoats hung. Aliette sloughed off hers and added it.

No window. No magazines in a pile. No escape. She sat. Glanced at her watch.

The receptionist looked up from her bookkeeping, suspicious, a guard dog trained to sniff impatient people glancing at their watches.

Aliette offered another smile. In vain. The woman glared as if smiles were rude, then reached around and rapped twice on a cupboard door directly behind her. A voice behind it called, 'Do please come in!'

… Well! One had thought it *was* a cupboard.

In lieu of a word, the doleful woman at the desk made a jerky move, gesturing behind her:

Get in there, you.

Aliette moved automatically to comply. It was a strange sensation.

INVESTIGATIVE CONSULTATION

It was like a cupboard, if a normal room has windows. And a disorientingly large one—after the confined space of the waiting room. Behind the psychologist's busy desk was shelving lined with masks, a diverse collection, from Sarkozy to Batman to Tintin, tribal gods and virtual demons, eyeless papier-mâché skulls with painted grins, and carnival masks, sexy, sad, extravagant and enigmatic. An angel mask enjoyed pride of place front and centre—complete with floating Botticelli hair and rosy cheeks, all she needed was a pair of loving eyes. A home-theatre-sized television was mounted on the side wall. Three rudimentary wooden chairs were grouped in a triangular configuration, as if waiting for a table, a pitcher of water, three glasses of pastis. A closet in the corner was open, revealing colourful garments hung in a row: party costumes? What kind of place was this? An open sailor's chest beside the bathroom door spilled over with brightly coloured accoutrements—hats, scarves, belts and beads.

'Inspector Nouvelle…' Gabrielle Gravel rose to greet her. Plus forty, possibly fifty. Treated blonde hair pinned in a careless chignon. Austere space-age black metal glasses balanced the escaping strands and tangles while setting off her chosen colour and matching her thin eyebrows. A rather stern gaze. Her eyes were myrtle blue. Her bearing was full, but trim, healthy. Not a wrinkle to be seen. A not unhandsome woman, if confoundingly generic. In those first moments, the psychologist's unlined face reminded Aliette of nothing so much as a police composite, the kind of drawing that conveys a shape, but rarely a personality. Add the vague scent permeating the airless space and it was a presence encountered a million times, most lately where? Processing fast, Aliette's olfactory memory found

a match in the woman overseeing the *soutien-gorge* fitting room at
Galeries Lafayette...She wore a slate-coloured jacket and skirt, a
plain white blouse. As plain as a teaching nun's...These were first
impressions. The environment was new.

Aliette held out her hand. 'Doctor Gravel.'

After the handshake, perfunctory welcoming smile, a caveat: 'I
do have a doctorate in psychology, yet I am not a doctor. Which
makes you a client, not a patient. You can call me Doctor, but I do
not prescribe medications. Just so we are clear, Inspector.'

To which the inspector responded, not so brilliantly, 'Chief
Inspector. And this is not my idea. Just so we are clear, madame.'

Gabrielle Gravel had heard it before. 'It's a rare person who
volunteers to sit in this room, Inspector.'

'Chief Inspector...So, what is it that you do?'

'I help you come to terms with your role as an officer of the law.'

'They told me this, but not exactly how.'

'We talk. We play in the sand. We talk some more. I should add,
it is not an exact science.'

'We play in the sand?'

'Unless we need to take it further...' gesturing behind her.
'There are many ways we can attack a problem.'

'Do I get a mask?'

'If you want a mask...that is, if you need a mask, you find one
that feels right and bring it. Or...' swivelling in her chair, she pulled
a dead-white papier-mâché face from the drawer below the army of
masks and held it front of her own; 'you make it yourself right here.
It's always an interesting hour.' She stowed the mask and informed
the cop, 'But we start in the sand. Yes?'

The cop could only shrug.

Gabrielle Gravel got up and opened the credenza beneath the
gigantic television. Aliette had assumed it contained books, maybe
television equipment and office things. She was quietly astounded
to behold two top shelves lined with hundreds of tiny toys and
figurines representing all categories of human, machine, creature
and plant; made of metal, wood, plastic, pottery, bone china; and
mixed amongst them were trinkets: Christmas ornaments, costume
jewellery, bracelet charms, miniature flags, horns and drums, castles

and cakes … there was no apparent rhyme or reason to the collection. Below, waiting on expressly designed slots, six high, four across, were stored wooden boxes the size of small fruit crates. The psychologist pulled one out. Constructed of strong wood, sanded to the grain and varnished, it was filled with the whitest, finest sand. She placed it on the desk. 'This will be yours.'

'This?'

'Or one just like it. They're all the same. To start. Like people.'

Aliette noted that most of the other boxes had Post-it notes stuck on them, with initials.

'What will I do with it?'

'Fill it with objects of your own choosing…' from the top shelves, 'and play.'

'Play.'

'Arrange things. Then arrange them again.'

'This is the World Technique?'

'It's all world technique when you come down to it. But yes. Sand play. Very effective,' a motherly smile, 'even fun. If you let it be.'

'But…' But what? 'But how could that have anything to do with my life as a police officer?'

'Your approach to your life as a police officer has everything to do with the world, Inspector.'

'Chief Inspector. I actually happen to agree with that.'

'Excellent… A good starting point for us then, no?'

'But I still don't want to be here. I still don't see—'

'But you are. And you have to be.'

Gravel's tone was daunting, much like that spectral teaching nun's. Aliette withdrew from it, sinking into her chair, dismayed. 'If this is the world, why are there no windows?' Or air.

'Windows are a distraction. Here, the world is in the sand. The world is a concept waiting to be elaborated. You want a window, you can create one.' With a businesslike nod, she replaced the sandbox in its slot. Sitting again, she opened her notes. 'But first we talk.'

Aliette waited.

'A little bit about yourself. Age?'

'Forty-two.'

'Married?'

'No.'

'Children?'

'No.'

'In a relationship?'

'Yes.'

'Good… Nice to have someone to complain to when you get home.'

A small joke? Gabrielle Gravel smiled. Aliette did not.

'Do you take care of yourself, Inspector? Are you mindful? Do you go to mass? Meditate?'

'*Chief* Inspector… Yes!… No and no. I run.' But she hadn't for the better part of a year.

'I sense you're lying. But running is good. I suggest you take it up. Or take it up again.'

'What does this have to do with playing in the sand?'

'Mind and body, Inspector. Part and parcel of the process.'

'Do you meditate?'

'That's not your concern. I am a non-person here. There is only you. We are here to change your mind in relation to your gun.'

'My gun is not part of my body.'

'It will be. Your mind. Your body. Your attitude… All your constituent parts. Ending in your gun. You see? With my help, you are going to learn to see things more as they are, you are going to develop more realism in your default mode perspective, and in so doing you will improve your effectiveness.' She waved a piece of paper. 'The fact of the matter, the reality of the situation, here, now, is that you must carry your gun and be prepared to use it.'

Aliette glimpsed official SRPJ letterhead and assumed a memo from the Divisionnaire laying out the facts and reality as they perceived it. Looking away, she had to admit, 'I can't dispute the facts as such.'

'I.e., the reason you are here.'

'I can only say that my superiors were not *there*. They never are. The reality of *my* situation is that I have never needed my gun to accomplish what was required.'

Prompting Gabrielle Gravel to ask, 'And what is your situation, Inspector?'

Aliette retreated for another moment, pondering it. Then she leaned across the desk. 'I like to think of myself as the centre of the universe.'

The psychologist leaned forward to meet this, fingers tightly laced. 'Do you feel all right?'

'I feel uncomfortable. As I said, this was not my choice.'

'Where did you get this notion?'

'What notion?'

'That you are the centre of the universe.'

'I got it from... I've always known it. One day I woke up and I knew it. It was after something rather large. But it was J-P who helped me understand it. J-P Blismes. Perhaps you know him?'

'Why would I know him?'

'Same line of work as you. Specializes in junior offenders. Also consults to my former brigade. Up north... A conference, maybe? I gather you people go to a lot of conferences.'

Gabrielle Gravel indicated negative. 'Never met him. Those things are mostly a lot of faces.' She unlaced, then re-laced her fingers. 'He told you that?'

'He didn't tell me. I told him.'

'Even so.'

'Even so, I think he saved my life... He's always smiling. Huge shiny teeth? Hard to miss.'

Gravel silently denied a second time knowing J-P Blismes.

A veteran cop could see the psychologist was not averse to lying.

'It is not an exact science,' Gravel repeated.

'No... But you, what do you tell your clients?'

It was here that Gabrielle Gravel, peremptory and categorical, laid down the law such as it was in that airless room. *She* would be the one asking the questions.

It stung. Normally it's the cop who asks the questions. And there was the existential issue at the heart of it which needed to be put squarely on the table. Aliette confronted the psychologist who now, by virtue of a piece of paper, suddenly had such control over her life. 'There are so many people out there. Really, what good is a gun?'

'But that's exactly it,' Gravel replied, prepared to allow this basic query. 'So many people, so many of them angry, medicated, lost and volatile, erupting through the fragile veneer of civility—no warning, human explosions, just like that. The public lives in a state of fear, they depend on the likes of you to be prepared and able to respond in kind.'

'It's chaotic out there. From what I've seen, guns only make the chaos worse.'

'Or these people are simply evil, Inspector. Monsters in disguise, living amongst us. And breeding.'

'Do you believe in evil?'

The question compelled Gabrielle Gravel to answer the other she had dodged. 'I don't care what my clients need or don't need. I don't judge. I try to help them move forward with their lives.'

'Well, that's the problem. My gun does not make me feel that I'm moving forward.'

'Which is why you are here. And why we cannot fail.'

'I don't see how.'

'They've ordered you to wear it.'

'Yes.'

'Or turn in your badge and seek other employment.'

'But what would I do?'

The question was not relevant. Gravel sighed, patient, but not forever. Advised, 'You must visualize a bridge and go across it.'

'Wearing my gun,' Aliette added matter-of-factly. She had no wish to alienate Gabrielle Gravel with more unsolicited questions, much less cop cynicism. Her job was on the line and she had to come to terms.

The psychologist appreciated the effort. 'May I suggest something right off the top here?'

Aliette waited.

'You call me Gabrielle, I'll call you Chief.'

'No.' That would not work.

...A bumpy start at PsychoDynamo? *Not*-Doctor Gravel shrugged, perused her initial notes. 'I do like this idea of the centre of the universe. I mean as a start point for our explorations. A very workable trope.' A smile. 'The universe in a sandbox? You will be part of my Tuesday-Thursday evening grouping. Let's say 7:30.' She scribbled on a page.

'Grouping?'

'I find it works best when certain types of clients are grouped together.'

'Are you saying this is group therapy?'

'Not at all. We don't do that here. I also treat families and couples—but no groups. As you can see from this environment, I believe in a creative approach to therapy. The real work gets done at a place of metaphor and imagination. I group my clients according to shared characteristics, and obviously their problems. The grouping is for me, my focus, my rhythm, my depth—bing, bang, bong. You see?' She rose, extending her hand. 'I will see you next Tuesday evening and we'll get started. And please don't forget to bring your weapon.'

Bing, bang, bong? Aliette got up, uncertain. 'But...strictly speaking, I'm off-duty at five.' Not supposed to be carrying a gun around when you're not working.

'Strictly speaking, I understand. But we both know rules like that don't matter to the likes of you. Your gun is central to your program, yes? Obviously we're going to need it. Have a nice weekend. Chief Inspector?'

'Just call me Aliette.'

Another smile to confirm that, then a hand gesturing her out, a quick directive murmured to the sour creature at the reception desk, the cupboard door shut silently behind her as Aliette stepped back into the waiting room.

Where she waited, staring down into the receptionist's flakey scalp as the appointment was entered in pencil on a smudged desk calendar; and waited further as the woman painstakingly filled out a card. It looked like she had a skin problem too, poor thing. That could certainly leave a person perpetually grouchy.

It was a relief to step back into the street. It felt like she had no idea where she'd been.

- 3 -

FAMILY SYSTEMS DISCONNECTED

Not long after Aliette Nouvelle left PyschoDynamo, the Petitpas family gathered in the office of Gabrielle Gravel. They each had individual programs on the go with her. There was intermittent interaction amongst themselves in the waiting room—of questionable value thus far. All the work was meant to come together in these Friday afternoon family sessions. '*Bonjour*, how is everyone today?' An ironic shrug. A listless nod … It must be said the Petitpas family gathered reluctantly, slouching into Gabrielle's office, eyes everywhere but on each other.

No one looked forward to Friday afternoon; lately, Gabrielle Gravel least of all.

Some families were more pessimistic than others. In Gabrielle's experience, regardless of a father's supposed leadership role, a family's collective state of mind was usually dependent on the mother's sense of hope for the successful reconstruction of her shattered nest. Madame Emma Petitpas was trying but having scant success with the personal challenge of mustering hope. Her sadly ineffective husband hadn't one iota of leadership in his genes. Their alienated adolescent daughter aggressively disdained both of them. Individually, they were three more unhappy people who clung to their difficulties with a stubborn tenacity—it was the only identity they knew. Of course, the success of each was dependent on the others, but Emma's situation was at the crux of it, and Gabrielle's hopes for success were closely linked to Em's.

Too closely, she knew. But you had to try new things now, push boundaries in search of new solutions in an increasingly unforgiving world. Some clients demanded it. Inspired it too.

Slowly, painfully, Em had been inching forward. But she seemed to have crashed again.

The three chairs were there—they took their customary places. The psychologist remained at her desk. She instructed Emma Petitpas, 'Could you please try to tell us what has been bothering you these past few weeks?'

She couldn't. Emma gulped and belched silently, struggling to compose her feelings, make a statement. Her brow tightened. She was physically unable.

Gabrielle suggested, 'Was it Christmas alone?'

Virginie Petitpas interjected. 'Me, I got zero for Christmas and I survived. Well, except for some great sex and excellent drugs.'

The girl's taunting scorn left her mother with her face in her hands.

The psychologist asked the girl, 'Was that useful?'

The girl asked, 'Are you?'

'I am trying to be,' responded Gabrielle. The girl could too easily provoke her. 'Humans have to try to be useful, Virginie.' Her professional smile held firm.

The comment prompted the girl to get up from her chair and go to the shelves behind the desk and take up the angel mask that had pride of place in the middle of the middle shelf and hold it over her face. 'But I'm not human,' she announced.

Gabrielle Gravel kept all the creative tools for self-expression she used in her work available during family sessions—self-expression being both the brass ring and the bottom line. Strictly speaking, Virginie Petitpas should construct her own mask. She refused—as she refused to add a single figure to her sand tray. Virginie refused to be proactive or positive in any way.

But at least, and as usual, Virginie got the conversation going.

Gabrielle turned to the father. 'How do you respond to that?'

Jean Petitpas only nodded as his eyes slid sideways. As if he might agree that his child was an inhuman thing.

Gabrielle turned to her mother. 'If you were her father, what would you tell her?'

Emma blushed deeply, the guiltiest woman in the world. She shook her head, quick and frantic. Role playing was beyond her ken.

To the father: 'If you were your wife, what would say to your child?'

Jean Petitpas was perplexed by the question. 'I don't want to be my wife. She's the last person in the world I'd want to be.'

Gabrielle Gravel wished they could try to see some issues from the other person's point of view. It was a healthy exercise in finding things to share. But they resisted ... And resisted.

She asked Jean, 'Don't you want this to work?'

'It'll never work,' said Virginie.

Jean Petitpas frowned. 'I want everyone to be happy. And I want a divorce. And some good luck, for once.'

'Never!' blurted Emma Petitpas. She glared at Jean. She meant the divorce.

From behind the mask, their angry angel added, 'You don't deserve good luck.'

Gabrielle asked Jean, 'But what do you feel you need to do to earn your family's forgiveness and respect?'

He rolled his eyes. 'Make a killing?'

The angel, now gliding in a dancerly way around the three adults, said, 'I want respect but I don't need forgiveness.'

Gabrielle challenged the angel. 'I don't believe you.'

The angel repeated, 'It will never work.'

'And why won't it?'

'Because we're useless? ... and we hate each other!'

'But we have to try, Virginie. We need to help each other here.'

'It's their fault.' Virginie sat, shrugged, and removed her mask.

She meant her parents. She was only here because she had to be.

Emma and Jean looked down at the floor. They were both uncomfortable in the presence of Virginie. In fact they were afraid of her. Helping Jean and Em alter that dynamic was central to the challenge of repairing the Petitpas family system. Gabrielle Gravel had invested time and energy and she wanted it to work. But some days it did seem futile, the constant pushing of the river, gently but firmly mining their resistance for the barest hints of any communication that might lead to healing interaction within this damaged family's soul.

Gabrielle Gravel made a note. And tried again. '*Alors?*'

They were here for an hour and they all knew it, and eventually they got down to it.

Jean said he had several important business projects in the works and he was under a lot of pressure and he needed their support, but if they were just going to complain and ignore him, then he didn't need that... Virginie said he never told the truth and her mother was a feeble *nul* and she hated this world and they were doomed... Caught between them, Emma battled deep anxiety. When she managed to speak, she said they were 'bad.' It was a generic word. It could mean all of them, or Virginie, or Jean. It was mostly directed at Jean. In many ways, Emma was bent on punishing her husband. But she still loved him. Or the idea of him... She despaired of Virginie but the only word she had was 'bad'... Jean's affection for his daughter remained vague at best. He was mostly interested in himself... Oh yes, and Virginie despised Gabrielle.

It could sound like progress, but it was much the same place they got to every Friday afternoon. Steadfast at her desk, Gabrielle Gravel redirected with questions, suggestions, and jotted notes. And thought they were so ordinary. It was a reflection she struggled with—less than caring; and the fundamental rule of thumb is that every client's problem—i.e., their pain—is unique. But she was a professional. She understood guilt as just another pressure and could live with it... No, the Petitpas family were ordinary, but they could be special, but they had to work at it. It was mostly up to Em. At the end of another ordinary hour, all she could tell them was, 'We have a lot of work to do,' and send them out. Gabrielle Gravel could not order the Petitpas family to make better use of their counselling time. That was for Emma to inspire. Somehow.

Or not. Lately, Em was failing.

- 4 -

QUIETER MODE

Chief Inspector Aliette Nouvelle's assigned territory was based at Saint-Brin, a wine town in a bucolic valley thirty-some minutes north of the city. Though she sometimes found herself bemoaning the slower pace, it had been her choice and she did not regret the quieter mode of life on the spacious second floor of the old Mairie with Inspectors Magui Barthès and Henri Dardé, her manageable and enjoyable team of two. (Her leadership skills seemed fine with them.) Mathilde Lahi provided prompt and neat secretarial services and a knowledgeable take on local affairs, current and past, an invaluable help when one has been parachuted in. They shared Mathilde with Deeds and Records, at the other end of the hall. (It was Mathilde who, by virtue of some savvy calls, uncovered the overlap with Faugères in the long-ago deeding of the party-drug-producing farm just then at issue with Chief Inspector Julien Lesouple.) With Mathilde's blessing—crime being by far the more interesting way to spend a day—the inspector had petitioned to have Mathilde assigned exclusively to her own unit. She hoped the request landed on a sympathetic desk.

The downside of the quiet life is rust. That edge, that instinct, the thing that is supposed to set a cop apart gets dulled. She had complained, privately to Sergio (during a rare but bitter crying jag), that surely a drop in acuity flowing from said life was the catalyst to the professional error which had brought her to a moment where she might have done better with a gun than without. It was a disingenuous complaint. It was not the environment. It was her choice, her deep-seated predilection to leave her gun at home that had resulted in the order to attend at the office of Gabrielle Gravel until such time as the psychologist deemed her psychological metrics adjusted and felt confident her aim was true. Figuratively speaking. Aliette would have to work on the literal aspects herself at the range.

Still, had she landed too far from civilization? There were no psychologists in Saint-Brin, no one offering psychotherapy, personal coaching, much less guidance in the World Technique. She had seen notices on the post office board and in the library announcing meditation groups, tai chi classes. Pilates? Another thing Mathilde knew about, but not her. Nor Magui or Henri.

In truth, her new patch was not so bucolic in winter. More a silent netherworld. All tourists and summering northerners had disappeared with the last of the October sun. That day, after the cramped and bustling maze of downtown Béziers, the town square seemed like an empty box, its treasures gone. The plane trees loomed huge and barren. She imagined witchy fingers reaching gleefully, caressing a pristine but deathly winter sky. The magnolia, fulsome and beautiful in July, looked embarrassed, mute and tangled and without a proper explanation, helplessly tolerating a stiff and chilly mistral tugging at the last of its dull and listless leaves. The poplars by the post office stood like a row of upended brooms. Stark. Scratchy. Below her office window, rows of carefully squared hedges lined deserted walkways bereft of people. The late afternoon sun glared against the oddly green carpet of lawn in the War Memorial square. Green but dead. It was still too cold for the local bench sitters to come out.

Up on the second floor of the Mairie it was so very quiet.

Gabrielle Gravel was fresh on her mind. Her team probably already knew about her disciplinary status, the gun order, although she would tell them, eventually, to make it official. Gabrielle, on the other hand, was private. Bitterly so. A quiet but cutting insult. A personal failure.

…Chief Inspector Nouvelle turned away from her window, adjusted the thermostat, sat at her desk, sipped tea…

She had told herself she wouldn't do it. Now, in one of those empty moments on the far side of resolution, she called the Materials department at Division and requisitioned a shoulder holster.

The man sounded happy to hear from her. He asked if she wanted it personalized.

That pricked the bubble. She asked, 'Like Annie Oakley?'

'Who is Annie Oakley?'

'Forget it, not your problem.'

He promised it would be delivered by Tuesday noon to a spare office in the sub-basement at the courthouse. He did not specify which one. Nor how he knew she would be there. He said she'd see it, a plain brown package, she would know. Her name had obviously been flagged and he was having fun with her. She played along, polite and cheery. She had to ... No, he had never been to Saint-Brin ... Until '*merci, monsieur,*' she looked forward to receiving her package, She let him go and got back to work.

Next up were meetings with Henri and Magui to discuss the judges' positions and plan next moves.

Inspector Henri Dardé was frustrated.

She asked, 'But what does your instinct say?'

'*B'eh,* I've got perjury, conspiracy, if not in the first instance, then in the aftermath of finding their companion's body ... manslaughter ... or possibly second-degree, obstruction, protecting a criminal—that could be for the bizarre mother of young Nicole, God I'd love to slap her with that. Or ...' Henri Dardé was a large man with close-cropped curly hair. He made a large gesture indicating all of the above.

'It can't be personal, Henri.'

'Sorry, boss. You know it is.'

She did. The death was suspicious: Four girls, all fifteen and exploding with hormones, drinking wine by the river, and one somehow falls into the fast-moving shallow rapids, cracks her skull and drowns, coming to rest in the branches of a fallen tree some three hundred metres downstream. Her friends come home in hysterics, claiming a horrific accident. They all have cell phones in their pockets, of course, but none has the presence of mind to call for help. They make you angry before you even start. Questioning reveals an argument, a history on the part of the dead friend of being a stealer of boyfriends. The more they're questioned, the more they each try to pass blame along the line, the more the parents feel a need to intervene. Perhaps mistakenly, Henri had started talking to neighbours, teachers, guidance counsellors, the priest. His pages were muddled as he tried to pull the thing together and Aliette's own pages reflected his. Children's Judge Claire Houde was still waiting for a coherent view pointing to a realistic charge. She had resisted intervening personally. But the judge was trained for utmost empathy when faced with exploding hormones and was now asking for a psychologist to be brought into it. 'Sorry to have to bring you that, Henri.' Would Claire ask for Gabrielle?

Henri fumed. 'But there are already two social workers!'

'Alternatively, I have suggested we convene a group meeting with the Children's Judge.'

'Oh, God ... Parents included?' Henri's face fell further.

'No. Relax. Just the girls. And Claire. In her office. And you—as calm mediating presence.'

'What about you? You and Claire seem good together.'

'But they're your girls, Henri ... you know them.'

Henri was taken aback. 'Well ... but how?'

'Get the social workers onside first. Then go back to the parents ... give the girls a little break? Claire understands what you're up against. She's willing to give you time to try.'

Henri remained skeptical. But the community approach was a quagmire and he knew it.

'You get them alone with Claire in the courthouse, the lay of the land will change, I'm sure.'

'I'll work on it, boss.' Henri promised, then departed.

Magui Barthès arrived. She had spent a productive day at the cheese producer's farm ...

Before heading home, Aliette dashed across the high street (which doubled as Departmental Highway 612) and into the butcher's, where she purchased two thick mutton chops for Saturday night. Then into the baker's for Sunday morning treats. Two of each.

Everything in pairs now. She'd given him a pair of slippers for their first Christmas and he had left them at her place, at the front door beside hers. Romantic and realistic, her Sergio: these old houses were never really built for these raw, damp southern winters.

It was a six-minute drive to the top of her little street connecting the top of the village to the lane by the river. It had been deemed too tight for vehicles and so a birdbath-sized cement planter had been placed there to block passage. It did the job far more effectively than any traffic sign. And April through October it spilled with flowers, adding charm. She lugged her parcels forty paces down the wobbly—and these days slippery!—paving, checked her mailbox, waved at old Roland staring like a ghost from his dim *salon*, let herself in and turned up the heat (not too high; it cost a fortune) and slipped into her slippers, waiting by her new man's.

She changed into frumpy woollens. Opened a Friday evening beer. Looked out the window at the sun going down over the peaks of the Caroux range etched along the northwest sky. Orange and indigo. Lovely background. Drab foreground. There was nothing remotely 'charming' about her Midi village on a winter evening with the mistral blowing through. Not at all. Her village, properly called a *commune*, which is to say a suburb of a village, itself a suburb of Saint-Brin (which barely had 10,000 souls) was lonely. Deserted. Grey.

There were dread moments, feeling like she'd been dropped at the end of the earth.

Roland, the old man opposite, was still peering. Had been since December.

She did not call Sergio that Friday night. He did not call her. She did not wonder what he was up to. She assumed it was the same for him. It was surely too cold for his Friday evening bike sprint. Whether out with the boys, alone with his *télé*, or sharing a moment with someone else who could never be her, this was not Aliette's concern. They were at the point where they spent chunks of time together, his place or hers, and then they didn't. The gaps were respected. She had her own *télé*. She had a book from the library in the annex behind the Mairie. She had not met anyone else who could ever be him.

Those gaps were necessary, the better to gauge the space between a pair of slippers at her front door, and how her coat lay over the kitchen chair at his (much warmer) home in town.

What would happen to that balance when Tuesday and Thursday night became automatic?

She would not insist. But she knew he would.

Saturday morning, the mistral continued. The day was dazzlingly bright, fantastically cold. She rendezvoused with Magui at the church at Villespassans and followed her up a mountain road for a proper talk with the goat cheese producer, also a philandering husband, and now a grieving widower. He was off the hook for murdering his wife, but they needed a clearer view on where he stood regarding his lover's desperate action. Beside her, urging her on? Or in the dark? The man was already facing charges for obstruction of justice and perjury—indeed, appeared willing to go to prison for someone else's deadly act. 'She's too young!' he had finally sobbed when the inspector informed him that his girlfriend had admitted it. She did look young, this murderess. She seemed even younger, a distraught teenager in love. In fact, she was twenty-five.

Aliette and Magui turned their cars in at the sign, crawled up a narrow track to a cut in the ridge, then descended toward the house and outlying buildings in the lap of the rift. The small brown goats at pasture were pretty, finely sleek. And completely skittish. They ran from the approaching cars, through a gate in the pasture fence and over the ridge.

Except one little thing, so unnerved she had to stop, squat and pee...

... before she went bounding after her friends.

Inspector Barthès joined the boss in her warm car to confirm their strategy.

His children had been sent to relatives. 'It's just him and his goats,' said Magui.

And a gendarme, to make sure he didn't do himself any further harm. And ensure he stayed clear of the rest of his staff, who were still making cheese and manning the little shop.

'How are they coping with it?'

'They know everything and probably more, but swear they don't.' Magui shrugged. Afraid of losing a livelihood? That was normal. She was working on it.

They went in. Two sombre ladies in white overalls and hairnets worked the counter in the shop adjoining the production area. Aliette counted four more attending to the process on the other side of the glass. On a Saturday morning they were busy serving a steady stream of day trippers who had no idea why a gendarme was parked in the lot, and probably some loyal local customers who knew that a murder in the family does not preclude the need to continue doing business. Nor does murder change the taste of cheese, and this cheese was apparently renowned.

The widower was alone in the main house. Miserable. Feeling neglected. Magui assured him his children would come back soon. 'And do you really want them to be around at this sad time?' No. But he was desperately lonely, that was clear, and it sounded like a cry for help. Aliette made sure Magui made a note of his mental state … This man would always be alone. He had ruined everything. But apart from making a note and alerting the gendarme, who might pass it on to a social worker, those kinds of issues were not the inspectors' concern.

An hour later, Magui offered her opinion. 'I think she did it on her own.'

Inspector Nouvelle tended to agree. A not ungentle man caught between two women, themselves too close for comfort. Apart from his nine-year-old son, he was, from one week to the next, the only male for as far as the crack of a bullet could carry. The bucks were trucked in, then trucked out.

Did he imagine himself the resident buck? Did a place like this instill that kind of thinking?

Add to that a man now wracked with devastating guilt who had, gallantly, stupidly, made a second mistake to go on top of his first. He had tried to shield her, the way one might a child.

To prevent two women being destroyed instead of one?

Too late … He seemed to know that now—the futile, double damage of his gallant gesture.

Though he was still far from clear as to how it was between his wife and the girl who'd killed her for furious passion's sake. He had to know, Magui and she agreed on that. His employees too.

Six of them, all female, for a female sort of place. They drove up from various spots around the valley. But from morning till evening six days a week, this was an enclosed world.

There would be more interviews here. And with the defiant young woman in the cell.

In the meantime, it was Saturday. After purchasing some of the man's undeniably tasty products, Magui and Aliette stepped back outside and were hit by the mistral whistling down from the ridge. Magui gasped, '*Mon dieu*, it's cold up here!'

'And so isolated. Beautiful, but...' Too far away. Good for goats. Great for cheese lovers. Bad for a marriage. 'See you Monday.'

They ran for the shelter of their separate cars. The goats ran away again as they drove out.

Magui and her construction worker boyfriend and her two sons lived over at Creissan. At the top of the road, back at Villepassans, they went their separate ways.

– 5 –

NABI HAS A PROBLEM

The phone rang as Aliette walked in the door.

Sergio Regarri sighed before speaking. 'Sorry, tonight does not look good.'

'Ah. Why?'

'There's been another one.'

'Another stabbing?'

'Last night, early this morning, they're still working on it. They want me.'

'They've arrested someone?' The Procureur assigns an Instructing Judge when there is enough information to start a criminal inquiry.

'Not exactly. But they've got the weapon and ... it's complicated.'

That made three within ten days, now two on consecutive nights. A deranged street person with a kitchen knife. Horrific and messy—of course. But what did 'complicated' mean?

'It's complicated,' he repeated, in that quiet steady way Aliette had been learning to trust.

But it was Saturday night! 'We'll eat at your place.'

He relented cautiously. 'I might be late.'

'Surely they won't keep you all night. Just tell me what to do with this mutton.'

She turned down the thermostat, packed the food, filled an overnight bag with things for Sunday—a toothbrush, presented on her birthday back in August, was already next to his—and drove off, happy to leave the damp house, running from the moaning frigid wind, laughing at herself in the rearview, momentarily crazy and briefly ecstatic, looking forward to making love in Sergio's magnificent bed ...

Sometimes, in spite of everything, a tiny frenzy of joy quickens the heart.

Sergio Regarri's place was a hidden treasure. Hidden in plain sight. It was a five-minute walk from the courthouse, directly across from the famous cathedral. A small park on the panoramic promontory lay between, frequented mainly by tourists after visiting the church. From a bench on the lawn, the last house along the short street bordering the park was a faceless presence, completely unremarkable. A scratched but sturdy oak door set in an unprepossessing stucco façade gone grey from age. And only a door—no windows looking back at the park. You might briefly imagine a small workshop, or a warehouse, a practical space with a workaday purpose. Perhaps there was a garage accessible from the street behind. (There was.) But your eye wouldn't dwell too long. It would automatically return to the grand view of the rolling lands stretching northwest to the mountains. You'd never guess it was someone's home unless you happened to be sitting on that park bench when a stylishly turned-out man of swarthy tint emerged from that scratched but sturdy door, these days sometimes with a handsome woman at his side, she sometimes sporting a basic blue beret. In fact, 36 Rue Boudard had been a Spanish immigrant's modest home and *grenier* (storage loft), where he raised a family and built a decent living importing oranges from his homeland, supplying shops and market vendors in a city that could get cold in winter, but was safe from fascist politics. Señor Regarri had left the business to his sons, the property to his daughter, Sergio's mother. She had left the city to pursue the next levels of French life with her accountant husband in Pézenas. She shared the taxes on the place with his uncles, who continued to receive and keep stock there. Then they retired. It was slowly rotting when her son the magistrate bought it from her ('at a reasonable price') five years prior to the entry of a blonde chief inspector into his life.

With his widowed mother's hearty blessing, Sergio had the place gutted and transformed.

That sense of style you remarked upon when you saw him returning from work the other day? It went deeper than his taste in shoes. True, if you looked up from a parking spot in Boulevard d'Angleterre, you would see only another bland white wall. You probably wouldn't realize that the two large windows dividing it were made of the most modern, light-adjusting glass. If you were walking up the city stairs directly below, you'd be too close and beneath to see inside.

But if you were Sergio's lover and you had a key, the scuffed-up door at the corner marked 36 would open to a comfortably spacious, subtly appointed space. Warm wood. Modern everything. The most spectacular view northwest—far better than from that park bench, because you'd be contemplating it from under the sheets with this interesting man. The bedroom looked over the low-lying edge of the city to the mountains, host to holy sunsets in every season. Not hard to imagine a happy life as you shook off the day and shed your clothes and climbed into his oversized bed. After making love, it was lovely to watch the vast night skies. Given the privacy of a high vantage point, you slept without the blind drawn down over the studio-sized window.

Aliette lugged her bags up the city stairs and let herself in. She got the meat dressed according to his instructions and cut the carrots he said she would find, then put her coat back on and went out for bread. Returning, she opened a beer, read the paper. Snoozed ... Put the meat in the oven. Sergio was not so late: closing in on eight, but it was Saturday. They opened wine, prepared the table. Shared news. Her day first: an account of the sad man up on the plateau until ... Ding!

Mutton à la Aliette. Not bad at all. She even managed to keep it a bit pinkish.

Her Vichy carrots were fine. He toasted her. She got the story.

The third stabbing victim was discovered by a pair of uniformed officers in the alcove of the derelict Église Saint-Aphrodise. The police had gone in to hush the noisemakers. A regular stop. Alcoholics and addicts, runaways and the homeless would all crawl in there for the night, a diverse crowd, varying degrees of mental stability. Things often got out of hand. Last night the mad shrieking had been especially shrill. They found the motley gang gathered around a man with a knife buried in his stomach. No one had seen anything. At least nothing clearly remembered.

'And no link to the others?'

'None apparent. It's a cop.'

'Ah ... Those poor uniforms sometimes have no idea of the risks.'

'Not a uniform,' corrected Sergio. 'One of Nabi's guys.'

'*Mon dieu*! Poor Nabi.' Aliette Nouvelle had seen her share of colleagues go down. That was before rising to boss. Now? The sense of responsibility was too much to think about, but she carried it every day. 'But what was he doing there?'

'Exactly.' Sergio refilled their glasses. 'And worse. It's Nabi's knife.'

'Nabi's knife? What do you mean?'

'Nabi has admitted it.'

'Are you saying—' And Nabi had been so stressed yesterday.

'No.'

Sergio explained: 'The two uniforms find and identify Inspector Pierre Tropéano—his warrant card and other personal stuff is all right there in his pockets. They call PJ headquarters, who call Nabi. He pulls himself out of bed, rushes to the scene. They've cleared the place, Annelise and the SOC people are doing their work. Nabi IDs his guy for the record. Then Nabi takes a closer look—at the knife. Horrible. It's still buried in Tropéano's gut, hilt's protruding. It's old wood, very ornate, it's no kitchen knife, at least not one from this past century... Nabi hovers there, riveted. That seems normal, his man's down, he's in shock. But he keeps reaching toward it. Poor Annelise is trying to do her work and, well, you know how she has a hard time connecting with Nabi on a good day.'

'I do.' Aliette did not like the Medical Examiner much. She knew Légiste Annelise Duflot had an ingrained distrust of Chief Inspector Nabi Zidane. And anyone else who looked like him.

Sergio sipped wine. 'Obviously Nabi knows not to touch the knife. They said it was like he could not *not* put his hand on it, like he was mesmerized. Then he begins to bawl, which isn't normal. And then he collapses, falls to his knees, which is a bit scary—you'd think it was his son or... who knows? They try to help him, try to get him out of there, but he insists on staying. Annelise carries on, doing her usual *in situ* exam, pictures. Nabi's sitting on the dirty floor, whimpering, no one can understand a word... shivering, weeping. Till finally Annelise is done and it's time to remove the knife, take everything to the lab. Nabi suddenly jumps up, tells her, No! like she's about to touch a bomb, and muscles her out of the way... He leans over Tropéano and grabs the knife and yanks it out, holding it in front of his face like it's the cure for cancer. Blade's as long as the hilt, just as Annelise said from looking at the first two victims, and now it's definitely no kitchen knife. Sharp pointy turn at the tip. A dagger of some sort. Nabi's clutching the thing, hands all bloody, he's really wrecking up the evidence. Annelise screams at him. He screams back, This is mine! Then he faints.'

'Faints?'

'Right out. They said he almost put the thing in his own gut when he went down.'

'That's horrible. But how did he know? I mean…'

'*B'eh*, it's a traditional Kabyle *flissa*. He knows.'

'Surely it's not the only one in a city like this.'

'Of course it isn't. But it's Nabi's. They take him to the hospital for the night. Hugues Monty sits there with him this morning. And his wife, she's there too. Nabi's got a lot of pills in him but he insists it's his knife. Says he hasn't seen it for about thirty years, but it's his.'

'Where has it been?'

'At Vincent Spanghero's house.'

'Oh, God.'

'Oh, yes. They were partners… well, we all heard about that. Seems Nabi gave him the knife as a wedding gift way back when. His wife confirmed it.'

'That's so sad. Like Spanghero was giving it back.'

'Indeed. It fits too well.'

Yes, complicated…

Inspector Vincent Spanghero had quit the force last spring, very suddenly, then disappeared. No one, including his wife and children, had seen him since. The weeks and months leading up to that day had been tempestuous. Aliette, working through her first year at her new posting, was still a stranger. She had been aware, but from a distance. But it was no secret Vincent Spanghero had tried and apparently failed to live with the fact that Nabi Zidane, his former partner on the street, had won the top city job. The situation had been simmering for more than a year, since Nabi had moved into the corner office on the third floor at Hôtel de Police. Openly bitter,

Spanghero had grown stubbornly maverick. His volatile temper even erupted during instructions—Sergio had felt the brunt of it more than once. 'It rarely had to do with the case at hand. It was simply and crudely to make a point. In giving the job to Nabi, they had made a big mistake. Vincent seized every opportunity he could to let them...us, everyone know.'

Aliette had not known Sergio then, except as a face in the hall at the Palais de Justice.

Sergio ventured that Vincent Spanghero had probably sealed the deal five months before his sudden departure, when he'd ignored a direct command from Nabi, and sent his men into a dangerous situation. One was killed—Inspector Menaud Rhéaume. In the aftermath, Zidane and his group had tried to cope and carry on in what amounted to a failed attempt at solidarity. Politically iffy, psychologically impossible. 'But Nabi tried. Not easy... It was mainly for Spanghero, his career, if not their friendship. And Vincent tried too. For a bit. Tried to calm down. He *did* calm down. Got kind of silent, is what I'm hearing. Then he walks in one day last June, drops his warrant card on Nabi's desk and that's it. Gone. Totally gone.'

Was Vincent Spanghero back, wreaking revenge? The obvious evidence said yes.

'Positive forensics?'

'Not yet... Gloves. Hats. Cold out there these nights.'

'Another note?'

'Not this time. No note on or near Inspector Tropéano. Or at least none found. It's possible one of the crowd may have picked it up. Then forgot.'

'They do that.' Scattered brains filled with too many noxious things. 'But Nabi. They going to bring it to him?'

'Of course not. Nabi can't have anything to do with it now.'

'Thank you... I *meant* to his group?'

Sergio looked up, abashed. Sometimes he said things the wrong way, things that implied she was a junior—and he was a judge. He smiled and adjusted his reply. 'No. Not yet.'

'So why you, then?' If it was not yet an officially assigned case.

'They're panicking. Almost. I mean, apart from Nabi's claim, there's still really nothing to build a case on. Maybe the notes.

Hugues is hearing from a lot of people in Nabi's division and others who know Spanghero that the notes sound a lot like Vincent's ranting. Before he went all quiet. Even Nabi mentioned it. They figure Tropéano noticed too and went out looking. Menaud Rhéaume was Tropéano's partner. Good pals. There's really no other explanation for him.'

Aliette mused as to how that fit with Nabi's fretting over the notes the day before.

Sergio stared into his wine. 'Nabi's nightmare has resurfaced—in spades, I'm afraid. Last spring, trying to work it out with Vincent, some people started stirring up a lot of shit. Mario Bédard? Not nice, some of things Mario was starting to say.'

'Yes?'

'Political stuff. Ugly.'

'Mario can definitely do ugly.'

'But people hear him, especially now he's up there on the third at HQ.'

'Makes me glad I'm not.'

'Makes me wish you were.'

'Nabi's stronger than Mario.'

'Let's hope so… He managed to walk past it last spring. Now this.'

'If it really is Nabi's knife,' mulled Aliette.

'It is… But that is not being shared,' cautioned Sergio. 'Nor Vincent's name.'

'But Tropéano. They can't keep that—'

'They'll announce it Monday. But it's a still a crazy street person. That's the official line. No one wants people thinking there's a rogue cop out killing people. Not good for the public's confidence. An angry cop killing his former colleagues is worse.'

'How long can they keep the lid on something like this?'

'Depends on who knows and how they feel about it.'

'Like Mario?'

'Like a lot of people.'

'But you—what are you supposed to be doing?'

'It might not be Vincent.' Though it surely was. And Sergio Regarri was to very unofficially work with top city police investigator Hugues Monty to determine which way the thing should head before any definitive public statement was made. 'I'm supposed to be quietly talking to relevant people, establishing what we all hope and pray isn't, actually *is* the case. Monty will continue working on the first two victims, looking for a street-related thing. Or whatever.'

'Poor Nabi.'

'Nabi definitely has a problem. But we all do. This gets out the wrong way, the entire house could come tumbling down.'

'Yes...' Aliette poured herself the last of the wine, mulling a city police force in panicked disarray. She tried to spin a positive from Sergio's grim scenario. 'But if it's Spanghero and he's returning the knife, maybe that means he's done. It's over.'

Sergio gave his head a glum shake. '*And* it's complicated because Tropéano's gun is missing.'

'No!'

'Yes.'

She got up to fetch another bottle and mulled the ramifications of that. Presenting bottle and corkscrew to Sergio, Aliette ventured, 'So maybe it isn't Spanghero. He'd have his own gun.'

Sergio confirmed, 'Vincent's service arm is unaccounted for—like him. He quit, but he never turned in his gun.' He pulled the cork and tasted. Shrugged. Filled his glass. 'But if the knife's a gesture—returning Nabi's gift, as you say—so is taking Tropéano's gun. Like a warrior taking a scalp?'

She blinked. 'Nice image.'

'The more interesting question is, was Tropéano tracking Vincent? Or vice-versa?'

'Why would he target Tropéano?'

'Tropéano was on the operation that brought it to a head. He saw Vincent put his phone on a window ledge, still open, and go in with Rhéaume while Nabi was still in the process of giving orders. Total insult, not to mention blatant disregard for orders. He said as much to the enquiry, if not to the media. Rhéaume was young, next generation, like him. Tropéano couldn't wait to testify. I'm told Vincent hates Tropéano as much as he hates Nabi.'

'But the other two?' Two homeless kids.

'That's the hard part. The notes? Maybe Vincent needed some bodies to communicate his cry of pain? Didn't really matter who. Now the notes have been … noted? And it's a good cover.'

'You're saying he doesn't want to kill the whole city, just his old friends from work?'

'It's a theory.' Magistrate Regarri could be just as mordant as any street-hardened cop.

'So they may have sent him out expressly. Poor Tropéano.'

'Maybe. Though obviously not on the clock. I'll have to talk to some people about that.'

'Including Nabi.'

'Nabi most of all. But we need to let Nabi rest, get over the shock, I'm sure he'll have some things to tell us.'

They worked through the next bottle, exploring the possibilities of a bitter cop on a deranged murder spree, a cop pissed that a swirly-haired *burr* had won the top job, a job he'd assumed was his. A cop who knew how to kill. Who'd snapped. The last thing a city needed as it lurched politically rightward, struggling to adjust to new French realities. Aliette kept Sergio talking …

They did not get to Gabrielle Gravel, the ramifications of *that*, till Sunday morning.

- 6 -

SUNDAY, MOVING FORWARD

The indoor market at Les Halles was packed on a Sunday morning. They held hands as they navigated the teeming lanes. Sergio knew all about her order from Division. Magistrate Regarri had also been admonished for not ensuring that the cop under his instruction toe a closer line to her assigned murder mandate and leave the anarchists to the DST. Though gently circumspect when listening to her anti-gun-philosophy speeches at the table or on the pillow, he had promised his unstinting support while she was undergoing her enforced regimen at PsychoDynamo. As predicted, when she told him about the sessions she'd be obliged to come in to the city for, he said, 'Of course you can stay! Can't guarantee anything too special to eat on a Tuesday night. Thursday either. Might be working late—you'll have to fend for yourself. But the bed will be warm when you get home. Or you can warm it for me.'

'Thank you. I will.' She bestowed a kiss on his unshaven Sunday cheek.

Their string bags bulging with groceries, they stepped back into an overcast winter day. The mistral had finally blown away, but had taken the sun with it. Place de la Madeleine was filled with the usual crowds, families with well-scrubbed faces on their way to the late mass, sleepy couples heading for a brunch at one of the many eateries on the square. And people like them—just walking.

Sergio put a lover's arm around her waist. Then stopped. Released her. 'What is that?'

'Practising?' She had slipped her new gun into her pocket before setting out.

'I can't believe it.'

'Neither can I.'

'But you're not on duty.'

She chirped back, 'And neither are you.'

'Dissociation is the first phase,' he commented, a knowing twinkle beaming from his dark Spanish eyes. 'I hear this all the time.' Magistrate Regarri meant when he was interviewing those disbelieving ones who had somehow picked up a gun and pulled the trigger with disastrous consequences. They would not recognize the impulse—'That wasn't me!... not like me at all...' They denied even as they admitted the result. He told her how the conflicting pressure could squash all traces of personality from their voices. 'It's as if the gun stole their soul.'

Inspector Nouvelle had often been party to the same strange moment. 'I'll ask Gabrielle.'

'I should hope so.' He was teasing, she was making light, but it was Sunday and they were having fun as he directed her up a tight, curving street off the square. The city knew about the latest killing by now and many Sunday wanderers were headed in the same direction.

'And you should put your hat back on,' she advised.

He did. A James Bond driving cap added distinction. And anonymity. She tugged her beret down over her ears, fluffed her scarf up around her cheeks. An off-duty cop with a gun in her pocket? A judge unofficially but deeply involved? Not at all. They approached the scene, just another couple, one showing the other around.

And there was some history for a local son to share with a newcomer from Brittany via Alsace. Église Saint-Aphrodise, ancient, long abandoned, was named not for the Greek goddess of love, desire and beauty, but for a priest who, according to legend, had found his way from Egypt on a camel. Who became archbishop of the city. Who came to a rather bad end, his head chopped off by pagans. There were statuary and paintings depicting Aphrodise carrying his head in his arms, and an annual spring festival celebrating the saint, the faithful dressed in medieval costume as they led a wooden camel on wheels through the streets. But the congregation itself had dwindled to irrelevance and the church had been closed for years. It was opened only to curious professionals and consulting restoration experts. The work had yet to be done. The City always had more important problems.

The Diocese too, one supposed.

Although the large iron-trussed doors kept squatters from the inner spaces, a demimonde of marginal types and runaways climbed the fence and camped nightly in the garage-sized entry area. 'Very popular. Like a port of call...' No one liked it. No one did much about it. 'Beat cops shoo them off, they flow back within hours. Like water.' PJ Inspector Pierre Tropéano's was not the first violent death to happen there. Far from it.

'Could Vincent Spanghero have been reduced to sleeping in this sort of place?' Aliette hadn't met the man, only heard the gossip—and that from a newcomer's distance.

'It's possible. Vincent's a very high-strung guy. That kind break hard and badly.'

Media vehicles lined the street. The murder scene had been cordoned off, a spinnaker-sized dropcloth installed to create a makeshift blind. Despite it, arc lamps set up inside spilled exaggerated light into the grey morning. Uniformed officers patrolled the tape. Onlookers were speculating. Camera people were circling. Reporters bearing mics and note pads were pestering the uniforms or listening to locals who claimed to know what was up.

But, body long since removed, there was really nothing to see.

Aliette pulled him by the hand. '*Allez, monsieur*, our lunch is waiting.'

As she was guiding her judge out of the throng, Aliette suddenly came face to face with a pair of washed-out eyes. '*Bonjour?*' The woman froze. She looked familiar. Where?... A pause to let the memory synapses find the proper juncture... '*Bonjour!*' It was the receptionist from PsychoDynamo. She too toted a string bag filled with market groceries. Perhaps her memory synapses were not as well tuned as a cop's. Those bleak eyes just stared. 'Small world,' prompted the inspector. The woman did not reply; she stood looking at Aliette as if fearing she'd be asked for money. Another try: 'Busy morning?'

Finally registering, the woman blurted, 'I don't have to talk to you!' And hurried away.

Of course she didn't. But she didn't need to be rude either.

Sergio asked, 'Who was that?'

'Receptionist at my psychologist's.'

'I wonder what her problem is.'

'I think she needs a boyfriend, poor thing.' Aliette decided it had to be that.

They returned to a quiet lunch. A nap … no sex, just the afternoon sky.

Finally a cup of tea, quiet, talked out, watching the evening sun drop through the clouds.

Then he walked her down the city stairs beneath the lookout. They found her car parked along the boulevard. They kissed in the gloaming. He waved... *À bientôt*! She headed back to Saint-Brin and another Monday.

Moving forward? Aliette was feeling comfortable with this man. She enjoyed sleeping with him. She enjoyed walking with him, and sitting with him, sharing wine. Yes, part of her remained vigilant. Her heart had been devastated the time before. Her instincts had signalled wrongly, had left her soul in free-fall. Somehow, through grace or luck, she was now with Sergio Regarri. She was loath to bring emotional baggage into their still-forming love, but in painful moments she remembered. She looked hard at love, searching for signs that history might repeat.

So far the coast was clear.

Ensure the bed is warm if she got there first on a Tuesday night? Absolutely. Thursday too.

She could see it: 'Got my gun thing this evening, don't wait up for me.' He would nod, 'See you in bed,' and leave it at that. Where her ex-partner Claude had allowed her love to turn his love rigidly traditional, Sergio did not insist. He was not being casual—he was trusting. He was fitting with her way of loving. He did not push it in directions she didn't want to go. They lived their life together when they could, extending their days forward one by one. And it was working… A shame it hadn't happened sooner.

But life never happens sooner, it happens now.

She looked forward to Tuesday night, to coming home to Sergio.

BACKGROUND CHECK

Chief Inspector Aliette Nouvelle began her week with a call to an office in a dull but prosperous mid-sized city on the Rhine:

'*Salut*, J-P!...it's Aliette...Nouvelle? No, I know, how could anyone ever forget me? I'm fine, just fine. But I need some professional advice... Yes, sure there's someone in the area, but no one I can talk to, at least not like I can talk to you, if you know what I mean... Yes, I know you know. It's why I called, *monsieur*.' Child psychologist Jean-Paul Blismes loved it when she flattered shamelessly. He knew she knew it, which made it that much more enjoyable for both of them. 'Well, what I need to know is, can you tell me about this sandbox thing?'

'By all means, Inspector!' J-P smiled.

He always smiled. On the wrong day, it could be pure torture. Today it was fine—he was at the other end of France, after all. But she could hear J-P Blismes smiling like the Sahara sun as he briefed her on this non-verbal method of 'sand play' therapy, also called the World Technique.

It had been around for half a century. J-P differentiated between a 'sand tray' and a 'sandbox,' a sandbox being something one could actually step into. A tray on a table was the usual tool, such as Aliette had been presented with in her interview with Gabrielle Gravel. 'But it could be a box,' J-P advised. 'Why not? Be a lot more fun, you'd have to think.' Fun being related to play. Play being the operative concept.

Playing silently in the sand with miniature toys and sundry objects provided to the client—yes, of any age, J-P Blismes assured her—was a medium through which clients could construct their own microcosm reflecting their life and attendant issues. 'They do groups too. Couples, families… football teams that aren't performing.' That last item was a J-P joke. Aliette imagined a huge smile to honour it flashing all the way from Alsace and warming the barren square outside her southern window. 'It's meant to help people communicate, with each other and with the therapist… Never been my cup of tea,' he added. 'But what do I know?' he asked, playfully rhetorical.

'You know lots, J-P. But what's it supposed to do?'

'The usual stuff. Remove conflicts. Instill some order. Help a person connect with their inner child. Enable her to recognize the beauty of her very own soul. And communicate it.'

He inquired, Did that help?

Immensely. Sort of. And there was one other thing.

'Yes?'

Casually, she mentioned that she was intrigued to hear his take on Gabrielle.

'Gabrielle?'

'Gravel. I believe you two met at a conference in Iceland. She speaks very highly of you.'

'It was actually just across the river in the Rhinelands.' Noting, 'Never the best liar, you.'

Aliette's turn to smile. 'I keep working on everything we covered, J-P. But this is not about me.'

'Everything is about you, Inspector. Centre of the universe, remember?'

She confessed she'd already shared that. 'Gabrielle seemed pleased. Said it was a very workable trope.'

'Then I'd say you two are away to the races.'

'Please, J-P …' For the briefest instant, Aliette allowed the heart of her heart to show.

And J-P Blismes could see it all the way from his window in Alsace. 'She likes the centre of the universe? That's good,' he counselled. 'She likes your language. It's all about talking, yes?'

'Tell me more.'

He smiled—but remained oblique. 'She was interesting. Into lots of eastern stuff, not afraid to try new ideas. I mean at work… Not everyone in the profession would be amused. Perhaps she's not as mindful of barriers as our tradition dictates she ought to be…but

I thought she was fun. Those conferences can be deadly boring. Sort of looks like la Bardot?'

'You like la Bardot?'

'Well, not so much now. I'm talking about then.'

'I suppose she still does. A bit.'

'Why do you need to know this?'

Aliette hesitated. What to say? Because her life was on the line? 'It's like she has no sense of morality. Like I'm a motorcycle that needs to be tuned.'

'Yes, that was definitely there. It's not meant to be personal, what she does. What any of us do … I felt we were communicating well enough. (And it was only for a magic weekend.)'

(Aliette heard J-P's verbal parentheses loud and clear. But:) 'How can it not be personal, J-P? How can using a gun as a way of controlling a person not be personal?'

'There were no guns in our relationship, Inspector.'

'I feel she's going to gut my soul.'

'So now you're a house?'

'On fragile ground.'

'I like that. Gabrielle will too …' That smile, large, completely confident. 'Keep giving her tropes to chew on, she'll be happy, you'll be fine.'

'What about this sand?'

'Sand, finger painting, role playing, hypnosis, whichever way you turn, it all comes down to talking, I assure you.'

'*Merci*, J-P.'

'You call me if you need me.'

'Can I convey your wishes to Gabrielle?'

'Not the best idea, Inspector.'

'Understood. But you can give my love to all up there.'

Even to a certain Claude? J-P did not ask and she left it open.

She knew J-P Blismes always enjoyed the open side of things, especially the things of love.

Then she buzzed Mathilde, arranged for coffee and pastry, and prepared to welcome Sergeant Nicolas Legault, head of the small Saint-Brin Gendarme unit. A body had been discovered the day before in a gully in the hills above the vines near the village of Bouldoux. Or what was left of it—it had been there for months. Some Sunday hikers had had their day seriously disrupted. Nicolas had come to provide initial details, pending the forensics. Forest creatures had taken the best part of the body, and some of the bones. But they'd left the head, which had a large hole, and the only thing with a bite strong enough for that was a bullet.

- 8 -

My *PSY* is private

Béziers is second in size to Montpellier in a line of cities strung westward along the Golfe du Lion to Spain. Though you could be forgiven for thinking so from glancing at a map, Béziers is neither on the sea, nor a port. The sea is fifteen minutes away (when there's no traffic). Rather, Béziers is a busy end point for the Midi canal system, which works its way south and east from Toulouse. It is also at the mouth of the River Orb, a major artery of commerce and population flowing down from the Caroux mountain range. And the Languedocienne A9 autoroute brings much Euro and Euro/Africa traffic through its environs.

All of which makes Béziers a small city that feels major.

Then again, most cities do once they swallow you up.

Béziers swallows with a cunning grin. Built around Cathédrale Saint-Nazaire, huge on a west-facing promontory, the city's original layout is vaguely circular, accent on vague and tending to unfathomable, and the traffic is bizarrely difficult. It had been over a year and Chief Inspector Nouvelle still hadn't figured it out. But if she stayed organized, left time for the inevitable walk—she liked walking—she could park on the edges and get to where she was meant to be.

Tuesday, early afternoon, Aliette headed into town.

After Marraussan—at the southernmost limit of her jurisdiction, she headed west, negotiated the roundabout, passed the new prison. The cathedral was straight ahead, looming high and massive. She found a parking spot in Boulevard d'Angleterre, climbed the stairs, ducked briefly into 36 Rue Boudard to leave her overnight bag and some pasta makings, after which it was literally a five-minute stroll across the park into the shadow of the church, thence to the Palais de Justice.

Magistrate Martine Rogge had considered Magui's report from their Saturday visit with Robert Benech the cheese producer, and she had conducted her own interview with Justine Péraud, the woman who had killed his wife. She was ready to discuss next steps. It was not a question of who did what. It was about how to frame it for the court. Justine's attorney would be there too.

Then Medical Examiner Annelise Duflot would brief her on the forensics gleaned from the remains found in the woods at Bouldoux. The pathologist had generously suggested a meeting at the courthouse, saving Aliette a nerve-wracking drive out to the morgue at Centre Hospitalier, on the eastern edge of the city. Very generous. A belated gesture of good will? Aliette was no fan of Annelise. The always stylish little *légiste* (she couldn't weigh 100 pounds) exuded that France-for-the-French! hard-right mentality which was becoming increasingly counterproductive to peace and trust in the streets. Annelise, a finely tuned woman, would no doubt have sensed a natural enemy in Chief Inspector Nouvelle. Could there have been a softening on her side of the barrier? Aliette made a note to henceforth do her best to extend Dr. Duflot a more open-hearted response.

The Palais offered equipped offices in a hallway in the sub-basement where visitors could prepare, recharge, report, communicate back to their own offices, and conduct their own meetings before or after their business on the upper floors. Leaving Martine Rogge, Aliette went down, happy enough with the meeting, albeit still not certain *crime passionnel* fit the circumstances at the goat cheese operation in the hills.

She tried all six office doors along the hall, hoping for a package from Division with her name on it waiting on a desk. All she found was one Italian cop eating something with much garlic in it. Ah well… Aliette sat at the desk in the room farthest from the Italian and began to review her notes while waiting for Dr. Annelise Duflot to finish her other business upstairs. She was about to call Magui Barthès and relate Magistrate Rogge's next directives when there was a knock on the door. A man stepped in and handed her a package. 'Sorry to be late. This place has the stupidest traffic I've ever seen.' She forgave him, signed the voucher, put her notes aside.

The holster and rig were blond leather, still stiff. They had stamped *AN* on the actual sheath. Her first thought was for a custom-tailored silvery undergarment bearing the same monogram, a souvenir from her previous life, which she still had. Which Sergio hadn't really noticed. No, but nothing is perfect... Removing the staid navy blazer worn in respect for the formal courthouse ambience, Aliette cautiously tried it on. Made adjustments—at her shoulders, along the curve of her lower back, trying to position it in the soft area above her left hip.

She stood there. It did not feel right.

...Yes, of course: The gun. She retrieved it from her case—yes, she had been carrying it, all day yesterday too—and inserted it in the sheath. And stood there.

She reached across her belly and drew her gun. Replaced it. *Bon*...

She put her coat back on and repeated the exercise.

She buttoned her coat. She wished she had a mirror.

Chief Inspector Nouvelle stepped out of the borrowed office, headed for the Ladies to better assess the new bulge at her side but was stopped in her tracks as Chief Inspector Zidane came shuffling into the hallway, head bowed, a mopey posture, no doubt searching for a place to hide after being ripped apart upstairs.

He might have walked right past her. He was there, but he was obviously somewhere else.

Who could blame him? His knife. His enemy. His inspector, so brutally killed.

'*Ça va*, Nabi?' Her most *sympa* voice.

That stopped him. Perhaps he recognized a friend. 'Not fun, that's for sure... I suppose you know all about it.'

'Some.' And possibly more than Nabi, at least concerning Sergio's assigned task.

'It's whether they can keep it under wraps till we find him.'

'Can they?'

'I don't know. I've no idea how this could ever...' Pursed lips, baffled shrug, a desolate man.

Where was the sly twinkle she enjoyed? Aliette felt its absence. She *wanted* him to recognize a friend. 'If there's anything I can do,

Nabi...' Which was a nice thing to say, but of no practical value, she knew. The Spanghero conflict had played out long before her arrival. Beyond Sergio's cursory facts, she knew nothing about it. The murders were not even remotely close to her patch. Still, she meant it. Nabi Zidane had helped her. She owed him.

Nabi actually considered her blithe offer. She saw it—for an instant, that softly calculating thing flickered in his eyes. 'Maybe...'

'Maybe?'

'Maybe you might ask that woman if she has any ideas as to where he might be.'

'That woman? His wife?'

'That *psy*. Vincent spent about half a year with her. An order from the enquiry after we lost Menaud Rhéaume.'

'Oh...I didn't know.' It was all Aliette could say. She felt like screaming in frustration.

But she listened politely as a melancholy Nabi filled her in. 'Vincent should have quit after I got the promotion—if it really bothered him so much. He kept coming to work, but he wasn't helping. The Lone Ranger, complaining about everything, exploding in the middle of meetings. We were all on pins and needles every day.' Nabi sniffed. 'When he fucked up and Menaud went down, they made him go to therapy. If he didn't go to her, he was out. So he went. But then he started becoming really withdrawn, quiet. Which was almost worse, if you know him. Then he quit. But her report said he showed up for his appointments till she felt he was better.'

'Better?'

'Who knows? Said she was satisfied he'd gotten a handle on his emotions and ended it. She cut him loose, he severed ties with us, he disappeared. She's probably the last person to have seen him—at least that we know of. Catherine, that's his wife, she gave up, couldn't reach him. Apparently he walked out on her a couple of months before. This *psy*... Hugues sent his guys to talk to her, but she just repeated her report. Vincent had moved past it and would be fine. She refuses to say anything more specific. Client confidentiality. A very tough nut by all accounts... Maybe Sergio will pry something out of her.' But a woeful shrug said Nabi doubted it.

'Sergio?'

'She's on his list.'

Sergio's clandestine mandate to double check. Clearly, even if removed from all involvement in the matter, Nabi Zidane had been informed. He was assuming, quite correctly, she knew too.

She could only nod, she hoped not too stupidly.

Nabi's smile was self-deprecating: my problem, not yours, ' ... and, well, since you're seeing her ... I mean, if you sense a window there? Maybe you could somehow...'

'Sure.'

'Thanks. You never know.'

'Her name is Gabrielle.'

'Right. Gabrielle.' He shuffled off, found an open door along the line and went in.

Aliette forgot about seeing how her new holster hung beneath her jacket. Stepping back inside her borrowed room, she flung the door shut—heard it echo in the hall. Her face was boiling.

Another cop about to explode? My *psy* is private!

Who should she be angry with? She spun around, exasperated.

She hoped and prayed not Sergio. Surely he would not—

Another knock on the door. Aliette snarled an angry 'Oui?'

'*Bonjour?*'

... But Dr. Annelise Duflot had arrived and Aliette had to put it from her mind.

9

TRANSITIONAL STREETS

The bullet extracted from the skull of the decomposing body found in the hills at Bouldoux was a 200-grain round, typically used in the .35 bore rifle favoured by most of the local hunters for bringing down wild pigs. Likely a Remington 700, very popular among the many hunters in the area. The body had been there since before the freeze, probably November, height of the season. No one had tried to bury it, making it feasible the shooter was unaware that he (or she) had made a hit, much less a kill…

Dusk was falling when the inspector left the courthouse.

She was feeling calmer after an hour of emotion-free forensics with Dr. Annelise Duflot.

It must have been Divisionnaire Doquès who'd divulged her order to attend at the office of Gabrielle Gravel to Nabi Zidane. Or some Human Resources functionary doing a search for Nabi, an off-hand remark when PsychoDynamo popped up in the file on Vincent Spanghero. Aliette would give Sergio the benefit of the doubt on this. She had to. And to scream at Gael Doquès, or HR for that matter, wouldn't help. Live with it, she commanded herself.

Could she trust Nabi to manage the information honourably? She sensed she could.

A tramontane had arrived to replace the mistral. It wasn't as cold, but it was dryly northern, biting in its own right. She walked quickly through the shadows of the cathedral, crossed the small park—empty, no tourists at the look-out railing snapping pictures on a blustery Tuesday evening in late January—and let herself in Sergio's door. She prepared a bowl of pasta and sat in front of the local news. The pictures of a fallen Pierre Tropéano, his widowed wife and two children had filled last evening's broadcast, along with a vacant-looking Chief

City Investigator Monty standing with the mayor, who vowed the perpetrator would soon be apprehended. Tropéano's face was there again tonight, but the reporting was back to the investigation's lack of progress. A city police force PR mouthpiece blandly explained that the main hurdle now was to determine a motivational link that went beyond the fact of stabbing. Indeed … Aliette left the news, went up and brushed her teeth. Strapped her gun back on.

It was fully dark when she left for her appointment. Calculating the direct route from Sergio's to Place de la Madeleine, adding Friday's walk from there to Rue Argence, she gave herself a good hour and deliberately set off the other way. The medieval configuration of the inner city was a maze and she knew she'd probably get lost on the way to Gabrielle's.

Check that: She *would* get lost, it was almost certain. Getting lost would be an experiment—some personal prep for the next phase of this order to get bonded with her gun.

She made her way down the stairs, up the next stairs, around the school, the ugly HLM. The streets were tight and the lighting inconsistent, overly bright one moment, murky the next. She navigated damp pavement strewn with haphazard garbage, the horrid leavings of dogs. Climbing slippery cobbles in Rue Calvaire, she had to use the handrail. She turned left, came out into the open of a small square, passed a row of stately bourgeois apartments overlooking the boulevard and valley, turned back into a side street with no doors at all. Up the next, she passed artisanal shops—handmade shoes, dentures, dusty useless bric-à-brac absurdly called *objets de collection* (collectibles), an empty-looking *épicerie*. Dwellings on the second floors of each. The deeper into the labyrinth, the more For Sale signs on the boarded-up doors and windows of properties falling into ruin, value tumbling, waiting for a different demographic to make an offer. Some people called these streets 'transitional.' Some politicians liked that term—easy code for territory in the process of being claimed by the steady influx of newcomers who lived a different way. A growing Maghreb diaspora had claimed entire enclaves, adding extravagant colours, patterning, intriguing scents on passing bodies, lightning-cadenced dialects, that whining, seemingly formless music. Even on a winter's night with windows sealed, a barrage of spicy fragrances escaping from kitchens let Aliette know she was in another world. Another world taking root in the heart of France...

Around the next corner, the music had a different beat, quick, with major tuning. And the supper smells were different too. Côte D'Ivoire? Senegal? Togo, Guinea, Mauritania? No idea... Aliette was watchful as she turned one dim corner after the next, feeling her gun, attuned to reactions, hers, theirs, aware of questions floating up from somewhere in her heart. It wasn't fear, was it? It never used to be. What was this feeling? Did a gun on her person alter her presence in this street as she passed this klatch of chattering ladies, all of them heavily veiled? It did not appear so. She was ignored as if invisible, not a soul amongst them was inclined to accord her the slightest glance as she passed by.

Which allowed a darker question to arise: For other citizens, less inclined to exotic spices, who only speak one language, could this invisibility be construed as a slight, a cultural insult?

A mood, political or otherwise, is plastic. A gun is immutable. An off-duty police officer is just a private citizen. The weapon in the holster riding not so smoothly on her hip was illegal.

...Not true, Inspector: A cop is always a cop. Off-duty only means you are not being paid.

Instinct was the soul's anchor. Why should a gun change your navigation skills?

The first two victims of Nabi's knife had been killed in the general area. The two found notes conveyed the fear and rage of the loss of something more treasured than the value of a house. But both those boys were very French—or, pending absolute ID, at least Caucasian—one of 'us,' Vincent Spanghero's people. And Inspector Pierre Tropéano was a real French cop, as the TV news reporter had so solemnly said—aware of double meanings or not. But a deranged street person could be from anywhere. And be anything—including an ex-cop. It's the *deranged* that sets them apart... Mulling variables, Aliette had a feeling she was the most vulnerable soul in the neighbourhood. Gun attached to her hip or otherwise.

At a certain corner in a particularly dilapidated street, she stopped to contemplate the chalked crime-scene outline of a body. It was beginning to fade. Ditto the remnants of blood where it had seeped into cracks in the paving. As she stood there, two ragged-looking youths stepped out of the door of an abandoned house opposite and shuffled warily past her, smelling of beer, marijuana, the perpetual lack of basic grooming. Sad: hardly twenty and lost to the world.

This would be the scene of the first killing. Those two boys may have known the victim. If not them, someone inside this shambling house—a squat, the news had said, until its inhabitants were rousted, the doors boarded over and the windows re-nailed. She stepped close, heard sounds on the other side of the door, smelt the reek of humid plaster. Then drew back. No…

It was not her case, not her patch. She had an appointment with Gabrielle Gravel.

Aliette Nouvelle moved on, hand on the bulge at her hip.

Afer two more blocks, she crossed a major street. She was glad to be reoriented, and almost there. Turning into Rue Argence, she noted a man at a window on a second floor. He was watching her and didn't hide the fact. White guy. Skeptical. She hoped he was simply there at his window, an empty moment, waiting for his evening *télé* shows to start.

The way he looked, she suspected he was watching out for a killer invading his quarter.

Sorry, not me, *monsieur*… Smiling briefly up at him before stepping in at PsychoDynamo.

10

TUESDAY-THURSDAY PEOPLE

'*Bonsoir*, madame.'

…but the sad receptionist did not look up from whatever it was she was doing. Stepping forward, the inspector placed the appointment card on the desk, directly under the lady's nose. To no avail. 'Won't be long. Take seat,' the woman mumbled. She was studying a blank page. Any sense of readiness Aliette might have gained from an hour's march through the streets with her gun was instantly negated. Chagrined—was this woman part of Gabrielle's strategy?—she hung her coat and sat, leaving an empty chair between herself and the man ensconced in the corner.

He was deep in a book. Or pretending to be, a lock of greying but long and lush hair falling down over his nose as he focused. Aliette nodded hello, though he wasn't looking.

Although he was… *Bonsoir* to you as well, *monsieur*. I'm a Tuesday-Thursday person too.

She tried to get comfortable, soon wished she'd brought something to read. She tried—because she couldn't help herself—but could not catch the title of the man's book. His large hands were wrapped around it, as if purposely shielding this information. But he sensed her prying eye and glanced, quick, furtive—then instantly let his eyes fall back to his page. It irked. What book? Aliette peeked again. She was as curious as he, though she knew she mustn't be.

Not here.

He glanced again. She caught him—met a pair of grey sloe eyes assessing. Her age group, more or less, lean face, nervous, sensual mouth, a straight and strong aristocratic nose. Actually a very good-looking man. In the instant before his eyes dropped back to his page, she smiled a neutral smile.

Then checked it. The receptionist was observing. And not approving.

He shifted slightly in his chair. To ensure the title of his book remained obscured? In the effort of the movement, the ghost of a human sound that came with it, Aliette thought she detected something sad, frustrated, like an animal that's bored but can't understand the emotion. He was another depressed person, like the poor woman at the desk. He had come to Gabrielle Gravel for a blast of psycho propulsion. The impression... and the supposition it evoked seemed feasible. But what does such a person read? It was getting to her.

And what do I share with the likes of him?

An inner voice commanded, Stop this. The man was waiting, reading. It was not for her to impute character into that, let alone a problem.

But he would not be here if he did not have a problem. Like me?

Next time she would bring her own book. And she would hide the cover...

The sound of a door disturbed her absurdly vengeful train of thought.

'*T'es une pute!*' You whore... A nasty growl jolted the inspector to her feet, cop instinct kicking in, on high alert as a lanky, evil-eyed teenaged girl stomped out of the cubbyhole door to the therapist's office.

Evil-eyed and in black from head to toe: chopped-up hair, ratty wool sweater, ripped denim, clunky boots. She grabbed the scuffed-up bomber jacket from the overloaded coat tree. Worse than her murderous look or her uncouth language was the odour of the angry girl. Wielding her jacket over her shoulders like a cape as she pulled it on, a wave of sweaty female fug wafted through the space. Inescapable. Awful. The inspector was repulsed and must have shown it.

'What is your problem?'

It was a challenge verging on a threat. Aliette shook herself, met it coolly. Fanning the air in front of her nose, she held the hateful gaze. 'Gabrielle still alive in there?'

'*Connasse!*' Bitch. Snatching the proffered appointment card from the trembling receptionist, the stinking girl bolted from the room, infuriated, slamming the door behind her.

Silence: the man with the book still pretending to read, the receptionist deeply wary.

Aliette said, to no one in particular, 'Lovely. Just lovely.'

Did she really belong with these strange people? What exactly made Gabrielle Gravel think she should be part of the Tuesday-Thursday cohort?

PROPERTY OF THE STATE

'Hello. How are we tonight?'

'Is it going to be like this every Tuesday and Thursday, Gabrielle?'

A shrug. 'We all hope not.'

'I find your attitude less than professional.'

'I'm just a mirror, Inspector... Sit, please.'

Turning, indignant, Aliette made to leave.

'Can you stop being such a diva?... Just sit down and deal with your life.' It was an order as much as a taunt—and clearly heard. Chief Inspector Nouvelle slumped into the chair. Gabrielle moved on. Folding her hands, leaning forward. 'Now, let's have a look, shall we?'

Aliette obediently reached inside her jacket, too aware how automatically she was responding to cues touching on obedience. She placed her sidearm on the table. PROPRIÈTÈ DE L'ÈTAT was etched on the side. Gabrielle touched it. Then tamped the oily film on her fingertip against the dryness of her thumb. 'Please pick it up.'

'Are you afraid of it?'

'Please.'

Another order. Feeling played with, the inspector did so, proffering it a moment in the manner she was trained, safely pointed away. Then, with an empty shrug, she moved to re-holster—

'Wait.' Gabrielle brusquely motioned her to stop. 'Just hold onto it for a bit, if you would.'

Obedient Aliette sat with her sidearm cradled loosely in her right hand at a safe remove.

Gabrielle said, 'To answer your question: yes, I am afraid of it. Any sane person is.' Eyes more on the gun (which was loaded) than on the one who held it, the psychologist sat back in·her chair. 'So. Let's consider your new position, as it were. I mean your new existential position, yes? I want you to tell to me what you think you could accomplish with this fine piece of machinery that you could not without.'

The response was direct. 'Nothing I couldn't accomplish without a few right words.'

'Sorry, that is a wrong thought. It will lead you to unemployment.' Gabrielle made a note.

Aliette asked, 'How does a gun in my kit affect my sense of a civilized approach to my job?'

In keeping with the classic style, Gabrielle Gravel met a query with one of her own. 'How do you define civilized?'

'Does a gun in one's pocket make one the most important person in the street?'

'In some respects, very much so.'

'Does one radiate power? I was thinking about that on the way over here. I do have my gun. Not a single person batted an eye when I passed.'

'Meaning?'

'Power would depend on my mood, not my gun.'

'Agreed ... Can you deal with that?'

'How can I know until the moment comes?'

'The confluence of mood and moment?' Gabrielle liked that. She made a note. Advised her client, 'Inspector, only the most simplistic gun-culture ideologue will cling to the instrumentalist notion that it's all down to the individual, that the gun is a dumb object innocent of any agency. You and I cannot allow ourselves to sink to that level. *Obviously* the human-gun relation transforms a situation and re-renders it a world away from a similar situation minus the presence of a gun in hand. Much less two guns in two opposing hands. Mm? We are talking about the power of life and death. A gun in hand confers this. That is agency, Inspector. *Big time...* as the Americans say?' This in English. Gabrielle allowed herself a tiny smile.

Aliette could not return it.

There was a small stack of magazines on the corner of the desk. The psychologist opened the one at the top at a marked page and read, again in English. '... *In a world inundated with violent images subsumed in heroic consumer fantasies, a gun is now the pre-eminent social catalyst. More than money, birth, even beauty—our culture's perennial gold standard!—the implication of impending violence trumps everything. It is not the gun per se—though it obviously is—but the bearer, the implied possibility of what could happen. We could say: The gun shines through like aura and defines the bearer.*' Closing the journal, she held it up. A glossy shot of a handsome golden retriever, a large male hand stroking its silky head. 'You have a large responsibility,' noted Gravel, replacing the magazine on the pile.

Aliette shrugged. 'It's sad.'

Gabrielle Gravel agreed. 'Sick is always sad, Inspector. But it's neither here nor there. A professional—you—will develop relationships with the tools at her disposal, never losing sight of the fact that she is at the crux of the situational nexus.'

Aliette saw an opening. 'Centre of the universe then?'

'I am willing to grant this trope could work if kept in proper perspective.'

Aliette persisted. She had to. Otherwise, who was she? 'Did you know I tracked down one of the most dangerous criminals in the history of modern France and none of it involved a gun?'

'None of it?' asked Gabrielle, something crafty creeping into her probing eyes.

'Look it up—Jacques Normand, Public Enemy Number One.' She cited year and place.

Gabrielle Gravel stared deep into Aliette Nouvelle for a disconcerting moment. 'Bravo, but your lack of a firearm has been directly linked to the murder of a federal agent, name of—' Waving the file, she licked her thumb, flipped the pages.

'Margot,' Aliette volunteered.

'By a man who probably killed at least two others and is still at large.'

'He *did* kill at least two others.'

'A very highly regarded officer, I'm told.'

'Not as good as she thought she was.'

'Should I keep that for the record?' Pen poised over her pages.

Aliette glumly indicated, No. Acknowledging that she was at their mercy.

And that Gabrielle Gravel had agency, totally and utterly.

Gabrielle put the file aside. 'You have this volatility. Up … down … Do you have mood issues, Inspector?'

'I'm a human being. I have moods. Issues? I don't know. My job is stressful, everyone knows that. Some days it's physical, other days it's like you're talking to God.'

'Well, we can talk about it too. And we will explore it in your sand.'

Gabrielle devoted the remainder of the session to ideas touching on the notion of less existential stress coupled with improved results through the agency of a gun, the right time, the right place.

'And according to my mood.'

'Moods can be adjusted.'

The inspector's only defence was a sporadic, increasingly meek reportage of facts harkening back to a time of perfect results, professional stardom.

'Of course we must deal with the past, see it clearly if we hope to move forward,' said Gabrielle.

Aliette realized her hand was getting tired. She replaced her weapon in its leather pouch reposing against the soft area under her kidney. Gabrielle saw and smiled spontaneously. 'And you've had it personalized! This is good.' She made another note.

It grated. The inspector heard herself asking, 'How many police fit in your sandbox, Gabrielle?'

A vague and ill-constructed question? Or a highly existential koan?

'Not relevant,' rejoined Gabrielle, a bit too defensive, following directly with a speech reiterating the law according to Gabrielle within Gabrielle's domain: She would not respond to questions outside the context of her particular mandate with a given client.

Aliette let it go by. She was bound to. But an experienced police officer will notice when the woman across the table knows exactly where a question points. And deliberately evades.

The thought occurred: I could pull my gun and hold it to her head and make her tell me about Vincent Spanghero.

But Gabrielle said, '*Bon*, I think we've made a useful start... For homework, as it were, I want you to dig down and bring me the absolute truth of this fantasy of the Public Enemy. I think it could be seminal, in fact I'm sure it is, and we'll need to clear it up if we want to avoid slipping backward here.' She rose. 'Next time, then?'

The reading man was still there when Aliette emerged. He had waited the entire hour she'd been inside with Gabrielle. Why?... But you were not allowed to ask. Donning her coat, pausing to accept another meticulously printed appointment card from the receptionist, the inspector felt his gaze. She ignored it. She tried again to engage the woman. '*Merci*. And do you have a name?'

Apparently not. Nor was a card really necessary. Next time was Thursday.

She headed back along the disjointed way she'd come. The veiled women had disappeared, gone inside to their kitchens, children. It was just their men now. Alone, in groups, shivering, muttering, rubbing chilled hands, they made no bones about watching her. Though none said a word, at least not directly, as Aliette Nouvelle passed. With her gun. Did they sense it?

Did she shine?

12

IMAGE CONSCIOUS

As promised, the bed was warm and her man was welcoming. Lying there with him, she felt an awful need to ask, 'Does a gun make a difference? I mean, in me?'

Like Gabrielle, he replied with a question. 'What kind of difference could there possibly be?'

'I don't know. I'm asking.'

Sergio Regarri was wise. Half a year into their love affair, he knew it wouldn't matter what he told her, she'd sort through it in her own time, in her own way. 'As long as you're honest. Why would a gun change anything?'

Honest? Did this man know how a word could prick her soul?

Some hold that some lies are necessary, even good if a good result is where it ends. Lots of police fall into this category. Many lovers too. But if the lie creates the myth? Fifteen years on, the image was too clear. Aliette remembered watching Jacques Normand, the legendary Public Enemy, running for his life. He had been so hopeful. Desperately hopeful. Doomed, but smiling. It ended a moment later, so mundanely, when he was struck and killed by a car. Exit one tired old French hero. If there had been no gun defining that moment, there would have been no lie.

Inspector Aliette Nouvelle had ignored it. Left it untouched. Forgotten it for years on end.

She was the myth and she had lived it. Or tried to.

Now Gabrielle, holding a mandate to bring an errant cop back on track, had brought it to the fore.

In fact, it was his gun, not hers. True to form, Inspector Nouvelle, soft-spoken, silvery-eyed, a rising star in the Judicial Police, did not bring her gun that night. True to form, she had talked him into handing over his weapon. Simple, if you know how. (Yes, J-P, it all comes down to talking.) She was something new, a kind of cop a man like Jacques simply couldn't fathom. He thought it was love. He'd come willingly, if warily, a confused and isolated man who believed the voice of a cop sounded like the voice of love. She received him gently, he had handed over his gun. Face to face with the Public Enemy, she had lifted it from his hands. Told him, 'We don't need this, you and I.' Like a magician with a bird, Aliette had held it up. One gun: not useful here. Then put it aside. *Voilà* ...

But it wasn't love, it was the turning of the wheel. The end of his story, the beginning of hers.

When he finally understood, his anger surged, the anger of a lifetime holding history in the balance. Fifteen years on, warm and safe in Sergio's bed, she remembered feeling that legendary anger flame one last time in the inarticulate space between them. How could she forget the anger in those large hands clasped around her delicate neck? He could have used his hands to choke her. Snap her neck. Pummel the beauty, silence the voice, destroy the things ... *my tools, Gabrielle?* ...that had charmed him into giving up the gun that defined his life. It was more than a possibility. It was who he was: Jacques Normand, Public Enemy Number One.

And a cop remembered: While she waited for the anger to leave him, to drain away forever, Inspector Nouvelle had maintained a firm, unseen grip on the surrendered gun, justly cautious of anger's second thoughts, and uncertain, not entirely convinced by her own magical voice uttering soothing words. The gun in her hand had bolstered her soul, helped her wait it out.

The crisis point had lasted, what? maybe a minute? (One minute in the history of modern France.)

How to balance the risk to life and limb against a sense of destiny? That night, fifteen years ago; this night now, here in a new life. Aliette knew it then, she'd known it all these years. *She would have used it.* The gun in her hand ... In the end, everything had worked out according to history's movement. But the fact she had relied on that hidden gun to push history forward put the lie to her larger claim: *I don't need that gun to be who I am and do what I have to do.*

Now Gabrielle Gravel's eyes reflect the lie back into the light.

Now a sense of destiny recedes.

Lying there under the stars with Sergio, Aliette Nouvelle saw history moving backward:

She could see her hand hidden in the folds of her coat, she could see herself make a decision to pull the trigger and blow the Public Enemy away. Could hear a flat bang, a hollow pop. She saw the jolt, total surprise, a moment of uncomprehending disbelief, saw him stagger backward, fall to the floor. Aliette saw it too clearly as she looked back in time. She saw herself, standing over him, interested but removed. She saw the mess of gore and blood, the collapsing of what was his eye into his brain. She saw herself delivering the *coup de grâce* when he reached out a wondering hand. Those about to die, they always seem to wonder…

Then she saw him disappear. His gun. Her gun. Who cares? Bottom line: Case closed.

Everyone knew this didn't happen. But it could have. It almost did.

Gabrielle was right. A powerful tool. Powerful agency. Set against history.

She whispered to the man beside her, 'I almost didn't meet you.'

'Impossible.' From somewhere in his dream, Sergio Regarri murmured in reply.

No. Too possible. If she had killed Jacques Normand the way she was supposed to kill him, *then*, where would she be now? The stars would have aligned differently. Inspector Nouvelle would have been a different cop, a different person. But here she was with this wonderful (and honest) man. Like a dream come true, but also a fact.

Did that fact connote forgiveness on the part of someone, some*thing*, somewhere?

Or would she pay for that little lie? One can't know. (Nor could Gabrielle.) Some days it's like you're talking to God.

Aliette held on tighter, fell in and out of fitful sleep.

She awoke to the aroma of coffee and the sounds of Sergio downstairs collecting his things. She waited till she heard the front door open, then fall quietly shut. Time to get going, Inspector.

The huge window presented a clear winter morning.

And that troubling question: Does a gun make a difference in me?

In the place between sleep and the world there was a mirror. Body length, life sized. Before stepping into the shower, the inspector stood in front of herself. Naked. There was the woman she knew and mostly loved. Still looking good at forty-plus, firm and full. Functioning…

Well, yes, patting her tummy, she really must get back to running. Preventive action.

But the gun. That could not be prevented. No gun, no inspector.

She collected the holstered weapon from the pile of things on the chair and strapped it on.

And stepped back in front of herself.

Naked is normal. Naked with a gun strapped on is something else. You could see the grip, a butt of black hard steel, flat, featureless, peeking from the pouch resting at her hip. The holster was minimal, strictly serviceable, not a fashion accessory. But it was there and it fundamentally changed the view.

She laid a tentative hand on the gun. The other instinctively had to touch her belly, a breast, move the hair from her eyes as she stood contemplating lines of leather bisecting and traversing. *Obscuring me.* She fretted, image conscious, image *bound*, still sleepy, still in that soft cocoon of sleep's protective gauze, but not so sleepy that she was able to deny: naked in a minimalist sky-washed space with this deadly thing appended, it was hard to recognize herself.

13

IN THE LUNCHROOM

Breakfast alone with the radio: Another killing, another street person, young male, perhaps a minor, Caucasian, yet to be identified, found in the lane outside the wall of Cimetière Vieux sometime before midnight, the cemetery being a popular place for these non-citizens to pass the night in relative peace. Another jolt: Aliette's way home from PsychoDynamo had taken her within a block of the scene. He had been shot, point blank through the neck, said the morning news.

'So we don't know if it's related,' said a spokesperson for the city investigators.

Arriving at Hôtel de Police, Betty, Chief Inspector Zidane's long-time secretary, informed Chief Inspector Nouvelle that Medical Examiner Annelise Duflot had worked through the night and everyone on the third floor now knew the killing round had been fired from Pierre Tropéano's missing gun.

'Another note?'

'Apparently.' Though it had yet to be circulated through the office.

'How's Nabi taking this?'

Betty shrugged, eyes wide. 'Haven't seen him since yesterday. He's hiding and I don't blame him.' She shook her head, slow and foreboding, as if to say, What a shame.

'What is it?'

'You'll find out.' Betty was uncertain who to trust. She went back to her endless typing.

Aliette went searching. She had wanted to share her impressions of Gabrielle Gravel's revealingly evasive reaction to a question at least three steps away from the name Vincent Spanghero.

'Seen Nabi?' No one had. Blank stares, some more blank than others, along the halls of the third floor.

Her search took her down to the second. Head city investigator Hugues Monty, stuck in the middle of four subordinates as they scrummed into the lift, was too distracted to give her anything but a brusque shake of his head: No.

'*Merci*, Hugues.' And fair enough: with the revelation of the knife in Inspector Pierre Tropéano's gut and with ex-Inspector Vincent Spanghero unofficially at the centre of their radar, Nabi Zidane was officially excluded from the investigation. Any personal attachment, actual or perceived, and you're out.

But surely there were a thousand other things a chief inspector could be doing to justify his rank and pay. Aliette wandered through the canteen, media centre, IT and switchboard areas, and all the way down to the basement holding cells. She couldn't find him anywhere …

She went back up to the spare office on the third where she conducted a second interview with Justine Péraud, murderous *fromagère*, this time in the company of her advocate. As pathetically passionate as she came across, it was sounding more and more like a well-planned assassination. Then, before heading home, another try down the hall.

Betty's sulky frown told her Nabi had not come in and he was not answering his messages.

So Aliette gathered her things and buttoned her coat. On an impulse, she glanced into the lunchroom. Her three regional counterparts were sitting around the table littered with the remains of sandwiches and pastries. Liza Fratticelli was peeling an orange. There was a grimy file folder in the middle of the table. They were well into something.

Mario Bédard smiled through a mouth full of tuna, gesturing, 'Pull up a chair.'

The others barely nodded.

Aliette remained standing. She had to get back to Saint-Brin.

Mario swallowed, gulped coffee and continued on, as if she weren't there.

Or was it that he wasn't worried in the least that she was? After all, she was one of them.

To Liza Fratticelli: 'Yes and no. Yes, we float Vincent's name. Of course the media will jump all over it. And yes, we can get the right people advancing our cause. That won't be a problem, not now. But Vincent will hide. I mean really hide. And Nabi's got his people too, we all know that. *Alors...*' Another large bite.

Liza said, 'The mayor's an ass but he's not an idiot. He'll work it from our side.'

Mario made a gesture, *Voilà*. He and Liza were on the same page.

Julien Lesouple stared, lost in thought, trying to see the end point. 'A lot of programs will fall apart,' he ventured, uncertain.

'We can make new programs,' Mario responded. Peevish—as always when presented with details he deemed inconsequential to the larger picture.

'But who?' asked Julien. Who will make new programs?

'The politicians will decide that.' Mario shrugged. 'Might even be you.'

As a replacement for Nabi Zidane? Julien shrugged back, noncommittal as to the possibility of himself.

Mario smiled. 'Think you could you handle it, Julien?'

Caught off-guard, Julien Lesouple blushed. 'Why not?'

'Good question. Big difference between wanting it and handling it, no?'

Mario's smile was not exactly friendly.

'First things first,' responded Julien, regrouping, meeting the beady stare.

Mario nodded *oui* to that and bit into his sandwich.

Aliette stood there. The worst part was how insouciant and open they were. Mario especially. He was enjoying his lunch.

Professional resentment is endemic to life in the institutional hive. Vincent Spanghero was not the only one who had a problem with Nabi Zidane's promotion. Only the loudest. Aliette had just passed the first anniversary in her new posting. One downside of choosing to operate from Saint-Brin, a step removed from Hôtel de Police, was that while pervading undercurrents were sensed, their depths remained unclear. It takes time to get to know people.

And vice-versa. As if guided by one mind, all three heads now turned her way.

She pretended ignorance. 'Can't really stay, I'm afraid ... Haven't seen Nabi? Anyone?'

Three more heads shaking. Three pairs of cool cop eyes assessing.

'Looked under a rock?' asked Liza, carefully separating a section from her tangerine.

Julien sipped coffee, grimaced, suggested, 'Algeria ... back to the mountains?'

'Wherever he is, he's fucked,' pronounced Mario Bédard.

'Why?' Aliette was feeling left out. 'I mean, I don't understand.'

'No. You're new and you don't understand.' Mario Bédard nodded, perhaps accepting this as he ripped another hunk of baguette with his teeth. The others waited while he chewed it in an angry way. He swallowed more coffee. 'Vincent Spanghero has lost his mind. And why?'

Rhetorical. Aliette waited, mute.

'Nabi,' inserted Mario.

Julien Lesouple and Liza Fratticelli nodded in unison to confirm.

Mario told Aliette, 'This would not be happening, if not for Nabi.'

She mumbled, 'You're talking about these murders.' For the record.

'Just so.' He wiped his lips. 'But Vincent's insanity is only the latest result of some very bad decisions, Inspector. Our city is falling apart and we all know why, and Nabi Zidane—'

'Do we?'

Mario Bédard wasn't used to being cut off mid-flow. His round head tilted to a skeptical angle. 'Because there's no more centre. I mean recognizable core values ... French values?' He sighed. In recognition of a fool? 'You know exactly what I'm saying.'

She met his eyes. Of course she knew what he was saying.

But he'd gathered a head of steam. 'People are losing confidence. Businesses are closing. You can't sell a house for beans, the whole place smells funny and Nabi Zidane thinks he can talk his way through to a workable solution.' Mario stared hard at Aliette. 'It's not working.'

'Can we let it be so personal, Mario?'

Everyone knew she meant the police.

Mario put his sandwich down. He nodded, searching for patience. 'My brother-in-law had a little haberdashery, over by the theatre? Three summers ago—'

'I wasn't here then.' And she didn't want to hear it.

'But our burgeoning little Africa was. Too many, and with nothing to do. And two of their nasty kids were pissed or high and they threw a rock through his window and put a knife in his gut when he screamed at them. And he died.' He shrugged—yes, personal—and picked up his sandwich. 'For a fucking pair of pants. Ask your friend. He'll tell you all about it.'

He meant Sergio Regarri.

It offended her that Mario would bring her personal affairs into the discussion. The way he said 'friend' wasn't quite right. She stayed steady, but very much on her guard. 'I'm sorry.'

'It's OK. I didn't even like him much. But it sure messed up things at home. There's a ripple effect to these things, Inspector. That's the bigger point, yes?'

Liza Fratticelli smiled sympathetically.

Aliette asked, 'What will you do?'

'*B'eh*, come down hard, clean it up. Make it very clear whose town this is.'

Aliette allowed a hint of a smile. Chief Inspector Bédard obviously assumed *he* was Nabi's natural replacement, if and when. 'I mean about Vincent Spanghero. First things first, Mario?'

His reply was distinctly guarded. 'At this point, we can't do much for Vincent.'

Now Julien smiled mordantly. 'We can't do *anything* for Vincent.'

Liza muttered, 'I don't like Vincent.'

'And why would we?' asked Mario. 'A very hard man to like.'

Three faces signalled grim consensus.

Mario sniffed, 'But we can do something about Nabi.'

'So how?' Julien Lesouple pushed, nervous, a side Aliette had felt but not yet seen.

The question left her suddenly extraneous again.

But it pricked Mario's impatience. He was taking the lead here. 'One way or the other, we have to find Vincent.'

'And then?'

'And then we put those two together, so to speak.'

'Nabi and Vincent?'

'Exact.'

So to speak. It was the touchiest of police moments. It was lunch. There was no official record and never would be. But no one was hiding. They didn't need to. Chief Inspector Nouvelle heard what she was meant to hear—which was everything and nothing. The fact she'd heard was their protection. It was her choice as to whether she would be a part of it or not. Whatever *it* might be.

She asked, 'What do you mean, together?'

Mario Bédard was a short man with close-cropped fuzzy hair. Solid. *Costaud*, as we say. Something about his face, the way it fitted on his fuzzy head, always reminded her of a tennis ball. But Mario played rugby, or so she'd heard. And he was a slow, meticulous eater.

Mario put his sandwich back on the table.

Tapped out a pensive tattoo with a meaty finger.

Laid it out. 'It will depend on how and where Vincent presents. Might be dead by then, or running, or holding a gun to some poor slob's head with a hundred sharpshooters lining him up and a thousand cameras trained...'

'Tropéano's gun,' noted Liza Fratticelli. Quiet. Always quiet, figuring things. A lot like Nabi. But then she had worked with him, been part of his group in an earlier reincarnation.

'Whatever.' Mario's impatience flashed again. 'Or maybe another one of Nabi's guys will be hanging in the balance, maybe Nabi will be the one trying to talk Vincent down... Together means just that: side by side, cause and effect, two peas in a pod. However it plays out, they have to be there together. If the world sees it, all the better. The idiots at City Hall won't ever let this happen again.'

'Good cops. Bad peas.' Liza again. She had worked with Vincent Spanghero too.

Aliette said, 'It's not absolutely certain it's Vincent.'

They all looked at her as if she'd just got back from Mars.

She dared to argue. 'Would Vincent Spanghero be so hysterical? I mean, the knife: What? Five, six blows? And stabbing downward? I don't know him, but I assume he'd know how to use a knife... once, twice, into the gut. Clean. Gone. No? As for the gun...' She shrugged. 'Anyone can pull a trigger.'

Mario Bédard nodded sagely, as if giving this his deepest consideration. He enjoyed playing the role of wise cop. Removing a sheet from the folder, he proffered it, repeating, 'You are new and you don't understand. And no, you didn't know Vincent.'

It was another photocopy of the two scraps from pages torn out of a lined notebook.

We must learn to live a better life This world is absurd, is falling apart People like us we are burdened by clarity Are we brothers? sisters? People like us we are not kind to people in our way We have no time to spare nor heart to wait People like us must step up must sacrifice must take steps we must show you who you are

How in the world did he get so far from where he should have been?

'And last night's...' Mario handed over a separate page.

Aliette read another note, scribbled in the same large, round hand:

Does France need another child like this? We can do better We must

No argument it was the same author. 'Is that his hand?'

Mario was rueful. 'It's his head, no question. Or what's left of it.'

'Dissociation,' prompted Liza, pulling another page from the folder. '...physical anomalies.'

Aliette held another photocopy, this one ink-blurred and smudged. A police report of a fatal collision from almost thirty years prior, signed by V. Spanghero, Cpl. The hand was large and round, like a kid's. And too much like the blocky script on the scraps of lined pages they'd been finding with the victims. She recalled Sergio's glib remark about Vincent needing bodies to get his message out. Sergio was allowed to be glib—she loved Sergio, she knew he would not rush to judge. Mario, she didn't like at all—she doubted any amount of personal tragedy could change that. And she couldn't stop her face from twisting. 'No question?'

Mario Bédard eyes bulged momentarily beyond the smooth contours of his thick face. 'That is Vincent, madame. Completely and utterly. We listened to it for a year.'

Julien Lesouple corroborated. 'Hysterical is putting it mildly... Savage?'

'Let's just say poor Vincent's well and truly lost it,' sighed Bédard. 'And I can understand that.' He smiled at Aliette. But it wasn't friendly. 'How about you, Inspector? You losing your mind too? I'm definitely losing mine... We heard you were having some difficulties.'

Aliette could only fight to suppress a blush and try to meet his gaze.

'Don't be embarrassed. It's hard out there. And we're all in this together. The likes of Nabi Zidane only make it worse.'

'I like him.'

'I like him too. But he's still the wrong man in the wrong place at the wrong time.'

The other eyes told her this was true. Though perhaps not the part about liking Nabi too.

— 14 —

RIPPLE EFFECTS OF UGLY PEOPLE

As she drove to Saint-Brin, Aliette cast her mind back over the lunchroom scene. Mario's problematic personality had suddenly taken on larger context. No big surprise, but...

Julien's cool commentary touching on Nabi's decisions and programs came into high relief. That suppressed agitation he carried had shone clearly. Maybe diplomatic Julien was not what he seemed.

And Liza... Aliette would have to have another lunch with her and get a few things straight.

So many layers in each life, revealed when least expected. When she arrived at the office, she tried Nabi again—no luck. She left a message, sent an email, brooded over a solitary lunch at her desk. None of the ugly politics at HQ had any bearing on her work and she couldn't let it. But it was a blow and she was in a mood, distracted. Difficult to think straight when it dawns that your colleagues are... unsavoury?... No, let's not put too fine a point on it. Ugly was the word. She was still mulling the bitter taste of it when she drove out to the village of Bouldoux later that afternoon with Inspector Henri Dardé.

Légiste Annelise Duflot was right: Henri's initial interviews had confirmed that almost everyone in the village was a hunter and they all used a Remington 700 in pursuit of the boars. And they had no idea who the victim was. Male. White, 'but certainly not northern,' Annelise had advised. Tissue density and remnants of his clothing suggested not that old; not a sporty-kitted hiker either. Or a hunter. Sergeant Nicolas Legault at the gendarmerie had a dozen regional files on missing persons; he'd made enquiries but found no takers. He had access to a database with thousands more... it could take years. But a fading label on the unknown victim's underpants pointed east and it was actually bright Mathilde again who'd walked in with tea and said, 'A gypsy?'

More politely: a Romani. Though not for a growing number of French citizens.

With Mathilde's flash of insight, the notion of a reactive shot at a flash of movement in the leaves—i.e., an unremarked hunting accident—became more a hope than a possibility. They had to consider the darker choice: Had a gypsy, spotted wandering in the woods—'my woods! my vines! my land!'—been an almost irresistible target for a man feeling culturally invaded?

Henri Dardé had statements from a handful of villagers who, questioned privately by the police, said what they would never dare to in public. Egged on by Inspector Dardé (who was more subtle than he looked), these people, retired, transplanted city people mainly, declared their contempt for hunters. They complained about noise, the mess, the cavalier attitude to collateral damage, the absurd macho quasi-military mentality that emerged when hunters went out *en groupe*. And the obvious danger of an accident such as the one they were looking into. The name Fabien Fleury appeared on several of Henri's pages, described as an especially trigger-happy old *vigneron* who hated the boars that ate his grapes and the 'foreigners' who ventured near them with a loud and equal passion. 'Foreigner' could mean anyone Monsieur Fleury didn't personally know. Henri had established that even Fleury's neighbours, hard core hunters included, were embarrassed and not a little nervous where it came to the old man's volatility.

But they were neighbours, and loath to denounce him. Though the body was found in a wooded patch directly adjacent to Fleury's parcel of vines, of course they knew nothing about any incident. Fleury himself had shrugged. His wife had smiled…

Listening to Henri's report, Aliette could feel her temperature rising. Too many foreigners for the likes of these village folk, salt-of-the-earth citizens every one. Too many for stout-hearted cop Mario Bédard. The night before, walking the city streets, she had tried to gauge her presence as citizen-with-gun, the possibilities when joined with a paranoid hatred of so-called foreigners.

Her imagination had failed her.

This morning she had faced it in the lunchroom.

And now again, out here in tiny Bouldoux.

Her inner voice said, Calm down, Inspector, it happens all the time. Part of the job. People are always less than you imagine. Roll with it, apply the law. Sure. But—

'You OK, boss?'

'Fine. Let's go see what he has to say.'

But Aliette was in a controlled state of fury as they knocked on Monsieur Fleury's door.

No answer.

'He was there Friday. Swore he wasn't going anywhere.'

Indeed, grey mid-winter is when vine growers have nothing to do but dream of sun and a better world.

Unless they suddenly decide to visit in-laws in the south of Spain ... This from another smiling neighbour.

Inspector Henri Dardé was thorough. His notes said Albert Lépagnol had parcels on the same stretch of land. Not a business partner, but he and Fleury spent the better part of the year in close proximity.

Lépagnol was another one who'd had nothing much to say to Henri. But they could try again.

Albert was not home either. Gone to his cabin, said his wife, out at the vines. He liked it there in the winter, he and the dog, and she was glad he did. Aliette could see why he might. Sour woman. No doubt she hated foreigners too. But they got directions.

Driving out to their next stop, Henri related his progress on his other case, the challenges of wooing the social workers to the cause—the cause of convincing three pairs of over-protective parents to face the fact their adolescent girls may have conspired to kill their slutty friend. Aliette made an effort to listen, but it was obvious her mind was elsewhere. Henri fell silent ... till they rounded a corner and spotted a small Renault van parked off the road. The man they were investigating owned and worked two parcels of vines on this hillside. The man who'd gone to escape his wife on a bleak winter's day owned four ... They got out and walked down through the silent, hilly terrain.

The vines had been cleanly pruned of their branches. Despite the winds, there were some orangey leaves still clinging to the shorn stalks, solitary, improbable dots of colour, somehow hanging on in death. The stalks were all about waist-high, gnarled, twisted, headless, yet lined perfectly along uniform rows. It was like the inspectors had wandered into a dance, a private affair open only to twisted, stunted, headless creatures. The vines looked so cold, set against the thinned-out winter forest rising around them on three sides. And yet they danced... The place felt lost in time. Frigid gusts swirling down from the ridge through the huge natural bowl added to the feeling.

It could be beautiful when the winter sun was lowering, shining—Sergio and Aliette had done some enchanting Saturday walks. A dusting of snow might have added charm. This day was overcast, strictly grey.

The inspectors plodded toward two simple work huts at the far border of the vast field.

Inspector Nouvelle fingered her gun, waiting there inside her winter coat.

Near each other, but not too near, rudimentary one-room structures made of fieldstone and mortar, roofed with tiles. Normally they would be inconspicuous during the season of leaf and grape, but today the two huts were strangely central to the lonely scene. A faint stream of smoke rose from the chimney of the one to the left. As junior officer, Henri opened his coat, put his hand on his gun as they approached. Standard procedure. There is much in the way of standard procedure that precluded someone like Aliette Nouvelle from ever touching her sidearm, let alone using it. She let go of hers and knocked. 'Monsieur Lépagnol?' No answer. No windows. She tried three times.

The latch was not secured. Taking the lead, Henri carefully opened the door.

There was a chair in front of a tiny wood stove that was still smouldering, a snuffed candle that was still warm. That day's *Midi-Libre* lay open on the floor beside the chair. Work tools were stacked in the corner. Biscuits and bottles on a hand-hewn counter, cutlery, basic implements, a few glasses, cups and plates, a tin of condensed milk, a kettle on a small camper stove, a cup half full of tea, still warm. Two bowls on the floor, large, one with water, the other with a smattering of sandwich scraps.

Henri suggested, 'Maybe went for a walk with the dog?'

'Maybe.' Maybe alerted by his wife via his portable phone. Would he give her sour face a kiss?

They stepped back outside. Inspector Nouvelle called, 'Monsieur Lépagnol ... !' It echoed briefly.

They proceeded to the suspect's hut. It too was unlocked. But empty, nothing to indicate a visit on a day like this. Fabien Fleury had moved all amenities out for the winter.

They walked up the rows to the top of the cleared area. Here the forest opened in a path wide enough for a vehicle. There were no recent tire tracks. Inspector Nouvelle called again. Silence. They continued up the path into the forest and stopped on a rise about half a kilometre up. The path led down to a largish stream. The two inspectors descended carefully. Icy. No one to be seen in either direction.

There was a light but distinct cracking in the trees back up the hill behind them.

'Monsieur Lépagnol?'

More cracking. Steps. Someone fleeing.

'Monsieur!' Aliette drew her gun. Before Henri could do anything to help—or hinder, she aimed in the general direction and fired. Twice.

... A scrawny Jack Russell terrier scurried into the pathway and took off up the hill, back to the vines, and his bowl in the hut. But a good hunting dog will show you the way. They went up to that spot.

Monsieur Lépagnol was waiting, thirty paces off the path, prone, at the base of an oak tree.

Henri was worried. He managed to keep it politic, calm, quiet. 'Boss, that was not like you.'

And totally against all regulations he had ever been taught.

Aliette replied in kind, 'I'm working on altering my style, Henri. Re-inventing me.'

'*Bon* ...' Drawn out and skeptical, not satisfied with that at all.

'I wasn't going to kill him, Inspector.' She laughed, self-deprecating, not a little bitter. As if she could hit the side of a barn from five paces. 'I was just practising.' After all, Monsieur Lépagnol was merely a person of interest, someone they only wanted to talk to. There was no need to kill such a person.

Henri, who was a trusting man, dared to rebut this. 'Horrible technique, boss. Stance like that, you might hit anything.'

'But it did the trick. No?' This was rhetorical, not inviting any reply.

In fact, forbidding it. She knew she was being the worst kind of boss. Too bad, she thought, that's how it sometimes is. And she could have pushed it. She could have started blaming Mario Bédard, the way Mario was blaming Nabi Zidane. She could have blamed small-minded village people for twisting her soul in a knot. She resisted. Henri would have taken issue, and rightly so. But her mood was brought on by ugly people. If she continued to work with them, Henri would have to learn to live with that.

Gun in hand, she stood over their quarry. '*Bonjour, Monsieur.* Chief Inspector Nouvelle, Police Judiciaire. You've already met Inspector Dardé. We wanted to speak to you about Monsieur Fleury?'

Face buried in rotted leaves, Albert Lépagnol rolled an eye in her direction. He was terrified.

She added, 'Please... We only want to talk.'

Talk he did. Several useful things about Fleury, who loved his guns, who hated foreigners.

Aliette apologized to Henri as they drove back. After all, you cannot leave your people in the lurch. They want you to be steadfast. You need them to trust you. She complimented him on some thorough work that had helped move a major case forward. She offered encouraging feedback on his report on the three girls.

Confidence restored, Henri respectfully suggested she spend some time at the range.

She agreed that she should. She did not tell him what a horrible day it had been.

PART 2

A GROWING LIST OF SINS

15

READY TO CARRY ON

A night alone. Pyjamas. Slippers. Three beers … four. No harm done. Thursday morning, Chief Inspector Aliette Nouvelle sat down with Inspector Magui Barthès. A question of understanding their suspect and the murder of a cheese producer's wife. *Passionnel?* Or *Assassinat?* There is often a genuine world of difference, which is why the two concepts exist in the law. Many a perpetrator has been released outright on the strength of *Passionnel*. Who better than we French to know what passion can do? But in this instance, there was very little space between two views of a clearly premeditated killing.

Justine Péraud was not an exceptional woman in any discernible way except by virtue of that one brutal act. She had started working at the *fromagerie* at sixteen, direct from school (where she had not done very well). By all reports a hard worker who got on with the other staff, was never late, rarely ill. Who still lived with her parents. And nothing fatefully beautiful there. Robert Benech, the man who led her to her downfall, was a lanky, brooding sort, yes, but it was not a scenario from Flaubert. She may have looked good bending to stir the whey… But Justine insisted, 'We loved each other the moment we met.' The day he'd hired her some nine years before.

'She does say he instigated it,' noted Magui.

Whoever, however, it had taken time. Fact: Justine had given herself to Robert (Bobby), in a bed of goaty straw on the far side of the ridge. They had started a relationship. It had gone on for a year or so till the wife had told her she was being let go. Her Bobby had not intervened.

'But he continued to call her, we know that.'

And they continued to meet. Till Justine had taken her father's hunting rifle and gone to the house on a January evening when she knew her love was in town with his friends.

'But when I ask her why, she keeps saying, So it would be final,' Aliette said. 'It's not: Because I love him. Or, Because he's mine! She goes straight to the gun. The tool, the act. Final.'

Magui saw where Inspector Nouvelle was headed. She protested. 'Not fair: all she did was fall in love and lose her head. Her muddled head told her she needed the gun to solve her heart's problem.'

Aliette was with Magui: she too wanted to recommend a charge of *Crime Passionnel* to Instructing Judge Martine Rogge, for her to recommend to the Procureur. But she doubted the recommendation would be accepted. The judge was conducting her own interviews with Justine Péraud. She would be hearing the same underlying and damning thing. '…so it would be final.' Magui said Justine was lost in the thing she believed. 'He was meant for me… Martine Rogge will hear that too.'

Yes, Martine surely would. But the suspect's too-straightforward, too-practical sense of the gun would tip the scale. 'If we can get more out of him…' Justine might have a chance.

'He's already said it's all his fault. Refuses to see it any other way.'

'Easy to say. He didn't pull the trigger… Was he pushing her? Or even suggesting?'

'He stops short of that.'

'Keep trying, Mags. The ladies…' If Justine's co-workers didn't open up, forget their worries over their small jobs, it was a good bet Justine would spend her best years inside a jail.

'I will let them know the stakes.'

After the meeting with Inspector Barthès, the rest of the Saint-Brin contingent of the Police Judiciaire gathered at Mathilde's work station, where, over mid-morning tea, Chief Inspector Aliette Nouvelle officially divulged the order from Division to wear her service arm. She showed them her new gun, her new holster. There was no point continuing to avoid this moment, not after her display in the woods at Bouldoux. It was her duty to apprise them. Before Henri mentioned it to Magui… who would tell Mathilde? Which had surely already happened... In any event: '*Alors,*' she concluded, 'from here on in, I will be armed and dangerous. Just so you know?'

She felt better, less encumbered. Now that it was out in the open, if they sensed her unease, they would understand. Not that she would parade around the office naked, seeking affirmation, but they were a family, in a way; they saw her every day from an intimate vantage. She had pledged to go through the adjustment process with professional equanimity. She had made no mention of Gabrielle Gravel. That remained private—for her, if no one else. Though she would not be surprised if they knew all about it. It seemed everyone else in the system did.

It was also, after a year as a unit, normal that she would complain out loud that the idiot thing did not feel right. What are families for, after all?

And so they made a fuss trying to help the boss adjust her new holster to fit her slender shoulders. Chafing where it draped her left. Slipping off like a difficult bra strap on her right.

Henri tugged gently, this way, that... No luck. 'This is old technology, boss. And it's brand new—not supple, no give at all.' He recommended a night in a bucket of water, then lots of saddle soap. For the holster, not her. His was a pliant space-age plastic.

As was Magui's. She suggested, 'Why don't you just keep it in your bag?'

'Have to do it the way they like it, Mags.'

Henri kept trying... 'Boss, it's not my business, but it should be as, um... not there as your underwear, you know what I mean?'

'My underwear is there, Henri. And it is not your business.'

'We want you to be comfortable, boss.'

Mathilde stepped forward with a tea towel from the pantry. 'Like a shoulder pad?'

It was tried... then tried in the mirror, and rejected. 'Makes me too lopsided.'

'We could try a piece from my Pilates mat,' offered Mathilde. 'Very soft. I don't mind cutting off a little strip, really, I don't.'

'What exactly is Pilates?'

'You have to come and find out. Be good for exactly this sort of stress. Muscles too.'

Was she stressed? Aliette snatched a handful of tissues from the box always available on Mathilde's desk and stuffed it into the problematic area. Flexed her shoulders. Drew her weapon. 'Not so bad.' Donning her jacket, she posed in front of them, a final check for off-kilter slants.

Everyone agreed, 'Not so bad, boss ... not so bad.'

She thanked them and headed out. She was due in Béziers. Meetings. And Gabrielle Gravel.

16

Up to Em

Gabrielle and Emma had their daily time together during the tea and sandwich break before the evening appointments. Em's sandbox was always present on the desk, waiting for her to build a story. But it requires a certain energy to kickstart the imagination. Or maybe hope? Either way, you need imagination to play in the sand. Or to play at all ... After months of patient work, Emma's sandbox contained a house from a board game, a rudimentary icon fashioned in green plastic, and two mother-like figurines made of the same soft lead as toy soldiers. They were from the same collection (Gabrielle had no idea where she'd picked those up) and wore similar long skirts, one blue, one army green, hearkening back at least three generations, and white blouses with a line of painted buttons the same colour as the skirt. Their hair and faces were identical. And there was a baby, a cheap dolly made of spongy material, and a miniature wooden television, and a tiny tea cup, finely made but chipped. Pretty basic images. Emma was a mother with a child and a house. She had a mother and a mother-in-law who were dead. And a husband who had ruined her life. She still refused to choose a figure for him. He had broken every rule there was to break; she insisted she didn't want him in her world. Gabrielle Gravel knew Emma did, but still lacked the essential human gumption required to re-imagine her man. A matter of a fragile soul formed of long-set rules and deep-seated expectations having been destroyed. They were working on it. Reclaiming her child's respect was both intrinsically linked and a painfully separate challenge.

Until Emma Petitpas got past the fear and brought her sandbox into the present, well ...

Imagination is the soul's communicator. Without a sense of the possible, you cannot play.

Emma was resolutely hopeless, miserable, consumed by her anxiety.

The family sessions ran from futile to disastrous.

But against all odds, Emma's problematic place at the reception desk had yielded some primal-oriented movement. Tiny steps. Then bigger steps. A small miracle. An exciting new approach…

Now threatened. 'Did you have an episode, Em?…Can we talk about it?'

No. Emma stared, tea untouched. Gabrielle paged back through her notes.

Emma had been weeping steadily since she'd come in, and not for the first time in the last few weeks. She'd been in a downswing since the return from the Christmas break. Her crying jags regularly erupted into hysterical anger. Not that Gabrielle Gravel put any stock in outmoded notions of hysteria, but it was an image that fit Em's perpetually distorted face. It seemed a sort of PTSD, heaping stress on the stress Emma bore each day. Gabrielle had put it down to emotional fallout from spending the holiday season alone, which could be hard on even the most stalwart souls. But it had continued. It was concerning, after some hard-won progress in the waiting room.

Two years prior (after a devastating Christmas), the social worker had dumped this defeated, distraught, anxiety-ridden woman at PsychoDynamo. Marriage shattered. Child out of control. Sense of self-worth obliterated. She was barely coherent, afraid to open her mouth, her mouth was in constant pain due to inflamed nerves making her teeth hurt to an intolerable degree, a sad case trapped in a closed circle of ongoing pain. Mistrustful to the point of acute paranoia… *like a half-drowned cat rescued from a sewer.* An initial observation in Gabrielle's notes.

But it was not acute paranoia. She was not bipolar. Once clear of the cocktail of pacifiers and painkillers, her scans and chemistry were normal enough. Severe anxiety linked to self-esteem issues, coupled with bouts of near-debilitating depression. The psychiatric ward had said, Try Gabrielle Gravel.

Presented with a sandbox, Emma froze, mortified by fears of making the wrong choice. *Her imagination is locked in the basement of her soul,* wrote Gabrielle. Em mutely, angrily... despairingly rejected all modalities. Costumes, masks, the empty chair, nothing in Gabrielle's catalogue of creative options could make a dent. Emma was too sad, too hopeless to play.

Offered a pencil, and much coaxing, Em painstakingly printed out terse notes. I am useless. I have failed... Nothing original, nothing helpful. Six months later Emma was still printing out her agony in laboured messages, Gabrielle was frustrated, on the verge of giving up, handing her back to the shrinks, an almost certain path to a quiet room in a drab hall in a neglected building too far for anyone to bother visiting.

Then: eureka? Gabrielle saw an idea in this simple act jotting notes.

While the World Technique is not the world, it reflects the existential fact that people live in the world essentially alone. Emma was too alone inside her traumatized soul. Stuck there. Perhaps a bit of pressure—real world pressure (people?) could help bring movement. Perhaps one way to bring Emma out the far end of her soul's dark tunnel might be to push rather than guide. When Gabrielle's receptionist left to have a baby, Gabrielle sat Emma down at the front desk, instructed her, evoked the dead end that was the hospital route, and let her try. She did not have to do much. She sat in front of clients. She (painstakingly) printed out appointment cards. Her real job was to interact. Talk? Gabrielle instructed Em to consider the waiting room as her territory. 'Your space, Em. Like your kitchen. You are in charge, the way it works is up to you. I want you to see it that way—and engage. Communicate with the clients. Yes?'

Emma balked. She was petrified. Gabrielle drew up some waiting-room rules Em could use to keep control and stay in charge. She was relentlessly positive, watchfully supportive. 'You must try, Em. For the health of your soul! It's safe, I'm here... It's the only way back to your child. Your husband.'

So Emma tried. She was in charge of the waiting room.

Gabrielle could control it, to a point. Beyond that, it was up to Em.

Gabrielle observed Emma receiving mothers and their sulking children, knowing her child was infinitely worse than theirs. And Em sitting there with bitter wives having problems with their gormless men. Then, with those same husbands, who drank and drugged themselves and went running after dangerous sex. Wednesday afternoons Emma received the so-called troubled adolescents who were pussy cats compared with hers. Emma spent the better part of her time in tears. Occasionally she lost control and screamed. No one's life was as horrible as hers. Some of it was halfway healthy. Most of it was pure anger. At least it was finally coming out!

And though steadfastly miserable, Emma kept at it. On edge. Mistrusting. Anxiety crushing her. Teeth aching. But Em held her ground, such as it was.

Answering the phone was a huge step forward.

Gabrielle lost some clients, the ones who took the worst of it. She didn't worry, there were plenty more where they came from. Emma was by far the more interesting challenge. Indeed, observing Emma interacting with clients, alone, or better, when they happened to overlap, Gabrielle believed she saw the larger possibility in the waiting room. *Volatile but fascinating… definitely new ground!* Emma's file became the Waiting Room Project. *(Projet Salle d'attente.)* Gabrielle saw the elements of a ground-breaking case study. The social worker cautiously agreed it was something different. Gabrielle declared the waiting room was the new front line.

Fate has made poor Em my guinea pig… Gabrielle wrote, excited.

They had a base to work from. She had gently eased Em into her sand.

Now her guinea pig appeared to be relapsing into crisis. Em's new pain was a worry. Often a downswing like this was the last darkness before the proverbial light. The thought was exciting.

Gabrielle Gravel was uncertain. 'Are we ready to carry on?'

They had to keep pushing. … *If Em can stay the course.*

17

MY SAND

Aliette Nouvelle walked a different maze of streets to her appointment with Gabrielle Gravel. The miserable receptionist barely glanced up when she came in. Same sagging, tea-spotted orange sweater, same grim mouth pulled tight, grinding. '*Bonsoir, madame. Ça va bien?*' The woman responded with a quick, violent shake of her head—as if fending off something repugnant.

Leaving Aliette shrugging. 'Fine. If that's how you want to play it.'

The good-looking man with the book was there once more, sneaking clumsy glances again while pretending to mind his own business. And good evening to you, Monsieur Creepy Weirdo, unbuttoning her overcoat, already irritated, yanking her arms from the sleeves...

Which pulled her sweater up, inadvertently exposing her gun.

The receptionist gasped, 'And you have a gun too! Oh, *mon dieu, mon dieu, mon...*' She shuddered. Tears gushed. She sat clutching her pencil, mortified.

Oops... The inspector made a show of casual indifference, hanging her coat, taking a seat. 'Don't worry, I won't kill you, madame. It's part of my program... Unless you want me to?'

Which wasn't nice at all. But the woman was absurd, tiresome. Not helpful.

We *are* here to be helped. Yes?

Aliette settled into the chair. This evening she chose the one directly beside the furtive reader. He kept his eyes glued to his page. She made a point of staring openly. A *policier*—a bestseller from America. 'Good read?'

So he confronted her, smiling strangely through perfect teeth. 'I have the series.'

Behind the star-quality bone structure, she saw uncertainty. Like an empty space—a gap between his natural gift and the wherewithal to use it. He was a timid man. Beautiful, but scared.

Yes, well, guns scare people… She had no wish to frighten anyone. She couldn't blame him for being curious. She felt a need to atone for her presumptions. 'I've haven't read it.'

He leaned forward, too eager. 'I could loan you one.'

'No!' The receptionist smacked her desk.

He blinked, retreated back into his chair like a chastened dog.

Aliette asked, impish. 'No loaning books?'… and smiled at the man.

Who was staring at the angry woman.

Who glared. Warned, 'Just mind your own affairs.'

The inspector bowed. She felt she'd just won a small victory—over what, she wasn't sure.

But it was fleeting. The cupboard-sized door behind the receptionist opened and the same awful adolescent girl stomped through. She hadn't changed her shirt since Tuesday. Or her jeans. Or socks! She had not washed or even brushed her hair. This was too apparent as a pungent fug with telling notes no polite person would mention pushed all breathing space away.

Aliette held her breath and stared. Grabbing her ratty leather jacket from its hook, the girl demanded, 'What is your problem, bitch-head?'

Before the inspector could respond, the woman at the desk hissed, 'She has a gun!'

The girl whirled to face her. 'Do I care? Do I care about any of this stupid crap?'

'It's part of my program.' Aliette's most reasonable tone bounced off the girl's broad back.

'But she has a gun!' The receptionist insisted.

The girl took two steps, put her face in front of the weeping lady. 'You have to stamp my form and give me my appointment card. That's all. I am not interested in your insanity!'

'But—'

'Do it!' The girl stomped her heavy foot, impatient, on the verge of a tantrum.

Aliette repeated, 'It's part of my program.'

'Fuck yourself.' This without turning, leaning over the traumatized woman.

Who managed to find a stamp and apply it to a paper in front of her. The girl snatched it up. The receptionist seemed to be in absolute pain as she applied her pencil to an appointment card. The girl threw up her arms. 'I can't stand this! ... I don't *need* a card, just the fucking form, so will you just—

'I *need* to give you a card,' whimpered the receptionist. Then screamed, 'It's the rules!'

'Fuck the rules!'

'You have to obey the rules!'

The argument was escalating. The man in the corner sat motionless, riveted to his reading.

Aliette was clutching her gun and didn't even realize it till Gabrielle Gravel appeared at her office door and made a motion signalling her to enter.

Giving wide berth to the battle at the desk, Aliette went in.

'What is wrong with that girl? She's grotesque!'

Oblivious to the disruption in her waiting room, nodding calmly at her client's consternation, Gabrielle shut the door and took her place behind her desk. 'Good evening, Inspector.'

'She told me to fuck myself.'

'She's just a child ... Please take a seat.' She turned a page in her book.

'Do I deserve that?'

'That's a question we'll get to ... First, tell me how it felt displaying your gun.'

'And that poor, creepy man. He ... What is he supposed to be doing there?'

'He is waiting for his appointment. I will remind you again, Inspector, and I hope for the last time: I am not prepared to discuss my other clients'

'And your receptionist! What is her problem?'

'Obviously she is experiencing some distress at the moment. But it's not your business. This is only about you.'

'It's like a room in hell.'

The psychologist allowed a flicker of a smile. 'I like that … Centre of the universe. A room in hell. You bring interesting tropes. Now—'

'Why do I have to put up with this?'

'*B'eh*, it's part of your program. The moment you walk through that door, not this one, that one, you are in my world, in my keeping.' She waved a piece of paper. 'I have a contract from the State … Now if you'll just sit, we can get on with it.'

Aliette would not sit. 'I would like to change evenings.'

Gabrielle ignored this with the same dry nonchalance she had ignored the war in the waiting room. Perusing her page, she mused, 'It seems we left off with you promising to meditate on the truths underlying your *grand succès* with the Public Enemy. Did you do that for me?'

'I said I want to change evenings.' Aliette steamed. 'And I did not promise you anything!'

Gabrielle sat back in her armchair, bemused, as the inspector stood in front of her venting her pique.

—which ran from rashes on her shoulder and above her hip ('Look! Look! This thing is hurting me!') … to shame at how she was reacting to the pathetic people on the other side of the office door ('I am not like that, I am a caring human, I really am, it's this environment, it has to be!') … to guilt over an irresponsible action during an operation in the field that undermined the trust of a colleague ('Which is life-and-death crucial!') … to unfairly induced uncertainty as to her role in the history of modern France ('It was in *Paris-Match*, for God's sake! It doesn't get more real than that, madame. It just doesn't.')—

When it petered out, Gabrielle nodded blandly. 'All very germane and duly noted.'

But moot. Tuesday and Thursday was how it was going to be. 'Now sit, please.'

They had wasted fifteen minutes' worth of France's investment in better policing.

Reducing Aliette to plead, 'Are you really so inflexible?'

'That's not the point …' It was a matter of professional principle. 'It has to be this way or we lose a crucial working dynamic. You see?'

No.

'I believe one should learn to adjust within minimal parameters. Think of Tuesday-Thursday as a world with limited options. Yes, a room in hell. And there's no way out.' That professional smile crept back. 'Except with your gun?'

Aliette gave up. She sat.

Gabrielle assured her, 'You'll feel better once we get you started in your sand.'

Then, challenging the inspector's defences masquerading as a noble cause, Gabrielle introduced the concept of an essentially virginal mind. 'Are you really so special?'

It was not a fair question.

If one was the least bit honest, one had to answer Yes.

If one had a shred of humility, one had to answer No.

Aliette balked, aware of a seismic shifting in her righteous heart. She started mumbling about an uneasy night spent trying to revision her life-altering encounter with Public Enemy Number One. She stopped short of renouncing the experience. It *was* logged in the public domain. She resented 'virginal' and said so. She was unable to admit posing in front of her boyfriend's mirror, stark naked but for her holstered gun.

Gabrielle made a note. 'I think you are dangerously unaware of the game you've allowed yourself to become immersed in. I suggest you make it a priority to activate your jungle senses. I have to say, the aggression you displayed when you came in tonight — that makes me hopeful.'

'Perhaps I should shoot that girl, put her out of her misery. And that poor woman.'

'You mean put yourself out of yours?'

Aliette gave up again. Giving up seemed to be part of the process. 'When do I get my sandbox?'

Gabrielle put her pen down. Touched the tip of her nose, thinking. Finally shrugged, 'Why not right now? You've put your gun in play. Perhaps this is where we put you in the sand.' So saying, she rose and opened the sideboard, selected an unoccupied sandbox and placed it on the desk. Gesturing toward the sideboard, she instructed, 'Choose a dozen pieces, anything that strikes your fancy. Don't think about it too much. You're already playing against yourself.'

Aliette stared at a square metre of perfect sand. Silvery. Fine as sugar. Virgin sand for a virgin mind? She flinched. 'I cannot believe a man like Vincent Spanghero went along with this.'

For an instant, Gabrielle Gravel appeared perplexed. A flash of worry? But with a shake of her head she dodged the reference, coolly advising, '*Everyone* goes along with this, Inspector—as you quaintly put it. It is not a party trick. We are practising the World Technique.'

'If you say so.'

'I do. And this is the world…' the sandbox. 'You can't not go along with the world. Mm? Not if you want to be part of it.'

Aliette heard a veiled warning. The psychologist's certitude filled the space. The sand in front of her was waiting like the portal to a formless desert. Her will to fight was disappearing. Should she get up and leave? Perhaps Vincent Spanghero had done just that. And disappeared.

Chief Inspector Nouvelle sat there. She had to. She had no wish to disappear.

'Tell you what,' said Gabrielle. 'You choose eleven, I'll supply the gun.' Rising from her chair, she returned to the shelves, found a tiny toy pistol and brandished it between her fingertips with an encouraging smile. A six-shooter, made of long-tarnished metal, miniature but realistic—you could actually spin the cartridge. Which Gabrielle did, then dropped it in the middle of the sand.

… *Thunk!* Aliette experienced a quick but profound twinge of disappointment.

She did not want to see the perfect sand disturbed. Because it disturbed her virginal mind?

Sitting, Gabrielle pulled another thick professional journal with a glossy cover from her collection, found a page and read in her well-practised English. '*A gun culture can take hold in society only when social mores and cultural conventions validate it. We need to clearly understand this phenomenon if we are to be able to respond appropriately.*' Putting the magazine aside, she faced her client. 'Much literature from America these days. Not all of it's wrong… Mm?'

Her client nodded dumbly.

'Understanding begins in the heart,' said Gabrielle. 'Please: Eleven pieces. According to your feelings. We'll build a world around this gun. An image of your reconstructed heart.'

Aliette got up and began searching the toys, baubles, miniature statuary for signs of life. Her life. Her eyes wandered, her fingers touched, tentative, then moved on. Amongst the hundreds of gathered human and human-ish figures, the only one that really resonated was a grinning plastic child clutching the famous yellow Banania tin in her triumphant hands. But somewhere between Gabrielle's office and an innocent moment enjoying cocoa in her mother's kitchen, the tin with the image of the smiling Senegalese sporting the scarlet fez had been deemed racist *and* colonialist and banished to the ranks of the politically incorrect. That connection to her life was closed.

There were legions of animals. She choose a cat, carved from a black wood, in a stalking pose, in remembrance of a long-time friend. And a wooden bird, head cocked, alert to the cat. A horse made of glass—which used to be expensive, but had lost a leg, leaving him only useful for service in the sand ... What else? Not easy trying to second-guess your soul. And with Gabrielle Gravel observing, commenting sporadically, airy, calmly urging her on. Try as she might, Aliette could not choose on impulse. Sorry, never one for those psychological tests where you say the first thing that comes to your mind. Fretting, assessing, rejecting, feeling the next possible candidate in her fingers ... A deceptively difficult exercise. Growing woefully circumspect, unsure.

Gabrielle assured her this was the hardest part.

Painfully, one by one, they were selected and placed in the sand. Her sand.

She paused to make a hole for the gun and uncovered a bright blue painted bottom panel. 'Pretty,' musing, oddly separated from the woman observing from the other side of the desk; 'Makes me think of the sea ...' She looked up at Gabrielle for reaction, guidance?

She barely nodded, not involved. 'It's your world, Aliette—you do as you want.'

So she left the gun at the bottom of the sea. Went back to the shelves and found a tiny plastic sailboat. It made her think of her father, summers at Belle-Île ... her mind was wandering.

She had gathered only seven pieces by the time the hour ended. Apart from totemic links to her past, she had no idea how they might serve to reconstruct her heart, much less what Gabrielle Gravel might read into her choices.

'It's odd, your lack of spontaneity,' murmured the *psy*. Not mean; simply clinical.

She returned the sandbox to its shelf. She jotted a note. 'We'll try again Tuesday.'

Aliette received her next appointment card from the receptionist's trembling hand.

The horrible girl was completely right: a useless thing. But part of Gabrielle's holy rules.

The reading man was watching surreptitiously as she put on her coat.

The receptionist appeared to be holding her breath.

Tugging her beret down over her ears, the inspector left.

18

JANGLED

Stepping into the street, feeling jangled, unnerved, a wretched knot unsettling her gut, Aliette Nouvelle immediately looked up. The man in the second-storey window across the street was on watch again tonight. She held his gaze and caught a glimpse of something that was of a piece with the waiting room in PsychoDynamo. That man was dreading something. Hoping for it too. Spreading the draping of her coat like heavy wings, she tugged at her sweater, exposing her gun. When she saw that he saw, her wings fell back. She patted her hip, nodded coolly up at the man, and walked away. Best way to keep a citizen in line is to keep him at a stasis point between his beliefs and his desires, no? Did she hear him tapping on his window? The inspector did not turn around. Gabrielle had been happily intrigued that she had displayed her gun in the waiting room.

She had made it sound like progress.

It was milder, and blustery, a gusting wind ruffling the compact silence of the tight streets. Walking helped the jangly thing subside. Walking where? Not home, not yet, she did not want to bring this feeling home to Sergio. Aliette walked for an hour or so, repeating her steps, repeating her thoughts. Though it wasn't late, she encountered no one till she saw a figure, indistinct in a long hooded coat, step out of a door at the far end of a street.

The figure sensed something and moved briskly away, around the near corner.

It was the same street, it had to be the same door. Aliette advanced, grasping her weapon.

But … ear to the door, then knocking: the house was empty, the squatters had moved on. The washed-out chalk outline on the street pointed at a blank wall. With the wind swirling, a brace of fire sirens now rising in the middle distance, there was no hope of picking up the sound of steps.

'Where have you been?' Sergio was in bed, reading a file.

'Walking … She gives me all this stuff to sort. Makes my head spin.'

'I was going to call the police.' He watched as she unbuckled herself from her gun, let her clothes fall to the floor.

'Very funny.' She crawled in beside him. 'Have you seen her yet—Gabrielle Gravel?'

'Tomorrow.' He tossed the file on the floor, put his glasses aside, turned off the light and settled into the pillow. 'Why? Were you discussing me?'

'No. Only me.' She rolled onto her side, looked out at the endless night.

He stroked her back. 'Well, you're far more interesting than I'll ever be.'

'Nabi says she's the last person to have any communication with Vincent Spanghero.'

'You really shouldn't talk to Nabi about this. Nor he to you.'

For my sake, as well as yours. She heard him clearly.

She had to say, 'Nabi is my friend.'

He touched her hair. 'Nabi's my friend too, you know.'

'Then help him. His other friends are … not.'

'It's not about friends. People get nervous.'

'People get ugly.'

'Not you.' He moved a millimetre closer.

'Do I have a virginal mentality?'

'Not that I've noticed. Maybe we should make sure?'

So they made love and she felt better.

19

JULIEN'S INSTINCTS

The lights in Regarri's place went out. Chief Inspector Julien Lesouple retreated, back through the twisting streets to his car, nervous, imagining the pillow talk just now in the judge's bed. He had volunteered for the task of tracking his new colleague's movements. He knew Chief Inspector Nouvelle was on an order from Division to see that fucking witch Gabrielle Gravel. It intrigued Julien. He could not say what might be gained from it—it was just an instinct arising from the fact that he'd been through a strange kind of hell in that same office. He had followed her, watched her wandering the streets for almost two hours, going in no apparent direction ... till she'd finally let herself in at Regarri's door. Why? Julien Lesouple had no idea. Except that Vincent Spanghero had been through it too, before he'd disappeared and started killing people.

Aliette Nouvelle was an unknown commodity. She was not onside with Mario Bédard's plans for Nabi Zidane. The risk she might pose was unclear. Mario was sanguine. In his opinion, Chief Inspector Nouvelle's grasp of the politics at play was formed of knee-jerk liberal fluff, and her knowledge of Nabi and Vincent's personal war was nil. The people who ran the city knew Nabi Zidane was a mistake and would be pleased to see it corrected. What's more, the blonde inspector's status with Division was precarious at the moment, she could ill afford to make waves about a matter that was none of her business. Whatever her naïve sympathy for Zidane, keeping her in the loop, 'up to a point,' while keeping her in their sights, was the best way to neutralize her. 'When we have Nabi with Vincent on the front page, I doubt she'll want to be anywhere near him, let alone start making speeches.'

Julien Lesouple was not so sure about Mario's strategy. Julien did not see the world with Mario's drastic eyes. He was fifteen years junior to Mario Bédard. Next generation. Fifteen years newer. Smarter? In the Nabi-and-Vincent mess, Julien saw systemic inefficiency. It would be no big loss if Vincent were put down—it would be a relief, probably for Vincent most of all. But did Nabi really have to go with him? All they had to do was leak Spanghero's name and the fact of Nabi's knife in Tropéano's belly, and that would pretty much do it. Tropéano's gun would not add much. It was just another gun... As long as they moved Nabi out of the picture, the world could get back on track. Julien wanted that, no question.

But Mario had this notion of a big public moment, a photo op, 'a nice poetic ending to a very meaningful story about how we live,' he said. Whether 'Nabs and Vince' were grinning, crying, or both stone cold dead, 'we'll wait and see how it plays out.' The ending would be the same, Mario was sure.

There was an anger behind Mario Bédard's blasé certainty. It was not Vincent Spanghero's bursting, violent anger. It smouldered. Julien Lesouple worried Mario's calculations could create another bloody mess. He'd had no problem arranging for a tracker to be fixed on Nabi's holster. For both their protection, he'd been thinking... Julien had refused to consider the same tracker for Aliette Nouvelle. She was already problematic to Julien's hopes. He could not risk her having something like that to hang over him. He would attend to it personally—and carefully.

Julien thought Mario Bédard was not worried enough about Aliette Nouvelle. Fluffy liberal sentiment had nothing to do with it. Her style was beyond Mario's ken—Julien wondered if Liza saw it too. Negotiating territorial rights to a drug bust that could be a major feather in Julien's cap and put him on the inside track to Nabi's city job had revealed a canny in-fighter. If she put her nose in it, it would be for Nabi's part. Nabi would be lucky. Mario should know that.

And there was this personal element that was playing hell on Julien's nerves.

Julien Lesouple was thinking Gabrielle Gravel had pushed Vincent Spanghero to a crazy place. Julien got nervous thinking about it. He'd been nervous for almost two years now, since his wife had left. Marie would not admit it, but Julien knew it had been on the advice of Gabrielle Gravel. He knew it was his own fault—one bad day dealing with scum, one bad night trying to make Marie understand, one stray fist to her nose, one call to the HR office at Division, where Marie's sister was just a secretary but she knew the signs and who to talk to. They'd kept it quiet—Julien was smart and young, he had a future worth preserving. But there was a problem that had to be addressed and HR ordered them to go to Gabrielle Gravel. Together. What a bloody joke. Playing in sandboxes with toy soldiers. Wearing masks and pretending to be strangers. He couldn't pinpoint the moment Marie had actually become one—a complete and utter stranger, but he knew it was in that office and that he'd been powerless to turn it around.

Two weeks after Gravel had freed them, Marie was gone.

Her last words, on the kitchen table. *Let's just be thankful we didn't get around to children.*

Her very last words. He still had no idea where she was. Gabrielle Gravel did—she surely did!—but she refused to say a word. Julien had even followed her home and climbed the gate and pounded on the door of her big bourgeois house on the boulevard, demanding information.

She'd threatened to call the police.

Having talked to poor Catherine Spanghero, Julien had a feeling it had been much the same with Vincent. The witch had made their spouses disappear from the face of the earth.

…Julien frequently woke up sweating. He had a recurring dream of Vincent chewing on Marie—they'd found each other, like two zombies. He would wake up sweating, tears rolling down his face. Julien missed his wife. He felt all nerves and he knew it showed. And that made him weak. This thing with Vincent was making his head spin.

Julien Lesouple detested the psychologist.

What would she do to Chief Inspector Nouvelle? She was different, very possibly strange, wandering the streets for two hours—like another zombie.

Of course she went home to Regarri. They all knew that's where she slept.

But between the *psy*'s office and the judge's bed, what?

Julien Lesouple knew there was nothing rational in his feeling. But he couldn't shake it. Vincent Spanghero was somewhere in that witch's world. So was Marie. He felt the inspector, blonde and floating slowly, was headed to where they were.

She was odd, but strong—he liked the way she faced down Mario. Liza could never do that. Nor could he. On the other side of it, Julien was nervous of the way she could finesse the situation when they were sitting in front of Judge Martine Rogge. Julien wanted that drug lab. It would be a huge step, maybe even past Béziers and straight to Divisional HQ. First he had to do it right with her. Chief Inspector Nouvelle was a lot of things and Julien's instinct told him he could benefit by staying close and seeing which way she fell when they finally flushed Vincent.

First things first ... Julien and Aliette Nouvelle agreed on that.

He would be Mario's tracker, the one to know what she was doing with—and for—Nabi.

He would be sitting better when it came to Mario's big move.

And there was nothing else to do these nights ... Alone with the sound of his shoes on the paving, Chief Inspector Julien Lesouple was entangled in a web of nervous figuring. He walked right past a hooded figure, out alone, even more nervous than he.

20

RANGE

Friday morning, Aliette Nouvelle stepped out of the lift at Hôtel de Police. She nodded workaday *bonjour*s to Liza...Mario...Julien...and was met with same. But nothing was the same. They knew it too. Nabi Zidane had not come in. He had yet to respond to her calls. An hour later, after a meeting with the *fromagère*'s attorney and the resulting paperwork, Nabi's office remained disconcertingly empty. Next door, Betty shrugged, but the veneer of protective distrust was softening. 'I wish he'd deal with it... Things are piling up here.'

Aliette correctly perceived Betty's concern for the backlog as concern for her boss. 'They've chased him away, Betty. Help me. I need him back too.'

Betty decided to trust. She suggested the range. 'When he's worried, he goes there. Can you blame him? Got no one to cover his back.' Betty knew exactly how things were.

'*Merci.*'

The police shooting range was in a reclaimed warehouse behind the SNCF railway station by the canal. The inspector thought she recognized Nabi Zidane's bashed up Audi in the range parking lot, but she could not spot him in the ebb and flow of cops coming and going from the lockers to the booths, or at any of the tables in the lounge area. Wary of drawing attention to her search, she did not ask as she signed in, collected a packet of rounds...

Aliette was feeling alone, compressed inside a pair of ear protectors, shooting at paper targets shaped and drawn to resemble a generic man. The statistics said it was usually a man. They had made her put on a grimy grey American baseball cap retrieved from the lost-and-found with I'M LOVIN' IT stitched on the brim in lurid vermillion. Protection against ejected shells.

She popped off half a dozen rounds. The man fluttered. Was he dead?

Changing cartridges, she glanced at the snouts of weapons extending past the blinds on both sides of her lane. Glimpsed hands: steady, muscles obeying thoughts, fingers squeezing triggers, hands jolting, reacting to the kick that came with each muted, metallic crack; no hand along the row was strong enough, focused enough, to prevent this. At the far end of the lanes, rips were forming in the chest area below glowering pro-forma faces, generic men were being blown away.

There were perhaps twenty other shooters in the booths lined along the gallery, lots more coming and going in the club-like lounge on the other side of the glass, all of them cops. Her people, supposedly. But the ear shields created a sense of isolation. Maybe this was essential to the practice experience—necessary to learning and relearning the aloneness that descends and envelops when wielding instant death. I am alone, the man I want to shoot is there.

She pushed the button, sighted her lane. Man pops up...drops down...slides by.

She missed most of the time. If she scored a hit, it felt accidental. Born to miss? The jolt through the nerves in her shoulder, the adrenaline spark to her heart was not natural and never could be. Could it? The sound, though expected, remained a surprise each time: A hard, dry, blunt report, the crack of metal on metal, implacable, a nail piercing steel.

...The feel of it on the receiving end unimaginable till it happens. The burn. They spoke of the horrible burn. Oftentimes it was the last thing they spoke of. So hit the brain. No pain. But you have to be good to hit the brain from any distance. Far better than she...

Aliette pushed the button, locked her body into position. The paper man popped up, she cracked off shots till he fluttered. She pushed the button, the blasted sheet flew toward her like a ghost. She unclipped it, like underwear from the line on Saturday. Two lousy hits by his hip.

She reloaded. Pushed the button, locked her body. Waited a moment.

He dropped down this time. She fired again.

With each series of fusillades — six shots, eight shots, twelve, she improved. Once she actually landed a cluster, a hole near the heart began to rip. Perhaps there was some instinct there.

Bonding with my gun?...She plugged away, for the sake of herself.

After an hour, Aliette holstered her weapon. Made a tidy stack of sheets.

She had signed out and was heading for the bathroom to wash her hands when a guy sidled up beside her, in shirtsleeves, holster unsnapped, a plastic cup of coffee in hand. 'Looking for me?' His face was obscured under the peak of a Béziers rugby team cap — white with blue and red flashing. He raised it briefly, smile beaming to a manic degree, a film of sweat under his black eyes. Like he was on some drug?

Sure, a drug called stress. 'Salut, monsieur. I didn't see you ... A bit of practice?'

A guarded nod. 'In the theatre.' Gesturing at a door across the lounge.

The situation simulator. 'Haven't tried that yet,' Aliette admitted. 'You don't return my calls.'

He took a breath, calming himself. 'Not returning any calls, Inspector.'

'Hiding won't help fix this, Nabi.'

'But a bit of practice might... Come. Big fun in there. Let's see what you can do.' Taking her by the arm ... clutching it with a strength that surprised and almost hurt — yes, manic, he escorted her to the simulator.

A German-designed interactive virtual environment, it *was* like a small theatre in size and function. But instead of rows of seats for passive viewing, the floor space between herself and a screen on the far wall was laid out with randomly placed blinds and barriers of varying height and shape. A shooter uses her own service arm and fires real rounds while engaging 'targets' in a variety of settings requiring strategic decision making. And good shooting. The technology, aided by an operator, reads hits and misses, positioning, movements, even vocal commands. If you are not doing it right, you're doing it wrong. Which means you're dead. Hostages and/or innocent bystanders too, depending on the scenario selected.

Nabi signalled to the control booth. A disembodied voice enquired, 'Where?'

'Park. Alone.'

The lights dimmed. Aliette was suddenly on the edges of a pleasant green space ornamented with trees and bushes, a pond, pathways, benches, a picnic table. An ambient sound track provided a bird singing. A dog yapping. Then a man stepped out from behind a tree.

Nabi's voice cut in, 'There's your target. Draw your weapon and hail him.'

'Shouldn't I get closer to be sure?'

Behind her, Nabi's voice boomed, 'Police! Drop your weapon. On the ground! Now!'

She glanced over her shoulder; she had never heard Nabi raise his voice.

Mistake. In the space of a glance, the man by the tree was now three steps closer. He aimed a gun, fired off four shots and ran for the trees. She returned a single shot in his direction while moving into a crouch behind the nearest barrier. She peeked over, took aim—

Everything stopped. The lights came up. Nabi advised, 'Forget it. You're already dead.'

'I am?'

'You were a good officer, but you were too slow to react.'

'Sorry.'

'The dead don't apologize, Inspector.' Nabi signalled toward the booth, spinning his hand, as if rewinding a spool. 'They rise up and try again.'

Lights down. Same scenario. Aliette hailed him … No reaction.

'Louder, please.'

She took in a chest full of air. 'Police! Drop your weapon and get on the ground. Now!'

The target had been engaged. He took aim—

She fired. Several times. Missed … the target was in flight toward the trees.

Nabi hissed, 'Advance!'

Without thinking, Aliette moved into the open space and tip-toed toward the next blind.

The target had found a position behind a bush. He aimed.

Nabi ordered, 'Run!' as the crack of exploding ordnance filled the space … 'Dive!'

The industrial carpeting burned her knees as she slid to safety.

Or maybe not … the target froze, the birds fell silent. The lights came up.

Nabi looked down at her, rueful. 'Third time lucky?' Offering a hand up.

When they left the theatre an hour later, Chief Inspector Nouvelle was dripping with sweat. Limping, knees like jelly. Not a great outing: She'd been killed six times by the 'target' and left some tragic collateral damage in her wake. She retreated to the Ladies, washed as best she could, sponged warm water into dust blotches on pants and sleeves, despaired of eating lunch in a soaking bra and shirt.

Nabi Zidane's roots were in a village in the Atlas mountains, but the defining moments of his life had occurred in the streets of Béziers. Regardless of what his grandfather may have thought about it, Nabi believed sometimes a cop (and his soul) will need a drink. The right or wrong of it was in God's keeping. Aliette found him waiting at a table in the lounge with a beer, a sandwich, and same for her. He had a Gauloise on the go.

'Some things to work on, Inspector,' he noted, clinking his glass against hers.

No point replying to the obvious. A stack of printouts supplied by the unseen simulator operator gave detailed measures of her marksmanship, engagement strategies, decision-making, timing. More correctly, her lack of each. Aliette took a swig of her beer, stared at the sandwich, exhausted.

'An hour in there twice a week, they'll bring you up to speed.'

'I'm not very good.'

'You have to be good.' Nabi drained his glass. 'Another?'

'I have to get back.'

'Me too.' He signalled the girl behind the counter to bring two more.

Aliette did not protest. Being killed six times will make you thirsty.

And Nabi needed to talk.

21

A MAN LIKE THAT

Gabrielle Gravel was comfortably ensconced in a stately leather *fauteuil* in an office at the Palais de Justice. She informed Magistrate Sergio Regarri that she was not the kind to trust in the notion of an absolute conversion and would never claim to have effected one. The Saul-to-Paul effect? Spiritually speaking, she didn't buy it. An alcoholic could stop drinking, but could he ever forget the feeling? 'A soul retains its entire life,' said Gabrielle. 'Otherwise it's depleted. Vincent Spanghero is a very complex man.'

'Is?'

'I hope so.'

Magistrate Regarri tapped the file. 'And you have no idea where he went?'

'I believe he said something about fishing… It was several months ago, as you are aware.'

The judge was aware. 'Did you offer any advice? I mean by way of ending the program?'

'I told him fishing sounded perfect.'

'You weren't worried?… It was quite sudden. Impulsive? His superiors. His colleagues… they were all taken by surprise.'

'I was not. As it says on the page in front of you, it was a natural step.'

'To go fishing?'

'To leave the force.' Gabrielle smiled for the judge. 'It's not my job to worry. I do the work. If there's a natural end point, good. More often than not, there isn't. Either way, the clock stops, we shake hands, I wish them luck.'

'… and you file your report.'

'Yes. Though in this instance, strictly speaking, it wasn't needed. He decided to retire.'

'Walk away ... go fishing.'

'Therefore no longer his employer's problem.'

'Nevertheless,' reading ... 'you did file and you say were pleased. That he had come to a solid place and made a sound decision.'

'Yes. Which makes me wonder why I'm here.'

'We're reviewing his case.'

'Has he asked to come back?'

'No. But we might want him to come back.'

'I'd be very surprised if he said yes to such a request. Last time I saw Monsieur Spanghero he was headed a very different direction.'

' ... a spiritual awakening.' The judge was reading from her pages.

'Yes.'

'Is fishing spiritual?'

Gabrielle shrugged. 'One hears it might be. There was a book ... *Fishing in America?*'

'Ah yes ... you mean, *Trout Fishing in America.*' (*Pêche à la truite en Amérique*)

'*Voilà*. And that movie with that blond man who was an outlaw? Who jumped into the river?'

'Sundance ... Sundance Kid.' Magistrate Regarri smiled.

'That's him ... myself, I thought he was better with a gun than with a fishing pole. But yes, there must be something spiritual in fishing if the Americans put it up there with their guns.'

'So, better a fishing pole than a gun for Inspector Spanghero?'

Gabrielle considered and conceded, 'Yes. Vincent was intense by nature.'

'Was?'

'Is ... Better fishing than the pain that had him sent to me.'

'Did you feel he was cured of that pain?'

'Pain is personal, always relative. Officially? Sure. But no, not completely. He'd seen too much. But I believe he was well grounded in his new perspective and ready to move on.'

'No word from him?'

'No.' Gabrielle added, 'For what it's worth, I would recommend not asking to him to come back.'

'I will note it, madame.' And he did so. Then asked, 'Why not?

It took an hour. She was intrigued, at moments discomfited. They wanted Vincent Spanghero but they had no idea where he was. They were worried; should she be too? This was not stated in so many words, it was gleaned from the judge's hesitations, his questions leading into tangent areas such as anger and vengeance, his constant mulling as to where a man like that would go next.

A man like that: people's presumptions about their fellow humans were Gabrielle's stock in trade.

It concluded with a cautionary advisement: 'I trust you realize his file is still confidential.'

'All my clients enjoy lifetime confidentiality.' Gabrielle would not breathe a word.

He thanked her for coming in. It was her pleasure. He had a very attractive face.

– 22 –

Mario's war

As Gabrielle Gravel was leaving the Palais de Justice, Chief Inspector Mario Bédard was sitting down in the lunchroom with a tray from the canteen. Fridays, they did a decent croque monsieur.

He had barely tucked in when his cell buzzed. He wiped his fingers. 'Yes.'

'So they're having beers in the lounge at the range.'

'How nice …' Mario felt a flush of heat at the base of his neck. He knew that Chief Inspector Nouvelle was not his friend. He could live with that. But it angered him that she was Nabi's. He sucked it up. Friends were always fluid. 'Send them one from me.'

'I'm at Bédarieux. Someone torched the bakery.'

'Ah.' And Liza was leading an operation at Saint-Thibéry.

'Maybe I'll drive down there for some practice.' Though he was expected at the gendarmerie in Capestang at two.

Like in any war, people still had to attend to their daily business. Or try. The more so in this business. Stay steady. Build trust. It was good that Nabi was hiding from the world. Exactly the optics Mario was needing. But an appearance at the range would—

'Don't crowd them, Mario,' Julien advised.

Mario sniffed at it. 'Nabi works best under pressure.' Sometimes Julien provoked the same heat under Mario's collar. Liza was the only one he really trusted.

'Perhaps. But she's not Nabi.'

'No.' He had to agree. And he asked, casually, 'How do you read her?'

A pause. He heard Julien searching for words.

Finally, and not so casually: 'I don't know. You?'

Bon ... Mario sat back from his tray and looked out at busy Place du Général de Gaulle below, the buses endlessly arriving, leaving, people flowing in every direction, no fixed point at the hub of the city, ever. 'I'm not sure,' he admitted. May as well be honest. He sensed Julien was—for once. 'Just not sure how to work with our new friend.'

'So we give her some space. She's not stupid.' She would see it, mused Julien Lesouple, easing assiduously away from an argument over the phone.

Fine. And Mario wanted to eat his lunch. 'You're right.' Let her have some beers with Nabi Zidane. Let her see him good and close. Then go back to her. 'OK, good work. Thanks.'

'Not a problem. All for one, *quoi?*'

'All for one ... You going to stay with it over the weekend?'

'I'll give her the weekend off. She'll be with Regarri... I think we have Nabi covered now.'

'Right.' Julien had his friends and systems. And Regarri stood to lose too much if his new girlfriend screwed up. 'Keep me informed.' Mario ended the call.

... and after the interviews at Capestang, there was a team practice at Narbonne that evening, a big Round 16 Rugby Union match to watch tomorrow, his own match Sunday morning. And he'd coach the junior team Sunday afternoon—all good strong French boys he'd selected himself.

And Liza. Supper with Liza, Sunday night.

Life had to go on despite the war.

Chief Inspector Bédard got back to his croque monsieur, eating slowly. Enjoying it.

Mulling the notion of Aliette Nouvelle commiserating with Nabi Zidane over a glass or two, Mario thought of his father, the original Mario, a grimy and eternally skeptical man who was good at fixing cars. It was automatic, and a comfort in these tricky times. Mario had listened closely to his father, who'd fought in Algeria in the ugly years before Mario was born. Bédard *père* was a legionnaire, which meant he had served with lots of foreigners and embraced them as brothers in arms—lots of good men from everywhere fighting for France, it didn't matter how they'd got there, he loved them and they loved him. Burrs were something else again. Mario Sr. had been with the Pioneers. Sappers—engineers and the like—there to support the warriors. His battalion had been paired with the airborne infantry, elite soldiers trained in counter-insurgency. He had taken part in brutal operations against the insurgent, pitiless FLN and he had no end of horrible, riveting stories to tell his son. There was an abiding thread that ran through all of them, and which he'd kept in his heart to the bitter end, just as he'd kept the full-fledged legionnaire beard: burrs were dishonest, cunning people, it was bred into them, and when they tried to draw distinctions amongst themselves, they were only lying again.

A burr is a burr, point final. Don't trust him, admonished Mario's papa.

Whenever Nabi Zidane dropped in the fact that he was Kabyle and that was different, Mario thought of his father. It was just one more way Nabs would try to split the defence.

No go. Not with Mario defending.

Before he died, bitter and discouraged at how the politicians kept failing him, Mario's father said, *You have to keep at it, make sure life goes on. Our life…*

Mario took it to heart. If you can't believe your father, what's the point?

Life went on after they put bombs along the train tracks at Paris, and blew up factories in Toulouse. If you did not keep going, you lost. Life went on after the politicians gave the job to Nabi Zidane. Vincent Spanghero was a thorn in everyone's side, but at least he stood up and told the truth. His father had been in Algeria too, though not in the Foreign Legion, and Mario and Vincent were never really friends.

Not easy for two cops who both wanted the same thing.

So Vincent was a casualty of war.

… and Mario thought of himself as a counter-insurgent, pushing back, fighting for his father's disappointment. For Vincent's truth. And for the loss of his wife, poor, defeated Jeanne.

Jeanne was another casualty. Cracked apart by the pictures of her brother lying in the street in front of his shattered shop window, she retreated to the Carmelites. She was sorry, but all the hatred was too much to bear; the only sound she could live with was the silence of the Lord. Jeanne took a vow of separation and now lived her life behind a wall.

Liza wasn't Jeanne, but she was tough, realistic, she saw Nabi clearly.

Still, Mario wondered if they ever enjoyed croque monsieur at the convent.

If they ever enjoyed anything... He didn't visit. She didn't want visitors. She wanted peace.

Mario could do nothing but choke down his grief and rage.

Betty looked in. Her eyes clouded. Mario blushed, dabbed his lips. 'Haven't seen him, Bet.'

Betty did not come in. She was with Nabi. Some were. Most weren't. This was the war.

...he thought, But why not a quick coffee at the range?

If only for a picture. A picture was always useful, could tip the balance, help a person make the right decision. Would Julien have thought of that? Mario Bédard knew Julien Lesouple was afraid of their new friend. But he was not.

23

BEERS WITH NABI

Nabi stubbed his fourth Gauloise. 'Look, when I got this job, not everyone was happy about it. I know that. Guys like me are all right on the team. Just never at the top.'

'Will you stop it with the whining?' She didn't like this side of Nabi.

He didn't hear, he rambled on. 'I swear I never said a word by way of self-promotion. I didn't expect to be considered. It's the politicians. They decided I'd be a good bridge to the new Béziers,' he explained, finger raised, a cautionary gesture, 'their words, not mine. But it makes sense. I have the right face, know the language, what *they* believe, and how they expect to be treated... Mm?'

Aliette sat chewing on her stale baguette, nodding, Yes, yes, yes...

'And I *do* know the job. Thirty years on these streets, I know the job as well as anyone, and that includes Vincent Spanghero. Not bragging—just a fact.'

'You're a good cop, Nabi.'

'Yeah.' Gulping beer. 'And once it was mine, I wanted it. Once they pointed my way, even I could see that I wasn't the worst choice. Logical. The demographic? Right?'

'Right... please calm down.'

'Sure. Calm.' Throwing back more beer... 'Well, Vincent hated it and said so. Loudly. Every day...' His Kabyle eyes had a moist quality, dark sparkles floating in darker waters. Now they were on the verge of tears. He closed his eyes, breathed, controlled it. Asked, 'What was I supposed to do? Say, "Here, you have it; I don't need it?"'

'Of course not.'

'Vincent hated it, but he stayed put, and maybe someone wasn't very smart to let him. Smarter to just clean house.'

'But you didn't.'

'He was my friend. My partner… And it takes a while to learn how to be the boss.'

'It's not your fault.'

'Then Vincent does his Lone Ranger thing with two young guys and we lose Menaud. And Pierre Tropéano tells them exactly what went down, even if I was too spineless.' That was a hard one for Nabi to admit. 'And now this.' This killing spree. 'If it's not my fault, whose is it?'

'Did you send Tropéano out looking last week?'

'Of course not. Never.' He smiled sadly, lost and woeful, despair creeping to the fore. 'But I surely said some very wrong things… I know I did.' Squelching the tears, swallowing his drink like awful medicine, Nabi Zidane immediately rose from his chair to signal for more.

Aliette put an arm out. 'Just talk, Nabi.'

He eased back down. 'I don't know what to say.'

She communicated gentle scorn. 'So you come here and practise killing imaginary men.'

That touched a nerve. 'Whatever else, I will be ready for fucking Mario Bédard.'

'Talk to them, Nabi. You can… Talk past Mario—that's no big challenge.'

Nabi threw her a don't-be-stupid look. 'Mario's got the world behind him, Inspector.'

'Aliette…'

'Aliette. They all think I got something I don't deserve.' Another awful smile. 'And not because of my Solve record.'

'I don't think that. Lots don't.'

'What do I know about deserved rewards?' Nabi stared at the table. 'Talk to them? I can't talk to them because they don't want to hear from me! They want *this*. Now that it's happened, they want it… Can't you see that?'

She silently confirmed that she could. *She* called for more beer. When it was served, she ventured, 'I know the knife is… what it is. And I know Tropéano's gun was taken. But—'

'A war prize for Vincent.'

Exactly what Sergio had said.

'Vincent and me, we took down some very nasty people. He used to laugh when it got ugly... I suppose I did too. Very nasty...' Nabi was getting sentimental again. 'Those were some days, I'll tell you.'

She didn't want to hear about it. 'But would Vincent stab a man he doesn't know, so wildly? Hacking away like that?'

'I don't know. He can lose it. Completely lose it. I've seen it.'

Which echoed Mario, Liza and Julien... Perhaps her gut instinct was wrong where it came to the logic of Vincent's supposed rage. 'I asked Gabrielle, my *psy*?... or tried to. Twice. She dodged. There's something there, I'm sure of it.'

'Well, you tried.' Nodding a glum thank you, sitting back in his chair. 'Maybe Sergio will get it out of her. Whatever it is.'

'He's seeing her today... he thinks I shouldn't be talking about this with you.'

'He's right.' Nabi sniffed and started up another cigarette. Stared into his beer. Waited.

She finally asked, 'His wife—what's her name?—what does she have to say about all this?'

'Catherine? She thinks like the rest of them. She blames me.'

24

CATHERINE AND THE SCHEMING BURR

Rue des Paradisiers was in Pech des Moulins, off Boulevard du Four à Chaux and handy to her way out of the city on a Friday afternoon. While nothing like a new suburb, it was visibly newer than the cramped and byzantine city centre on the hill, a more spacious quarter built on the low grounds adjacent to the Orb. Not unlike where Chief Inspector Aliette Nouvelle had come of age in Nantes. Wider post-war streets were lined with homes on properties with gardens, some with pools. Aliette parked down the street from the Spanghero residence, closed her eyes and drifted in the residual fuzziness of beers with Nabi for twenty minutes. Then she lowered the window, breathed in fresh air and tried to arrange her thinking.

But Nabi Zidane's lugubrious self-pity was a dreary mirror that left her staring at her own precarious situation.

From where she sat, the inspector could see the wall of the cemetery on the crest of the hill, the forested parklands spread below. She realized she was looking at the very spot at the corner of the wall where another young street person had been taken, this one shot point blank with Tropéano's gun. Three kids, one cop. To Aliette, it seemed clear that the kids were the target: where they were taken, how they were killed. Alone. In places where only they tended to go. The third kid proved it, gun notwithstanding. Tropéano was an anomaly, a cop who happened to get in the way, paid the price, and inadvertently provided the killer with a gun. If Vincent Spanghero had wanted to kill police officers—with a knife or a gun or an axe or his bare hands—he would have started there. Cops were just as readily found in the city at night as street kids, but in different places. This killer went where the kids were. Whether randomly, or hunting a specific kid, was obviously a tragically crucial question. She doubted it was over …

Her police colleagues had a different theory and Nabi Zidane seemed to share it. A bitter ex-cop fit their bitter agenda. The knife, the gun and the notes were like gifts to the likes of Mario Bédard. In lieu of a specific kid, Vincent Spanghero had to be accounted for. For clarity's sake. Before he and Nabi could be framed publicly together. Alive or otherwise, it was all the same to Mario.

But how to approach the wife of ex-Inspector Spanghero without compromising herself? Or Sergio. It was not her business. To pursue it was to walk a fine and potentially destructive line. Everyone knew about her and Magistrate Regarri. He had not been assigned any of her cases since the autumn, and not because of the summer's debacle. It was unstated but clear: you can sleep together, but you will no longer be considered a professional team. Because love tends to get in the way of hard legal decisions, not to mention the need for absolute discretion. Which was a pity, because they were a good professional team.

Forget work. Love brought on the harder question: was she disrespecting Sergio? His advice to back away from Nabi's problem was not an instruction issued from his official desk. It was a lover's friendly word, delivered in trust, and infinitely more fragile.

What Nabi was facing was ugly and unfair. Aliette hated that. She knew in her heart she was not going to stand down. She knew Sergio would know. Where would that lead?

Nowhere good.

It was wearying. It wasn't fair!

… No, but you still need a strategy here, Inspector.

Aliette left the car and walked. Motion, endorphins — in the space of a block she left behind her fretting. She decided her own predicament was her best cover in approaching Catherine Spanghero. There was no point pretending she was not who she was.

Be up-front. Mostly. But personalize it …

The white stucco house on the corner lot was a change from the cream tones lining the block. A palm and a mulberry graced the front yard. The dead palm fronds and mulberry leaves had been swept up. The lawn was winter sparse, but clean; the place looked cared for, in good shape.

The woman who answered her knock was not. 'Madame Spanghero?'

'I'm not interested ...' already closing the door. She was cross and clearly very tired; raccoon eyes and dullish skin were dead giveaways.

'Not selling anything, madame.' Aliette flashed her warrant card, knowing the woman would recognize it immediately. 'I have a problem at work, I need to contact your husband.'

Catherine Spanghero blanched. Tall, straight, strong, lots of thick black hair tied up for work at home. She'd look great when she needed to. When she wasn't weighed down with worry.

'He's not here. And you must know that.'

Aliette nodded honestly. Pleaded silently.

Perhaps Catherine perceived a similar stress. 'What is your problem?'

'Nabil Zidane.'

'Oh Lord! ... Come in.'

The house was typical. One large bright area extending from the family room at the front to a sliding glass door in the kitchen, leading out to a back patio. A narrow pool, good for laps, had been covered for winter. More palms and a fig tree in the back garden. There would be an office and toilet in the hall off the stairs, three or four bedrooms upstairs. A laptop was open on the kitchen table, and a spiral notebook. Aliette appraised the page surreptitiously—it was not uncommon for an outraged wife to seek redress on the part of her wronged husband. But the woman's handwriting was nothing like the childish script on the found notes. 'Busy day?'

'There's work out there, you just have to find it.'

'What are you looking for?'

'Just secretarial. Administration? I have experience. I thought I was free of it. Now it looks like maybe not...' A large sigh, decompressing for a visitor. 'Sit. I have wine. Or another beer?'

Aliette smiled. So this woman sees something she understands. 'I'd rather water. Tea? Have to get a handle on things here.'

'Vincent couldn't.' She put the kettle on, found a packet of biscuits, asked over her shoulder. 'And so what's that scheming burr done now?'

The query jolted. Distaste made it easier to ignore any lingering guilt Aliette might have felt about deceiving Catherine Spanghero. 'Nabi's doing a number on me.'

'Political stuff?'

'And worse... Tries to push me off to the side, I resist and now he recommends they push me off to some *psy*. I'm powerless. Forgive me, I know it's personal, but I gather your husband went down a similar road? This Gabrielle Gravel? I was hoping he could...' A gesture.

'Help you avoid what happened to him?'

Aliette indicated an open-ended yes and eased the conversation forward. 'I hear they were partners.'

'Twenty years, off and on. Very regular at the start.'

'And good friends.'

'Don't ask me about men and friends. That man has wrecked our life.' Catherine Spanghero folded her arms across her breast as if to steady her heart. Closed her tired eyes. Breathed. Then poured tea. 'It never felt right to me. I know those people...' Those horrid burrs. 'My mother thought I was out of my mind having him at the wedding but Vincent insisted...' A weary shrug. 'It's not right. Yes, Vincent made mistakes—'

'Who doesn't?'

'Vincent's a better cop.' Catherine tasted her tea. 'But Nabi had the numbers. Right man for the new demographics. *Mon dieu*, the way they think. It broke Vincent's heart. He was so angry. He unravelled. They sent him to that woman. He had to go or they'd have forced him out. That was pure hell, I'll tell you. He retreated into himself, barely spoke anymore. But you could feel the anger. And guilt about poor Menaud Rhéaume. I was used to that part... After all these years, if you want to hang onto your marriage, you accept the nature of the business. But this was scary. My kids were watching him like he was some kind of mad dog.'

She sipped more tea, bemused. Her mood was settling. Talking was helpful. Aliette waited.

'Absurd,' quoted Catherine Spanghero in ironic imitation of a growly male voice. 'That was his new word. Vincent would sit here making speeches about the absurdity of his life, what he wanted, what he couldn't have, all because of his ex-best pal, the burr. For three months we sat here watching him being torn in half, trying to work with this Gabrielle person, trying to carry on with Nabi as his boss. It was like the Vincent we knew started to disappear before our very eyes. I mean before he actually left.'

'But did he talk about it? I mean beyond his speeches?'

'Hardly. Gabrielle says this, Gabrielle says that. All this psychobabble. Vincent was on the verge of violence. Between that and my kids, I was on eggshells every minute. Horrible life. Then one day he left. I should have seen it... Silent all morning, not a word, clearing out his drawers and desk, his shelves, his pictures, all his little knick-knacks, mementos, everything... all of it into cardboard boxes and garbage bags and out to the side of the house with the trash, like a silent, angry machine.'

'Everything?'

'Everything. I couldn't stand it. I went downtown just to get away from it, I come home to prepare my family's supper and he's gone. No note. Not a word since. Not even to my kids. I don't know where he is. He could be dead. He may as well be, *merci*, fucking Nabi and your *maudite* new face of Béziers.' Moving to the far side of anger now, struggling to keep it together.

Aliette's sympathy rebounded somewhat. 'Not easy.'

'We thought he'd gone fishing, and maybe that was a good thing...' She chewed a thumbnail, lost in the awful recollection. 'The worst part was looking out the window in the middle of the night, at the people who come by ahead of the City with their trucks and wagons, scavenging. I have no objection, why waste good stuff? But it was so sad... First the grim little men trying to make some money, and then these street kids, in packs like animals, I couldn't bear it, watching them, all of them so silent, as silent as he was, stuffing Vincent's life into their pockets. I pulled the drapes and wept, prayed my kids weren't watching too... In the morning it was all gone.'

All gone. Aliette's antennae twitched. But she did not dare let on she had any idea as to any of Vincent Spanghero's personal effects. She stayed on topic. 'But were you not involved? This therapy thing? You're his wife. This Gabrielle Gravel. What does she do?'

'Bloody voodoo? I don't know.' A despairing glance at her tea. 'She made him disappear. I called a few times, even went in there after he left. She was polite, I suppose, but cold, not too helpful, in fact, not in the least. Said Vincent wanted it private, totally private, and she had to respect that. Wouldn't budge ... Strange place. It's like she has this zombie answering her phone.'

The inspector could only nod to that. 'You're making me scared.'

But Catherine Spanghero's story dovetailed with the scraps gleaned from Sergio and Nabi:

Inspector Spanghero was last reported *in control of his issues*, comfortable with his decision to leave the police, looking forward to spending a quiet summer fishing in the Tarn.

Aliette finished her tea and sighed. 'I really wish I had an ally in this.'

Catherine echoed it. 'And I'd like to see my husband ... ' She had sent her son up to the Tarn to bring him back, or at least talk. 'Not a trace. They know him. They hadn't seen him. That was last summer.' But she could relate to an isolated cop. 'I'm probably speaking out of school, but I was called to talk to a judge. Just yesterday.'

'Oh?'

'Regarri. You know him?'

'Yes.'

'He was wanting to locate Vincent as well. Wouldn't tell me why, of course ... Think it could have something to do with your problem?'

'It may, madame.' Aliette leaned forward, commiserating, looking to hear more about Catherine's vanished man. 'I mean, it could. A lot of things up in the air at HQ these days.'

Her host repeated, 'Political stuff,' in a tone that was dry and dark, then refilled their cups, and they talked about the situation at Hôtel de Police. And in the city. And in France ...

25

SOME GOOD ENERGY?

Gabrielle had two investigative consultations scheduled this Friday: a man who flew a little red antique airplane back and forth over the beach at Valras in the summer trailing advertising banners had nothing to do in the winter and confessed to fears of drastic action. Another man, who appeared with his dismayed wife, had become addicted to pizza. Gabrielle Gravel decided to take on the flyer—something poetic there she thought she might enjoy. She referred the pizza man along to her friend Pierre Depierrerue, a hypnotherapist known for his success with the Erickson method.

Then the Petitpas family came in for their Family Systems hour. '*Bonjour*, thank you for coming. Everyone fine?' She did not expect responses. At least Emma had stopped whimpering. They took their usual places, avoided looking at each other, everyone pretended not to smell Virginie. 'Before we start, I want to apologize for the incident in the waiting room last evening. To be sure, guns do not belong in our waiting room. But I have discussed it with the client and she assures me it was an accident and, for what it's worth, she apologizes too...' Not exactly true, but a proactive suggestion. 'We all hope it won't happen again. And just so you know, the gun is actually part of her program. And we are working to—'

'Did she kill someone?'

Gabrielle faced Virginie. 'You know I won't discuss another client's situation. But perhaps I could ask *you*, I mean all of you, if you would like to say anything about what happened. A gun is a very serious thing. If it disturbed you, please, that's why I'm here... That's why *we're* here, mm? Anyone experience any repercussions from the presence of that gun? An unsettling dream occurrence?... rashes, upset stomach, disrupted bowel rhythm, constricted throat... Em? It's very normal, and actually important that we know. If you have something to share, I for one would like to hear about it. Because I care about you... yes, and because this is an issue that society in general should be talking about. Guns. In public... The waiting room can be construed as the public square and we are all individual citizens at the end of the day, after all, and so—'

'I thought it was supposed to be her kitchen.' Virginie got up and perused the masks.

'It's *supposed* to be a place where people communicate, Virginie.'

'What about cook? Did she ever cook anything worth eating? Not for me. So useless...'

Emma hung her head. Jean stared at the ceiling.

Gabrielle closed her eyes. 'But most tragic gun incidents occur within the family context.'

She opened them to confront the hysterically coloured demonic face constructed by Gerte, who came on Tuesday afternoon, and who, at eighty-three, suffered from debilitating sexually violent nightmares. 'And so?' said Virginie.

Gabrielle held steady. 'And so we should talk about it.'

She waited.

As was the pattern, Virginie Petitpas spoke first. 'I'm pretty sure I hate her.'

Gabrielle Gravel raised her finger, about to make a point—

But Jean pre-empted her, shrugging. 'I think she's interesting.'

Prompting Emma to rise up, glaring. 'No!'

Jean took issue. 'Why do you automatically react like that?'

'Because you automatically want to take her to bed!'

'You always think that.'

'Because it's always true.'

'She was interested in my book. I told her I'd lend her one. Is that wrong?'

'You're lying.'

'I'm not lying... It's an excellent series.'

Poor Emma huffed and stewed, blurted, 'I threw them away!'

'That's great,' sighed Jean.

'Too bad!... just *too* bad!'

Virginie laughed at her parents. Gerte's horrific mask made it echo.

Gabrielle Gravel sat mesmerized for a few beats longer than she knew she should. Emma was actively fighting Jean. Her motivation appeared to be paranoid jealousy; on the other hand, there was much good reason for Em's outburst in Jean's file. The useful thing was that Emma was expressing herself, as opposed to collapsing in tears. If she really wanted to reclaim her errant man—or her demonic daughter for that matter—she had to show some backbone. This was good energy, but... 'But this is not about the client,' instructed Gabrielle. 'This is about the presence of the gun. This is an excellent opportunity to analyze the issue as three indiviuals, and as a family.'

'We are a bad family,' intoned the demon, mimicking her mother.

Emma started crying.

'Come on, Emma, respond to that. Please...' Gabrielle urged her.

Emma sobbed. She couldn't.

Jean looked at his watch. 'There are so many other things I could be doing.'

And it devolved from there.

And then, mercifully, it was the weekend.

... but Em had lashed out. Before she left, Gabrielle made some notes.

26

ROND-POINT MOMENT

Aliette Nouvelle eased into the afternoon traffic, dodging qualms, telling herself she had not lied to Catherine Spanghero. Nabi Zidane really was doing a number on her. OK, more accurate to say Nabi's situation. Still: every word had been substantively true, from the ugly politics of city policing to an uncomfortable order to attend at the pleasure of Gabrielle Gravel and her related need to locate an alienated cop who had gone to ground. Aliette's feelings toward that cop's wife were double-edged: sympathy, even a measure of admiration; but if Catherine Spanghero had to think that way about reality—sorry madame, but Nabi Zidane is reality—well, what could you do with that kind of thinking except stand back and let it burn? A quiet chat over tea with a racist wife made the hole in this cop's heart one turn wider, deeper. But she had learned something. Maybe. Had Vincent Spanghero tossed out Nabi's wedding gift with the rest of his forsaken life? Or had he kept that one item for purposes of revenge on the horrid scheming burr? She was convinced it couldn't be Vincent. After hearing his bitter wife fill in the backstory from the family side of it, Aliette's conviction was wavering. Her thoughts went back to Catherine, a big woman, and as bitter as her man, apparently. The notebook. Everyone tried to disguise their handwriting. Were the woman's bleak eyes a sign of a much deeper distress? Killing kids to lure cops. To kill them ... Or her son, his son, old enough to drive to the Tarn alone, looking for his father. She imagined a big boy carrying a father's angry pride. Should she talk to him too?

She probably should. But under what pretext? And he would surely tell his mother.

And that would not be good for a cop needing at any cost to fly under the radar ...

The possibilities made her yawn. Time to give it break, Inspector. It had been a long day, a difficult week, and she was tired of thinking about these kinds of people. Time to get home, to a peaceful, empty-headed Friday night.

Yes... yawning, hands tight on the wheel, heading home, the *rond-point* came into view.

No. Aliette realized she did not want to spend Friday night alone.

Alone, she would only continue gnawing at it. Entering the *rond-point* at the edge of the city that would put her on the road to Saint-Brin, her village, her slippers, pyjamas, maybe another beer (or two?) and her warm bed... the inspector made a full circle and went back the other way.

Aliette knew she was about to commit a sin. Friday night was Sergio's, carte blanche, no expectations, no questions asked. She yawned again and kept driving. She needed to be with him. For her sins, Chief Inspector Nouvelle drove straight back into traffic that was quickly getting seriously awful. An hour later she lucked into a spot on Boulevard d'Angleterre, climbed the city stairs and let herself in. '*Cou-cou!*' But the house was empty.

She called Mathilde, who said things were quiet and passed her to Magui Barthès, who said she would visit the cheese producer in the morning to confront him with the reality of his tragic lover's status (an almost certain *assassinat* charge) and see how he reacted, then passed her to Henri Dardé, who said he had taken two gendarmes and a warrant and done a search at the domicile of Fabien Fleury, but they had found no guns or ordnance—not normal in the house of a long-time hunting enthusiast (who professed to hate 'foreigners'), and tomorrow he was going with two social workers to see one of the three girls who had probably pushed their boy-stealing friend into the river, the (now judge-approved!) strategy being to separate and scare (a little) then bring them back together in the judge's sombre office for the moment of truth.

'Good. Good luck... See you Monday.'

Reassured that her own small world was holding steady, Aliette went upstairs, took a long, hot shower, washed and hung her shirt and underwear, then crawled into Sergio Regarri's bed.

'*Quoi* …!' She woke with a start.

He was buttoning a casual shirt. He had changed to jeans. 'You were far away.'

'What time is it?'

'Seven or so.' Sergio waited for her to explain.

Aliette smiled at the beautiful man. She was not going to explain that she had been to talk with Catherine Spanghero. *After* listening to Nabi Zidane spill his guts and display his hopeless fears. She could not, because she was breaking the rules and being dishonest and would not risk revealing a woman who could not keep to her own affairs. No. Impossible to even hint at any of this after a blessed three hours of oblivion under his comfy quilt.

Her bad faith would leak through his feelings for her and cause him unfair pain.

She reached and held his hand. 'I had a big day … and a drink … and I just thought …'

'Good instincts, Inspector.' But it was Friday night and he had a date.

'With?' A friendly query, not prying, merely interested in his life. She blushed through sleepy eyes.

Sergio asked questions all day long. He understood. 'Well, Misha. Architect … designed this place. Alain … owns that big pharmacy on Les Allées? Friends since …' spreading a palm flat down by his knee to signal since we were very young. 'And Marc, from law school … does defence work, you may have seen him at the courthouse.'

'Do they bring their wives? Girlfriends?' She was a girlfriend.

'Actually, Misha's gay. But, no. It's Friday. We just drink and eat … and drink. You know?'

'Of course.'

But she could make some soup. There was wine, lots of cheese. 'You remember that thing we were discussing—about keeping the bed warm?'

She did. She told him to have fun and let him go.

27

THE KILLING SPOT BY THE CEMETERY WALL

Two hours later, after soup and cheese, the evening news, Aliette's underwear was dry. She stole a soft T-shirt and a cashmere sweater from Sergio's drawer. She strapped on her gun, buttoned her coat, tugged her beret down over her ears and went out. Shouldn't take long; she just needed to see. She would be back in lots of time to warm the bed for Sergio.

She went down the city stairs to the boulevard. She had been to the old church where Pierre Tropéano had died violently. Coming home from Gabrielle's, she had wandered down the lane behind the bistro where the second victim had been killed while scavenging the bins for food. She had stood on the chalk outline marking the place where the first victim had bled out on the street, in front of the squat where he may have lived. She had seen another person stopping at that same door. A killer, still searching? For whom and why remained a puzzle.

The logic of it fell both ways. The notes and Nabi's knife said one thing: a killer seeking vengeance on those who'd wronged him, who'd left bait in a trail he knew they'd see and follow, so he could follow them. Aliette had to concede that Pierre Tropéano, like everyone in the Police Judiciaire brigade, had seen the hand of Vincent Spanghero in the notes. And he had followed the trail to l'Église Saint-Aphrodise, an obvious possibility—where he'd been cruelly ambushed. Cops were cunning. And vengeful. It was possible.

But the murder scenes said something else. Take away the trail of notes, a cop of Tropéano's rank was not likely to be encountered at the abandoned church. Without the notes, the PJ cops on third floor at Hôtel de Police would not have had the slightest interest. A city thing, street level, for Hugues Monty to fix. In and of itself, *where* the killer was striking showed a pattern built on homeless kids. With one wrong cop, sadly, intervening.

Aliette mulled it again … and again, heading for Cimetière Vieux.

It was a twenty-minute stroll. The boulevard curved along the edges of the high ground, an avenue of several schools, hospices, a retirement home, one or two elegant private homes built on the slope. Between, there were views of the Pech des Moulins neighbourhoods, the river, lights of towns spread across the valley. She had misjudged the weather, the milder air was holding, there was negligible wind. She adjusted her beret, loosened her coat, eased her pace and her natural guard. A safe street, a decidedly different walk from the neurotic jigsaw streets and lanes of the inner quarter. The doors were regularly numbered as she neared the corner. Denuded plane trees exposed upper windows, rooftops, the sky. There were not many people out — one woman, nightgown showing under the hem of her greatcoat, urging her dog to do its business before retiring, a pair of kids arm in arm. Turning left, another hundred paces past more private residences, a purveyor of memorial stones, a well-situated florist, and a Ville de Béziers maintenance garage, she arrived at the cemetery gates. They were locked for the night, but the inspector had no intention of making a tour through the rows of tombs.

Going left again, senses back on high alert, Aliette proceeded along Sentier Belbezet, tracing the cemetery wall on her right. To her left: garages, garden walls guarding the back of properties along the boulevard, whence she had come. At this hour, the road was empty. About a kilometre further, it dead-ended at the southwest corner of the cemetery. Killing spot number four.

A direct reversal from her position in the car, earlier that afternoon: the inspector found herself gazing down at the lights in Vincent Spanghero's neighbourhood, where his wife and family waited. One would hesitate to walk down from this point. From here, all paths were provisional, no signs, no lighting, leading into the forest spread down and across the hill behind the burial ground. The woods were parkland, a great place for joggers, adventurous walkers, weekend picnickers — and a known refuge for people of no fixed address. Down through the years, the woods had been the scene of many violent incidents.

The cemetery itself was another popular stop for the marginal. It was no big challenge to climb the wall, it was a peaceful place to party. Some would sleep there.

It was just here, under the last dim city lamp, that the fourth victim had been shot through the throat. Another chalk outline, still intact, marked where he'd slid down against the wall and died. There were stakes in the ground, remnants of crime scene ribbon lying in the unkempt grass.

It was a good place to kill someone. A gunshot would have been just another distant noise. The assailant may have tracked the victim from the darkest streets of the inner city. Or come out of the woods. Or did he (she?) come up the paths, a daytime jogger who knew the way, a psychopath by night in the grips of a dark side that had broken free?

Forensics probably knew which possibility was best by now.

That information was beyond her reach. It was not her case.

Aliette took tentative steps into the woods, realized it was futile, the more so at night, and came back to the spot. Where she could only stand and speculate.

An angry cop had abandoned his life and family in the house at the bottom of the hill. Could he be hiding in the woods, emerging to wreak revenge for his broken heart, the 'absurdity' of it all? Vincent Spanghero would know how to use a knife with precision—he would not stab hysterically. If he had his target cornered, five paces away and dead to rights, he would not shoot him in the throat. But Aliette Nouvelle did not know Vincent Spanghero. Those who did said it was commensurate with Vincent's rage… She tried to feel it. The moment of a murder. Why that poor lost kid? Not much older than his own son. It was hard to imagine.

Easier to imagine a bitter man renouncing his past and ridding himself of its echoes. People do throw things out. Things that no longer carry meaning. And things that carry meaning too painful to retain. And other people wander by and find those things and give them a second lease on life. Lots of people out scavenging the streets in a postmodern medieval world.

Had Catherine Spanghero mentioned Vincent's soul-clearing day to Magistrate Regarri?

Aliette was imagining Nabi's knife on the other side of the equation, in the hands of homeless people, their kind of life on the edge, and Pierre Tropéano suddenly amongst them, following an assumption, scaring them, coming face to face with a seriously deranged personality... When her thoughts were shattered by the heavy *callump!* of a body hitting the ground not five paces away.

She froze. Another figure dropped from the ledge of the cemetery wall. Then a third, almost on her shoulders. '*Merde!*' Aliette sprang back.

The first two boys stared, unsure whether to run or to help their comrade.

The third kid rolled and stood, close enough to kiss, stinking of beer, eyes lit. '*Bonsoir?*'

'Who are you?'

'Who are we?' The first boy seemed to laugh at the very idea of such a question. '*Allez!*' he commanded his friends—let's get out of here, turning toward the woods.

Grinning stupidly, dusting his jacket and the seat of his pants, the third kid edged past her.

'Wait!... please.'

'Please' sometimes works. They all three stopped. Waited. Two suspicious, one in a daze.

'Did you...' She gestured at the outline on the wall. Half an outline, really. 'Did you know this person?'

'Jaco,' murmured the third boy.

'Jaco...?'

He shrugged. Just Jaco.

'Did you see anything or any—?'

The first boy spat, 'Who are you, his mother?'

The notion boggled her. She was feeling in her pocket for her warrant card when they ran.

'Police! Stop!'

Pointless... Standing there, she realized she had not given the slightest thought to her gun.

Then again: pull a gun on three lost boys? Absurd.

... 'Absurd' was Vincent Spanghero's new favourite word, according to his wife.

- 28 -

LIKE A HUMMING SOUND

Aliette Nouvelle was idly perusing the arranged offerings in the flower shop across from the cemetery gate, fatigued and fed up. She had in fact drawn her gun and walked into the woods and muddied her shoes—and found no one. Of course. She had come back up the lane and stood at the cemetery gate for twenty minutes, peering in, a lost soul who'd got home too late. If there was a party in progress, it was respectfully quiet. She had briefly considered pulling herself up and over the wall, but then shrugged, dismissed the idea, her will dulled by ever more doubt that a disaffected cop would kill relatively harmless, mostly helpless people he didn't know for something that had nothing to do with them. Unless the trauma of failure spun into betrayal had popped a fundamental connection in his angry mind? Again: possible.

But surely Gabrielle Gravel would have seen this.

Any thought attached to Vincent Spanghero brought Gabrielle with it. Gabrielle had declared her client to be OK and sent him back into the world. If he had truly come to terms with his issues, he would not be out killing. If he was sick, Gabrielle had to know. That was her job. She would have kept him. Kept him in his sandbox, helping him sort through it, or recommended psychiatric help within a more secure environment. Gabrielle was difficult, to say the least, but she wasn't stupid. Or malevolent? Aliette's own professional instincts were under attack and Gabrielle Gravel was the enemy's front line; yet a cop could still sense a serious woman who believed in her work and was trying to do it. Yes? No? She stood, staring at flowers dedicated to death, puzzling the presence of Gabrielle Gravel in the possibilities surrounding Vincent Spanghero. Gabrielle, who evaded questions...

The inspector couldn't fathom it, her concentration was drifting.

… Her mother always said fake flowers were more practical. Plastic lilies. Far cheaper. Mama had badgered promises out of both her daughters not to waste money on caskets or flowers for their papa or herself. And if she went first, not to let Papa take care of it because *he* surely would …

A cloud of sound filtered through this sombre reverie, a sound like a humming moving toward her. Aliette distractedly glanced up the short Avenue du Cimetière Vieux toward Boulevard d'Angleterre, a hundred or so steps away. There was no one. The sound must be further than it felt, deflected by unruly architecture across the high street. The boulevard was a boundary separating her senses from the maze. She looked skyward, the way one instinctively does, as if a cloud of sound could be seen above the dense warren of streets on the far side of the line. The sound remained indistinct, a hum, another blot of urban tumult.

She shook herself and set off. Time to get home and warm that bed for Sergio.

Approaching the corner, Aliette paused, instinctively cautious as the humming sound suddenly grew distinct. She recognized the swishy, softly abrasive mix of people moving, the brush and scrape of coats, rough jeans, the syncopated rubbery thump of marching feet was now clear, as if they had emerged onto the boulevard.

… No. They were in Rue Ermengaud, which met the same corner, but still somewhere around the far bend. There was an excited shriek. Laughter. She deduced a gang of girls out on a Friday evening tear. Then a profanity in a lower register indicated at least one boy. And another profanity in response, the way boys will. Aliette was not aware of any urgency or fear. It was just a bunch of kids.

Then a quiet crack, a brief scraping noise of metal brushing plaster …

She knew that sound too. A gun? Aliette stopped in her tracks.

A voice, male, confirmed it, commanded loudly: 'Hands in the air, *putain de connard!*'

There was laughter as they came into view, rolling forward in one dark clump.

She saw an arm extend into the air, heard another blunt crack, not loud; it quickly dispersed in the night and was covered over in more laughter. An angry female voice broke through. 'Don't waste it, asshole!' This was met with more laughing. An exultant whoop. Dancing, spinning, it appeared they were passing a bottle ... Aliette stood in the street, transfixed as they crossed the boulevard, *en masse*, enfolded in their own noise. When a male voice from a bedroom window somewhere above shouted, 'What the hell do you think you're doing?' it was like an automatic button: simultaneously, like goats on a hillside, they broke into a run.

Straight at Aliette, maybe twenty of them, a human wave.

The lighting was dim and her brain was locking, they were shrouded in bulky coats, woollen scarves and caps. All she really saw were eyes, intent and bright above the masking scarves. They were carrying more than bottles—sticks? clubs?—raised, ready, clutched in fists. She saw a glint of silver in a hand. A knife? And then another. Where was the gun she knew she'd heard?

Crowd control? ... She had to fix on faces, at least one face at the head of the pack.

There were only disembodied eyes as they came rushing on, flowing forward relentlessly.

She could see no way past them. She knew they would not give way.

She turned and ran, back toward the cemetery gate.

Not quick enough. The steps behind were closing fast. The door to the flower shop was indented into the step. She stopped and flattened herself against the shop door, pressing against it, face to the glass, heart racing as they stampeded by, a flock, a swarm... a *humming*, something primordial. A hard shoulder bumped her back. Another almost knocked her over.

Aliette sank to her knees, pushing herself tighter to the door.

A hand touched her head. She felt her beret removed. Another hand glided over her hair. She cringed, submerged in it, willing herself tighter, smaller, not daring to look up, awaiting worse as the mob flowed by ... She realized that she smelled them—clothes redolent of tobacco, wine, beer and urine; rank, unclean bodies melded in a ghastly wave.

It probably lasted all of five seconds.

Then they were gone, past the gates and down the deserted back lane along the cemetery wall and into the woods, the sound of them receding, growing indistinct, moving upwards again into the night sky, back into a vague cloud of humming clatter—till a loud curse capped it like a grace note, '*Sacrée pute!*' Holy whore? Like a cry of revolution.

There was another flat report of a gunshot in the midst of shrieks of bizarre, outlandish joy.

The inspector got to her feet, stunned and shaking, feeling her hair. One of those filthy hands had actually… And her beret! Where was it, her treasured cap? She stood in the lane, a bundle of reactions—fury, fear—embarrassed, scanning the dark pavement for a patch of navy blue.

She flung herself back to the ground when yet another crack from a gunshot close by split the air. A rangy, stick-like figure in a knit cap and flapping greatcoat appeared to sail across the space in front of the cemetery gate. Aliette saw his arm extend and—CRACK!—fire off another shot before gliding out of view… not running, gliding, strangely, floating vertically like the mast of a boat or the tail of a cat. The coat, the movement, Aliette knew it was the same person she had seen stepping out of the derelict house from the far end of the street the night before.

She struggled to pull herself together. There was no physical damage, not that she could feel.

A foreign hand had played in her hair. Another had taken her beret. That was a violation.

She felt her gun: there, loaded. Waiting. Twice in a single night this instinct had failed her.

Chief Inspector Aliette Nouvelle was huddled in the doorway of the flower shop dumbly processing her incompetence when a third figure came lumbering around the corner and up the avenue, right past her and on past the cemetery gate. A uniformed cop, gun raised, the gear attached to his belt banging: truncheon, lamp, cuffs, spray…

In pursuit of the shooter, she presumed.

She felt like retreating, never showing her face again. That would be the smarter move. But he might need help. Drawing her weapon, she went cautiously into the open area in front of the gate, and followed, tight to the cemetery wall, gun at the ready, heart unclear.

RANK SHAMELESSLY ESTABLISHED

'Halt right there! Put your weapon on the ground! ...I have you. Don't even think about it ...' The uniformed officer stepped out of the shadows. 'Just stay calm and put it down.'

Aliette stopped, slowly laid her gun on the pavement. He moved closer, gun aimed straight at her. When he was close enough to read his eyes—and he hers, she informed him, 'I'm police. PJ. I have my card ... my right pocket.'

Inching closer: Tall, young, his face was white, thin, unhealthy, big sockets under nervous eyes, short blond hair askew. He too had lost his hat. 'Do I know you?'

'Can I show you?'

He nodded. But his gun was trained.

She did. He relaxed. 'We were sitting in the car, that guy runs past, gun out and not trying to hide it. We yell at him to stop. He didn't even turn. Like we weren't even there.'

'I've seen this person before ... You know him?'

'We think we've seen him around. Crazies love the cemetery. Some even live there.'

'He was after those kids.'

'Which kids?'

She told him how she'd been almost trampled.

He sniffed. 'A game.'

A game? 'They have a gun.'

The officer nodded dryly at her consternation. 'They've got all sorts of nasty things, Inspector.' He called his partner, in the car somewhere on the far side of the cemetery.

Before he could ask, Aliette attempted to explain her presence. She did not have to, now that rank was established, but felt she must.

In case she ended up in his report. *Alors*, she'd been walking, thinking of a funeral in the family that was going to happen soon. She had turned up the street to look at flowers, monuments... 'Have to be ready for these things. Otherwise, it's total panic and you make mistakes.' She smiled. 'I've promised my mother I won't let them steal our money.' The young officer nodded to that... The gang of kids had surprised her, scared the life out of her. It did not sound like a cop speaking, let alone working. It was not meant to. That she was window shopping for funeral arrangements well after shop hours with a gun in her pocket, well, rank *had* been established. He could challenge but probably wouldn't.

No, he did not seem worried about her gun. In fact he retrieved it and respectfully handed it back. Politely advised, 'Not the safest place after dark. These kids think it's a free zone. Party central. We get calls every night.'

That opened a door she could not resist exploring. 'You were here Tuesday night? The street kid. Jaco.' Dropping the name, shamelessy implying she was in the loop, if not on the team.

'We found him. I mean, after someone called it in.'

'These kids have phones?'

'Inspector, some of them have everything. They just hate their mums and dads.'

'You knew him. Jaco?'

'Only to see... Still think it's the same guy switched to a gun?' This young cop may not have been privy to the name Vincent Spanghero, or the issues, but he was obviously hearing some things.

Forcing a compromised (and shameless) inspector to extend her reckless charade. 'We have some competing theories,' she hedged. 'And you?'

'I don't know. Lots of people leave notes on tombs, you'd be amazed. Monty seemed a bit desperate. He sent us through the tombs. Find the note?' He was dubious. 'I found a dozen. We all found some. Ten of us. If there was a note, you'd think it would be on him.' The victim. 'Or on the wall?' He shrugged. 'I guess the forensics guys will sort it out.' He was a street cop, not an investigator.

Headlights washed over them as the car rolled up to the cemetery gate, blue light flashing. He conferred with his partner. The guy with the gun was long gone. So were the kids. The radio was going non-stop on a Friday night, they had a million other things to do.

They offered her a ride. She accepted. There might be more to learn between here and Sergio's. She was settling into the back seat when another gunshot cracked through the night.

The young officer looked toward the cemetery. 'That was inside for sure.'

His partner agreed. And apologized. 'Sorry Inspector, but we should go and see.'

But she shouldn't. There would be more police arriving any moment. Hugues Monty's guys? Annelise Duflot? Not good. Pleading people waiting at home, Aliette got out, thanked them and left the scene. She did not tell them not to tell anyone about their impromptu meeting. They might not, but they probably would; and in writing. All she could do was wait for the fact to surface. She would deal with it then—if she wasn't fired first.

As she was walking away she heard a volley of shots. Screaming from the tombs.

She kept going.

The bed was warm when Sergio stumbled up the stairs, smelling of a full night at it with the boys. After a few clumsy moments in the bathroom, he rolled in beside her. She didn't say a word. In any event, within seconds he was snoring. And Aliette lay fretting: over her lost beret, her untouched gun, her deceit and what it might bring, and another piece of a strange puzzle:

A note on a tomb this time.

Which tomb?

− 30 −
BLEAK

Saturday was bleak, what with the rain that came and stayed all day. Warmer, but solidly grey. Bleaker still with the news that another street kid had been killed, caught in a 'shoot-out' at the old cemetery. A girl, possibly a minor—they still didn't know her name. Aliette Nouvelle headed for Hôtel de Police, rain in her hair, feeling naked without her beret, saddened. Guilty. Rightly or wrongly, she'd been carrying her sidearm and was supposed to know what to do with it. Could a right reaction have turned some swarming kids around, changed the flow of history enough to let one misguided girl avoid a useless death? Impossible to know.

Impossible not to add it to her growing list of sins. Bleak, bleak morning.

Sergio had gone straight from bed, in a flustered rush, hangover and all, responding to a call from lead city investigator Hugues Monty reacting to a call from Procureur Serge Ferland, who had received a call from a reporter saying she had been talking to Pierre Tropéano's widow and some disturbing background questions about her husband's tragedy had come to light. The name Vincent Spanghero had come up—an incident involving her late husband's late partner from a couple of years before, and its bitter aftermath. The reporter had been diverted—for the moment. That forensics had already determined the bullet taken from the previous night's victim had been fired from Tropéano's missing gun did not help. This detail was also being withheld from the public record. But for how long? Sergio's day—and weekend?—was suddenly full. As her harried man was rushing out the door, Aliette had called downstairs, promising to make supper.

The dispatch centre at Hôtel de Police was a perpetually busy hive and Saturday morning was no exception. She showed her warrant card, asked to see the record of the call-in concerning Tuesday night's murder at the cemetery. The woman responded automatically with a quick search. 'No name. Female. From a public phone near Les Halles.' She shrugged. 'At 22:19 hours.' Ten-twenty pm.

'I need to hear it.'

The woman tapped some keys. The voice was almost a whisper. Flat. But definitely female.

A man at the cemetery, not doing well. Please.

Aliette listened five times. Impossible to deduce young or not so young. A sniffy sound, barely there as the call was cut, suggested someone with a cold. Or crying?

Back through the rain to the house at 36 Rue Boudard. She tried Nabi. He had promised to answer, but didn't. And what was she going to tell him: It's not Vincent Spanghero?

That all she had was circumstantial but she was thoroughly convinced?

It didn't matter if she was convinced, much less what Nabi might say...

She tried to read the weekend paper.

Her trusting judge finally called at noon. As expected, he foresaw a very long day.

Trying to sound conversational as opposed to miserable, Aliette asked, 'Another note?'

He turned distinctly cool. 'This is classified, Inspector. Very fragile situation.'

'I understand.'

'Do you?' Cooler still, not so trusting.

'Of course.'

'Then what were you doing there?'

She took a breath. It was not a time to start lying about funeral flowers. 'I wanted to see. Tuesday's? By the wall. I've been to the scene of the first two ... And you know all about the church. I acknowledge the notes, Nabi's knife, of course, but there is an obvious pattern that is not being—'

'And what were you doing at Catherine Spanghero's?'

'Talking...' Before he could hit again, she blurted, 'Nabi needs a friend!'

Icy. 'This is not your problem.'

… then, in spite of himself, an exasperated sigh which let her know his disappointment.

She knew it was his job to tell her this. She knew it was her job that was at issue.

But she was disappointed too. 'This is all wrong, Sergio. Tropéano was wrong and—'

'Tropéano is dead, Inspector.'

'The victim of his own mistake. And if you continue with this inquest to confirm it has to be Vincent Spanghero, someone will decide it *is* him and that will give the wrong people a free ride to a bad place and you will be a part of it. Are you ready for that?'

He did not respond.

His silence tipped the balance. She exploded. 'Well, I'm not! This is not about Vincent Spanghero's big anger gone out of control! That is a pretext for small-minded people with political axes and a lot of fear for their pure fucking French credentials!'

Nor did Magistrate Regarri respond to that—to his credit.

'Talk to me, Sergio! Ask me what *I* know.'

'No.' Nor did he argue or try to dissuade when she said she'd see him Tuesday.

… Chief Inspector Nouvelle drove back to Saint-Brin in the rain and a mighty sulk.

31

SAD ONE

On Sunday morning Aliette walked up the hill behind the village. Left her phone, took her gun. She aimed it at a tree and fired. Scattered some birds. They resettled in a moment, like the shame that wouldn't leave her. She knew her aim could be fixed with practice, but she wasn't so sure her heart could be transformed. 'Perhaps,' she thought, 'I do need Gabrielle after all...' She walked all morning in the warmer air, returned to the house looking for a friendly message from the city. Forgiveness.

She got Magui instead. 'Sad one, boss. You better come in.'

It took six minutes to get to the office. 'Well?'

Magui was subdued as she handed over the gendarme's notes. 'Double suicide. Or looks like it.' Two teenagers had been found on the lookout at Notre-Dame de Nazareth.

Another historic chapel, ten kilometers from town—still functional, the priests unlocked the doors once or twice a year and the faithful drove and some even walked up the steep, broken road for mass to mark a special day; otherwise, a tourist destination with a glorious view out over the valley. Tourists of faith enjoyed the legend of the Virgin appearing there in the oddly specific year 840—she had left a divine footprint to prove her divine presence. A growing community of weekend climbers enjoyed the sheer eighty-metre challenge of the rock face. Nights, local kids went up to party, lovers went to make out.

'On the lookout?... Means they didn't jump.'

'No, just lying there near the boy's car. An early morning pilgrim found them. He thought they'd froze. Seems they'd been there all night, or a good part of it. Gendarmes saw indicators pointing to drugs.' Making a spaced-out suicide pact a possibility. 'Saddest thing. Lying there holding onto each other. Could life really be so hopeless looking?' Inspector Barthès was the mother of two boys—though both still too young for romantic passion and its many pains.

'Perhaps it's that a drug makes heaven look better, Mags. Where from?'

'Boy, Cessenon; girl, Cazedarnes.'

A town, a village. The smaller the place the bigger the loss. 'Parents know?'

'Nic's taking care of that, thank God…' Sergeant Nicolas Legault, head of the small Saint-Brin gendarmerie.

'Annelise been?' Suicides are always subject to police scrutiny.

'Still out there. Said she'll come in with the paperwork on her way back to the city.'

'You should get back home. I'll wait for Annelise.'

Magui didn't protest. The inspector retreated to her desk with tea, a quiet Sunday afternoon alone.

She thought about adolescents following their hearts and ending up in extreme places, recalling her own dark feeling after being left for another by that magical first love—riding her mobilette through the streets of Nantes to the Tabarly Bridge, staring down at the Loire, wishing to be carried away to somewhere better. It passed. She rode home, wept, her mother held her. Magui was right—double exits are more about despair than love. The world wasn't getting any easier, that was sure… The thought of couples needing hope made her reach for the phone.

…No! she told herself, Don't do it.

She was busying herself with paperwork when she heard clomping on the stairs, then along the hall.

The petite *légiste* tapped on the office door. Aliette called out, '*Bonjour*. Welcome.'

Annelise Duflot clomped in. She had donned Swiss hiking boots for a Sunday at the lookout. High-end, of course, the best available. Otherwise, the dainty doctor was looking chic as always in a black wool topcoat worth about a thousand euros, under which she sported a crimson silk blouse. From one of the more expensive boutiques off Les Allées. Aliette knew—she'd looked at that very blouse while exploring the streets with Sergio. She had refused to let him spend that kind of money on an impulse. If he offered ten years on, that would be a different matter. As for Annelise, it matched the laces of her boots. Aliette wondered if anyone had ever seen the pathologist in jeans. A T-shirt? A T-shirt would not suit Annelise. Too petite. She'd look twelve, or maybe nine...

The inspector wanted to like Annelise—and she hadn't forgotten the *légiste's* favour the week before. But it was hard. The doctor's dress code somehow perfectly reflected a point of view she could not condone. Sergio said Annelise lived with a financial whiz with the banking arm of La Poste who doubled as a bag man for the regional Front National. Law, medicine and money: a well-connected extreme-right couple.

'Cold up there?'

'Death is cold, Inspector.' A smile hinted this may have been a pathologist's joke. She took papers from her case, peeled away the duplicates of the forms and handed them to the inspector. 'I would recommend making some space in your week for this one. They didn't just go up and fall asleep watching the stars. For now, I'll guess Super Ecstasy—also known as Pink? Been a lot of it around the city lately, cheaply made, very dangerous. I will let you know tomorrow.'

Inspector Nouvelle immediately thought of a certain barn on a hill on a problematic territory line. Despite her personal feelings, she had to admit Annelise was very good at her job and she trusted the *légiste's* professional hunches. 'We're starting to see it out here too. I'm told they mix it with other things and dance all night.'

'And have psychotic episodes,' added Annelise, nodding gravely. 'I would be interested to know if there was anyone else from those kids' crowd up there last night. Or this morning? My two SOC guys can only do so much with a site like that. I've asked Division to send technical help. They should be be arriving just about now. Perhaps you could make a run up there before calling it a day?'

'Of course.' Making notes. 'You think they were dropped there?'

'I wouldn't be surprised. Bad drugs. Bad party...get rid of the evidence?'

'So heartless. It boggles the mind. Tea?'

'No, thank you. Have to keep going...' Standing, sliding back into her lovely coat.

'I imagine you've been busy all weekend.'

'It happens.' But Légiste Duflot was not about to share any details concerning a killing in the city with the likes of Chief Inspector Nouvelle.

Nor did Aliette expect her to. Nevertheless, escorting Annelise to the top of the stairs, she could not resist another sideways probe. 'Poor Nabi… I ran into him. Not doing so well. This latest won't help. I don't envy him at all.'

A sniff. 'He's made his own bed.' Definitely a political sniff; one learns to recognize them. Indeed, after shaking the inspector's hand in her businesslike manner, the doctor made it clear. 'If the universe were working right, none of it would be happening.'

Having lately been drawn into wearying debates about the centre of said universe, Aliette felt that one personally. 'We are living in a period of fundamental change, Doctor.'

'Fundamental is a good word for it.'

'How well do you know him?'

'*B'eh*, I don't know people like him, Inspector.'

'But you've worked with him for a while now?'

'Not the same… I am a professional.'

Aren't we all, you snotty… 'Mm, but do you believe it could really be Vincent Spanghero?'

Annelise Duflot looked askance. Like everyone else in the local system, she knew about Sergio and Aliette. She probably didn't care. But her arch look revealed she assumed he was divulging information he should not. Where else could Aliette's question have come from? 'I believe evidence, Inspector.' And she was privy to so much of it. Always. By virtue of her job.

The Inspector did not dare probe further… A shame: had Aliette and Annelise been anywhere near that place called 'friends,' a friendly chat would've been normal and natural, and might have led to any number of casual disclosures under the general heading of Work. But that mutual space did not exist and probably never would. Aliette and Annelise, who saw the world in distinctly different ways, would always be separated by a wall of polite antipathy.

Aliette knew that Annelise had her own instincts too. And her circle of professional friends. Actively defending Nabi Zidane would not be smart at all.

The inspector offered a professional hand, and sincere thanks for the good légiste's advice regarding two more tragic kids.

For the second time that afternoon she was tempted to call Sergio. He knew the political terrain far better than she did. Did he know she was sorry? She picked up the phone, then replaced it without making the call. Maybe she would call later.

First, she had to drive out to Notre-Dame de Nazareth to see how things were shaping up.

A sad one, indeed.

PART 3

TUESDAY'S HOROSCOPE

32

PERFECT STORM

No one called Monday summoning Chief Inspector Aliette Nouvelle to the Divisional office in Montpellier to surrender her warrant card (or her new gun). Neither did Sergio, to see how she was doing. It felt like either could happen at any moment. But you have to get on with your life.

Annelise Duflot's pathology report arrived as promised. It confirmed the presence of cocaine, sulphur, caffeine and various amphetamines in the systems of the two tragic adolescent lovers—primary ingredients in the preparation of Pink Ecstasy. They had ingested much alcohol. Heart failure. While not extremely cold Saturday night, hypothermia was part of the deadly mix. The report suggested a sexually intense marathon, after which they had probably passed out in each other's arms—outdoors or in an unheated space (barn, outbuilding?) was not clear, and never woken up. Drastic body temperature rise brought on by the intoxicants combined with hyper physical activity—dancing, sex—exacerbated by extensive perspiring while exposed to the night temperatures. It was not sure whether they had died where they had been making love, had not been discovered till too late, someone had panicked and taken them to the lookout, where they were cold-bloodedly left in each other's arms; or they were still breathing when discovered but deemed too much of risk to call *les urgences*, so they'd been taken to the lookout. And dumped. Either way, the presence of the boy's car at the lookout did not fool Annelise.

Cheap, careless chemistry pointed to the barn on the problematic geographic line dividing two cops' patches. Chief Inspector Nouvelle contacted Chief Inspector Lesouple and Magistrate Rogge. Then she wrote up a report.

And yet more paperwork as Magui returned from another round at the cheese producer's with a revelation that changed everything. The Chief Inspector contacted the attorney for the suspect and arranged a meeting for the next day. She was preparing her report for that meeting when Mathide Lahi buzzed. Chief Inspector Bédard was on the line.

'Yes?'

'We were wondering if you could help us communicate with Nabi?'

Instead of hanging up, she asked, 'What should I tell him?'

'You don't have to tell him anything. Just let him talk away… We're thinking you could wear a listening post? Maybe some more beers at the range?'

There was not a glimmer of guile in his voice. Mario was jokey, ingenuous, collegial, like it was a matter of course. Just a small favour between colleagues? His presumption threw Aliette, left her confused. 'But why would I do that?'

'*B'eh*, all this pressure? Vincent's going to be crawling out any minute now. He'll call Nabi.'

She stared at the phone in her hand and realized she was shaking. 'I don't understand you, Mario.'

'Sure you do. I'm not that complicated, Inspector. Just trying to fix a problem here. Just want things to be the way they're meant to be. But to the point: you can see a perfect storm as well as anyone. Vincent knows Nabi's the only one who will listen to him without shooting him first.'

'And so?'

'We need to be there.'

'Who is we?'

'All of us.'

'Not me.'

'But you will be… Aliette. Even if you're not, you will be. You're too far into it to not be. Very perfect storm here. No? We're counting on you. See you at HQ tomorrow morning, then.'

They even knew her schedule.

- 33 -
VIRGO

Tuesday's horoscope advised getting used to living with ambiguities for the next little while.

That morning she drove to the city, first to meet with Instructing Judge Martine Rogge. Her counterpart Julien Lesouple failed to show. Martine had received a communication pleading scheduling conflicts and asking for 'more time to confirm some things on my side' of the unclear territory line. Martine furrowed her brow. 'Julien adds that you know exactly where the line falls and everyone looks forward to hearing your thoughts. Clear?'

Clear enough to understand Julien's problematic schedule had something to do with Mario's requested favour. Sometimes her horoscope was bang on. Martine's too? Together, they moved forward with a plan for a raid that could avoid the errors of long-dead functionaries and the nit-picking of soulless advocates who acted for heartless men. Two cruelly deceived kids demanded they must. Julien Lesouple was not required.

Then she walked over to Hôtel de Police.

No sign of Chief Inspector Zidane. 'He was here for about ten minutes,' reported Betty. 'Got some stuff from his desk, said he'd be right back ... ' She shrugged. 'There was a reporter waiting for him at reception. Down the fire stairs, I'd guess.'

Mario Bédard and Julien Lesouple were in the lunchroom, sipping coffee.

Aliette poked her head into the room. 'Seen Nabi?'

The two men looked at her. Was that a joke? Aliette smiled, ambiguous—maybe it was, *messieurs*, maybe it was—and kept moving. No point bringing up the lab in the barn with Julien just now. Liza Fratticelli was in the Ladies. On an ambiguous impulse, Aliette suggested lunch.

Liza's eyes went wide. 'Sure. Why not? ...Let me just check my daybook and get back to you.' An hour later she appeared at the door to the spare office. 'Fine.'

Aliette knew it was not Liza's appointment book that made it fine.

Before her lunch with Liza, Aliette convened a brief meeting with Justine Péraud and her lawyer. They were advised that a co-worker at the cheese producer's had informed Inspector Barthès that Justine had been carrying the murder weapon back and forth to work in the trunk of her car since the summer. Justine screamed denial. Then eternal hatred for the informing woman. (She knew who it *had* to be). Her lawyer seemed lost. The feasibility of a plea of *crime passionnel* for his client was growing very faint indeed. The inspector left them to confer in the spare office, freshened her face and met Chief Inspector Fratticelli in the lobby.

They walked around the corner in silence, sat by the window and ordered tuna salads.

A carafe of white was set on the table, Liza poured for both of them. '*Alors?*'

Aliette did not mince words. 'Apart from perhaps inadvertently providing the knife, Vincent Spanghero has nothing to do with these murders. Someone, maybe even you, because I don't think Mario has the right communication skills, should have a talk with this reporter who seems so intent on blowing up the castle.'

Liza seemed amused by that. 'You sound like you've been investigating.'

'Not investigating. Just talking. Off the record. No instruction, no reports.'

'I think you're a bad influence on Sergio.'

'Sergio is the most discreet man I've ever met.'

'And I think Nabi's a bad influence on you.'

'Do we need a rumour like that just now?'

'We?'

'Us.'

'Are you one of us?'

'Like it or not, it seems I am.'

'*Seems* being the operative word here, Inspector.'

Aliette would not allow herself to be goaded.

Liza smiled. 'Mario has already communicated with this reporter… For what it's worth.'

'What *is* it worth, Liza?'

'Hard to say. These things take on a life of their own at a certain point. Seems she somehow also knows about the knife.'

'Oh, no.'

Liza nodded, shrugged, sipped wine.

Their meals arrived. They ate. Aliette spelled out the logic of a recurring kind of murder scene and the people associated with such places. Pierre Tropéano had got it tragically wrong. 'This is about homeless kids and the like. They're the ones who are dying. And what could they possibly have to do with Vincent Spanghero's problem? Really, Liza, do that reporter a favour. She'll only end up looking a fool to her bosses, not to say an uncaring bitch for putting Tropéano's poor wife through the wringer twice.' She managed to imply the same for Mario Bédard. 'This is not Vincent we are looking for. Friday's proves it. I'm convinced.'

'You're convinced.' Liza sized up her colleague, perplexed, as if observing an unknown bird. Police do it every day. They don't much like it when someone does it to them. Aliette suffered it with a calm stare, a taste of wine. Taking a sheet of paper from her bag, Liza handed it across the remnants of their lunch. 'This is Friday's note.' Another photocopied image of another scrap of paper: *Do I matter? Am I solving anything? I am sorry for who I am.* 'And that is our Vincent.'

'That is thousands of people, Liza.' Aliette handed it back.

'…rhetorical, self-pitying, raging. A good shot, too, I might add. Right between the eyes.'

With Tropéano's gun. Aliette supposed Liza knew that too. 'Who's feeding you all this?'

Chief Inspector Fratticelli only shook her head.

Aliette pushed. 'It's not your case either. None of you.'

'But it's everyone's problem.'

'I agree. And are we dealing with it in a rational way?'

'Rational?' Liza waved the note. 'What is rational in the face of this?'

'Exactly. We could start by seriously asking why he is hunting street kids… The more we ask, the more rational we might get.'

'What we have to be is realistic.' Then Liza shrugged. In that moment, some guard she'd put on for lunch fell. Her eyes betrayed disappointment. Or perhaps it was fear… But she looked away, musing, not a little sour. 'Killing kids? I'm no *psy*, Inspector. Just a cop. A colleague?'

Her challenge hit deep. Aliette had to fight. 'Are you really a part of this?'

'Part of what?'

'Or are you just going along because you're a girl?'

Liza repeated, 'Part of what?'

'Nabi Zidane is a good man, Liza. A good police officer.'

Liza sighed, processing this statement. Frustrated? 'No one's saying Nabi's not good… No. It's just he's… a mistake.'

'Nabi's as French as you are.'

That landed. Liza threw back the last of her wine, put her glass down with some force. 'You know, I resent that. My grandfather was mayor of Sète.'

'Ah! Good Communist family, I take it?…' Humming lightly, with a smile: *This is the final struggle / Let us group together and tomorrow / The Internationale / Will be the human race…*

Sète had a large Italian-rooted community descended from fishermen and their families, many of whom literally sailed and rowed away from desperate lives a century before. And during the mid-century, as in many French towns, small cities and Paris suburbs, a well-organized PCF had controlled the Mairie. But that was then. The Communist Party's presence was fringe now, and becoming irrelevant. Liza Fratticelli winced scornfully at her colleague's rendition of the idealistic anthem, and sniffed at her implication. 'I am as French as you.'

'I doubt that. How could you be?' Aliette asked snidely. '…And now here you are in cahoots with an extreme-right xenophobe *connard* like Mario Bédard. What would your grandpa say?'

'Oh for the love of… It is not politics! It's politically correct stupidity. Which is bad for all of us—and that includes you!' Aliette blinked. Liza pressed her point. 'It's moving down through the ranks, Inspector. In our business, we need everyone on the same page.'

'You sound like Mario.'

'Mario's not wrong.'

'Because he's realistic?'

Liza would not reply. Her gaze held steady.

'Mario's an anal police pig, if I ever met one.' And Aliette had met lots.

Now Liza blinked. And blushed? 'You have to learn how to talk to him.'

'Been trying for a year, madame. Perhaps you could help?'

'Why would I help you?'

'How does Mario propose to fix the mistake?'

Liza flashed a mean grin. 'That's not something a girl should talk about in public.'

Prompting Aliette to kick hard. 'Please tell me you're not sleeping with Mario.'

Liza rolled her eyes and wiped her hands, preparing to leave.

Aliette feigned shock. 'Oh, God! Liza… I can't… You really could do so much better.'

Chief Inspector Fratticelli rose from her chair. She was tall, almost a head taller than Chief Inspector Bédard. And remote and cold as she stared down at Aliette. 'Think they'll send me to talk it out with Gabrielle?'

'They might. They sent Vincent. They sent me.'

Liza let her serviette fall on her plate. She was fiddling distractedly with her shirt cuff. 'This was fun, but not that much.'

'Just because you want it to be Vincent Spanghero, doesn't mean it is.'

'No one *wants* it to be anyone. Are you really such a child?'

Aliette was trying to hold Liza's much darker eyes. 'You people make me sad.'

'Sorry, but it is a sad world…' She succeeded in removing a tiny item from her cuff and placed it on the table. 'From Mario… Over to you, Inspector.' With that, Liza Fratticelli took her coat and left. She neglected to leave money for her share of the party.

Aliette picked up the miniscule listening device. It fit just as well on the button of her shirt cuff. She wondered if it was activated, if Mario Bédard had been an invisible presence at their lunch. Part of her hoped yes. The better part of her was ashamed at her own lack of professional comportment at a key moment. No need to insult to get to the truth, Inspector. Liza had worked with Nabi, she probably knew him better than anyone.

There had been a moment when Liza Fratticelli had been looking to connect, a door—

But Aliette had missed it. Done it wrong.

…Hard to like yourself after a lunch like that. Hard to like anything.

A good time to get down to the range and blow away. some virtual men?

Have a beer with Nabi. Let Nabi talk away? If he was even there.

And if he was, would he only moan and cry some more? Better if he stayed in hiding?

What did Nabi deserve? The inspector was of two minds. Her horoscope was holding true.

34

A NORTH AFRICAN POLICEMAN

Gabrielle Gravel received the sad-looking North African policeman. 'I only have ten minutes.' Till Madame Dormevil and her lousy sex life. Tuesday was always a long and demanding day.

'I need your help.'

'Personal or professional?'

This confused him. '*B'eh*, both?'

'Inspector, you know I am not going to discuss my work with Inspector Spanghero.'

'You have to help me.' The man's liquid eyes implored.

'Help you?'

'Help *us*.'

'I have already spoken with a magistrate at the courthouse. I have nothing more to add.'

'Do you *know* where he is?'

Gabrielle bared her teeth. 'I have nothing more to add! These are confidential matters. I told the magistrate and I will tell you: Vincent Spanghero left here in a considerably better frame of mind than when he first appeared. Which is what one aims for. I was pleased, but I did not pursue the matter of his future plans. Not my business. And the things we discussed are not yours.'

'Fine, I understand.' The North African policemen accepted this morosely. He asked, 'What about me?'

'What about you?'

'I have personal issues.'

'Relating to Inspector Spanghero?'

'Partly, yes.'

'Partly?'

'He was my partner … I … it went beyond work.'

'Then I can't help you. Conflict of interest?'

'But it's getting bad. I know you understand us.'

'Us?'

'Police.'

'Everyone is unique, Inspector.'

'I need some … some counselling.'

'I suggest you talk to your imam.'

Gabrielle watched the North African policeman gaze momentarily heavenward, as if praying. He appeared to collect himself. His voice was a tone softer. 'We don't really attend. Mosque. Sure, weddings, funerals, but not in that sort of way.'

'Maybe you ought to. There is a cultural element at play in these things. I fear with me, we'd both be wasting time, not to mention public resources. Mm?'

'The cultural element is the law, madame. It is the same for everyone.'

'Except yourselves.'

'Ourselves?'

'The police?'

'Yes,' he acknowledged, almost a whisper. 'That's the problem.' He sat there, helpless.

Gabrielle felt badly. 'You get a note from your boss and come back to see me. We'll talk about it. About you. But remember: I will never reveal anything to you about my clients, police or otherwise. The culture *here*, in this room, extends into the rest of a person's life. I made my report last spring. I went to see the magistrate this morning. And I am telling you now. Clear?' He acknowledged. She smiled. 'But seeing you are here, will you tell me why everyone is so interested in Vincent Spanghero?'

'No.'

'And neither would the magistrate.'

'It's a police matter.'

'And I respect that.' Gabrielle rose, extended her hand. She recalled the ugly bile Vincent had unleashed in his name. 'Nice to meet you. *Bon courage*.' Adding, 'I'm serious: I've heard some of the local imams are incorporating some very forward-looking techniques into their pastoral work and helping a lot of people. Worth a try?'

The North African policeman shrugged and left, a sad-looking man indeed.

Some people slammed the door. He was the kind who left it open wide.

Gabrielle heard Emma asking him, less than politely, if he needed to re-book.

She heard, 'Maybe later.' Then the front door.

She heard Madame Dormevil comment, 'First one of those I've seen in here.'

She heard Emma snap at Madame Dormevil, 'Next!' … before Emma resumed her weeping.

Gabrielle fetched Madame Dormevil's chaotic sandbox and placed it on her desk. Chaotic and increasingly pornographic. '*Bonjour, bonjour.*' She tried to focus on sex.

… But *why* was everyone suddenly seeking Vincent Spanghero?

Gabrielle was distracted as she received her client.

35

NAMES & FACES

Chief Inspector Nouvelle failed to find an outlet for her feelings at the shooting range. The unseen operator in the booth running the simulator put her through some scenarios. Aliette fired, ran, slid, flopped, fired, ducked, fired again. The virtual gunman on the screen continued to win more than she, the cheeky disembodied voice implied not so subtly that her strategies were verging on clownish. She called, '*Je m'en fous!*' ... I don't give a damn, and slammed the door behind her. Nabi Zidane was not on the premises. She left the listening device received from Liza Fratticelli in an ashtray on the bar in the lounge. They might pick up something useful, hopefully about themselves. Cretins ... The day was wearing on, and she was in an ornery mood when she parked in front of the cemetery gate, walked into the office at the rear of the maintenance garage and flashed her warrant card. 'The murder Tuesday night, other side of the wall: a note was found on a tomb. I need to see the place. Now?'

A man in a dusty suit sighed and put on his overcoat. Squinting at a printout filled with numbers, he led her to a plot with a chunk freshly broken off the corner of the granite slab, three dead potted plants placed against a time-stained headstone. FAMILLE SYLVESTRE. 'This one.'

Any signs of forensics activity had been removed. Aliette considered the names Paul-Michel Antoine Sylvestre, 1898–1963, Marjorie-Marie Lucette Cantin née Sylvestre, 1904–1975, Janette Rejeanne Savoie Sylvestre, 1932–1999. 'Exactly where was it?' The killer's note.

'Under one of those pots, if I heard correctly' His pinched face pinched tighter. 'People are so careless, disrespectful. They bring these things, then forget them. They die within three days. A year later, they're still there, rotted. The entire community suffers for it.'

She assumed he meant the community of the dead. 'Why don't you remove them?'

'This is not our property or our responsibility. We open and close the crypts when instructed. Clean out old bones ... Otherwise, we do the public areas, the drives, the trees. *C'est tout.*'

Immediate neighbours to the SYLVESTRE family were the FAMILLE PETITPAS, with its own inventory of names and collection of rotted potted plants. She took his point. And her mother's. 'Artificial flowers are better.'

The cemetery manager did not react to that.

'This is an old family?'

'They are all old families. You can't buy a plot here. You want to be buried here, you'll have to marry someone who is.'

She looked at him.

'I mean someone whose family is.'

'Is there a Regarri family here?'

'Offhand, I wouldn't know. A name like that, I'd bet not.'

'No ... And the girl, Friday night?'

'They found her over on the other side.'

Aliette gestured: lead on.

'As you wish ...' He huffed a cranky sigh. 'But that note was left here too.' Then, pointing at the FAMILLE PETITPAS stone, he qualified it, ' ... actually, they said it was on this one.'

She left her car and walked it. But there was no criminal record attached to anyone called Sylvestre or Petitpas in the files at Hôtel de Police. Which meant another walk. Before heading over to the central library in Place du 14 Juillet to search family names, she went back up to the third. No Nabi. Looking vacant, Betty shook her head. Aliette went to the spare office and called Mathilde Lahi. 'Any word from Chief Inspector Zidane?'

'No calls.'

'Can you check my mail? I'm in a bit of a rush here ...'

'Surely ... Just a second here ... No, can't see one. Three judges ... and —'

'Sergio?' A surge in her flagging pulse.

'No ... Martine, Claire and Martine again. Your sister. Doctor Nguyen. Chief Inspector Bédard, and—'

'Open it. The one from Bédard—and read it for me ... Please.'

Another moment of clicking. Mathilde read, 'Thought you'd be interested in sharing this.'

'Sharing what?'

'There's an attachment ... It's a photo ... you and someone wearing a Béziers rugby cap, he's smoking ... I suppose that could be Chief Inspector Zidane ... and some beer.'

Mathilde waited ...

... as the boss's pulse raced again, but in a different direction.

Then asked, 'Are you still there?'

'So far ... *Merci*, Mathilde.' Now opening her own machine.

'You all right?'

'Fine. I'll see you tomorrow.'

Aliette breathed slowly as she beheld Nabi looking stupid, elbows on the table, in deep conversation with her—hair in damp strings, more than a bit bedraggled after a workout in the theatre, but definitely her. Who would she want to share this with?

She decided against a visit to the library. Had she thought of securing her search downstairs?

No ... Not smart, Inspector.

The day was getting the better of her. Leaving, she let her eyes linger on the diverse faces met coming and going along the hall. Just faces. Like names on tombs. She was still a stranger, there were far too many cops for her to know, friendly or otherwise, here on the third floor. And more in the lift, packed and stuffy at the end of the day. She knew Liza Fratticelli wasn't just talking when she warned that Mario Bédard's support was filtering down through the ranks.

- 36 -

MOVEMENT IN THE SAND

Sandplay therapy can be remarkable in the immediacy of revelations provided to the therapist in the configuration of the sand 'world' the client fashions during a session, or over the extended course of treatment. Sandplay bypasses verbal barriers formed on both sides of the intrapsychic exchange known as psychotherapy. Unprompted … just aimlessly playing with the sand in her fingers, the client might clear a patch revealing the blue-painted floor of the sand tray. Blue is emblematic of water—which in the poetics of psychology is the element of dreams. The client may not realize where she has directed her psyche's story; but her therapist will immediately see the inner narrative changing. Or it might involve moving a 'character' into a different position or alignment: the mother figurine has spent weeks lying face-down in the sand. In an almost whimsical action, and without verbal explanation, the client turns the mother over. Or stands her up. Or two characters change positions in relation to each other. Apparently random, 'playful' action in the sand signals psychic movement. The meaning may be obvious. Or it may be enigmatic, difficult to read. In any event, the therapist does not immediately regale her client with an interpretation. She knows the client's story; she merely observes as her client's sandplay continues from this new vantage, and then proceeds to direct their conversation accordingly.

Because eventually we do have to talk about it. Mm?

Or perhaps the client suddenly adds a *new* character to her world.

Emma had been crying for most of the day. All day Monday too. This, after exerting herself so angrily on Friday afternoon. Gabrielle Gravel was becoming seriously worried about the waiting room experiment. Tuesday evening, over tea, she asked, pointedly but gently, 'Shall we stop this, Em?'

Emma's reply was a sorrowful gaze into the unknown and unchanging distance of her sand.

'You don't have to. If it's too much.'

'But I do.' Barely a whisper.

'Don't hang onto a ghost, Em. Not healthy.' How many times had she advised this?

'But he's my husband.' How many times had Em replied?

Emma's heart was not realistic. The hearts of most of the people who sat in front of Gabrielle Gravel were not realistic. The job was to gather broken pieces, to reconstruct a realistic heart.

Even when the dialogue was mostly empty sound...

'But he's not good for you.'

And Emma knew this intrinsically. Her estranged man was too toxic to be allowed a place in her damaged psyche—as reflected in the meagre mother-dominated tableau painfully created in her sand tray. As always, Emma complained woefully, 'But it's the way it's supposed to be.'

'It's not the law, Em... Who says it's supposed to be?'

'My mother. His mother.' Those two carefully painted metal figures in the sandbox waiting on the table. One blue skirt, one green.

'Be your own woman. That's your starting point, my pet.'

'She needs us.' The dolly in the sand that was her child.

Gabrielle Gravel had a duty to advise, 'The number one killer in the world today is not cancer, it is repression, the unhealthy pressures it unleashes. Anxiety of your kind and degree is a large red flag.' Emma looked up. Momentarily drained of tears, her grey eyes were so empty. 'What I'm saying, Em—all this horrid crying, frankly, I'm fearing for your health.'

Emma nodded mournfully—to herself. She whispered, 'I can do this. I'm strong too.'

And so back to Gabrielle Gravel: her sense of what was needed, and what was safe. Em had borne much pain. 'Strong' was debatable. But she was tougher than she allowed herself to believe. That was the point here—to push her to believe. Gabrielle offered a smile. 'Good girl, proud of you...' and made a note.

Refuses to bend. Good! But we are at a precarious...

Gabrielle was interrupted when Emma murmured, 'I'm not.'

'Not?'

'A good girl.'

'No?' And so much horrid crying. 'Does that mean bad?... Em?'

A cogent question, because it was always the others who were 'bad.' Emma was the one who'd followed the rules, done exactly what was expected, had been disastrously wronged. And because *bad* could mean almost anything. There was a world between PsychoDynamo and the barren house down by the river where Em sat in front of the *télé* waiting for her family to be reborn. Perhaps she had started meeting strangers and taking them home? Or worse. Whatever she was doing, it was obviously not making her happy. But every client was still a free agent, until needs be otherwise. Trust. Safety. Boundaries... Freedom to continue living in the world was part and parcel of the contract.

Gabrielle Gravel could only ask, 'Can we talk about it now?'

No. Emma sat rigid, Her brow knit, the way it did. Gabrielle had learned this meant Em literally, physically could not talk about it. She made another note. *Why are we suddenly bad?*

Then asked, 'How's your sand looking tonight?'

Normally this question brought more dull, blank misery, an hour of coaxing, usually ending nowhere. On this evening, Gabrielle watched in quiet amazement as Emma actually got up of her own volition and went to the shelf.

... Emma's was a family-oriented trauma. Her challenge was to find it in herself to reassert her place. As wife. As mother. Or as mother, then wife. Emma's ongoing befuddlement made it difficult to understand her heart's priorities. The two were inextricable, of course, but Emma's sandbox needed that missing man—the husband-father she had so far refused to include—before the picture was complete. Before they could really hope to move Em forward.

Now Emma had declared herself 'bad' and was going to add a figure to her world. Gabrielle Gravel realized she was excited.

But she winced when Emma returned with a doll—another doll, silky blonde, its plastic female body fully formed—and carefully put it in the sand.

Em's own presence in her sand world was another shifting problem. Some days Em would situate herself in one of the two metallic figurines—blue skirt, green skirt, mother and daughter as eternally reflecting twins. Other days, the two ladies in Emma's tray were the double-mother power of two friends who'd forced a marriage that exploded—leaving Em not there at all.

After some moody contemplation, Emma took the new doll by the head and used it as a sort of rake to clear away the sand. In the process, Em's tableau was pushed away to the edges, effectively destroyed. She placed the shapely new arrival on the hard blue bottom of the box.

Gabrielle kept her peace. It was for Emma to explore, then articulate. If she physically could.

37

RAPPROCHEMENT (NOT)

Aliette dared to go 'home' before coming to Gabrielle Gravel. She badly needed a shower, if not a nap, before facing Gabrielle. Sergio arrived in time to share simple noodles and butter. He did not tell her to go away. Didn't say much of anything. Cordial, bland, removed. 'Good day?'

'I've had better.' In the interests of peace, she did not elaborate.

He did not mention Friday's sins. Nor his interview with the psychologist.

… Horrible, eating in silence. May as well eat alone.

Sergio must have felt it too. He finally pushed his noodles aside. 'All right, tell me what you know.' In response to a certain look, he added, 'Please?' And listened. Even smiled in a judge-like way as she explained her thinking. Then he folded his hands.

'OK, let's suppose Vincent Spanghero throws away the knife Nabi gave him and some deranged soul finds it and uses it to kill three people, the third being Pierre Tropéano. You're right—the places, the kind of people one usually finds there: Pierre Tropéano would've been an interloper, a threatening presence, one way or the other, almost asking for it, as it were. But his presence makes sense. Given the pattern, the notes, and what the police are thinking because of Nabi and Vincent's shared story, Tropéano fits. An anomaly, maybe a mistake, but not a total accident. And possibly the victim of a well-thought trap.' He paused. 'Is that OK with you?'

'I suppose.'

'Thank you. And so our killer trades Nabi's bloody knife for Tropéano's gun—which also has a double-edged logic. One: more effective killing. Two: the story of Pierre and Vincent. And he continues on, hunting these homeless kids. More carnage, more notes. Tropéano plus histrionic notes make the Spanghero possibility totally clear to all the wrong people. Or the *right* people, depending on how *he* happens to see it. And so, please tell me, Inspector—'

'Stop it, Sergio.'

'—if it isn't Spanghero, why is he hiding? Hiding is exactly the wrong thing to do here.'

'Because he doesn't know he's wanted?'

Sergio Regarri offered a dubious look in reply to that.

Aliette breathed in, breathed out, exercising fragile patience. 'If, as his wife will corroborate, Vincent Spanghero threw his life out with the garbage and then walked away from everything, he could literally be too far away to know what is occurring back in his home town, much less care.'

'Ah. The fishing theory.'

'Whatever… You don't know for sure he's hiding.'

Sergio looked at the ceiling—his own way of marshalling patience. Then asked, 'That uniform you were talking to: he said you seemed to know all about the fourth—the kid at the wall. What exactly does that mean?'

'Were you this much of a bastard with Gabrielle Gravel this morning?'

'Please… Inspector? Seeing that you are telling me what you supposedly know.'

'It means that I lied, Sergio. Though not in so many words.'

'I see…' An assessing nod. A gaze aimed slightly past her. 'Well, I tell you this, Aliette. Your friend Nabi's a big boy. Whatever else, however you manage it, your lying won't help him.'

A patronizing pat on the head was the last thing she needed. The day's frustrations boiled over, their brief moment of rapprochement fell apart. 'Not so big he can't be splashed all over the news and have his career torn to shreds. Make Gabrielle Gravel tell you what she knows!'

'You know I can't do that.'

'Yes, you can!'

He smiled at her fury—a mean thing, rarely seen, but there when he needed it. 'Why should Gabrielle Gravel compromise her professional values? Would you compromise yours?'

Trick question: Aliette already had. 'Do I deserve this?'

'You might.'

She swore some. He didn't budge.

Slamming her dirty plates down beside the sink, she went up to brush her teeth.

He waited at the table, watched with those same eyes as she was putting on her coat.

It was all she could do not to slam the door. Damn him!

Sergio was warning her. Yes, and so was Mario Bédard ... Stupid men. She did not need to be warned. She was an adult. She was a professional. She detested being warned.

38

TEARS AND VIRGINIE

'Are we sad tonight?'

'That's not your business.'

But it was. Tears could be a sign of progress. 'Can we talk about why you've been crying?'

'No.' The girl pulled a filthy sleeve across her face, needing to hide any trace of weakness.

Gabrielle Gravel made a note. Virginie hadn't cried in ages.

The girl whispered, 'I hate this rotten world!'

Virginie's hatred was ever-present. Nothing new to work with there. Taking a lilac-scented hankie from her pocket, Gabrielle held it to her nose. A gesture meant to provoke. It drew a bored smirk, a flicker in Virginie's defiant, tear-bloated eyes. She pulled the small, crushed notebook from her back pocket, snatched a pen from Gabrielle's desk and scribbled something.

A note for a note. This was one of the girl's usual manoeuvres, meant to provoke right back.

Gabrielle smiled—because it was a game. 'Can we talk about why you still cannot bring yourself to bathe? A nice hot bath will sometimes wash away much more than dirt.'

'My body is not your business.'

'It can do wonders for the soul.'

Virginie was huge—large, solid and mean enough to play scrum for the Béziers first fifteen. It belied the fact she was just fifteen and still under the purview of the Children's Judge. Not that the judge and an army of social workers had accomplished much before handing the girl on to Gabrielle. Yes, but... Apart from kicking her math prof in the testicles, refusing to attend school and neglecting to come home for days on end, Virginie had not broken any law they knew of.

True: there's no law against hating your mother. No law against acting as if your father does not exist. No law against being filthy... Gabrielle breathed in lilac. 'And if I tell them you should be sent to training?' *Maison de redressement.* A low blow, but the bath issue was wearing on her patience. All Gabrielle had to do was sign a form and send it to the court. Virginie would be rounded up and shipped to a training facility near the Italian border. Where she *would* have a bath.

'You won't,' the girl taunted brazenly.

'Won't I?'

'Because it means you've failed.'

Which induced a certain heat under Gabrielle's collar. 'It's your life, Virginie, not mine. In the long run, you won't get away with it.'

'Get away with?'

'Stinking.'

'My life belongs to me and no one else.'

'It belongs to the world,' advised Gabrielle.

'Don't you listen? I. HATE. THIS. WORLD!'

'Refusing human connection is not a healthy choice.'

Big nasty smile. 'I'm getting stronger every day.'

'No argument there, my dear. You smell, Virginie.'

'This is just bullshit consumer-culture brain-fuck talk.'

'It's disgusting. It indicates madness. Madness is self-destruction.'

'My friends love me. They love my soul the way it is.'

Friends. Love. Perhaps the notion of her soul? The tears were gathering again. Gabrielle moved to take advantage of a momentary chink in Virginie's armour. 'I thought we'd try a sort of thought experiment this evening?'

The girl sighed, looked so sad through bleary eyes. 'Like what?'

'Like what you think your life should be. Like what it would be if only—'

'My life is fine. You should do that with my mother. She's the one who needs a new life.'

Virginie came from a decent but disastrously dysfunctional home. Her mother lived in fear of her. Her father was a passive, self-absorbed blank. Her frustration level had effectively swamped her ego. She was a pure id creature with high communications skills. Gabrielle enjoyed the challenge more than she let on, she only wished the girl would have a bath and change her clothes. 'It's just a game, Virginie … Play. An exercise in imagination.'

'I hate exercise. More bourgeois bullshit.'

'Your friends won't like you if you get fat.'

'Then I'll kill them.'

'Surely not.'

'You said it was an exercise in imagination.'

'What about fun, Virginie? You *have* heard of fun?'

'I had more fun last night than you'll have in a year … Ten years.'

'Then why were you crying?'

'I said it's not your business!'

Gabrielle watched Virginie's resistance flowing back like water. In a year of battle, Virginie had refused to acknowledge the sand tray with her name on it. That did not mean the girl did not enjoy playing. Though she would not descend to making her own mask, she often got up and went to the shelves behind Gabrielle's chair and took another client's mask and wore it for the duration. Then forgot about it. No continuity there at all. Very disconcerting arguing with the gentle Botticelli angel. And worse when Virginie donned a mask for the futile family sessions Gabrielle had tried—if she did not completely disrupt whatever fragile thread of dialogue with her near-violent outbursts, the girl would sit silent behind whichever mask had struck her fancy until she flung it down and stomped out, pleas and warnings be damned.

But that evening there was no denying the sadness hanging in the fetid air. Perhaps this was an opening. Tears instead of anger as a start point? Gabrielle bent and lifted the box onto her desk. The fine white sand was spread evenly, untouched.

'So maybe we're finally ready for this?'

It was a challenge with an edge—sadly, the only approach that worked.

'Are you joking?'

'I don't think you would get my jokes, Virginie.' Gabrielle took a silk jewellery bag from her drawer and emptied it over the box. A colourful selection of figurines and objects fell into the sand. This was a proactive move, risky, not advised, sometimes necessary. Otherwise, resistance could go on for years. 'You set it up. As you please. Your world, your move, Virginie.'

Virginie snorted her contempt, pulled out her abused spiral notebook, and made another note.

'You can kill as many friends as you want,' advised Gabrielle. 'Enemies too.' Even her mother and father. There was a miniature machine gun amongst the many trinkets. *Star Wars* vintage.

As her client stared sullenly, and fussed and scratched—to be sure, the bath issue played both ways—Gabrielle waited. A crack in the girl's resilient shell would not happen till Gabrielle found a way to her heart. Or till Virginie realized that she had to play. Either way, Gabrielle was prepared to wait it out. Yes, advising a year or two of *redressement* was tempting; but there would be no calls to the court professing futility, demanding they take her client off to training school. The girl was unnervingly uncanny: Gabrielle would never let a stinky brat bring failure to her project. Too much was riding on success with Virginie.

It took an hour.

When Virginie took up the tiny gun and used it to inscribe **Virginie** in rounded childish script across the virgin sand, Gabrielle saw it as progress.

That and more tears falling, leaving tiny stains like rainrops in the sand.

The other pieces remained untouched, spread willy-nilly around her name.

- 39 -

IMPISH & BLOODY-MINDED

Pausing to let her systems cool after a conflicted march through a humid, misty evening, Aliette sent a baleful glare up to the stony man staring down from his window like a declawed and neutered cat. And how was your day, *monsieur*? He blinked first, looked away.

Stepping into PsychoDynamo, she met the sorrowful eyes of the woman at her reception post beside the wilted daisy, clutching her gnawed pencil, tear-mottled cheeks sagging. The inspector did not bother with a *bonsoir* as she slung her coat onto an unclaimed hook and slumped into her usual chair. 'Are you going to let that plant just die?'

The woman blinked, seemed surprised to see it at her elbow. She declined to reply.

The creepy man was hunched in his chair with his American book. Third week, same book. Was Gabrielle teaching him to read? She wondered if he remembered the offered loan.

A low murmur: 'Did you bring your gun tonight?'

She turned to him. 'Why?'

'Protection?'

'Stop it!' The ragged wreck pounded her desk.

Ignoring her, impish and bloody-minded, Aliette nodded yes and flashed her gun.

The woman gasped, enraged. The man was delighted.

More than delighted. Smitten. The inspector, also a woman of well-travelled instinct, looked into the eyes of a man who'd fallen in love. Yes, well... It happens. Not all the time, and far less than it used to. But it does. Normally one moves past it: a demure smile, or a flat, downcast gaze. Or a warning, depending. Tonight (impish and bloody-minded) she asked, 'What's your name?'

'Jean. You?'

'Aliette. Did you bring me a book to read?'

His eyes slid sideways as he shook his head. Sideways toward the reception desk.

She wouldn't blame him. She understood... Introductions done, Aliette settled in and waited, feeling his fawning gaze, ignoring the pathetic weeper.

She was focused elsewhere.

It was not her anger at Sergio's recalcitrance, or a presumptuous threat sent by Mario Bédard, or her frustration with the day. It was the odour in the room, and for a perplexing moment she thought it was herself, the grubby redolence of her own scent against sweaty clothing after a bloody-minded forty-minute march.

But it wasn't. Her nose was telling her something she had known since Friday night.

Moments of trauma will heighten the senses, but Aliette Nouvelle had been too confused with fear to process an elemental clue. The smell, here, now—if you can remember the scent of your grandma's sweater from thirty years ago, four days is child's play. It was from Friday. It was the coats... It was the ripped-up bomber jacket hanging from the coat tree, looking like it had been dragged behind a car.

Just so: When the door to Gabrielle's office opened and the huge, scowling, grossly messy girl emerged, the waiting room was immediately permeated with the rank notes of a reeking body wrapped in unwashed clothing infused with stale tobacco, beer, rotting earth...

The inspector's olfactory perception was confirmed, magnified by memory into a malignant wave washing through a tight, dark city street. Impossible to forget.

The girl hovered over the receptionist, impatiently twiddling an unlit cigarette, waiting as the charade of the next appointment card was laboriously enacted. Snatching the card, she turned to retrieve her coat.

Aliette stood, letting her hand drift to the bulge above her hip. 'I want my beret back.'

The girl ignored her, shrugged on her ratty coat. She was a head taller, and solid.

The police could use a girl like her. Tonight she was the enemy. Aliette repeated, 'My beret.'

'You're fucked up.' With dismissive disgust, she turned to the door.

Aliette drew her gun and put it between the girl's shoulder blades. Hard. 'Without my beret, yes, I am fucked up.' She jabbed. 'And if you don't hand it over in five seconds...' Jabbing the barrel twice again. 'Five, four, three...' It felt good. What better way of getting past the bitter taste of being warned than by warning the next person down the line?

Apparently the girl had been through this drill before. She very slowly moved a hand inside her jacket, the beret dropped to the floor.

'Thank you. And now your gun.'

'I have no gun.'

Aliette dared to frisk the gargantuan frame...up inside the musty jacket, down her oily denim legs to her putrid wool socks. She felt the girl tensing as she moved her hand. There did not seem to be a gun. *Bon...*' standing, another hard steel jab. 'So now you'll take me to your friend.'

'I'd rather die.'

Aliette said, 'Fine.' She pushed the barrel deeper. The girl arched her back.

The receptionist croaked, 'Virginie!'

Aliette heard it—a reaction as elemental as...what? 'Virginie?' She repeated it. What was it in the way that poor woman said her name? Distracted, she eased her pressure and turned...

In a split second, the door opened, the girl was gone.

The woman at the desk brought her hands to her face and collapsed on her blotter.

Gabrielle Gravel was standing at her office door, arms folded. 'You're next, madame.'

Without further comment, the psychologist went back into her room.

Without a glance behind her, the inspector holstered her gun and followed.

If

Jean closed his book. 'She's brilliant!'

At the reception desk, a mournful scowl. 'She's evil.'

'How can you say that? You don't know her.'

'She threatened our child!'

'I think she's the one.'

'I knew it, I knew it … You are sick.'

'And you are hopeless.'

'And who could blame me?'

Jean ignored a question he'd heard too many times. 'I believe I love that woman.'

'You don't know the meaning of the word.'

'She's strong. Aliette?'

'It's her gun.'

Jean seemed to agree. 'She's not afraid. You can feel it.'

'A gun proves nothing.'

'What would you know?'

'I know.'

They stared each other down.

Gabrielle was training Jean to say what he was feeling. 'I need someone like her.'

'Yes? What about the little woman in the store?' Gabrielle was helping Emma be more assertive, even combative when required.

'Solange?' Jean shrugged. 'She minds the store.'

A sniff. 'If I had a gun, would you love me?'

Jean could not answer.

'If I could save that poor girl?'

Jean looked down at his book.

If, if, if … like they'd been sitting here for a hundred years.

– 41 –

STAND-OFF

'And so?...are you proud of yourself?'

Proud? '*B'eh*... It's my beret. I've had it my entire career. That disgusting girl can tell me to fuck myself or whatever, I can handle her adolescent bile. But I will not let her walk away with something that's part of my life. I don't see what's to be proud of.'

'I'd say you've made a big step in the right direction. Good reaction. Strong presence. I can definitely report real progress.' Gabrielle Gravel sounded like the faceless technician controlling the virtual scenes at the range that afternoon. A dry positive to his machine-like negative.

'But I wouldn't *shoot* her. I lost my temper.'

'You might have. She thought you might shoot. That's what counts. You used your weapon to gain control. That's what it's for. Mm?' Nodding... the answer went without saying.

Aliette deflated. Actions speak. The gun strapped to her body had usurped an essential space at the core of her, a new ballast point redefining everything. 'I've no idea what I'm turning into.'

'That's part of the process. I would hope you might find it exciting.'

'It's pathetic! That poor girl, she needs major help.'

'We're working on it, I assure you.'

'Virginie... Her name is Virginie. The receptionist, she...' What? Aliette remained confused by the woman's emotion.

The psychologist confirmed. 'Yes, Inspector. And she steals, flim-flams, scavenges, lives on the street for weeks on end. Promiscuous to a dangerous degree, I hope she isn't selling herself... obviously not too mindful of basic hygiene. She was slicing herself when she came to me. Many issues...' She hovered between thoughts. 'I wonder if she learned anything from your moment in the waiting room. That will be something to explore.' She opened her notes. 'Now, where did we leave off?'

Aliette said, 'I'd like to hear more about Virginie. Scavenging, you say?'

'Let it go. This is your hour, we focus on you.' Gabrielle focused on her page.

And Aliette regretted to inform her, 'I'm afraid it goes beyond our moment in your waiting room, Gabrielle. It goes beyond me and my beret.'

Because Gabrielle thought Virginie had been caught going through the pockets of Aliette's coat. Because Aliette had expressly neglected to mention how and where the theft had occurred.

Now she had to take that risk.

The *psy* looked up, professionally wary. 'And where does it go, Inspector?'

'Whatever I say stays in this room, yes?'

'To a point. Obviously we discuss certain things, I report progress. Or not.'

'What I disclose is confidential. Yes or no?'

'What are you saying?'

'That I need to be protected if I disclose something you need to hear.'

Gabrielle assessed. Nodded. 'I'll stand by you. That's my role.' She gestured, Go on…

Aliette related her outing Friday night. About being caught off guard and nearly trampled in a wave of ragged street kids swarming down the lane. She admitted experiencing fear to the point of paralysis, a hand swiping away her beret. When the corner of Gabrielle's mouth turned up in a skeptical grimace, Aliette leaned across the desk and waved the beret in her face. Gabrielle recoiled—she recognized the stench infused in the wool. Clearly, the beret had been out of the inspector's keeping for longer than a minute in the waiting room. 'All right. And so?'

'And so someone in Virginie's gang has a gun. I heard it—they were shooting it in the street, for fun, I suppose, by the sound of them… I smelled it too, actually, when they ran past me. They were headed for the cemetery. So was a person chasing them. That person also had a gun. I saw it, Gabrielle. A few minutes later, shots were fired in the cemetery. Another kid is dead.'

'You're talking about these killings.'

'You've been following the story.'

'Of course I have.'

'Then you know it started with a knife.'

'Yes...'

'And you know the policeman killed at Saint-Aphrodise was from the same department as Vincent Spanghero. Pierre Tropéano. A former colleague. They hated each other.'

A questioning nod. Gabrielle may or may not have known that. 'What are you implying?'

'And did you know the knife was a gift to Vincent Spanghero on the occasion of his wedding thirty or so years ago? The gift of another ex-colleague, it so happens. This has been confirmed.'

'I heard nothing about that.'

'Almost no one has. And they won't until they find Vincent.'

'Find Vincent?' Gabrielle closed her notebook. 'This is absurd.'

'I happen to agree. But the fact is, the person who killed the officer left the knife and took his gun, which was used to kill the girl on Friday night—this is also beyond arguing, Gabrielle—and the way this tragedy is playing out, at least to the investigators, it does not look good for your client Vincent Spanghero. You follow me?'

Gabrielle retreated to her basic line: 'I cannot divulge—'

'But I happen to know Vincent was in a certain mood last spring and he may have thrown it away. The knife. Along with his former life.'

Gabrielle cautiously conceded, 'He did talk along those lines.'

'It's a good possibility that knife may have been scavenged from the heap of unwanted things former Inspector Spanghero tossed out.'

'Scavenged?' Now she could see where this was going. 'But how do you know this?'

'His wife.' Aliette held the psychologist's worried eyes. She had her full attention. 'Vincent Spanghero's wife saw them, a pack of street kids, among others, picking through, taking things. It's turning into a major subsector of the economy, which seems sad to me... Then again, I guess it always has been. In any event, what is odd is that not one, but two clients linked to this office appear to be dangerously linked to the murders. Don't you find that odd, Gabrielle?'

Gabrielle frowned. 'I can only report based on what I hear and see in this room.'

'On the other hand, Vincent may *not* have thrown the knife out with the rest of his past. It's not clear. Even his wife can't say for sure.'

Gabrielle's eyes turned hard. 'Your point, Aliette?'

'The only thing clear is that it was the knife used to kill Vincent's ex-colleague. And that the killer then upgraded to that man's gun. So to speak.'

Gabrielle got flustered. 'How do they know it's the same person? I mean, if people are buying and selling discarded things.'

'Certain forensics, Gabrielle. Trust me, they know.'

Gabrielle lashed out. 'It could not be Vincent!'

Aliette held up a calming hand. 'I agree. What matters is, *they* think it is. They're keeping his name out of it— they believe it keeps the potential panic level down. But the media is closing in. From what I'm hearing, as early as tomorrow Vincent's name and face will be front and centre on everyone's *télé*. Then all bets are off.'

'But it's absurd. It's—' Gabrielle left it hanging.

Aliette nodded. 'I hear that's what Vincent kept saying last spring. Absurd, absurd, absurd?'

Gabrielle blinked... Aliette deduced something like panic, or at the very least, a deeply baffled moment. Emotions speak too—to cops as well to psychologists. Interrogation was not therapy, and an inspector's listening skills might not have been as trained as Gabrielle Gravel's, but they were acute. As were her eyes: Gabrielle was guarding information. What's more, it pained her.

Gabrielle collected her wits. 'When he left here, Vincent Spanghero had renounced the use of violence in his life. I have to believe he has kept to his word.'

'But you don't know this.'

'But I do ... You may not like what I do, Inspector, but I am good at it. They would not send me the cases they do if they didn't think so. And when I sign off with a client, I have the highest confidence the solution we have found will last. If not—if I feel the results achieved may only be provisional—I will say so in my report. I have to. My credibility depends upon it. With regards to Vincent Spanghero, I am certain he has changed and for the better and will remain so.'

'How can you be so certain, Gabrielle?'

'He went through a remarkable transformation. I saw it. I felt it.'

'But the investigators did not.'

'But they have my report.'

'And they have the knife used to kill Pierre Tropéano… That, and much more circumstantial evidence which points directly at Vincent. They hate cop killers, Gabrielle. For them, the best justice is in kind. Sure, they'll try to root him out, corner him, bring him to trial. But it will be embarrassing for our trusted police. Much better for all concerned if he's… not. Am I making myself clear?'

Gabrielle processed this for a long minute. Finally said, 'So you talked to his wife. Are you saying you're involved in this investigation?'

Aliette took the next step into trust. 'I'm saying I've been making my own enquiries.'

Gabrielle sat back, contemplating. 'Professional curiosity can be problematic, Inspector.'

Forcing Aliette back to her start point. 'This room is sacred space. Yes?'

A vague, 'Yes…' was the best Gabrielle would offer at this moment.

'It's serious, Gabrielle. And you're sitting right in the middle of it. Two clients?'

That brought something markedly resentful to Gabrielle's calculating gaze.

Aliette was flatly professional. 'If you have any information, you should share it.'

To which Gabrielle responded, 'It is not Vincent.'

'If not for his sake, for Virginie's—I mean, if it matters.'

Another dart. And it had the desired effect. 'Of course I care about Virginie!'

'Good. Because she is in a very dangerous place. By which I mean in the streets with a gun, her gang, her attitude.'

Gabrielle considered it. 'She'd been crying when she arrived this evening.'

'Friday's victim was probably one of her friends.'

'Virginie would not kill a friend. She is a loyal type, if nothing else.'

'The police are not looking for Virginie. Or anyone like her...' Aliette directed Gabrielle back to the crux. 'They're looking for the person *chasing* Virginie and her friends, gun drawn, the person who chased them into the cemetery. They think that person is Vincent Spanghero. They believe he's the serial killer.'

'But he's not.'

Again Aliette agreed. But. 'The thing is, Gabrielle, if they keep looking for the wrong person, these tragedies are likely to continue. Virginie's an obvious target. You see?'

Gabrielle reopened her book. 'Virginie will be here Thursday. She and I will explore this. As for you and I, we are wasting precious time on things that have no bearing on our work. We must get on with it. I have a report to write. As we both know, much depends on it.'

Aliette could only sigh at another threat. 'Tomorrow could be Vincent's worst day ever.'

'Vincent Spanghero is not responsible for this.'

'Whoever has Tropéano's gun is responsible for this. Logic and forensics say Vincent. I can protect him. I can get Vincent Spanghero to the right people. He will have to demonstrate his remarkable transformation. And probably somehow prove he threw away his knife. But he'll be safe. So will you ... I mean your credibility. Please trust me.'

'I do.' Gabrielle stared coolly across the desk.. 'You are my credibility, Inspector.'

Stand-off. They both knew what a few well-placed words could do to each other's careers.

Aliette Nouvelle was disappointed. She studied her hands. 'So what do we do, Gabrielle?'

Gabrielle responded by rising, stepping over to the sideboard, retrieving Aliette's sandbox, and setting it on the desk. 'We play it out in the sand. You've made a breakthrough tonight and we mustn't lose sight of it. What exactly happened out there in the waiting room? Take me through it again using these figures you chose to populate your world. Break it down into as many isolated moments as you can. I call them instants of perception—leading up to, during... Start before you got here. Start back on Friday. The moment you saw this stampede. The instant your beret was snatched from your head. It is completely up to you. I want you to see how you got there, to that moment in the waiting room. So we can lock this thing in place.'

Aliette considered the toy pistol in a blue spot in the centre of her sand. 'I can't.'

'Of course you can. You already have. This is an exercise. Call it a debriefing.'

'I don't like what I did out there.'

'You don't have to like it. Liking has nothing to do with it.'

'I don't like *myself*! The person who felt the need to act that way. That is not me!'

'But this is you in front of me, here and now, Inspector. Please?'

NOTES TO THE WORLD

Virginie exhaled pungent smoke, then traded the joint with Elf for the bottle. She took a deep gulp of wine and confided, 'I know who killed Fanny and Jaco.'

And François, Knut, and probably the cop. Not that anyone cared about a cop. This was about their friends, their people. No one really knew each other, people made up stories about themselves, faces changed every day, but they were a tribe. Didn't matter where they came from. Or why. They all lived in the street.

And they were being hunted.

Elf held the toke … Finally exhaled. 'Let's kill him!'

'Her.' She took the weed and puffed.

'A bitch?'

'Total bitch … ' Exhaling. 'You have the gun?'

Elf reached into his coat. He held it up—the gun he had lifted from Fanny's lifeless hand. The gun Fanny had removed from the pocket of Patrice the dealer after he was shot dead at the lookout on Passage Canterellettes by two guys who said Patrice was stealing from them. He probably was. Patrice was slime. Still, it was unreal how people could just shoot someone. They'd all just sat there, not their business, too wrecked to run or even be scared. The one guy gave them some free pills and a piece of paper with a number, said they had great stuff, always, and always something different, always the best price. Then they'd left … left Patrice where he lay. Fanny found cash and the gun. They'd split too. It was in the paper for a day. That was way back in October, when it was warm and they were camping in the woods behind the cemetery.

Fanny had waved the gun around sometimes, and talked the way she did. Guys liked it. Jaco really did, and Fanny had liked him.

Now they were both dead and Virginie was crying again, wishing for spring. They'd head back into the woods. If there are any of us left, she thought.

Virginie wished life was simpler. It was simpler in the woods.

The problem was, she really did know who it was and knew she had to do something.

'Give it to me.'

Elf passed her the gun.

She was already composing a note in her mind. Something like *I can't live with this anymore because…*

Because why? The answer would be there with a bullet.

Virginie had always kept a diary. Even during the worst of the insane times with her parents, she would force herself to write something down. Not for the social workers who pretended to care. Not for the icky, chummy profs who were beneath contempt. Definitely not for Gabrielle. She scribbled in front of her *psy* as a way of fighting back, but would never share because she knew it would all be used against her. No, she wrote down her thinking so her head would not explode. And if her head exploded, which it felt like it would every day since she could remember, well then, Virginie wrote her thinking for the world: Remember me? This is how I felt about you.

This shitty world.

Sometimes her notes were nothing but a tit-for-tat release, an alternative to punching. She looked at the page she had started that night sitting in front of Gabrielle. *Egoistic bitch…* And, *You have such ugly hair.* Of course it would be used against her. She tore the page away and set it alight against the ember of the joint. She and Elf watched it flame and crumple. The faces in the room appeared briefly in the glow. Without electricity, it was darker in the squat than in the street. Or in the woods, for that matter. At least there they had the sky.

…Or Virginie's notes to the world came like an explosion of emotion and she could not write fast enough to contain her feelings.

Three weeks ago Elf had looked out an upstairs window and seen François sinking to the pavement in a pool of blood. Poor François, out of his mind like always, but harmless. And too friendly. Elf said a person in a long coat had stopped at the door of the squat where they'd been crashing that week—'one of those totally bourgeois puffy things that makes them look like the stupid Michelin Man?' François was standing in the street with his bottle of wine. He'd approached, offering the bottle, always up for chatting, and got his heart stabbed to pieces.

Elf sounded the alert, they'd all moved out within ten minutes, panicked. There was nothing to be done for François, there would be only trouble for themselves. On the way out, Virginie had scribbled a desperate note, a thread of jumbled thoughts about how the world was getting too insane—absurd! that was the word now—the world was falling apart and it seemed like she and her friends were the only ones who could ever see it and how they had to keep going no matter what or who got in the way, against all odds, and make people know this even if it meant more pain, more anger, more desperation…a note written in a flood of grief…

Virginie had tucked it into François's shoe and run.

They would read it. A message from the street. Virginie hoped they understood that whoever would do something like that was sick with hatred, infinitely more fucked up than poor François.

A week later Knut was found by the bins behind a bistro. Same horrible death. For what? Did anyone even know Knut? He was from Norway. Why? Who would do this? Virginie had crept under the barrier and left a simple note for Knut in a bin just down the lane. They would find it. Maybe they would think, *How in the world did he get so far from where he should have been?*

And care a bit. And try to fix it?…It was just a desperate hope.

After François and Knut, people in the street started saying *oui*, they'd seen him, wandering at night, wrapped up in a Michelin Man coat, staring from under a dark toque, moving slowly, as if searching, as if floating by, low and hungry like some awful bird. And they wondered, should they tell the police? But they hated the police. Then the cop was killed at Saint-Aphrodise and the Michelin Man coat was the only thing anyone there remembered. And it was getting scary.

But it was not the coat, it was what Fanny heard that made Virginie want to die.

Fanny had been with Jaco at the cemetery wall, but on the other side of it, and helpless. She was short and always needed a boost. He'd boosted her up and she'd gone over, was standing there waiting for him to follow when she heard a voice, and Jaco arguing, denying, getting mad the way Jaco did ... then getting shot, just like that, shot through the throat and killed.

Fanny came screaming, frantic, and found them in the tombs. Partying, wrecked like every other night. When she told Virginie what she'd heard, Virginie went and hid by herself and wept like she hadn't wept since she was nine.

In agony. A lot of agony in the place between hating and needing to help.

She left a note in the flowerpot on top of her *grand-mère*. Was she trying to help the police?

She *hated* the police. But she knew, and she needed to do something. Virginie remembered all those hours with her first therapist, all those years when she'd thought it was all her fault.

Does France need another child like this? We can do better We must

Friday night they'd been high, running wild, shooting the gun in honour of Jaco on the way to the tombs to party with the spirit of their friend. But they were followed. They were cowering in an unlocked tomb, watching the killer floating by, aiming a gun dead ahead ... floating by ...

Searching.

Fanny took them all by surprise. No one could stop her when she suddenly burst out with her gun and started shooting. Crazy. The killer ran, Fanny chased after, they'd followed and found her dead. Elf took her gun. The sirens arrived, they ran, over the far wall and into the woods, and did their crying there.

Except Virginie. She found her way back to her grandmother and left another note.

Do I matter? Am I solving anything? I am sorry for who I am.

Weed and wine dulled the pain of what Virginie knew.

'Hey! Wake up.' Elf wanted the weed back. She traded for the wine.

Elf understood the gun. He showed her how to check the bullets. '*Voilà* ... Still five shots left.'

'We only need one,' muttered Virginie, and swallowed wine.

And then they'd need another. She saw how it could work.

How she could fix it *and* get sweet revenge on the blonde bitch in the waiting room.

Elf blew smoke into the dank, unheated room. 'But how do we find her?'

'Not a problem. We go out, we go for a ramble, make some noise… She'll find *us*.'

They'll *both* find us, thought Virginie. And they would be found together.

Elf said, 'Cool. Let's do it.'

- 43 -

DOGS AND CATS

Jean Petitpas watched as the woman who called herself Aliette and carried a gun and was not afraid of Virginie snatched her appointment card from Emma, grabbed her coat and left without so much as a glance, let alone the cheery *bonsoir* he'd been craving for an hour. Something had gone wrong. Gabrielle could do that, Jean knew. Gabrielle required five minutes to prepare. Jean timed it to the second, got up and went in, sat without any of the usual niceties and demanded to know, 'That woman, the blonde who has started showing up? ... Beret and mac? Fighting with the girl?'

Gabrielle was engrossed in her notes and did not look up. 'I do know the one you mean, Jean.'

'Who is she? I mean exactly.'

Gabrielle was reviewing her pages containing observations related to former Inspector Vincent Spanghero. She shrugged, distracted. 'No one is anyone *exactly*, Jean.' And suddenly thought she might be talking to herself.

'I understand that, Gabrielle.'

And maybe he did. They had focused on this issue for several sessions.

'But what is she? Why is she here? I need to know this. Please!'

Jean's urgency forced Gabrielle from her mulling. There was a dread in Jean's plea. His fine thin hands were trembling. Jean Petitpas was a small businessman on the edge of ruin, addicted to fleeting dreams of glory. He had a new plan every week, and a blazing smile to match it. But no follow-through. Not much behind that smile. His sense of what he expected, what he was meant for, what he deserved and what he *needed* made him his own worst enemy. Perhaps because of his natural beauty? The man looked like the second coming of

Alain Delon. Men who looked liked that sometimes grew too used to an easy ride. Indeed, he blamed his failure on everyone else, most specifically his wife, whom he no longer believed in 'because she won't believe in me,' and their child, who rejected him out of hand. So what Jean Petitpas claimed he needed was suspect. The man's presumptuous impulsivity was the source of his problems.

But the incident in the waiting room was bound to send ripples. Gabrielle Gravel sensed a cogent passage pointing beyond this man's wayward dreaming, his chronic whining about his wife and child, the big potential no one noticed, the support he deserved but never received.

She was loath to tamp the energy flowing from her client. The inspector's run-in with Virginie had to be thoroughly dissected and built upon from his perspective. But calmly and methodically. She fastened on Jean's sloe eyes. 'You know I won't discuss my other clients.'

Which brought him up short and reduced him, as intended.

Gabrielle waited.

Jean burst through the silence. 'Her name is Aliette!'

'Yes, Jean. It is ... And so?'

'She has a gun.'

'We know that. As I told you, it's part of her program. Virginie provoked her, Jean—you know what that's like... Mm? It was not supposed to happen but it did..' She smiled. 'But let's talk about it. Please. Tell me your feelings. Were you afraid, Jean? It's normal. And did you fear for your child?'

'Was I afraid?' The question did not compute. Jean shook his head, quick and violent, very confused. Then clasped his gut. 'Afraid? Gabrielle, I feel like I've been punched.'

Gabrielle lifted Jean's box onto the desk. 'Let's see how this plays in your sand, shall we?'

Jean's sandbox was a busy place. China figurine Papa in red shorts and blue vest, his estranged wife and child in the form of two Russian-egg figures in babushkas, some nights one inside the other. Most of the action in Jean's sandbox was played out by the dogs and cats assembled around the central tableau, all cute, all charming, and he was constantly going to the shelf for more. Jean Petitpas kept no pets. These were his feelings. There were far too many to be meaningful and Gabrielle had quickly recognized a childish attempt to hide from her. But Jean Petitpas *was* childish, and he was hiding from himself. She said nothing as he added cats and dogs, and let him play... Some nights he had them fighting each other. Some nights the dogs attacked the Russian eggs, the cats watched or slept (according to Jean). He was attracted by models of huge buildings: castles, skyscrapers, he had three different Eiffel towers. He carefully changed the positioning of his architecture every session. And there was a black plastic crab from a cereal box he had chosen to represent 'our family problem.'

Gabrielle knew the crab was simply Jean; the father figure in red shorts never figured much in Jean's play. Before Christmas, in a dreary fit of self-pity, he had flipped the crab onto its back, leaving it metaphorically helpless... some nights Jean got himself totally right.

A tiny brass cauldron was set off by itself, on a space of blue where he had carefully cleared the sand. This was his pot of gold, the 'killing' Jean imagined he was always about to make. Or, depending on his mood, where Jean was going to be boiled before being eaten by his enemies.

Jean Petitpas was ever equivocal, his life was mundane, his dreams extreme.

As Gabrielle leaned forward, studying her client's world, he folded into himself, bewildered.

Gabrielle prompted, 'Do we have everything we need to do this?' She was intrigued to see who or what Jean would choose from the shelves to represent the blonde client with the gun.

... seeing that the blonde doll had been claimed by Em.

He didn't move from his chair. He hugged himself. 'I don't feel well, Gabrielle.'

Gabrielle heard Jean resisting. She tried to move him forward. 'How do you see her, Jean? The blonde woman. How does she fit here?' He was shaking his head, in a muddle, resisting. Somewhat peevish, Gabrielle suggested, 'And I'm thinking we should get that poor crab back on its feet?'... Claws? Whatever. Gabrielle wanted movement.

He shrugged, listless under his own psychological weight. 'It only moves sideways.'

Gabrielle nodded, 'True.'

He stood, wobbly, sweating now, pushing the theatre. 'I have to go.'

Gabrielle flared. 'Sit down, Jean!' He did. 'Stop fighting against yourself. If you feel pressure, release it... Talk to me, give it some room to show itself in the sand. I want you to tell me what happened out there in the waiting room. And how you feel about it. There was a gun drawn. I want to hear your thoughts.'

He stared, in a sickly daze, not at all beautiful in these dread moments—a very frightened man.

She coaxed, more gently, 'Come on, Jean... That's why we're here. Tell me about... Aliette?'

In reply, Jean Petitpas leaned over the side of his chair and threw up. Gabrielle froze.

He lurched out, feverish, mouth dripping. Emma screamed at the sight of him.

Gabrielle recovered, hurried into the office, but he was gone. There was only Emma, weeping piteously. 'What happened? He can't just leave like that. He has a court order.'

Emma sniffed, 'He says he loves her.'

'Madame Nouvelle?' Gabrielle felt an existential slap. 'But that's not right.'

'She has a gun,' Emma whimpered ' ... She threatened Virginie!'

Gabrielle was distracted. 'Love? He said that?'

'Why can't he love *me*?' Now Em was sobbing.

The notion of love floated in the waiting room. Gabrielle couldn't deal with it. She had to get her thinking organized. If Jean had said that to Em, that meant they were talking. That was good.

But love? That was wrong. Gabrielle returned to her desk, stepping carefully around the mess on the floor, pushed by a professional need to get it down while it was clear. She flipped her pages, stopped at JEAN and made a note: ... *a fascinating dread in expressing what he thinks he needs for a better life. The blonde woman? Or: The blonde woman with the gun?* The difference was something to be pursued. The gun was the central thing, the prime behavioural indicator, the shaper of the psychological dynamic pervading that flash moment in the waiting room.

Love was not the right result.

THREE CORNERS CONVERGING

Aliette Nouvelle stood at the place where the first victim had been killed with Nabi Zidane's gifted knife. The chalk outline could barely be seen now, washed thoroughly with the weekend's rain. The door and windows of the erstwhile squat were boarded over. She stepped close, listened. Empty. But the sound she was tracking was close, maybe in the next street over. That same sound from Friday night—the thudding mash of boots on pavement, the swish of coats against each other. And there was a voice hovering above it tonight, as if mixing in the soupy light clinging to the skyline, a solo singing voice repeating enough for her to recognize the doleful melody of 'Requiem pour un fou,' an ancient and much-loved tune by Johnny Halliday.

… *un pauvre fou /Qui meurt d'amour …* a poor madman who dies for love.

Aliette loved Johnny as much as anyone. It was almost as if they were calling her on.

They? She knew it was Virginie.

Right instinct would have pointed the inspector toward the boulevard, back to Sergio, their bed, perhaps some conciliatory love, and much-needed sleep at the end of an awful day. Leaving PsychoDynamo, a different instinct called her into the labyrinth. She had followed it, a cop inside herself, and comfortable there with an inkling of anticipation. The temperature had risen, a mist was drifting through the streets. The people in Saint-Brin claimed February was the door to the southern spring. Look for the mimosa, they advised. There were no mimosa along these streets, only the detritus of the city. But sure enough, she had come upon this sound—and followed.

Gabrielle Gravel had left her drained, mood at the zero point, neither up nor down. Not clear at all as to her feelings toward the girl called Virginie. What the inspector felt would not coalesce into a serviceable word. She did not hate the girl. On the other hand, she felt no sympathy either. She resented Virginie for provoking her. And for scaring her on Friday night. Was it a question of making some things clear—who was stronger, a question of respect? Strength and respect joined in the notion of power… Aliette did not know if those feelings were defined by the gun she carried. She suspected they might be. Wandering toward the sounds in front of her, she had tried to sort it out, then let it go and plodded on. In any event, if Gabrielle was right, about understanding beginning in the heart, what then? Aliette's heart was in a cupboard back at PsychoDynamo, waiting stunned in a box of sand. If your heart's not available, emotions are pointless. *And she was good with that.* Emotions would only be a drag on the matter at hand, muddle up the thing that felt inevitable. She sensed a rendezvous with Virginie. Much simpler when it's down to raw anticipation, an abiding sense of direction, this plodding momentum.

And when you are long past turning back.

At the far end of the murky street three corners almost met. The distance was closing, the crossroads looming. The noise in front of her was separating into speaking voices, distinct steps. Aliette realized the singing voice had stopped. She picked up her own step, no big hurry, a measured pace… Purposeful. Let her hear me. Me and my gun.

…Aliette unsnapped the flap securing her sidearm and clasped the grip. She had Gabrielle for backup. Yes? That promise of protection. Though you can't know till it happens. Who will come through, who will freeze, who will turn and run. Gun or no gun, that never changed. Aliette would stand her ground. She visualized the impending moment, the way they'd taught her: Virginie's face, set and bitter, hands in pockets, one hand on *her* gun, *their* gun, the gun from Friday night. She would have it. This was between Virginie and her.

Could it be Tropéano's gun? It could.

Strangely, but not so much, she heard herself telling Gabrielle, I'm going to lose my virginity tonight, my gun virginity, come what may, like it or not…

And Aliette heard Gabrielle telling her, *Liking has nothing to do with it, Inspector…*

No, it didn't.

She would draw her gun, point it at Virginie, order her to stop. Once, to no effect…

And then a second time, confronting Virginie, who would be standing there, defiant.

Visualization is an exercise in preparation based on the power of imagination. Aliette went through it again, riding the inevitable momentum, the engineered weight of her gun, these elements carrying her forward to the moment: Virginie, making a move, her right hand moving from her pocket…trying to see it, *needing* to see it, the moment she would pull the trigger, put a fatal hole in Virginie. But she was failing. Again?

Aliette Nouvelle could not see it in her mind's eye. The killing moment. It wasn't there.

Cutting down a human being remained a blank. Something in her soul had to leave it empty.

The basso drone of the gang's steps fell silent. Aliette was twenty paces from the zero point.

She walked on, resigned to live or die on the strength of a reaction. At the moment faces were glimpsed at the corner on her right… 'Virginie?'—the inspector hit a wall. And stopped.

'You?' It was a man, emerging from the third street, there in the mist to her left. Aliette did not pull her warrant card and shout a warning—'Police! Back off!' She only waited, flummoxed, as Jean, the man from the waiting room, approached, haltingly, long stilt-like strides on spindly legs extending under his oversized coat. 'You've been following me.'

'Not following…searching.' Jean stood in front of her, gulping air. For the first time, Aliette realized that he was tall, so much taller now out of his chair crammed in the corner of the stuffy waiting room in the confining space of PsychoDynamo. He'd been running. His brow shone from the exertion, his eyes were wide. She recognized needy eyes. There was a wrong amount of hope there. And fear. He panted, demented. 'And look, I found you! It really is like fate!'

Fate? Men in love always had to say that. Aliette glanced at her watch. 'But your hour isn't over yet. Is it?'

Between gulps of humid, misty air, the man called Jean acknowledged, 'I ran away.'

'You ran away from Gabrielle?'

He nodded forcefully, panting like a dog. Yes! Yes!

She dared to ask, 'But why?... Jean?' Knowing that 'why' would be merely the beginning.

He reached toward her, urging. 'Come!... come on with me.'

'Where?' She made it clear he mustn't touch her.

He retreated half a step. 'I want to show you my gun.'

'You have a gun?

'SIG Sauer SP2022. Just like yours.' A sly conspirator's smile.

Just like mine. 'Is this something you've been working on with Gabrielle?'

His voice dropped a tone, into the confidential. 'No. It's a secret.'

Aliette understood. Giving every last illicit thing into Gabrielle's benighted care would be an irredeemable mistake. This handsome, nervous, almost empty man had resisted. 'Show me.'

'It's not here.'

'Where is it?'

He gestured, This way, and headed off.

The noise around the near corner had disappeared. Aliette peered into the mist, heard nothing, sensed no one. Virginie had retreated. For now. So, instincts shifting, she followed Jean.

He had a secret: a gun like hers. Like Tropéano's? And he desperately needed to share it.

– 45 –
So uncool

Elf kept saying, 'There! Do it!' But Virginie kept insisting she had to get closer.

She had rallied everyone and led them out. Fun!... tracking the blonde bitch, making some noise and Georges's awful singing, hiding, watching her come, splitting, circling, waiting in the next street, leading her in circles. The bitch was looking lost. She'd walked right past them twice.

Then Jean Petitpas appeared. Why? How? It stopped Virginie cold.

This was not how she had imagined it. What were they doing together? The question was too difficult. The gun in her hand was real, the wine and pot in her head were fading. She fretted, unable to decipher it: *Why are they a pair?*... And while she fretted, the others grew bored, began drifting off. Word was going round: party at the lookout on Passage Canterellettes. There was some Pink Ecstasy coming in and people wanted a taste. Virginie heard them muttering, That would be more fun than this...

Elf stayed with her. They were a team. Sometimes.

Jean Petitpas and the woman disappeared at the corner. She and Elf set off again, cautious now, no more game, no more singing, no longer leading; tracking, close, unseen. You could hear their steps sounding on the paving, their muted voices in discussion. Jean Petitpas was talking more than her. Minutes later, from the shadows of a doorway near the corner of Cuvier and Benjamin Franklin, Virginie shook as she took aim. There: the bitch was passing.

Just now, NOW!... with a nudge from Elf, Virginie tried and failed again to pull the trigger.

The pair in the street walked past another open shot.

Elf was frustrated. 'Give me the gun!'

'If you don't shut up ... ' Virginie was sweating, pissed at herself.

Elf wanted to do it, but Virginie insisted this was her special job.

Elf smacked the wall. 'You are being so uncool!'

Virginie turned the gun on Elf. 'Just fuck off.'

'Cool, be cool ... ' raising his hands. Then he snatched it from her hand. 'Safety? ... stupid.'

Elf pointed to the button on the side. Again.

'Right. Sorry.' She *was* being stupid. She told him it was nerves.

And Elf was a like puppy. Before they'd gone another block, she had the gun back in her hand. They circled back a few more streets, found a next position, watched them approaching.

Virginie imagined the distorted lies and idiot dreams he was laying on the bitchy woman. She could hear his voice. She knew she ought to shut it out but could not. Never. She knew that voice too well. Jean Petitpas was messing up her concentration, dragging down her will.

46

PETITPAS COLLECTIBLES

Jean led the way, nodding to himself, deciding something. After two blocks of uneasy silence, he said: 'There's something wrong with Gabrielle.'

Aliette was not sure whether to agree. It could be used against her. 'She's just doing her job.'

'I'm going to show you.'

'Show me what?'

'First we need to get my gun.'

'Where are we going ... Jean?'

'The shop. It's at the shop.'

His stilted, vertical stride was quicker than it looked. Aliette hurried along half a step behind, noting street names as they turned corners, forgetting them before they'd reached the next. She had her phone, if need be. And her gun. *I* am in charge here, she kept reminding herself.

This man had walked out on Gabrielle Gravel and somehow found her in the streets.

Apparently her gun was his inspiration. His breath smelled like vomit.

How to engage? The thought occurred: Did Gabrielle know *why* this Jean had left?

'*Alors* ... Jean, so what are you working on with Gabrielle?'

'Oh,' a tired sigh, 'the usual stuff. Gumption. Responsibility. Focus ... that's important.'

'Yes, it is. Self-esteem?'

'Me? No, it's more about family issues,' he muttered. 'You?'

'More like self-image. Not quite the same.'

'We spend a lot of time on that ... My ex-wife, my kid don't see me right. Both against me: big battles, never-ending war.' His ex-wife and kid provided a springboard to a meandering rant about his plans and projects, important things he wanted to do but never could because the world kept letting him down, the world beginning at home. He seemed honest—too honest. Completely self-absorbed and heedless of saying as much, blithely arrogant, socially awkward. Erratic—but a threat? Hey, Aliette, come on over to my place and let me show you my gun!... Who was this good-looking, weirdly needy, seemingly... *empty* man called Jean? Who claimed to have a gun that she might be very interested in seeing? Was she strolling with a hair-triggered killer with a bizarre need to share?... Before lashing out? She knew it was a common element of the extreme psychotic tendency. Too much was unclear. She remained on high alert.

When Jean ran out of complaints and large ideas, they fell into desultory chat. The change in the weather. The filthy streets. 'Forty-seven thousand. One-twenty...' Quoting the price of every place they passed with an *À Vendre* sign on the wall. 'Two hundred. Dreamers!... Value's dropping like a stone. Sad, sad, sad.' She deliberately mentioned the rising risk, statistically confirmed, of going into these streets alone at night. He grumbled, 'France is coming apart at the seams.'

A sentiment echoed everywhere, most particularly in a serial killer's quasi-cryptic notes.

'Here,' said Jean, stopping, gesturing.

Objets de Collection Petitpas. She beheld a Second Empire sitting room recreated in the shop window. A dull feeling invaded. 'I don't think I've ever been by here.'

'We've been here for a hundred and fifty years.'

'You are Monsieur Petitpas?' A dull feeling spiked with a twist of dread.

'I am.' His eyes seemed to mirror it—an instant of dull cold fear gazing back her, before shifting away, as if his very name was a lie. With a shopkeeper's ceremonius bow, Jean Petitpas ushered her inside.

'See anything you like?'

Nothing. Old things. Tea and coffee services, champagne flutes. Faded prints of people long forgotten. If anything touched a chord, it was a cluster of porcelain figurines on an old side table, the tin soldiers lined up on the next. Tools for the World Technique. Did Gabrielle Gravel shop here? Aliette made an absurd show of browsing, instinct screaming, Do *something*. Call Sergio, at least!

'Tea? Or wine?' He stood by a door to the back area. His awkward presence did not balance. He seemed as adrift and out of time as all his useless things. He seemed crazy.

Indicating no to the drink, she said, 'Your gun, Jean.' She had to see it first.

'Of course.' There was a ladder on wheels against a wall of drawers, hundreds of brown wood slots, none marked. Jean Petitpas rolled it, climbed, removed a certain drawer, came down and placed it on the counter. The gun was lying in an oil-stained tea towel. 'Exactly like yours.'

Yes, SIG Sauer SP2022. PROPERTY OF THE STATE etched into the slide. A police gun, just like hers. Tropéano's? Petitpas smiled weirdly. Aliette slid her hand inside her coat, telling herself she should make an arrest and end it. It took a moment to realize he was smiling because he was proud of his gun. She offered only an appraising nod. 'Where did you get it?'

'Oh, I picked it up,' he replied, suddenly cagey. 'Just the other week. Been looking, got lucky.'

'Lucky?'

'*B'eh*, I always wanted one. Finding one's the trick. No?'

She challenged, 'If you don't speak the truth, this can't work. Jean?' She meant, you and me.

He agreed. But his eyes slid sideways.

She added, 'Guns are truth shaped to fit the hand. Eh, *monsieur*?'

He nodded knowingly. 'Everyone wants one. If they ever change the stupid law, I know what I'm going to do with the store.'

Petitpas Guns. New, Used and Otherwise…

'And so?' Seductively low, quietly encouraging.

'I bought it from a guy.'

'Which guy?'

'No idea.'

'Here?'

'In a bar…well, out behind. It was actually the night you first showed us yours.'

She hoped that was the truth. Difficult to read this man. 'You go to the bar after Gabrielle?'

'Can you blame me?'

She shrugged. No, not really. She said, 'They're not going to change the law.'

'Don't be so sure… It's just politics. Not the bible… It's what people want.'

Aliette did not respond. She heard movement on the other side of the door. 'Who's that?'

'Just Solange…' He asked, 'You work for the State?'

She dodged. 'Not just now.' Strictly speaking, true.

He grinned at her and confided, 'I don't want to come to Gabrielle. I have a court order.'

She assessed this. A court order. There was obviously more than met the eye with Monsieur Petitpas. 'So do I,' she lied, but not exactly.

'I thought so. We can work together.'

'Maybe… So? Better tell me now.'

'We have to free someone.'

'From prison?'

'From Gabrielle… She has him hostage in her basement. There's this sandbox, it's huge.'

Before Jean Petitpas could expand on that—she knew. 'You know where he is?'

He nodded, complicit and thrilled to be. 'She's done something to his head. Who is he?… He never told me his name.'

She responded with a vague and leading shrug. 'A friend.'

'Does that mean you're working?'

Aliette held his eyes. 'I'm not supposed to be.'

'Brilliant!' Jean Petitpas was smiling broadly, the pieces falling into place as he pulled his coat back on, took the gun from its bed in the drawer and put it in his pocket. *His* pieces, self-selected for the sandbox in his mind.

Brilliant? She blanched, unsure if she should disabuse him of his fantasy. Could he really lead her to Vincent Spanghero? The man was hard to read. Ingenuous, far too eager; then, on a word, the edgy, shifting eyes. Psychopath? Or harmless dreamer?

… Make that harmless dreamer with a gun. And a court order.

Aliette was badly wanting to make a call, summon help, but she had to ride it out.

'Jean?' A whispery voice. A woman stood at the door to the rear, clutching her bathrobe tight to her throat, cream on her face, sleepy and worried. 'You had me scared. I thought it was her.'

An enquiring look at Aliette. Who obviously wasn't *her*.

'It's all right, *chérie*. This is … my associate.'

The woman timidly acknowledged the guest. '*Bonsoir.*'

Jean cut off any niceties. 'I have to go back out. Everything's fine. Go back to bed. Please.'

She did not look too assured. She pulled the door shut. Turned a key.

'My ex-wife scares her.' Jean was vexed, but focused elsewhere. 'Come on! Let's do this,' he commanded, as if heading out on an operation like a hardened gun for hire. Or his idea of one.

'Right.' Aliette followed him back into the street.

47

NOT AN EXACT SCIENCE

Is my mistake with Em? Or the environment we have fashioned here?

Gabrielle Gravel did not normally practise group therapy. Scenarios enacted in the sand were filtered through a client's individuated imagination. But Gabrielle was highly attuned to group dynamics, which is another way of saying social interaction, as she guided clients through the micro world of their sand. You had to be — if you wanted to send a person back into the world in a halfway functional mode. On the strength of Emma's progress, Gabrielle now saw her waiting room as an effective staging area between the world and her office, which in turn was a portal to the sand.

While Emma attended to the putrid mess on the office floor, Gabrielle sat in a waiting room chair puzzling over a year's worth of notes. Psychology was not an exact science. There would always be mistakes. She had made a mistake, that was clear. The problem was defining it.

Was it the gun? Or the Chief Inspector?

Vincent Spanghero had brought *his* gun into the grouping — with no problem.

Vincent had had no effect at all on the Tuesday-Thursday grouping …

Placing Emma in the receptionist's chair had been an almost whimsical move (if whimsy can be born of deep frustration verging on desperation) but it had appeared to be working. Em had held her ground with Gabrielle's clients, the pure strain of it forcing her out of her shell. The strain was hard, but good — exercise for the soul with the goal of building willpower. Reacting, bitching, enforcing the rules about space and boundaries, giving them a piece of her mind, Emma was making progress, albeit on a crude level. Of course, the rules were arbitrary—but Em needed them. And they did no harm. And a whim had turned into an interesting, even innovative idea. The Tuesday-Thursday evening grouping was the deliberately constructed flashpoint: Emma, Jean and Virginie, the shattered Petitpas family regrouped in a quasi-controlled environment. Judging it safe, Gabrielle had arranged it with the social workers, and used her connections in the court system to secure it. Jean and Virginie had to attend or face the court. There was no divorce because Em refused—'in our family we believe in marriage!'—but Jean, branded an unreliable provider by a long parade of social workers, was legally obliged to contribute to the upkeep of their daughter—herself on the very edge of being deemed a ward of the state. Their case files were transferred into the care of Gabrielle Gravel. A Family Systems program built around the World Technique, with the waiting room experiment tacked on.

Gabrielle expressed big hopes for Em and set about drafting a case study she would submit to a respected journal, to be reviewed by a jury of her peers.

Too much? Emma had been gaining ground dealing with strangers—clients she would never know. Faced with her own family—the monstrous Virginie, whose main emotion was contempt, a gormless Jean who no longer 'believed' in her—Em's progress ground to a depressing halt.

The Friday family sessions painfully confirmed it. Em sat there dumbly and got beaten up.

Gabrielle Gravel wanted the waiting room to work for Emma and her family. And for herself. It was not an exact science, but there was a logic to the concept. She had invested energy and credibility. She looked to improvise. She reasoned, *If Emma can do well with strangers, let's put strangers back into the mix.*

But who? A certain type. To fit the grouping.

…They kept sending her these damaged police to fix. It was always a challenge matching them to a grouping. Every client's damage was unique to his or her personhood. That was a given. But in Gabrielle Gravel's experience, the stress level police brought when they first presented was on a different level than most other people's.

Understandable, if difficult—they lived in a different world. They brought anger, hard walls constructed to protect their humanity, the resulting deep isolation, abiding trauma. That was Emma Petitpas in *her* world comprised of Jean and Virginie.

In the waiting room Em had proved she could exert her fragile will. She had rediscovered courage, regained some confidence (if not grace) through strangers. Yes, it was solid logic based on *in-situ* observation. It was worth a try. Gabrielle wrote, *If we want movement, we shift the balance, we alter the dynamic in the room.* Dated last spring, the week they consigned Inspector Vincent Spanghero to her care.

Gabrielle assigned Vincent his hours between Jean and Virginie. On paper, Inspector Spanghero was a disaster—a hard and violent man burdened with a dangerously heightened sense of self-importance and a building paranoia stoked by (and which deepened) his anger and feelings of victimization and isolation. But he wasn't Emma's family. And he was trained in rules, and (still lacking personal grace) rules were Emma's life blood. If Em could confront a tough and miserable policeman and make him toe the line like she did moaning Madame Dormevil or nervous, chattering old Gerte, or so many of the other clients she had succeeded in confronting—the person in the chair beside him (her man; her child) might feel that strength in Em. And begin to respect it? There was a resurgence of hope for the project.

Vincent had presented as ordered... Then sat there like a lump, twice a week for five months, discreet if not polite, responding in monosyllables to Jean's prying gambits, impervious to Virginie's volatility, unmoved by Em's resentful misery, awaiting his appointments. To be sure, once through the office door, this policeman submitted to his program with minimal resistance and achieved some astounding results in the sand. He had turned his life around completely, Gabrielle believed, and moved on to a new level of sand (as she liked to say). But as a catalyst to progress in the waiting room, Inspector Spanghero had proved a total *nul*.

No frisson, no movement...

Vincent was released from his program in late June.

Gabrielle Gravel was left feeling just how inexact her science was—inspired by her success with Vincent Spanghero but discouraged by the experiment conceived for the benefit of Emma

Petitpas and her family, and, absent a next police officer, uncertain how to proceed.

…Not at all sure any of her other clients could deal with Virginie.

The Petitpas family languished in their unlivable status quo stasis until Christmas…Tuesday and Thursday evenings were frustratingly quiet out there in the waiting room—leave aside Virginie's eruptions. A wife who refused to give an inch and was too scared to take one; a husband who blamed his life on her. Then Emma went into her dark slide. Then they sent along another cop and where else to put her but into the Tuesday-Thursday evening mix.

She was the exact opposite of Vincent Spanghero: a healthy and by any measure successful woman, independently minded, if idiosyncratic—but interesting for that, after all the ordinary and ordinarily damaged souls passing through Gabrielle Gravel's domain. Indeed, not so much a damaged cop as one at odds with the rules and tools of her trade. There was a difference, even if a *psy* could not risk putting herself at a professional disadvantage by admitting as much to her client. So of course this woman fought back when Gabrielle tried to do the job she'd been hired to do: help Chief Inspector Nouvelle come to terms with the fact of her gun. And no big surprise that the inspector would complain about being subjected to the likes of the Petitpas family. Only a damaged person would willingly acquiesce to a damaged environment.

But she was police. And she was not afraid of Virginie. Perhaps the presence of this cop might bring the desired result in Emma's waiting room?

Barely two weeks into the Chief Inspector's program, Em, clearly in the grips of something serious enough for her to intimate that she is 'bad,' adds a blonde to her sand tray; and Jean rushes out, feverish, ill, seized by a passion for the client known as Aliette directly following a violent altercation with Virginie in the waiting room resolved by the client's gun.

Gabrielle Gravel sat pondering the ramifications. Jean Petitpas had a sorry history of provoking Emma's jealousy. Em's flimsy defence was to ignore it, to put it beneath her. Not useful, but Em was not the first wife to retreat to this strategy. So now Em's rectitude had been shattered by a blonde in the waiting room. A blonde with a gun.

On the other hand, if Jean was going to fall in love with anyone, it was supposed to be with *her*—after all, Gabrielle was his therapist, his guide and partner in personal salvation.

When transference happened, a professional dealt with it according to the moment, the client, her professional instincts. And so: could *she* be jealous? No ... No? No! Absurd.

Sure, the woman was probably attractive in her own way, Gabrielle supposed. Men saw what they wanted to see. Aliette. Not only had she wielded her service arm, she had shared her name.

Jean Petitpas was clearly desperate to know more about her.

But the inspector: how would she react to such a—

From Gabrielle's office, Emma wailed, 'I hate this! Hate it! Hate it! Hate it!'

Gabrielle pulled herself up, looked in on Emma, down on her knees scrubbing up Jean's vomit. 'Life takes a long time, Em. We can't stop now, my dear.'

'And I hate you!'

'I know, I know ... We're getting there, I promise.' Emma's agony was heart-wrenching. Gabrielle stroked Em's quaking shoulders, prayed for patience, then returned to the waiting room chair. And her mistake.

Jean Petitpas would come back, to sit in front of her with his failed life, to work at his issues in his sand. He had a court order—he had to. Chief Inspector Nouvelle was also compelled to attend. But in the meantime? Officially speaking, what Jean did when he left the premises was not her responsibility. But it was. Gabrielle Gravel had arranged for Aliette Nouvelle to be part of Jean's life, twice a week for the foreseeable future. And had hoped she would be. Somehow.

But love?

She feared more for Jean than the inspector. Where was he going, and in such an agitated state of mind? Would he follow her home? She had said she was in a relationship. With a man, assumed Gabrielle. But who knew? She almost laughed at the possibilities: An impulsive, ineffectual and irresponsible man in thrall to heroic fantasy; and a narcissistic cop with a gun strapped to her side which she had fulsomely displayed and recklessly used despite herself—as she herself had insisted. Gabrielle could not laugh. It wasn't funny.

Jean was asking for trouble.

And Em was tearing herself apart. Gabrielle called gently, 'Nearly done, pet? I'd really like to close up and go home.'

Emma moaned. Gabrielle was at a loss. Never an exact science. It had been a trying day.

- 48 -

THE ROOM AT THE END OF THE GARDEN

Chief Inspector Nouvelle and Jean Petitpas emerged from a warren of streets onto a small square. She realized they were passing Église Saint-Aphrodise, scene of Tropéano's murder. She watched him. He did not even give it a glance, nattering on about himself and about sharing time with the man in Gabrielle's waiting room the previous spring. 'Second slot, Tuesday-Thursday, after the girl. Like you. We talked a bit. I was amazed, he's so much like me.'

'Like you.' She was amazed at his presumption.

'People weren't recognizing him.'

'Recognizing him?'

'*B'eh*, for what he really is.'

Yes, that was Vincent Spanghero. 'But what is he really, Jean?'

'He never mentioned what line of work he was in.' But Jean Petitpas was adamant: it didn't matter if he never knew his name or what he did, it came down to the essentials of a man. 'I could feel it. The world was against him. Getting him wrong. Just like me. I felt for the guy.'

Leaving the derelict church behind, they re-entered the dim maze. Before they'd gone a block, Aliette felt a third presence. Virginie? She caught a glimpse of a face… Then it was gone.

She had to concentrate on the man beside her. 'Yes, and so?'

'You could see she was turning him into a sort of ghost. Gabrielle. It scared me… I can feel her taking me to the same place. Every time I sit in front of her. Like she's slowly but surely hollowing out my soul. You know?'

'Mm.' Aliette could honestly say she did.

'We're prisoners. The girl will fight it, but me?' Jean was grim. 'I try to keep her guessing with all my cats and dogs, but I can't hold out much longer.'

'Cats and dogs?'

'In my sandbox. I've got dozens of them, and they're all a little part of me. She thinks.'

'Ah.' Good strategy. Aliette made a mental note. 'But that receptionist—what's her problem? All she does is scream and cry. Never smiles. She won't even tell me her name.'

'It's Emma. She's in pain, a total mess. Afraid of her shadow, afraid of everything…' He sniffed. 'And her mouth hurts.'

'Poor thing. But I can't understand why Gabrielle would hire such a person. You'd think she'd want someone who calms a person down. I mean, it's not exactly easy walking in there to start with. It's almost perverse.'

Jean Petitpas jolted to a stop. 'But Emma's not *hired*. Working Gabrielle's reception desk is part of Emma's program.'

'Emma has a program?'

'Of course. Not that it's working… Some big experiment. We're all part of it. Like mice. So was he, I guess. Your friend. Maybe you are too?'

'I'm not allowed to ask about anything but me.'

'No, and we're not supposed to get too friendly in the waiting room. But he felt like my friend too. I liked him, but he kept withdrawing, quieter and quieter with each passing week, fading like… Then he stopped coming. I suspected something. So I followed her.'

'You followed Gabrielle?'

'I saw. It's horrible. Perverse is exactly right. You'll see.'

Aliette could hardly wait. Jean set off again. She hustled after.

'But what kind of experiment?'

'I don't know. It's for Emma, to help her get her head together.'

No, whatever the *psy* had in mind for Emma, it didn't seem to be working…

Jean took some turns she didn't recognize and suddenly they were coming out the far side of the quarter and crossing Boulevard D'Angleterre. Where he halted. 'Here.'

They were at the top of Sentier du Four-à-Chaux, a city stairway descending the steep ridge to the Pech des Moulins quarter. The stairs ran down between a school offering professional-stream tech programs and the garden wall of an old and elegant residence. Aliette had passed the place before, curious, but the entrance was protected by an imposing gate fifty paces up the boulevard, and the garden wall was twice as tall as she, probably embedded with shards of glass.

She followed Jean Petitpas down the stairs.

The wall along the end of the garden ran parallel to the stairs, growing higher as the stairs descended. Jean stopped just where a climb onto the stairway handrail would allow a man of his height to grasp the edge of the wall and haul himself up in relative privacy. Which is exactly what he did, ungainly but efficiently. Then, stretched on his belly, he extended a hand to her.

She hesitated. 'Is there glass?'

'Just be careful.'

She allowed herself to be hoisted. She felt the strength hidden in his spindly arms.

The shards embedded in the stone ledge were large, but time and weather had rendered them smooth, not so threatening. Nevertheless, taking no chances, Aliette very cautiously placed her bottom. And surveyed: the garden was long, forty metres or so, lined with small trees. At the far end: a pool, a terrace, a large room at the base of the house that appeared to be a conservatory—glass ceiling and walls extended onto the terrace. There was someone inside the glassed-in room.

A man... Was he naked? It was unclear what he was doing. 'What's going on in there?'

Ignoring her, Jean lowered himself in the cover of a garden shed, then helped her down.

They crept forward through a small orchard, a dozen trees, carefully separate, long nurtured, still barren save for the two olives. Thanks to picnic treks with Sergio, the inspector could now recognize a peach, a fig... cherry, apricot... she thought one might be a lemon. Turned flower beds and cut-back shrubs lined the perimeter. This would be a charming spot six months hence.

From ten paces she saw Vincent Spanghero. She had only seen photos of him, but she knew it was him. He was drastically slimmed down. And his head was now shaved and it shone with an oily luminescence under the soft light within. And yes, naked.

He was squatting in a large sandbox. Pushing a stick. A small rake?

Gesturing at the odd scene, Jean whispered, 'Have you ever seen anything so pathetic?'

Aliette could not answer. She did not know what she was seeing. Not exactly. Indeed, there was a zoo-like quality to the strange tableau in the glassed-in room. A snake in a terrarium.

Jean Petitpas had his gun drawn. He shuddered, transfixed. 'I don't want to be that man.'

'No.' Vincent did not look happy. Neither does that captured snake.

Aliette felt a bemused sympathy for the shopkeeper crouched beside her. His imagination was boiling over. Did Gabrielle Gravel know she inspired such fear? Whatever his problems with the world, whatever damage he may have been inflicting on his ex-wife and child, this Jean Petitpas could never be Vincent Spanghero. Different world, different beast.

… but did Gabrielle inspire murder? Aliette Nouvelle was out of hunches. She could not fathom how this bizarre revelation connected to the knife Nabi Zidane had given to Vincent Spanghero, which had led to the murders and left a trail to Tropéano's gun.

Perhaps Vincent would show her. Everyone was sure he was the killer.

She waited, crouched in the damp darkness, watching an ex-cop's ruminating explorations with his child-sized rake. Like a brooding painter with a brush.

49

GLASSED-IN MAN

Gabrielle has taught him to try to be in the present moment. The past is broken and gone. As for the future, you have to build it but first you rebuild yourself and you do that here within a world that will move with your spirit, your imagination, a world that can be re-felt and reconfigured each and every day. Each now? Now repeating and repeating. Now here in a warm solarium, warmed to body temperature, naked in a life-sized sandbox. No more toys and bibelots. Only rocks, stones, sand. The idea of water, the values of wind. The light of day and the dim, calm glow at night. His reflection in windows on three sides. His hands. One tool. The wooden rake is rudimentary, crude-seeming, till you learn to use it. The white sand is simple and clean. Vincent pulls the rake ... then pushes it, building a swell like waves in the river in the evening wind.

Fishing is a good thing and he will get there. In the spring he'll return and test the air.

'You live here in the *now* for a year,' said Gabrielle, 'you'll never have to go back *there* again.'

It was a challenge. An offer. A plea of a sort ... And she knew it wouldn't be forever.

'I will look after everything. All you have to do is do the work. Mm?'

There. They'd spent much time talking about *there* as he'd pushed and placed the objects in the small tray filled with sand. And in the painted water underneath it, his dreams, she said, because he went there too sometimes—without even thinking. *There* equals his assumptions, expectations, his anger. Moving forward, he knows his life is dependent on channelling the anger into a time-free environment. Anger got the better of him one too many times. Those assumptions. Expectations. Past and future: broken past, wrong future. Gabrielle has helped him grasp this. He regrets Menaud Rhéaume. He regrets Nabi…

But Menaud is dead and you can't change Nabi. Gabrielle has helped him accept this.

The only way past it, she said, is through the present and out the far end.

She offered the tools and thoughts with which to effect an absolute change in himself.

Vincent needed everything she offered. Including herself.

It will not be forever because nothing is. Said Gabrielle.

There is no guilt in the present tense. Not if you hone it to essentials. Vincent is seeing this.

Would these things be possible in the house on the corner down the hill? He can't see that. His wife would laugh at him. But she would be laughing at a different man, a man she doesn't know and never will. Catherine seems… primitive now. His children would be baffled, probably to a dangerous degree. Vincent does not want to alienate any more people. He only wants to do this thing. To see where it takes him. He hopes it's back to the spot by the river in the Tarn. He will aim for there. He will see. The thing of it is: to keep it simple.

There's a stone here, one there. They are like a door.

Four more in configuration by the long bend in the river. The river in his mind's eye.

The sentinel stone rises behind them. It feels… beyond words.

Voilà. That's the goal, says Gabrielle.

When there is wind out in the garden, Vincent will mirror it, raking wind through the sand.

It feels exquisite, the fine line dividing breakdown tension and uncontrolled fury *there* from *now*, this far side of the soul, a place of observing, of minimal movement inside a design flowing from a feeling that will last till the very last day. This *is* the very last day. This is the only day. The only world. But you have to work on it.

He reads. He senses. He moves stones, adds stones, removes others, rakes the sand. Mulls.

In the afternoons the sentinel stone absorbs the sun but shares some of it, casting a shadow on the sand. The shadow on the sand is a cloud on the solarium window when the sky outside is clear. It can be a miracle. It's not always satisfying. Not *right*. But *wrong* is now an absorbing puzzle that takes all day.

Now is a puzzle, says Gabrielle.

When the night comes to the garden on the other side of the glass, then it is only here, this room, this space of white sand in dim light, and himself reflected, if he cares to notice.

Until Gabrielle joins him, naked as he. She is always interested in their reflections.

Vincent is not sure if he is being *spiritual,* a word Gabrielle uses probably too much. He feels it as a physical thing. He is a physical man and this is how he survives the burden of himself.

He has lost track of the days, but he can see the weather. A mimosa in her garden is getting ready. The garden goes to the concrete walls. Over the western wall and down the hill is the place he used to live. Whatever may be happening outside the garden walls no longer matters to the glassed-in man. He has taught himself not to be curious.

Gabrielle helps. There is no television in the reading room, no radio in the kitchen. There is a computer on her desk, but that's her room. It sits there like a proxy challenge if he happens to stop at the door during the course of a day. Ignoring the telephone is the easiest part. Now the ring of phone is just an occasional sound in the air. And Vincent knows it's not for him.

Still, he tests this new personal zone. He needs to know, to feel the limits. Gabrielle knows this. Barriers, she calls them. And he needs exercise, of course—exercise is basic food to a basically physical man. So he walks through the city at night, late, when there are fewer faces, but enough. He passes police scenes—collisions, robberies, rapes, domestic abuse, suicides, gang warfare, and murders. The gamut. No changes there, except the names, the bleak parade. He probably knows many of them, and he could know for sure in a minute. He resists asking because it doesn't matter who they are in the particular. More names, same place, same situation.

For what it's worth, Grabrielle brings him the latest news. Apparently there's a maniac out killing street kids. Sad news, but not worth much. Not new. We learn nothing. Good luck to Nabi and the guys. Go for it, boys! Fix this stupid world!

... For his part, Vincent now walks away from knowing who and why, and that is amazing, not to say a point of pride. 'Pride is a difficult thing to lose when you're made like me,' he has confessed to Gabrielle.

'But you can turn it a different way,' she said.

'Which way?'

'Inside out.'

Gabrielle is right. Vincent's so-called pride was always centred in other men's lives, which is absurd when you think about it—and Gabrielle has made him think. Now Vincent looks for things that last longer than the contemporaneous flux. Other men come and go from a life. Any face in the street will tell you that the world outside this warm room never changes much, and when it does, is it ever good? France is not improving.

Vincent feels he is improving. He feels a quiet pressure inside himself and he believes he is.

He moves stones, adds stones, takes one out, rakes the sand.

The phone rang. That would be Gabrielle, if it wasn't her mother. Vincent let it ring till it went to message. He was deeply immersed in his sand.

... A while later, it rang again. And despite all breakthroughs and severed ties, some instincts abide in the ringing of a phone. It had to be Gabrielle. She never called, no one else did either, not at night, not even her mother—Vincent knew her patterns and rules by now. It must be important. He left the sand, naked as he was, and went up the stairs to the phone.

50

A HOLE IN HER CONTROL

Gabrielle forced a smile. 'All done, then?'

Emma was beside her, hovering. Those sour eyes, that unfortunate mouth, poor Emma with her pain. 'I'm leaving.'

'See you tomorrow.'

'I mean, I'm leaving. It's finished. I can't do this anymore.'

'I understand.'

'No, you don't!'

Gabrielle watched Emma struggling into her coat. It was out of style, starting to look a little stodgy. Two identical down-filled greatcoats, his and hers from the 3Suisses catalogue, had been Emma's last pathetic attempt at bonding her gorgeous sad-sack hubby's soul to hers. Matching coats were not enough. Love fell by the wayside, pain went on and on. 'You don't want to talk about Madame Nouvelle? Her gun? Jean? Virginie? It's been quite a night.'

A defiant scowl.

'No? I think you do, Em. I think you must.'

'It's disgusting. A child should not have to be exposed to such things. I won't be part of it anymore.'

'But Virginie will.'

'Not if I can help it.'

'I totally agree.'

Emma left without a word.

'Good night, Em.' Gabrielle spoke to the door.

… They'd work on it when Em came back. She would come back. They all came back. Clients became addicted to their pain. They depended on their pain for meaning. Emma needed Gabrielle. And Gabrielle cared for Em.

But Gabrielle could get tired too. She did not expect her clients to notice, much less care; but she could worry like any other human being. She had her own interests to protect.

Gabrielle Gravel could live with a mistake because a mistake could be corrected.

Gabrielle could live with competing impulses. She was not a machine.

But Gabrielle hated doubt, the more so when doubt rode on trust.

When he'd first come to her, Vincent Spanghero was not a happy man, but then none of them were. Gabrielle vividly remembered the moment. Vincent: a strong man defeated by a surfeit of himself, spirit flattened by guilt, sad, burned out, a sorry sight.

Docile. Mechanical in his responses. But he responded...

Then gradually interesting as they'd got on with the work.

When it was apparent they had gone as far she could take him in the toy-sized sandbox on her desk, it was time to send him back into the world. Vincent had transformed his heart's fall-back position from volatile to stoic. A stoic warrior. Accordingly, he had shrugged stoically, prepared for the eventuality. But he was not interested in returning to the world—not the world he'd come from. It was clear to Gabrielle Gravel. And in fact he had nowhere to go except a cabin by a river in the Tarn. He had given notice at the pension where he'd been camping since moving out of his home. An outsized soul given to drama, Vincent had cut ties with everything.

Gabrielle Gravel saw this transformed man as a testament to her skills. And a window to a next level of personal achievement. His? Or her own? The night of their last scheduled session, she offered Vincent Spanghero new purpose—and the guidance to attain it, personal training toward a different level of sand. It was not offered heedlessly. She counselled clients on the notion of boundaries every day. Gabrielle knew—because she knew herself; the training demands it (and yes, she had heard certain colleagues talking)—that she had her own issues concerning boundaries. But as she told certain other colleagues she trusted (e.g., a smiling *psy* from Alsace), if you did not challenge the odd boundary, breakthroughs would be far and few between. She believed (she knew!) the culture was changing, which meant the human condition was too. The profession badly needed breakthroughs if it was to remain a relevant source of spiritual care, not to mention psychological exploration.

Which is why Gabrielle had signed all the forms, let him peruse her report and officially ended Vincent's program before proffering the notion of personal training and giving him a piece of very unofficial paper with a scribbled address. Whether feminine intuition, or a creative healer's glimpse of the next level, she was prepared to live with competing impulses. Was he?

The next day he'd appeared at her door—her private door on Boulevard d'Angleterre, the door to a house protected by a three-metre wall. With a woeful, warrior-like gesture (*Ave atque Caesar, those about to die...*), Vincent committed. Not forever. For a year.

She received his commitment, had looked into his eyes, seen strength and strength of will.

Their relationship was not love. They both knew that.

No, Vincent was not a happy man, and never would be. But anger can be channelled. That had been the main thrust of their work together, as mandated by the people who had run his life. The work had been a big success. But stripped to essentials, the man was still an extreme personality, Gabrielle had no illusions of ever changing that. Trust? There were no perfect human beings. His life was his own and Gabrielle knew better than most how a man could hide a malignant secret. Most were tiny, ugly, deeply cached. One came upon these foibles and faults, one forgave. Or one sued for divorce and moved on. Gabrielle Gravel could reference her own unregretted Gilles. Pathetic. Gone... Vincent was not Gilles. He went out each night when it was dark, to walk, to breathe, when it felt safe from a city filled with eyes. She couldn't stop him. Why would she try to? Gabrielle was no one's mother. She was not his wife. She was his guide for a year in the sand.

What the blonde inspector suggested was intolerable. It went past casting doubt on the integrity of Gabrielle's hard work with a difficult man. It left her instinct vague, a hole in her sense of control.

Vincent was suddenly, intolerably, too unclear, his status disconcertingly unknown.

Gabrielle Gravel groaned (a lot like Emma), bending to the weight of doubt. Hating doubt. But there was too much at stake. Laying her notes aside, she went back to her desk and made a call. The phone rang through to message, and two possibilities. Downstairs in the sand. Or out in the street. If he had gone out—then what? Was he fulfilling the violent profile Chief Inspector Nouvelle said the world expected him to? The thought was debilitating.

'Vincent...' What? What do I tell him?

The stress of the moment stopped her thought process. Gabrielle hung up.

There were no rules, no court order. There was a goal to work toward. And trust. Gabrielle and Vincent had built trust in their time together. He *had* transformed his life. At that last appointment, he had told her, 'Guns are an illusion, Gabrielle. I don't need this anymore.' He had pulled it from his pocket and placed it on her desk. And left it there.

...Now Gabrielle opened her desk drawer and contemplated Vincent's gun. The one thing she was certain of: Vincent's gun was here. She touched it, ran her fingers over the *VS* monogram embossed in gold on the plating of the grip. Theatrical. Precious...

Vincent's gun had been a central part of his identity—and he had given it over to her.

But the thing had started with Vincent's knife. They were looking for another man's gun.

It was impossible. But there was this doubt. And Gabrielle Gravel was too much the professional to kid herself: no matter what kind of life he might be living, Vincent Spanghero would always be a certain kind of man. She picked up the phone again. Still no answer. Squeezed by competing impulses, she left a message. 'Vincent, they are looking for you. They think it's you, this person killing people in the streets. They believe you are this poor, sick person. I am praying it isn't true. Is it?'

51

ONE CALL GETS TWO ...

Nabi Zidane popped a tablet meant to calm his stomach, if not his nerves. His wife had him on a strict regime of soup and bread and sleep. Or bed, at least. Sleep was not easy, but the overall effect of nine hours in bed was a net gain in rest, or should be. According to his wife.

The television was off limits, the Internet even more so. 'Read a book!'

'Which book?'

'Any book. Take your mind away from this horrid thing... Please.'

Nabi was already in his pyjamas and under the quilt. He stared at the page. Someone called Houellebecq. He didn't get it. More miserable people. Whatever it was, it seemed ridiculous.

His portable phone vibrated. Yes, well, he had cheated and brought it to bed. '*Oui?*'

'*Écoute!*'

Nabi listened. He knew the voice as well as he knew his wife's or his children's. He did not say a word, but waited as commanded while a machine at the other end of the line was engaged. He heard a woman's voice, low, almost a whisper. Nabi Zidane remembered the voice. He had heard it that very afternoon. She left an urgent-sounding message:

Vincent, they are looking for you. They think it's you, this person killing people in the streets. They believe you are this poor, sick person. I am praying it isn't true. Is it?

The machine was stopped. The voice of the caller was imperious and impatient. 'Well?'

Nabi felt compelled to throw in his hand with the *psy*'s. He repeated, 'Is it?'

'Of course it's not!'

'Where are you, Vincent?'

'Nowhere.'

'They will find you. You've just opened the door ... ' Nabi sighed, glanced warily into the hall for a lurking wife, then corrected. '*We've* just opened the door.' It takes two to make a call.

'Just like old times, yeah?' No nostalgia there. Pure bitterness.

Nabi Zidane refused to bite. 'But I believe you, Vincent.'

No reply.

' ... me, and one or two others. You should let us try to help you.'

Long pause. Big question. 'Why do you believe me?'

'Would you have called?' Chief Inspector Nabil Zidane knew that whatever else, for better or worse, this man did not lie.

Typically, ex-Inspector Vincent Spanghero replied to that with an obstinate order. 'I am nowhere and I am staying nowhere. You will share this call.'

'Nowhere does not exist, my friend, not as of two minutes ago. You should know some people are not interested in sharing this call. They've got what they need. There will be no more communications till it's over. And you know what I mean by over.'

'Bastards.'

'Aren't we all, Vincent?'

'I don't deserve this.'

'Mm, tell me about it.'

'I'll say it once more, Nabs. Record it.'

'I am. So are they.'

'It's not true and it's not my problem. Do you hear me?'

'Loud and clear, Vincent.'

'Now I'm hanging up and disappearing.'

'What, Fishing in Canada? Tarn's a bit close, I guess.'

'Get away from me! All of you.'

'You're a cop killer, man. There's nowhere you can go.'

'*Quel bordel!...quelle merde!*'

Nabi heard the phone crash against a wall. The line was still open. Just like the night Vincent decided to save the world all alone and Nabi kept talking, oblivious, until he'd heard the guns ...

Eventually there were steps. And breathing.

Nabi said, 'Position two... Say, thirty minutes? We'll work something out, I promise.'

The line went dead. Nabi Zidane closed his bestselling book and got out of bed.

Now he had to get past his wife.

- 52 -

PRESSURES OF THE SAFE SPOT

Liza Fratticelli was uneasy, feeling pressure from too many directions as she served Mario Bédard a second bowl of rice pudding to go with his glass of beer. Mario was getting on her nerves tonight, sitting there like a little king in front of his match without a worry in the world—a league game *en retransmission* from New Zealand. If there was a match available, Mario would watch it. But it wasn't his passion for rugby, it was his casual certainty about Nabi Zidane.

Liza had found a safe spot between Nabi Zidane and Vincent Spanghero as she'd worked her way up through the unwritten pecking order of the often unruly Béziers Judicial Police detachment. Safe meant being respected enough to be able to stand up and ask, 'Does this make sense?' and know both of them would hear. Both good cops, very different men. Liza hadn't known them in the earlier days—she'd been a schoolgirl in Sète. But she heard stories. By the time she came on board, they were two veterans who were having trouble being friends, let alone agreeing on tactics. She was always a calming influence and they seemed to appreciate it. They'd both been pleased for her when she'd been promoted up and out, to run the patch centred at Pézenas. Neither was jealous that she now out-ranked them. Neither wanted what she'd been given, not in the least—they were city cops, pay raise be damned. They'd both shaken her hand and given her a kiss in honour of her success. Well done, Liza, *bon courage*!

Though they all still saw each other on a daily basis, they went their separate ways. Because self-preservation looks one way when you are *in* a team, like something else when you are running one, Chief Inspector Fratticelli's instinct for self-preservation made her gravitate to other kinds of men. Three years later, when Nabi got the city job, she was pleased for him. Because she liked him. But it did not make sense, it wasn't right for what the police needed to do, to *be*, not in Béziers, not these days. And so Liza was sad but not surprised at Vincent's unchecked rage.

Liza wished, belatedly, her lunch date with Aliette Nouvelle had ended on a more cordial note. It was not her new colleague's reasoning. There was no doubt in Liza's mind that Vincent Spanghero was killing innocent people—in aid of what, only he knew, but the deranged notes confirmed it. Liza knew Vincent. But she knew Nabi too, and Mario's plan made her nervous.

She had wanted to reach out, not sure for what—some kind of professional support, which was also feminine, sisterly support that might help her ease Mario's implacable certainty?

Aliette Nouvelle's righteous scorn made it impossible. Liza Fratticelli resented the woman's hurtful insinuations. Who knows what her grandfather the mayor would have said? A different life in a different time. Not only was the blonde inspector rude, she was clearly another soft-headed, unrealistic left-wing fool. Not useful. Nor a friend... Liza had passed along the listening device, and retreated. Back to the safe spot.

Contrary to what she might have thought ten years earlier, Liza found she liked being with Mario Bédard. After two bad marriages to men who had no idea what she went through every day, it was a comfort being with a cop. She had heard Julien Lesouple had been down the same disastrous road. So many had... And Mario's was tragic. So now they were together. And they agreed on reality. Liza was no righteous blonde. But Mario's confidence seemed dangerous.

Liza had no more sympathy for Vincent. He was lost. Better off dead.

But Nabi... 'Nabi does not deserve to be hurt.' She meant killed.

'And I wouldn't harm a hair on Nabi's head,' soothed Mario, eyes locked on the action as he spooned his pudding. 'Besides, Nabi's too smart to get hurt, except politically. Which he already is. We're only going to make sure it's once and for all.'

Liza shook her head, Certainty and being realistic were not the same thing. Mario was in thrall to his beliefs. What he saw wasn't wrong. It was the place he saw it from that worried Liza.

He sensed her consternation and looked up—she saw that impatience he sometimes had trouble controlling. 'The plan, Liza?... we make sure Nabi is with the wrong guy in the wrong place and everyone knows it.' He shrugged, dry and calculating. '... The wrong guy is his old partner, our latest serial killer, the once and always Vincent—who will go down, one way or the other, and Nabi's position will be indefensible.'

'One way or the other.'

Mario nodded. He was glad she understood.

But Mario's plan was mostly emotional, Liza knew.

The *télé* caught his attention. 'Look at that bastard run!' Some huge giant with wild curls sprinting away from the pack. Mario was in awe. And rueful. 'It's not fair... France hasn't anyone near that guy.'

Then Mario's cellphone buzzed.

Chief Inspector Julien Lesouple had followed Chief Inspector Nouvelle into the streets again after her appointment with the witch and seen her hook up with some guy who looked like a film star, who'd taken her to some dusty bric-à-brac in Rue de Lorraine. Odd place to go to screw, but not his problem. Poor Regarri, thought Julien. But maybe one in the bank for me... He was heading glumly back to his car when he'd received notification from an ambitious young uniform in the call centre at Hôtel de Police. Vincent Spanghero had just communicated with Nabi Zidane. He in turn called Mario Bédard. 'Looks like this could be our window. Listen.' Julien played the call. 'What do you think?'

'I think Nabi thinks he's so smart,' Mario replied.

'Where the hell's position two?'

'No idea... Just a second.' Mario smiled across the kitchen table. 'Where is position two?'

Liza had been part of Nabi and Vincent's team for a few years, before moving into higher places. 'Position two? *B'eh*...' She was perplexed at Nabi's lack of guile. He was getting careless. Or he had a move in mind... Was she actively betraying Nabi now? He was definitely screwing up her mind. And Mario would not be denied. 'Cemetery. Old cemetery. The gates. Quiet there. Lots of room. Good place to sort things out if we had anyone in the back seat who needed sorting.'

Mario came back to Julien. 'Get that?'

'Yes.'

'Tagged his car?'

'Yes. And his wife's.' Chief Inspector Lesouple happened to live an easy walk from Nabi's place, out in la Devèze quarter. 'But he'll take a cab. I mean he knows. He must, yes?'

'Which is why he'll take his own car. Nabi wants this.'

'Vincent sure as hell doesn't, not if I'm hearing right.'

'Then why call Nabi?'

'Someone scared him. Or something.'

'But who?'

There was a pause as Julien pretended to mull it. Then ventured, 'His *psy*. Has to be her... She knows where he is. I know she does.'

'You know this woman?'

'It's private, Mario.'

Mario hesitated. He was uneasy with people knowing things he might not. 'Fine, private. But four different people have talked to her and got nothing. If she does know, why now?'

'I'm thinking Nabi must have said something to her this afternoon.'

'Nabi?'

'He went in there this afternoon.'

'You don't say!' That made Mario smile. 'Well, Nabi's good at saying things that get people going.' He sipped beer. '... What about our new friend? They have any contact today?'

'Doesn't seem so. Unless he was hiding in the Ladies at the shooting range. She went straight there from lunch with Liza. Maybe looking for him, but he was down at the beach again looking at birds, then he went to see the *psy*. She left the bug on the bar at the range and went to the cemetery, pestering them about the notes. Then she was at HQ searching through the records trying to match some names. Then—'

'Names?'

'On the tombs. Then back to Regarri's. Then off to her thing with the *psy*. She tried his cell a few times, sent an email, but he's not answering. As far as we know, she hasn't talked to him since Friday … I guess Nabi doesn't want to know.'

'She's Nabi's pal. I sent them both a copy of the picture. He won't jeopardize her further.'

'… Unless it was *her* that got that witch to make that call.'

'Whatever, we're covered. She likes it here. She likes Regarri, she won't screw that up.'

'No.' Julien Lesouple was not inclined to share his sordid little revelation as to where the peripatetic blonde had ended up that evening. Some information was his alone. '*Alors?*'

'You stay quiet. I'm on my way in two minutes.'

'Liza coming?'

'We'll see. Give me a call in twenty. I'll find you, we'll get set up.'

Mario cut the call. 'Did you know Julien went to that *psy?*'

'I heard something. He and his wife.'

'Private,' mused Mario. He took one last spoonful of his rice pudding. 'Beautiful!'

Liza nodded to acknowledge the compliment.

'Nabi knew you'd know where position two was.'

'Probably.'

'I wonder what he thinks he's doing here.'

'Just being Nabi. The more of us he can get going in different directions, the better for him.'

Mario acknowledged the wisdom of that. 'So … You coming?'

'I think I did my bit at lunch,' muttered Liza, carrying dishes to the sink.

'You think she'll be there?'

'Don't see how, but it wouldn't surprise me.'

'She can't keep her nose out of it.'

'She's convinced it's not Vincent.'

Mario sniffed. 'Our new girl is fighting windmills.'

'She scares me,' Liza admitted, quietly and frankly. She set to washing up, and confirmed, 'No, I might say the wrong thing.' She took a breath. 'And I'm not sure I want to see this.'

'Fair enough.' Mario wasn't forcing anyone from their comfort zone. 'We'll take care of it.'

He zipped his jacket and gave her a kiss. Liza heard him drive off.

Mario was strong, lucky to be so certain. She wished she could be.

Liza Fratticelli focused on the dishes until she couldn't any longer and threw a plate at the kitchen wall. Goddamn you, Nabi! causing all this trouble. No one hated anyone. They didn't!...she didn't. It was business!

Dirty police business and they had to deal with it. *Point finale.*

Chief Inspector Liza Fratticelli was feeling very alone with the situation. She wished they could have struck a different tone at lunch, she and Chief Inspector Aliette Nouvelle.

- 53 -

UP THE GARDEN STAIRS

The two voyeurs were caught in a difficult silence as the man in the sand left to answer the ringing phone. Minutes passed, he did not return. Aliette eventually rose out her crouch, rubbing aching knees. What now?

Jean Petitpas looked up at her. 'You see?'

She had seen all there was to see of Vincent Spanghero. But it was far from clear.

'And then she makes him have sex.'

'Makes him?'

Jean gazed skyward, embarrassed. 'When she comes home. He's in there playing with his little rake like some demented fool, she comes in, naked as him, he just rolls over and... It's not right. She's done something awful to his head. I mean seriously invaded. You should see.'

Aliette demurred. 'I don't think I want to see that, Jean.' But sensed he was telling the truth.

He stood, drew his gun, tried to sound like a man in control. 'We're going to get him out.'

Aliette tried not to roll her eyes. The gun was real. And it might well be Tropéano's. But the man in front of her was in another world. It added up to dangerous. 'Does he want us to?'

He waved his arm, dismissing the question, the barrel of the gun coming within a millimetre of clipping her nose. 'I'm telling you, he has been in there since June.'

'But he's not in any pain, not that I can see.'

'Pain? She's made him into a goddamn house pet!' He turned, wielding his gun, ready to go.

'Calm...' She put a hand on his arm. 'You want to work with me, I need to know more.'

'What more is there to know?' Jean Petitpas was agitated, confused by her blasé reaction to the scene in the glassed-in room. 'She's dangerous. We'll storm the place and bring him out.'

'Jean … get a grip! Maybe he likes it here. Something different? Every man's big dream?'

He started to move. The calming hand tightened. He spun, imploring. 'He *needs* us. He—'

'Shhh!' Jean Petitpas fell silent as they heard movement on the far side of the house.

A door was opened. Had Gabrielle Gravel returned? Aliette tugged Jean's sleeve, pulling him into the cover of the fig tree. A door was closed. Then steps, the large gate groaning as it was pulled open, pushed shut. It was not Gabrielle returning. Vincent was leaving.

She hissed an order: 'Be. Quiet!' Jean acknowledged. They went up the garden stairs, stopped short of the gate, peered over the wall in time to see him climbing the stairs across the boulevard, his shaved head obscured under a woollen toque, body covered by a long coat. She assumed Vincent Spanghero had put some clothes on underneath.

She surveyed the house. She saw no movement in the upper rooms, no Gabrielle peering out.

'Looks like Gabrielle's hostage has stepped out for an evening stroll, Jean. Off his leash?'

He stared back at her, inarticulate, on the verge of rage.

She waited.

Till he muttered, 'If I thought I could get away with killing her, I would.'

'Would you, Jean?'

He shrugged, losing steam. 'If I knew how.'

'So you enlisted me for the operation. A shopkeeper who wants to kill his *psy.*' She scrunched her face, as dubious as she could make it, pushing for a reaction. Adding, 'And you've been monitoring the situation since June? …Wonder what he'd say about that?'

Jean's face went cold, resentful. 'I'm no pervert … I want to help him.'

'And I don't think he wants to be helped.'

'And I want to help *you* …' insisting, imploring, voice rising in a frustrated whine. 'I need you to help *me*. We're in this together!'

'Are we?'

Hitting back, Jean Petitpas demanded, '*B'eh*, court order, you?'

Aliette considered this fine-boned man with the sleepy eyes. Like a clothes horse who'd just stepped out of a catalogue. The ideal face—but what was behind it? A self-absorbed, messed-up man with a real gun, a fantasy agenda? Or the worst sociopath, devoid of qualms, devious, drawing sympathy with his every word? Her instinct could not settle on a clear read.

Worse, Jean Petitpas had pushed some deeper buttons and hit squarely on her own abiding resentment for the order that had sent her to Gabrielle Gravel … her resentment for the *psy's* systematic attack on entire swaths of cherished identity … deep resentment toward a system bent on making her admit she had lived the defining part of her life all wrong.

The rational side of a calculating cop knew this was a skewed take on it.

But emotionally, she'd been pushed into a corner.

Jean Petitpas stood in front of her, waiting, gun in hand.

While another messed-up man who definitely knew how to kill headed off into the night. Apparently (very apparently) Vincent Spanghero had felt otherwise about Gabrielle. There was nothing irrational in feeling Gabrielle's role in this odd affair was problematic, to say the least.

Aliette gestured at the wall. 'Help me over. We have to keep going. We have to find out.'

Obedient, he put his gun away. He formed a step with his hands. Aliette went up and over.

Gabrielle Gravel did not shout out for the police when she saw two figures climb down from the wall protecting her home and head across the boulevard and up the stairs and into the quarter. She recognized them both. The fact they had been in her garden was one more bit of leverage, if need be. A quick pass through the house sent Gabrielle straight back out in pursuit.

Vincent's gun was in her pocket. She had her own interests to protect.

BRAVE ENOUGH?

Virginie's friend Elf was brave sometimes. Brave enough to lift the gun from Fanny's dead hand, the gun Fanny was brave enough to lift from the hand of the dead dealer at the lookout. How brave was Virginie? It's like a video game but life-sized and slower, so slow she can't really handle it. Waiting, waiting, moving closer. The awful woman and Jean Petitpas have come over the wall of the bourgeois home, they're crossing the boulevard, now they're coming up the stairs, following the man who'd come out of the gate.

Like an auto-prompt, Elf is urging her to shoot.

Virginie takes aim again and tries. But cannot.

Finally Elf says, 'Let me do it if you don't have the guts.'

Virginie snaps at him. 'Fuck yourself! Stop bothering me.'

'Give me back my gun.' He makes a move.

She makes a move—gun pointed at his face. And holds it. This time the safety is definitely off. Elf's eyes dim. Sometimes he's not so brave...

Virginie gives him the gun. They run to the next position.

Here come the woman and Jean Petitpas. Elf gets ready.

Virginie waits. Waits!... and puts a restraining hand on Elf's.

He lowers the gun. 'You want to do this or not?'

Virginie stares. She should say 'sorry,' but she can't, not to Elf. Not to anyone.

Elf prods. 'You never had this problem before.'

'No.' Stealing things at the mall. Rolling drunks. Doing drugs. Turning the occasional trick.

Elf gives her back the gun. 'You know what? That killer Pink coming in tonight at the lookout? Think I'll go check that out. This is your show.'

Virginie could say, 'But I need you!' But she can't. Just can't. It *is* her show, her situation.

'Have fun.' Elf is backing away into the thickening mist.

'You too.'

'You know where to find me.'

'Mm.'

'Don't forget the safety.' A last smarmy tease muttered over his shoulder as he pushes off.

Virginie watches Elf go slouching away. Excellent Pink. Definitely worth checking out.

This isn't fun at all. It *is* her problem. She isn't dealing with it very well.

…as Virginie circles, her hand can't stop feeling the gun, the weight of it, the pull point as she wraps her finger, her thumb fiddling with the safety, carefully, trying to feel it right. Elf has showed her. The safety button. On. Off. Some bullets in the cartridge. Not that complicated, but nerves will mess with your memory, make it tricky. It says Colt 80. Everything on it's in English. Colt like in a cowboy film, she supposed. An American gun. So why is it here? How did that dealer get it? Virginie shivers with the brief thought of a world so large beyond these dirty streets.

One fun thing: Jean Petitpas and his American cop books. If Virginie is brave enough, she'll walk up and show him the gun—after she shoots him. If she's brave enough.

Her mind keeps moving out of focus. Not easy to find the right space.

Virginie follows the blonde bitch and Jean. Scumbag. All his fault.

- 55 -
ON THE WAY TO POSITION 2

Walking through the city unknown and unknowing and not wanting to know had been a new feeling for Vincent Spanghero. Not exactly pleasurable, in fact quite stressful, like something unnatural the first few outings, until he'd finally walked past that and it was actually relaxing, a profound release. No burden of responsibility, no need to be involved. Half a year, a little more? He'd grown used to it. It seemed like half a life. And now this—like he was being sucked back in time, back to his life's square one after all those days and nights within the cocoon of Gabrielle's guidance. Gabrielle's message was a shock. They think it's you, this person killing people in the streets. They believe you are this poor, sick person... The anger had started up immediately, too familiar and overwhelming. Her demand to have her trust confirmed was deeply confusing, at once a challenge and a plea attached to something Vincent had left behind.

The quickest way to Position 2 from Gabrielle's gate was along the boulevard. Responding to fears he thought he had tossed away with the rest of his unregretted career in law enforcement, ex-Inspector Spanghero took a circuitous route. Vincent trusted Nabi, even if he hated him. He knew the man and always would. Nabi would be there, he would come alone. Vincent trusted Nabi to care—which was intolerable. But Vincent trusted Nabi to be honourable and do it right.

Vincent had to be there. Nabi Zidane's soft, ever laconic voice was a vortex drawing him to a meeting at Position 2, mind swirling as the past flooded in too suddenly, too soon.

Far more intolerable than Nabi's maddening good faith was knowing *why* they might be thinking it must be him. Vincent knew them—knew them like brothers—and how they viewed a man like himself. Sure. In his heart, Vincent Spanghero could still hear the ugly words, the incessant complaining, an entitlement he so righteously and loudly claimed had been abused.

Removing yourself from the world doesn't mean you stop thinking.

The point is to think more, Vincent. About yourself, mostly.

He knew he had ruined a delicately constructed harmony at headquarters.

He knew his righteous snit had resulted in the death of Menaud Rhéaume.

Vincent knew nothing of the investigation into the street killings apart from what Gabrielle casually reported, recycling the media-led drama built around savage knifings and the growing spectre of an enraged predator stalking the marginal, the fact that he'd lately upped the ante to cold, efficient bullets. Vincent hadn't wanted to know. That low level of human ugliness was no longer his problem. But *they* suspected him.

In his ex-cop heart Vincent could too easily suppose why Menaud's partner Pierre Tropéano had got caught in the middle of it at Saint-Aphrodise. A bitter cop had disappeared, a cop who spent the final months amongst his colleagues ranting and sulking, needing someone to hit.

Vincent knew he had left behind a mess. He remembered their faces in the lunchroom, tuning out, turning away. Even Liza had given up on him. So angry...no more friends.

He knew they could easily believe poor Vincent would harbour the need to create a worse mess. Spiteful. Why? To show them he was right. So loudly right. Those cops knew him. Their thoughts could easily turn to him. It was a perfect situation. They would be happy if it were him. Happy to dig him out and put him out of his misery, end it once and for all. Now, with one phone call they were closing in—Nabi wasn't stupid. They had the resources, they knew what to do.

Neither was Vincent stupid. But Gabrielle needed confirmation and he owed her that.

At the same time, Vincent could not help thinking, If only they could see me now.

At the same time, he could not help knowing there was no more *now*.

Now was in the sanctuary of a sand garden in a glassed-in room.

Now was timeless days alone in her library, reading those books, learning to be new.

Now was sex with Gabrielle. She had showed him how to make it last and last.

No, Vincent was time-bound again, doubling back, moving sideways, remembering how they would be thinking, anticipating his own emotions when they came face to face. He couldn't know who or how many they were, but he knew they were coming and they would be face to face again tonight.

The cemetery gate was problematic. Vincent was thinking he would go wide and over the cemetery wall and come along to the gate that way. He assumed Nabi would be considering variations of the same circumspect approach. As he skirted Saint-Aphrodise and headed up Rue Gayon, working out his on-the-fly strategy, he wished he could tell his brothers who no longer knew him: *I am a different man now…*

… He would have to cross into the open where Gayon met the boulevard.

It had been a while since he had run…

Vincent's calculations ended at the corner with a sharp blow to the back of his head.

56

PLANET PETITPAS

Vincent Spanghero had eluded them. Whether by design or dumb luck, Aliette couldn't guess. In this maze of bent and disconnected streets there were too many possible directions. She slowed the pace, for safety's sake, in anticipation of what might lie ahead. Jean Petitpas stayed in step. He'd withdrawn into a chastened silence, his plan to storm the house and free Gabrielle Gravel's helpless hostage on hold. Feeling foolish? Certainly unhappy. The inspector felt his trust withdrawn. Jean was wary now, like an animal, continually glancing from the corner of his eye. Unhappy, but following without question, as if he knew she knew exactly what she was doing.

Or what he was doing? Who was this man? Dangerous? Or a passive-aggressive fool?

… Their *psy* would have an answer. Where was Gabrielle when you needed her?

They turned a series of seemingly random corners, walked out onto Place de la Madeleine. It was not late, there were still lots of lights aglow in the bistros and cafés along the perimeter, many citizens out walking. Though none alone. A serial killer remained at large in their city. Ironically, with the soupy mist dispersed to mere gauze in this larger space, and with batteries of strategically aimed lights setting off the church, the *place* exuded a non-threatening postcard warmth. Surveying the scene, momentarily bemused, the inspector found herself wondering in passing, Were she and Jean Petitpas the only two citizens here packing guns? A cop's abiding sense of otherness came into high relief in the public square.

For Jean Petitpas, the open area of the *place* somehow signalled a break in their shared drama.

'So,' he ventured, clumsily casual, 'how did you get into this game anyway?'

'Game?'

'Contracts... Operations?' Code for killing. Professional shop talk.

The more he said, the more he left her floating. She took a breath. 'Love?'

'I can see it... sure I can. I'm glad you didn't say money. Then again, I knew you wouldn't.'

Vexed, Aliette pointedly ignored his blather, directed her steps toward the church.

Rebuffed again—that sidelong look, hurt, uncertain—Jean attempted to bring it back to the business at hand. 'But what will we do when we find him?'

'We'll find out what he's doing stashed in Gabrielle's sandbox and go from there. The first thing we need to do is establish the knife. He'll need to know. So will I.'

'Knife?'

She pounced. '*B'eh*, the knife you found in someone's trash, Jean. A beautiful knife, blue detail on the handle and sheath, bent, very sharp?'

He almost tripped. 'What are you saying?... How did you—? It's not *trash*! I resent that.'

They stopped, faced each other. The hopeful passion beaming from his eyes when he'd come panting out of the mist two hours before had been completely displaced by confusion, if not outright fear. Aliette was not surprised. There was a certain kind of man who reacted before thinking. She surmised many brief passions, like glittery pebbles marking a trail to nowhere in this man's life. 'I'm saying I need total honesty, *monsieur*. If not, we are done here.'

Jean Petitpas did not want to be done. With a guarded shrug, he divulged, 'Found things help me stay in business. You'd be surprised, some of the things I find. That knife was worth a lot of money. But how did you—?'

'I need to know what you did with it.'

Trick question. Basic method. Big answer...

'She stole it. My ex-wife.'

'*Bon*. And she is?'

'Please. This is not about her … She is not well!'

Aliette ignored his pleading. 'What is her name?'

'What do you mean?' Jean was caught short again.

'Pretty simple question, Jean. Your wife—'

'Ex. Divorce or not, she is no longer my wife.'

'OK, your ex-wife. Who is she? Where is she? I need to talk to her.'

Jean Petitpas looked at Aliette as if she'd just landed from another planet. 'B'eh, Emma.'

'Emma …' The ground on planet Petitpas shifted yet again. 'Emma in the waiting room?'

'What other Emma is there?'

'She's your wife?'

'Ex-wife, please. We no longer love each other. We have different goals. We no longer live in the same universe … We are no longer married. She's gone back to her family name.'

'Which is?'

'Sylvestre … Gabrielle says it might help Em validate herself.'

A cop consigned to therapy had to ask, 'Are you serious?'

He misconstrued her disbelief. 'I swear on my mother's grave. Ask Solange. She's terrified. Emma gets into these panics over Virginie, walks into the shop like some kind of angry robot, steals whatever strikes her fancy, I confront her, she says she steals from me because Virginie steals from her. To her, it's all very logical.'

'And Virginie's your daughter.'

'On paper, yes, I guess she is.' Jean Petitpas hung his head.

A cop consigned to therapy stammered, 'I cannot believe …' But hadn't it all been right in front of her? The his and hers coats, the physical size of mama and papa, the size *and eyes* of their angry child; the constant undercurrent of resentment and mistrust, the poisonous silence between two guilty people with nothing left to say … all right in front of her. And hadn't she heard it in a distraught mother's cry of alarm as she'd held a gun to her daughter's back? It was all too clear. Now. 'You're a family.' Family Petitpas.

'More like guinea pigs at this point.'

And so tragic. 'What do you steal from Virginie … Jean?'

'Affection?' His eyes bounced, slid away from hers. 'I've learned to block her out. You have to. She's a monster. But Em can't. It's a vicious circle. The girl's in and out of the house all the time, takes money, food, clothes, anything of value, gives it away to her horrible friends, or they sell it. Em can't do anything but steal from my store. Me, I can't go within three blocks of my own home. Court order…' Seeing a certain look, he blurted, 'No! I never hit her, it's Gabrielle's rule—says Em's too fragile, if we want to talk, it has to be in the waiting room, where she feels safe. So we try but nothing ever changes. When I confronted her about the knife, she didn't deny, it was more like she could hardly remember doing it. She just said it was gone.'

'Gone?'

'She has spells, it's when her anxiety's extreme. She gets so vague. What probably happened is Virginie stole it from her. Or maybe Em just lost it. I don't dare confront Virginie.'

'No. You sit there.'

'Gabrielle advises against it.'

'I'm sure.'

'Gabrielle says that's Em's job.'

Emma Petitpas. Née Sylvestre. 'But Em can't even—'

'But *you* did.' Jean's eyes brightened momentarily.

'That was a wrong reaction. That was—'

'You were brilliant!' The ludicrous fond thing flashed.

'Stop!' It echoed in the square… *Not* brilliant. Automatic. Like another guinea pig? *Putain de* Gabrielle! Aliette's heart was flipping over. 'Why did no one tell me?'

'We don't communicate very well,' admitted Jean.

'But why am I with you? Why me? Why!'

'Fate… it has to be fate.'

'Not you!' Did she scream it? 'Your family! Your sad and broken…' She took a breath. 'Why do I have to be part of your problem?'

His eyes reverted to bleak. 'How would I know? Part of your program?'

Me and my gun problem? It occurred that Vincent Spanghero must have been as well. What was Gabrielle playing at? Could a cop consigned to therapy be blamed for feeling she was being used? But for what? '…Did Vincent ever show you his gun?'

'Who is Vincent?' responded Jean, ingenuous as a child.

Aliette wanted to shake him. 'Vincent is the man you sat beside in Gabrielle's waiting room. The man we are supposedly following. Gabrielle's hostage? My friend?' She patted her gun. 'Stop playing games with me, Jean.'

'I am not playing games.'

'*Alors?*'

'No. He never showed me his gun...' Eyes clouding, shifting. 'He never even told me his name. Vincent?'

'You swear on your mother's grave?'

Jean pleaded, 'Why would I lie?'

Exactly what she needed to know. It seemed Jean's eyes were always clouding, moving the wrong way at the wrong time. Because he knew he was absurd? Or something worse. Could he blithely off-load five murders onto the shoulders of his absurdly dysfunctional wife?

...Ex-wife? Aliette was stuck between this man and the truth. Or a necessary part of it.

She ran a quick inventory of fact and supposition. Gabrielle Gravel had been sheltering Vincent Spanghero. Sex in her sandbox was interesting, if true, but incidental. If Jean's claim regarding Nabi Zidane's long-ago gifted knife had credence, it put at least one person between Vincent and Tropéano's gun, leaving the bitter ex-cop circumstantially in the clear. Jean Petitpas and Vincent Spanghero had shared the waiting room at PsychoDynamo. Jean said they had talked and formed a bond. This was obviously misguided, a figment of Jean's imagining. But Gabrielle's waiting room was not a normal place. Would Vincent Spanghero mention to the weird man beside him that he was putting his life's keepsakes out by the side of the road? Could an insinuating Jean find out which road? Was the knife a bizarre coincidence? Or a lie?

She asked, 'Is it the tomb in the old cemetery?'

'Yes...' Jean Petitpas was boggled, dumbfounded by what she knew about his life. 'We've been there six generations.'

Famille Petitpas. Beside Famille Sylvestre. 'Take me there.'

'You think he went there?'

'Someone did.' Someone was leaving notes there. '...*Allez!*'

Lost, passion shattered, Jean Petitpas grimly led the way.

57

JUST ONE PROBLEM

Vincent Spanghero felt a nasty throbbing in the back of his head. He had felt it before and knew he should move slowly. He carefully opened his eyes. Fog. He blinked. That hurt too.

Mario Bédard moved into focus. 'Vincent. Long time, no see. Looking good, I have to say.'

'Eating better. No more beer. Where am I?'

'Position 2 ... No more beer? But that's insane.'

It hurt to move his head, but a natural need to locate himself impelled Vincent to gaze around. The fog was real, not just behind his eyes. He could just make out the cemetery gate. There were flowers in the window beside him ... He realized he was in the doorway to the old flower shop across the square. Right: Position 2. What about Nabi?

'Nabi's almost here,' prompted Mario, reading his groggy mind.

Vincent blinked, mustering his wits. 'What does he want now?'

Steps. Julien Lesouple appeared, studying the screen on his cellphone. He tapped the screen; '...he's on his way.'

It hurt as Vincent shrugged. 'Nabi's got nothing to do with me. I don't need Nabi. I don't want to see him.'

Mario appeared amused. 'He wants to see you, Vince. A lot of people do.'

Julien interceded with a nervous smile. 'The knife, Vincent?—everything to do with Nabi.'

Vincent managed to smile back. 'What knife, Julien?'

Prompting Lesouple to slap his face. 'The knife you left in Pierre's gut, you fucking maniac!'

Vincent absorbed the slap. Repeated, 'Nothing to do with me.'

Mario grabbed Julien before he could land a punch. And braced him. 'You know, I'm thinking that was you talking to that reporter about the knife.' Julien denied but his eyes confirmed. Mario returned the smack on behalf of Vincent. '*Connard*!'

Julien was mostly brains, not much brawn. He staggered, 'We don't need to do Nabi!'

'We do what we need to do,' pronounced Mario. Then sighed. 'You want to leave, go.'

Julien stood there. He was staying.

Vincent mocked, 'Poor *petit*.' Advised Mario, 'I'd send him home. Doesn't have the balls.'

Julien attempted a kick at Vincent's face. Fending him off with an expert fly-half's stiff-arm, Mario acknowledged this might be true. But remained phlegmatic. 'Everyone's trying fix a problem, Vincent.'

'Sure. And leave it with me.'

A friendly shrug. 'One more won't change anything, *mon ami*.' He pulled his gun and put it to the back of Vincent's head. Just a touch. It hurt, they both knew it. 'There's just one problem.'

'So tell me your problem, Mario.'

'We need the gun. We've been all over your person, practically took your pants off. For some strange reason you didn't bring the gun.'

'I have no gun.'

'Come on, Vincent. You have Pierre Tropéano's gun. We'll need it.'

Vincent was surprised by that and couldn't hide it. 'Why would I have Tropéano's gun?'

And Mario Bédard was disappointed. 'So we'll have to go and get it.' He tapped Vincent's wound. Vincent gasped. 'The gun, Vincent.' Mario truly regretted hurting him. 'Please just tell us where it is. I mean, who needs this pain?' And he tapped again.

Vincent sucked up the flash of pain. 'No gun... nothing to do with this.'

'Vincent...'

'Guns are gone, Mario. Guns are an illusion.'

'Really?' Another tap. 'That was a gun, Vince, and I know you felt it. Yes?... Does this have something to do with stopping beer?'

Vincent had only tears for Mario. 'Nothing to do with it... *rien du tout*.'

Mario said, 'Here's how it is, Vincent. You're going to take a bullet for the team. And for your pain. One little bullet from Nabi's gun, over in a split second, all your pain, all this bad shit, you'll leave behind a better world. You see? And, sadly, Nabi will take one from Tropéano's. Over. *Fini.* Peace and order. So we really need that gun.' Mario laid the barrel back on Vincent's sore spot. Rubbed it gently. 'Where is it?'

Vincent shrugged, bewildered, helpless and in pain.

Julien Lesouple was not as patient as Mario Bédard. He lunged between them, grabbed Vincent and threw him hard against the door. 'Vincent, stop this stupid shit! Where is your gun?'

Vincent's hands were well secured behind his back. All he could do was roll and writhe, pushing his head against the surface of the wooden door where they had propped him. The door redirected some of his pain. '*My* gun?' Looking up, Vincent managed another smile for Julien. 'I left *my* gun in therapy.' He was proud of himself.

'Therapy?' Julien Lesouple had his own sore spot. 'The fuck, Vincent!' He put a fist in Vincent's face and made him bleed, planted a kick in Vincent's side.

Vincent lay face down. Whispered, 'I took my gun to therapy and left it there. Tropéano's gun? That's your fantasy… Kill me now, but that's the truth, you feeble little *connard.*'

'Feeble!' Julien bent and grabbed his collar.

'Stop.' Mario restrained him. 'What is he talking about?'

Julien backed off, fuming. 'That therapist. It's such bullshit… They sent me and my wife to see her. This couples therapy stuff. Weird, weird. Playing in these sandbox things like four-year-olds. Marie came out of it ten times more crazy than she already was. At least the Ministry paid. Eh, Vincent? You leave your gun in the sandbox? That where Gabrielle turned it into an illusion?'

Vincent Spanghero closed his eyes. He felt like sleeping.

Mario Bédard asked, 'Why did they send you?'

Julien hovered over Vincent. 'It's not your business, Mario.'

'Did you sock your lady, Julien?'

He turned, put his hand on his gun.

Mario raised his. 'Oh, stop… Don't worry, I understand. But who's this Gabrielle?'

Julien Lesouple sagged, impotent and miserable, caught in the emotional crossfire of his own anger and fears. 'Gabrielle Gravel. High priestess of witchy fuck-ups...' turning back to their prisoner. 'What?...oh, yes: PsychoDynamo. Great name, eh, Vincent?—for an insane asylum. Sure, Gabrielle Gravel totally sealed the deal for me and Marie. *Me*, I was the illusion. But Marie's the one who disappeared. Figure that one out...' Then Julien sobbed loudly as he stepped forward, planted another shoe in Vincent's lower back.

'Shh!' Mario grabbed him. '...Relax. We can work with that.'

Julien Lesouple wiped tears. 'Work with what?'

'Where is this place?...this shrink's?...Focus, will you?'

Julien tried. He looked up the street, into the fog. You couldn't see the boulevard. 'Not far, ten minutes... How?'

'We'll do this first. Then we go to this Psycho what's-it's place and get Vincent's gun.'

'PsychoDynamo.'

'It has a ring to it.'

'It's just more bullshit.' Julien managed another kick to Vincent's back.

He barely moved.

Mario holstered his gun. 'Doesn't matter. Wear Vince's shoes, it'll fit perfectly: break-in at PsychoDynamo. Then this...' gesturing at the broken man lying at their feet. 'And Nabi.'

'What if she's there?'

'Bad luck for her.' Mario shrugged. 'Still fits.' Muttered, '...even better.'

Julien considered it. He wanted to cry with the man on the ground. 'Sure, we'll do her too. Gladly. Chalk up one more for poor Vincent, totally deranged...' nudging the flaccid form with his toe. 'Lend me your shoes?'

Vincent whispered, 'Too big for you, *mon petit*.' And groaned and seemed to pass out.

'God, you're tough,' said Julien, hating him.

...Hating himself. These men made him feel too weak.

Mario asked, 'Where is he now?' Nabi.

Julien took out his cellphone and opened it, hit some keys. 'Almost at Malbec.'

'Give me that...' commanded Mario, holding out his hand, 'and make it so it stays on Nabi.'

Julien obediently hit more keys. He was wearing a tracker too. With Mario watching—without a clue, Julien knew—he thumped a quick code that would alert the reporter he'd contacted. And a second code linked to a television producer he was thinking of asking out. Mario would not kill anyone if they were here watching the takedown on Vincent Spanghero. All they had to do was show up in time... With another sequence of taps, the map came up.

With a red dot. '...OK, it's fixed on Nabi.'

Taking the device from Lesouple, Mario instructed, 'Just stay calm, keep him quiet, I'll be back in ten with Nabs.' Mario withdrew and quickly disappeared into the mist.

Julien pulled out his gun and stood in the doorway looking down at Vincent Spanghero. Week after week, Gabrielle Gravel had advised him, 'You are playing against yourself here,' and he had told her, in his own way, to go to hell. But she was right, and Marie proved it. And now here he was again, stuck in the middle with nothing but himself. '...You still with me, Vince?'

'I'm here, you fucking feeble *con*.'

- 58 -

IN A MUDDLE IN THE MIST

The muted sound of their steps, the gloomy privacy of a socked-in world of two as they re-entered the side streets where the mist congealed. Aliette could not see twenty steps ahead. Jean Petitpas had started talking again. His passionate impulse had imploded. He maundered on about his unrecognized potential. It was tiresome, oppressive. She felt trapped in his despondency, in a hole that was getting deeper, murkier. He came back to the spiritual cage Gabrielle Gravel was bent on building round his soul. Aliette was sick of it. She cut him off. 'Are we sharing here, Jean?'

'I hope so.'

'Good. Forget your big potential. What is your problem? Maybe you should start there.'

'Well, Gabrielle says I have to —'

'Take Gabrielle out of it. Pretend Gabrielle does not exist. Court orders too.'

'What do you mean?'

'I mean a world without Gabrielle. Just you and your life. Pre-Gabrielle. What is your problem? Can you pinpoint it?'

He moved away from her, silent, considering it (she hoped). She lost sight of him for a dozen steps. Then he was back up beside her. 'My life is not very exciting. I mean, at the heart of it.'

'And you thought I could save your life.'

'A guy like me doesn't meet many girls like you ... Aliette?'

'Were you thinking of sex, Jean?'

That one took longer. He veered away again. She stopped, waited. Unseen, he admitted, 'No, actually. It was your gun. Working with you. Contracts. Operations. The attraction was all there.'

…Reappearing, he added, 'Gabrielle makes me work on that kind of stuff.'

'Which stuff?'

'My impulses?'

So my gun is more interesting than my body. Thanks for that, monsieur…

Aliette bit her tongue, fighting an urge to tell him she was police. Not yet. She was anonymous and had to keep it that way. If there was a darker hand at play, she needed him to show it. She stared into the obscuring grey, forced her thoughts into cover, hidden and waiting beneath the sound of their steps. She felt him waiting for her to say something.

…*Are we sharing, Inspector*? Her turn.

What could she tell him? 'I was a hero once,' she ventured, tentative, whimsical, like a grandmama with a child upon her knee. And I was in *Paris-Match*? No. Aliette Nouvelle would not share that part. She needed to keep Jean Petitpas interested—but no specifics, please.

He didn't challenge. He latched on. Of course. 'What happened?'

'Wrong choices. The rules.'

'You mean rules like a code? Tell me.' He was counting on her. He was needing to know.

'Oh, Jean…' Exasperated. And haunted. Aliette Nouvelle has been here before, exactly here, coaching a doomed man trapped by a code prescribed in dreams, coaching him forward within his heart. Oh, Jacques… Oh, Jean… One famous, one foolish. They were too similar in what they thought they needed, and too easily transferred in the space of one cop's life.

He insisted, 'Tell me!'

Tell *you*? Yes. OK. The one thing she has is hindsight. 'There was this man. An overweight has-been. I went out to get him…and he went out to get me. I won. I was a hero.'

'Of course you won.'

Of course I won. But nothing changed.

…They walked on. She demanded, 'You, Jean Petitpas. Are you brave enough to kill?'

He responded smoothly, 'They say after the first it's not a problem.'

'Perhaps they're right.' What they said made her want to cry.

'I could learn. You could show me how.'

Could I? She thought, What if I have to kill you, Jean? Kill you to show you how?

But he couldn't hear her thoughts, and surely didn't want to.

He wanted more of the story. 'And so what happened? How did it go down? Don't they just send you a name in the mail? An address? A face? The overweight guy—what was it like, face to face, putting him down?'

'What was it like?' Historic... it was historic. But Aliette would not tell Jean Petitpas that, either. What would be the point? 'They gave me a file. The overweight man was a name in a file. Yes, we were face to face. But I didn't shoot him. In the end, I didn't have to shoot.'

'But you were going to. You had him where you wanted him, and you could have. Yes?'

'But I didn't!' Aliette snapped at him. *Mon dieu*!

'OK... OK.'

'And that changed everything,' she felt a need to add. 'For me, I mean.'

'Thanks for sharing.' But Jean Petitpas seemed disappointed.

Well, so was she. Walking the streets, brooding over the mechanics of the soul was one thing; this was the actual wheel coming full circle. 'Why do heroes always have to shoot their way out?'

He was close again, close enough for her to see him cast another wary glance. 'If evil isn't killed, it lives.' Simple.

'A zero-sum proposition then. I win, you lose.'

'Evil's evil,' muttered Jean.

'Evil makes me feel so old.'

'But you're not old,' he countered, shyly gallant.

'Too old for the likes of you,' she warned, weary of over-aged boys.

Yes, but...

Yes, but...

A former hero talking it out with the next desperate man. The quality of the discussion had suffered since last she'd been engaged. And the mist was now a bona fide fog.

Aliette felt her gun. Like a shadow, Jean Petitpas felt his.

Down the street, around the corner, the wheel was going to turn again, she knew.

Through their shared despondency, she sensed he knew it too.

MARIO ON MESSAGE

Chief Inspector Nabil Zidane had parked in the boulevard, climbed the stairs into the misty labyrinth and proceeded to Position 2. A fairly straight line. But no lines were straight in the heart of this crumbling city. That was to his advantage and Nabi played to the fact. The visibility factor was too ... Turning into Rue Malbec, he sucked on the last of his Gauloise and tossed it, paused to tap a next one, lit up and continued on, in no hurry, nor trying to fool anyone. He was too tired for that. He needed this to be resolved and moved accordingly. The mist revealed a figure loitering in an unlit doorway. He had his own smoke on the go, he was gesturing at an interlocutor who likely wasn't there. It looked like Mario Bédard, and it was. That neckless cannonball head was always a dead giveaway. *Bon*, here we go.

Nabi kept walking, minding his own business.

As he passed, Mario abandoned his little game. 'Hey, Nabs.'

'*Salut*, Mario.' Nabi stopped without being asked.

Mario was indeed alone, gun trained. 'Hands slowly out of pockets. Open your coat ... '

'Of course.'

With a veteran's efficient expertise, Chief Inspector Bédard put the nose of his gun against the back of Nabi's head, removed Nabi's sidearm from its holster, stepped back out of range of a kick ... And hesitated. 'A little too easy, Nabi.' Mario was glancing at both ends of the street, once or twice toward the roofline. But the mist was growing thicker.

'Nothing's easy, Mario. Some things are just inevitable.'

'That's exactly what I was thinking.'

'That's why we work so well together.'

'And that's what this gun will say when it comes into evidence.'

'Guns don't speak, Mario.'

'This one will.' Proffering Nabi's.

'What will it say?' ·

'That some things are inevitable. That you were in the wrong place at the wrong time.'

'Mm, and you don't just mean tonight.'

'It's not personal, Nabi.'

'Nothing in our business ever is.'

'Bad politics. We all get caught.'

'You do stay on message, Mario, I'll give you that.'

'Have to. Too much at stake these days. Can't walk around spouting any old thing. Have to be definite. People need certainty … No offence, but you never really got that.'

'I got the job. And I do it. My numbers?... I mean, if it matters.'

'I've got a majority, Nabi. Always have had. Shit, even Vincent had a majority, when you take it apart. But, *voilà*: bad politics—and now look where we are.'

'Right. And so where's Vincent?'

'Vincent is expecting you at Position 2, as agreed.' With a soft nudge of a hard barrel in the small of Nabi's back, Mario commanded, 'Let's go.'

Nabi walked, Mario followed.

- 60 -

ONE GIRL'S LOYALTY ISSUES

Qu'est-que c'est cette histoire de fou? Which translates literally as: What is this crazy story? More generally as: What the hell is happening here? Virginie was close by, perhaps sensed by the bitchy blonde with the gun, but unseen unless she wanted to be. Her only bit of control.

Oh yes: and the gun in her hand. Safety off!

And if I want to put a bullet through my own head?

Well!... But it's the same drill, ma petite. Safety off—or no result.

Virginie knew she was not far from that grim place. She'd been there before: A miserable nine-year-old, trying to get lost in the streets but failing. Again two years ago on her fourteenth birthday. She put her hand up her sleeve and ran a finger down the row of scars on her inner arm, down to the hand that held the gun. *Oh yes*, here she was again. From child to almost-woman, Virginie recognized the feeling. Elf had gone. So was the anger she always needed. Precious anger had snuck away while she had dithered. Too much thinking. Now Virginie's only friend was despair, which is no friend at all.

She followed them, silent, sad, clueless and outnumbered, as always, watching the blonde bitch and her feckless father, like pals, the two of them murmuring away, planning something.

What? Who was leading? Jean Petitpas was a long step ahead, but the blonde had a gun.

But Virginie knew better than anyone how Jean would say anything to score a point. She had watched him do a number on her mother too many times, she had been the brunt of it herself since before she could understand his useless words. If that woman knew the pain the man could cause without a thought for anything but his momentary whim, she'd run the other way.

Or shoot him.

But they chatted away and continued on.

Virginie could not fathom it. She could not see what good could come of it. They had lost sight of the man they were following. Gabrielle had lost sight of *them*. Virginie had watched Gabrielle pass, then take a wrong direction. Who was the man from the big house on the boulevard? Adults were not honest with each other, they always had to win.

If Gabrielle disappeared, Virginie wouldn't cry.

She cared even less about the blonde woman ...

It was Jean Petitpas. Virginie was caught in a bind, hating her papa, and so hating the feeling of hoping her papa would win ... hoping he'd be safe? Virgnie knew she was having what Gabrielle would call loyalty issues, and falling into despair.

Were they going to kill her mother? Put her out of her pain? How could she hope for that?

... My pathetic mother!

Virginie's scattered thinking was shattered by a crack. She froze.

Out ahead, her father and the blonde froze too. Then two more cracks.

By now Virginie knew the sound of a gunshot. She clutched her gut.

The world stopped. *Oh, Mother* ...

- 61 -

LUCKY FOR THE FOG

But it wasn't Virginie's mother.

Gabrielle Gravel had watched the short man with the round head walk right past her, cross the boulevard and disappear down Rue Malbec. She had taken her shoes off and moved closer. She stood in stocking feet, studying the gun. There was no switch indicating ON or OFF. But it was just a machine. As the man who'd been kicking Vincent moved away from the shop door, she grasped it and recalled bits of what Vincent had explained so dryly during their first sessions. She hoped it was ready. Her feet were soaked and cold, but she was soundless, and lucky for the fog. She clutched the gun with both hands. Vincent had said something about aiming at the feet because the gun would fly high with the force of the explosion.

Gabrielle did this as she stepped through the fog, pulled hard, and fired. At his feet.

The flower shop window shattered.

The man dropped on his belly. His gun went sliding. He jumped to his feet and ran to fetch it. Gabrielle fired again. She saw him clutch reflexively at his stomach and fall. But he recovered his gun. She fired again. And again ... advancing, no idea how many rounds might be available, but with the knowledge that she was enjoying the power of it, the echoes spreading through the night. Gabrielle Gravel was a professional, acutely aware of her every thought and feeling.

And she knew this man. 'Are you going to die?' She stood over Julien Lesouple. His eyes were exuding pain. She told him, 'Pain's an illusion too. I told Vincent, he'll survive. I told your Marie, and she believed me. Luckily. We worked on it, now she's fine, whether you believe it or not. She has a new boyfriend, by the way.'

Lesouple croaked, 'Call someone. Please?'

'I don't own a portable phone... Perhaps Vincent has his.'

'Wait!...Use mine...in my pocket...here.' He struggled but couldn't find it.

And she left him.

Huddled like a beaten dog in the doorway of the flower shop, Vincent Spanghero determined he had been about a head's length from being decapitated by a wall-sized shard of glass. He took it in stride. When Gabrielle Gravel came through the fog, it made perfect sense.

There was the pungent billowing of funeral lilies escaping from the broken window, marrying with the humid brume. There were disparate cracks of more gunplay somewhere close by. One, two streets away, it was hard to tell. They both scanned the foggy darkness above.

Gabrielle spoke first. 'I thought that was me, reverberating.'

'Nabi and Mario, no doubt. I wonder who will win.'

'I should call *Urgences* but I don't have a phone... I think I've cut my feet.'

Gabrielle did not believe in cellphones. Following her example, Vincent had long since thrown his away. No matter. It would be safer to use the phone in the store, in the event they decided to leave. Was Gabrielle up for climbing in through the rain of glass?

Of course she was. Stowing the gun, pulling her shoes from her coat pocket, wincing as she put them on. 'Wait here,' Gabrielle commanded. She covered her head with her coat and went in.

'Sure.' This was exactly where he was supposed to be. Position 2.

- 62 -

GUT REACTIONS

Jean Petitpas marched through the fog with this woman called
Aliette. Why were they going to his mother's tomb? His sense
of a mission had been stood on its head. She was not the woman
he imagined. She knew too much about him. Her story of the
overweight man confused him. What was she talking about? She
had her gun, he had his, but was he brave enough to kill? He had
to be. For once, Jean had to prove the truth of who he saw himself
to be.

She said, 'If only— ' A quick crack in the air stopped her.

Instinct froze them. She looked up, around … into the fog. Jean
looked at her and knew it was the sound of a gunshot somewhere
near.

Total silence. A gun discharged in the vicinity quashes all
ambient sound.

Call it spiritual physics.

Another shot. Then another …

'*Allez*! … Let's go!' she whispered.

'Where?'

'Shush! Be brave … please.'

The plea stung. Jean nodded a promise. They moved cautiously
around the corner.

And met two men.

He looked at her. She looked stunned. Jean's gut turned once.
He knew this was it.

Aliette Nouvelle said, 'Mario … Nabi. *Bonsoir?*' What else was
she supposed to say?

Nabi Zidane nodded. Simultaneously shook his head. Hi … Now
just keep walking.

A careful step behind him, Mario Bédard held her eyes. 'Stop right there, Aliette… And your friend.'

My friend? Grabbing Jean Petitpas by the sleeve, she obeyed.

Wrong sleeve. Jean Petitpas pulled his gun. 'Oh, Jean…'

Mario shot him in the gut. His gun discharged as he fell.

A moment of silence: empty. Another blank space in the world created by a gun.

Then Nabi said, 'Great shot, Mario. Fucking good. Lucky you're here.'

Mario waved the gun. 'Your shot, Nabi. Your piece, man, not mine.' Adding, 'It'll work.'

Aliette was kneeling, obeying a gut reaction. 'Jean…' Crack: Another gun shot, somewhere behind her. She felt the bullet go past.

'*Merde!*' Mario Bédard was hit. His hip? He fired back, twice, before collapsing in the street.

Nabi flattened himself on the pavement as two more shots were returned… to no effect. Mario returned two more and rolled according to the training, uttering oaths against the pain. A third shot came back. Aliette was holding the hand of Jean Petitpas, unable to roll anywhere. Then: click… click… click. The sound of an empty gun. Everyone heard it. A girl's voice: '*Bordel!*' Mario rolled into a prone shooting position and fired into the fog. Two more shots came back. The gun was blown from Mario's hand. He crawled to retrieve it, in pain, labouring, big mess, nothing to lose.

A figure stepped into view, not a girl, his gun trained on Mario. 'Don't move, Mario,' Magistrate Sergio Regarri commanded in a voice Chief Inspector Aliette Nouvelle had not yet heard. Mario obeyed. Sergio stepped forward, kicked Mario's gun to the far side of the street. Or Nabi's? Aliette's brain was still in lock-down as Sergio barked, 'Stop where you are!'

But Virginie Petitpas came running, ignoring the order, ignoring his gun.

Aliette screamed something at Sergio, but it was cut short in the sound of another shot. But it was a warning shot and it was ignored and the large, reeking girl charged forward and pushed her aside with one violent, perfunctory shove. The inspector was on her ass, backing away, still trying to process the moment as, kneeling, taking her rightful place, Virginie gathered her papa into her quaking arms.

Aliette's gun was still inside her coat. As usual.

Just not made for this, Inspector. Mm?

- 63 -

EMMA AT THE GATE

Emma Petitpas née Sylvestre was sitting on her mother's tomb. Jean's mother was just there. The two families had always been close, even in death they were close, and this had created a safe feeling, an abiding sense that this was meant to be. Petitpas Collectibles had been a city mainstay for more than a hundred years, all the best families had accounts there, Madame was Mama's dear friend, and Jean and Emma never really had a say. Then her mother died and Jean's mother died and Em found herself alone with a baby in a house on the flats and the creeping realization that the shop was in trouble. Em knew nothing of business, but she could see the gap between her husband's big dreams and the dust in the shop window. Jean insisted things were fine, would soon be a hundred times better, all she had to do was keep house and raise their child.

Emma worried for ten years, then started screaming. At Jean, too many times unfaithful and now out in the streets in the middle of the night going through the neighbours' garbage 'looking for inventory.' At Virginie, who was thirteen and six feet tall, growing angry at the dissonance in Emma's kitchen, not doing well. At the pain in her teeth that was constant now, which Jean regretted they hadn't the money to fix.

… Virginie got so angry that Emma could not fix the pain inside her teeth.

Emma was losing her mind in a cycle of pain, pain killers and television. And worry. Desperate, she took the train to Montpellier to have her teeth fixed gratis at the university, where four pairs of student hands tried but it went wrong. Desperate, Emma sent away to the 3Suisses catalogue for matching coats, his and hers for Jean and Emma. Then, desperate, she stumbled into the police station looking for Virginie and fell down.

'Anxiety,' said Gabrielle after they left Em with her. There was nothing to be ashamed of, it was happening everywhere. Not to worry, they would rebuild the woman she had been.

Not to worry? Emma thought (dimly) that might have been a joke.

And who was the woman she had been? Emma was a blank.

When Gabrielle put a sandbox down in front of her, Emma saw mirages reverberating with pain. She could not conceive of playing dress-up, or having a 'dialogue' with an empty chair.

So Gabrielle (who was not immune to desperation either, Emma sensed it sooner than you might imagine) went in a different direction. 'Something new. What have we got to lose?'

Losing Jean and Virginie forever. That was what.

...Something new had gone on too long. Now Emma was sitting on her mother's tomb, listening to the shooting in the streets beyond the gate, contemplating the inevitable. Sooner or later, Virginie would be hit. That would be the end of everything. Emma saw it all so surely, from a place removed, as if from heaven. Though heaven was surely out of the question now.

But it was calm here. Her newfound clarity had come slowly through the pain.

'Did you have an episode, Em?' Gabrielle asked, with a gentleness that could penetrate.

It was such a story-like word. An episode like on the *télé*? Emma used to watch so much *télé* with Virginie, waiting for Jean, hoping against hope to get lost inside an episode of this or that.

'Is it Madame Nouvelle? Was it her gun? Can you tell me? *Ma pauvre...*'

My poor guinea pig? Emma had stolen glances at Gabrielle's pages. The plan to reconstruct her deconstructed family—she knew it was up to her. It always had been, after all, and she had tried. And did she have a choice?

With mamas linked through generations, had Emma ever had a choice?

...You have to be proactive, Em.

Yes, yes, yes, but there in the waiting room it was always two against one and Emma did not have the strength to be proactive. She did not know *how*. She was helpless, a sitting duck, worse than useless in her role at the reception desk, an easy target for Virginie, a pathetic, uninspiring image of womanhood for Jean. Gabrielle said, 'It gets it out in the open, Em, we'll work through it in our family sessions, it will get better, you'll see.'

It was worse in the family sessions: two against one plus Gabrielle, watching, saying useless things Jean and Virginie ignored. It crushed her, week in, week out...

But Gabrielle insisted: even when nobody loves us we have to try.

So Emma tried.

Virginie refused to budge, not a single millimetre. Hatred, hatred, hatred. And worse than that, contempt. Rude, loud, violent... and disgusting, so unclean. Fuck off, they're my friends!

Those 'friends' were turning her child into an animal.

Jean sat there. All he wanted to talk about was divorce.

Gabrielle kept saying, 'We have to do this properly, Em. It will take some time.'

Time in the waiting room waiting for *results*, lost in anxiety, acting like a maniac in front of strangers, cowering in front of her raging child, stuck like a stubborn stone in the presence of her husband, who could not be forgiven, who could not be divorced, who was the only man she'd ever slept with and was still the most beautiful she'd ever seen? No. It wasn't working.

Jean was never coming back, nothing in Gabrielle's scheme could ever make that happen. Madame Nouvelle had proved it. That blonde with the gun had demonstrated beyond doubt that Jean's magpie heart would never resist the next bright thing.

The blonde with the gun had made it deadly clear that Virginie had turned toward the fatal.

Em had tried and failed in Gabrielle's waiting room. Failed absolutely.

Well, Gabrielle, as a matter of fact, I've had five episodes, three with a knife, two with a gun... Should she spill it out? Explain it? Watch Gabrielle note it down?

Emma couldn't bear being the object of another note. She had cleaned up after Jean and come straight here—where it was starting to feel like home. Cold, lonely, but calm, blessedly calm. And where the pain in her mouth subsided. And this clarity.

Her husband was a lost cause. Mama could sit in heaven disapproving, but there was nothing to be done with Jean ... But Em would try again to save her daughter. A mother has to try.

Emma knew what she had done. And would again. If this was hell, so be it.

Proactive? It was during the long Christmas holiday, three weeks alone, three weeks in limbo ('Call if you need me, Em.'), that Emma first went out into the night. The instinct to rescue Virginie overwhelmed her. She knew now that a sterile room and abstract words would never get through. Emma knew she had to go to where Virginie was and demonstrate some strength. And there was, to be sure, the strategic calculation: if I can do this, Jean will see. And love me.

She brought a knife. A horrible thing, sharp and pointed. Another instinct: protect yourself, or how can you protect your child? She walked into Petitpas Collectibles, past the vaguely pretty face of whoever she was, and took the knife that looked most like the one that she might need. Whatever else, she was Emma Petitpas, it was her knife too, her mother had worked long and hard (proactive!) to make sure of that. 'Of course you'll marry Jean!' Yes, Mama ... and now I'll save my child. Knife clutched to her breast, Em had walked, searching, terrified, the pressure intense, as if in a suspended state of shock at how her feet kept moving, at how instinct pushed her forward, almost delirious under the weight of her fear. But having to at least try. That first night she did not succeed, but she didn't die, so Emma went out again. Then again.

Till that night in frigid late January: now beginning to understand how they lived, following traces of Virginie to an abandoned house in a neglected street. The drunk appeared from nowhere as Emma stood at the door, shaking, willing herself to go through. Bothering her, distracting her from what she needed to do. Scaring her. She reacted, hit at him with the knife. Several times.

He fell at her feet. Gazing down at him, breathless, there had been a popping sensation in her head, like in her ear after a difficult bout of sinus. Like a miracle … like suddenly stepping out of anxiety's back door? There was clarity. This unexpected calm. The aching in her mouth had stopped. She'd looked down at him with an awful clarity as he gurgled blood and died. When Emma walked away from it, she'd felt herself floating like an angel through the streets.

It didn't last, was barely remembered …

'Did you have some kind of episode last night, Em?'

Emma didn't know. But she did. She had made a step toward a strength she needed if she was going to find and save poor Virginie. Gabrielle fussed and rubbed her shoulders. Emma sat there numb and weeping, and then went out again, found the boy picking through garbage behind the bistro, speaking gibberish like the puppet who cooked soup on the show Virginie used to love.

Emma remembered how they loved to watch together in the morning and laugh and laugh.

'Have you seen Virginie?'

But the boy spoke gibberish and Emma's anger boiled over. She lashed out.

Floated away …

Some lost days later: 'Virginie?' Emma Petitpas found herself in the foul-smelling entrance to the rotting church, inching toward a group of dissolute creatures lolling on the floor, petrified of coming face to face with Virginie but knowing that she had to—Emma knew coming face to face and proving her strength with all of them watching would be the only way … when a man walks in looking for someone called Vincent. Maybe it was his friend or his brother, *or his father*? Before thinking (because she had stopped thinking) Emma blurted, 'We had a Vincent at PsychoDynamo,' and the man grabbed her by the collar, too harsh, too mean, demanding to know more. She had lost her mind with fear, and flailed. The knife got stuck, and such a mess, and the gun was on the floor.

And there she was, as if beside herself, so calm as she picked it up and put it in her pocket.

Killing was like a drug—with devastating effects when it finally left her system. Emma bore the residual pain and continued to go out. She had to. It *was* like a drug. And it felt more useful than sitting in the waiting room like a shaking leaf.

Emma learned the kids came here, to the tombs. She was surprised by her ability to climb the wall—she could not remember ever doing such a thing. She never imagined holding a gun. And Emma knew, in the flicker of an adolescent's lying eyes, that the boy at the cemetery wall knew Virginie and exactly where she was. But plead as she might, he wouldn't tell her. Rude and stubborn and just plain mean, he pushed her past the brink. The gun was better than the knife. No touching. Touching them was the worst part.

Then Friday night made five. That poor girl—so angry. But Em was far past fear by then and flew straight at her with the gun.

Voilà. Five episodes for Gabrielle to enter in her notes.

And tonight: still more shooting out in the streets. Emma nodded at her mother. Virginie needs me. My child needs me. She patted the cold damp stone containing the woman who had brought her into this awful world and matched her with a hopeless man, then lifted the clump of dead flowers, soil and all, from the cracking plastic pot. The gun was in a shopping bag from Galeries Lafayette. Emma took the bag, replaced the flowers and headed for the cemetery gate. Feeling calm. Feeling better. Cured? Who knew? It was for Gabrielle to decree. But Emma felt better. She thought it might be the gun. The gun makes everything simpler, thought Em, strolling the sombre lanes of the dead, like she was walking home from shopping. Home to watch TV.

Approaching the cemetery gate, it seemed correct that Gabrielle would be there on the other side, standing with a man by an *Urgences* ambulance. Its lights were flashing. Emma was thinking they were here for her. Gabrielle had got it so wrong, but Gabrielle cared.

Gabrielle spoke gently through the gate, 'Emma? What are you doing? Are you all right?'

…Emma Petitpas smiles a *bonsoir* for Gabrielle, removes the gun from the shopping bag. Clean, heavy, inevitable. She has killed two people with it. It's not that difficult. It's mostly luck, of a kind. Were there any more bullets? You needed bullets. Oblivious to the voices screaming at her on the far side of the gate, Emma peered into the barrel and clicked the trigger, to make sure.

LAST PERSON IN THE WORLD

Patrol cars and medic wagons and media vans filled the square in front of the cemetery gate, motors idling, vehicle and camera lights flashing ceaselessly, creating a humming, gaseous shadow show of blue and orange and white against the canopy of mist. Uniforms with high-powered lamps passed back and forth, searching the paving for shells and whatever else might pertain. Others lined the barriers, advising people to go home. Annelise Duflot's first unit had set up in Rue Malbec. She had organized a second team in front of the flower shop. For efficiency's sake—both criminal and medical—she had ordered that all medical situations in Rue Malbec be transported here. There was an uncomfortable delay while they awaited a key to the gate, while Emma Petitpas lay there and a crowd watched ghoulishly and Gabrielle Gravel was seen to cry.

Virginie Petitpas had ridden over from Rue Malbec in the back of the medic wagon with her father, under guard. When she realized it was her mother on the other side of the gate, hell erupted. She broke free of her guard and crashed through the door of the wagon. It had taken three uniforms to haul her down as she attempted to scale the wall, snorting, hyperventilating, a frantic animal in leather and denim with her pale hips exposed. She had momentarily broken free again and rushed at Gabrielle Gravel—who ran. All present were shocked silent by the brute fury of the girl—inarticulate; just a tragic wailing scream that went on and on till, brought down a second time, Annelise put a needle in her buttock and she grew quiet. Virginie could now be seen slumped in the wagon, sedated but conscious, holding her father's hand. He was still alive. A pair of uniforms were standing by. Vincent Spanghero was in another wagon, head bandaged, but he was sitting and appeared to be arguing heatedly with Chief City Investigator Hugues Monty. Mario Bédard was strapped in another, being treated, while two of Hugues's people waited at the door. No one was waiting by the medic wagon containing Julien Lesouple.

The crowd was pushed back. A Ville de Béziers car arrived and the gate was opened.

Annelise was kneeling by the body conducting a rudimentary exam. Even obvious suicides require the *légiste*. Released from preliminary questioning, Aliette joined Sergio Regarri where he stood at a polite remove contemplating the figure sprawled on the wet pavement, the gun lying by her dead hand. It was a too-familiar sight, the gloomy backdrop did nothing to accentuate yet another act of self-annihilation.

Aliette said to Sergio, 'That will be Tropéano's gun, I'm sure of it.'

Sergio said to Aliette, 'Could you please stop being so sure? Let's just wait for IJ, can't we?'

Rather than argue—not here, not now, please—Aliette breathed and reached for his hand.

Nabi Zidane ambled over and joined them. He looked at the victim with the same jaundiced professional glance. 'I was talking to her just this afternoon.'

It was Sergio who said, 'We think that's probably Tropéano's gun.'

Nabi asked, 'Do we have any clue?'

'She's the wife of the guy who was with me,' Aliette informed him. 'He wanted a divorce.'

'Right,' grunted Nabi. That explained much to a veteran cop.

'She must have had an episode,' muttered Gabrielle Gravel, stepping into the dim glow of the cemetery entrance. She had regained her composure. She was available if they needed her.

'The girl's their kid,' added Aliette, somewhat superfluously.

'The girl smells bad,' said Nabi.

There was nothing to say to that. They stood aside as the hearse backed in.

Gabrielle said, 'She's the last person in this world who should have access to a gun.'

No response there, either. A lot of non sequiturs in the aftermath of something like this.

Gabrielle looked at Aliette ... and at Sergio, and nodded. As if she understood. As if she approved. Then she drifted back toward the wagon where they were questioning Vincent.

Sergio put an arm around Aliette. She did not resist. She had decided to forgive his incursions. 'You surprised me,' she murmured. 'You surprised everyone. But your gun. I didn't know.'

'Same as yours,' shrugged Sergio. 'We don't advertise. It's a precaution. Some of the people we sometimes have to go after—before you do?'

'Didn't surprise *me*.' Nabi sniffed. 'Right on time.'

Sergio shed light. 'Nabi came by. Came up the stairs and knocked on the door. Asked for you, actually. You were at your appointment. Got me instead. Pretty basic plan.'

'I'm proud of you.' At that moment Aliette wanted to kiss him, but refrained.

'I hope so,' said Nabi, leaving them, '*Excuse...*' Hugues's guys were wanting another word.

Aliette and Sergio remained there, waiting with Emma Petitpas as Annelise Duflot signed forms. Then a body bag was produced and the morgue guys lifted Emma in and zipped it up.

- 63 -

INVENTORY

The gun found beside Emma Petitpas was the service arm assigned to slain Inspector Pierre Tropéano. The forensics thread to the knife (which included Ex-Inspector Vincent Spanghero's claim that he had thrown it out) made it clear (or clear enough) that she was the killer.

The gun that shopkeeper Jean Petitpas claimed to have purchased from an unknown vendor was found to be the sidearm assigned to the late Inspector Menaud Rhéaume, who had gone down a year before, during a botched operation led by ex-Inspector Spanghero. Small world.

The gun surrendered by psychologist Gabrielle Gravel had been assigned to ex-Inspector Vincent Spanghero. It had disappeared when he had, some eight months ago. Gravel said she had relieved Spanghero of his gun after finding both him and Chief Inspector Lesouple in a very bad way. She claimed to have been on her way home from her place of work at the time. She had heard shots and the sounds of a man in pain. She had removed her shoes and gone to see.

Spanghero admitted to keeping his gun—'one last thing to connect me to my former life.' He had taken it with him when he'd gone out after contacting Chief Inspector Zidane. 'Of course I did. It's getting dangerous out there.'

Lesouple's gun had not been fired. Spanghero's had, several times. All the recovered shells matched the batch assigned to him a year before, including the shell from the round in Lesouple. Spanghero described being ambushed and beaten by his former colleagues. He said they'd taken his gun and tossed it on the road. When Chief Inspector Bédard left to intecept Chief Inspector Zidane, Chief

Inspector Lesouple had started in on him again, '...very angry, like hysterical.' Spanghero said he had momentarily retrieved his gun as he rolled away from Lesouple's kicks but was instantly engaged in a close-quartered struggle for possession of it and Lesouple got control of the trigger. Several rounds had been fired into the air, one shattered the shop window. Spanghero managed to turn the barrel back at his assailant at the decisive moment. Lesouple went down, Spanghero recovered his gun. The psychologist had appeared some moments later. Chief Inspector Bédard said, 'We all know Vincent's gun. You were allowed to marvel at the work, but never touch. You know?...some guys get personally attached. I don't know if that's normal, but it's part of how we live... We were looking for Inspector Tropéano's gun. Vincent's gun was not the one we needed. Perhaps we were careless in our zeal to uncover Tropéano's. Obviously Julien got caught in a mistake. But I was not there for that part of it. I can say that Vincent had provoked him. I thought he'd got control of himself.' Spanghero's wounds attested to a beating. The hands of Lesouple confirmed it. They were all over Spanghero's gun. Bédard's were clean in this regard. In the absence of Lesouple, Spanghero's testimony was accepted.

Chief Inspector Bédard's sidearm had not been fired. The gun found beside him on the paving in Rue Malbec was that assigned to Chief Inspector Zidane. Bédard admitted to relieving Zidane of his sidearm when he encountered him in the street. 'For his own safety. Nabi was excluded from involvement in the affair because of his problematic relationship with Vincent. Of course I *had* my gun.' Accused of shooting Jean Petitpas point blank with Zidane's weapon, Bédard claimed, 'I must have got mine and his confused in the heat of the moment. I mean, crazy people in the streets with guns? A guy draws on you out of the blue from four steps away, you grab the first piece available, no?'

Chief Inspector Fratticelli confirmed Bédard's main concern was Zidane's wellbeing.

Zidane could refute, but not disprove. Nor could Chief Inspector Nouvelle.

Ex-Inspector Spanghero was not asked for his thoughts regarding the incident in Rue Malbec. When asked to comment on any discord between Chief Inspectors Bédard and Zidane, he said, 'That's not my problem any more.'

Chief Inspector Nouvelle said she'd been returning from her appointment with Gabrielle Gravel and had encountered Jean Petitpas by chance. They knew each other in passing from the waiting room at the psychologist's. He claimed to have been searching for his estranged daughter. He was clearly agitated. She described accompanying him to his shop, where he had secured a gun. No, she had not disclosed her profession to Monsieur Petitpas. She was accompanying him out of concern for an at-risk child. They'd spent the time before the fateful encounter in Rue Malbec looking for the girl. She said the events in Rue Malbec happened too quickly for her to react. Her surrendered gun showed signs of recent use, though no shells from her allotted batch were found in the street. Her claim that she had been at the range that afternoon was confirmed by a technician, who added (extraneously) that she badly needed practice. She admitted to breaking the rules viz. carrying her weapon off duty, but noted that her gun was central to her assigned therapeutic program and that carrying it through the streets alone at night was a form of the aforementioned need for practice. Her story was accepted.

It was noted that many officers carried their service arms outside of working hours, and it was not the biggest crime.

Psychologist Gabrielle Gravel confirmed Nouvelle's statements as to Jean Petitpas's state of mind that night—'he threw up on my floor!'—and his daughter's increasingly precarious status. She noted that what her clients did outside their time in her office was not her concern or responsibility. When presented with the series of found notes, she said they were like Emma's blocky printing, only round. As for their meaning, she said she wished Emma had been able to open up and speak her mind, but these things could never be forced.

Two expert-witness psychiatrists agreed.

Jean Petitpas could barely communicate. His spinal column was shattered. He was too weak to be interviewed to any useful effect. The doctors said recovery would take several years.

Virginie Petitpas, properly bathed and on a calming medication, claimed she'd been looking for her mother; she said her mother had been in a state of severe distress for several weeks. She said they were 'not exactly friends,' but she cared and was worried. She blamed psychologist Gabrielle Gravel for her mother's woeful state of mind. She stopped short of accusing Chief Inspector Nouvelle of same, but said the inspector's presence in the waiting room had made 'a bad situation worse.' When one of the interviewing panel mused that Virginie had a very guilty air about her, she replied that she'd been feeling guilty all her life and gave a heartbreakingly open-ended shrug. They did not show Virginie her mother's notes.

Chief Inspector Nouvelle replied that she was only complying with the order from Division to attend at PsychoDynamo. She wished Virginie well. Psychologist Gravel said Virginie Petitpas was dealing with a range of issues including aggression, bad judgement and 'magical thinking' flowing from childhood trauma within a seriously dysfunctional household beset by fear and false expectations—'magical thinking within the so-called adult sphere,' she added. A social worker confirmed this, but noted Virgnie complied with the hospital rules and seemed genuinely attentive where it came to passing time at the bedside of her seriously damaged father.

Virginie revealed that the gun she surrendered had been taken from the body a drug dealer known to have been murdered the previous autumn in a matter that remained unsolved. Her friend Fanny had taken it from his pocket, with his cash. When Fanny, in turn, became victim number five during a brief gun battle in the cemetery, her friend Elf (also deceased; unrelated causes) had taken it from Fanny's hand. He'd later given it to Virginie. She'd been carrying it for protection. Coming upon the scene in Rue Malbec, she had wanted to help her father. The gun, a Colt Series 80, was not registered in France. It proved impossible to trace in America.

Magistrate Sergio Regarri admitted to packing his sidearm as assurance in responding to Chief Inspector Zidane's request for a witness to his meeting with Vincent Spanghero. He noted that assessing Spanghero's status in the context of the serial killings was his specific if unofficial mandate and that it would have been irresponsible to go to such a rendezvous unarmed.

Chief City Investigator Monty confirmed the unofficial hunt for Spanghero, based on events surrounding his leaving the PJ force. Monty noted that the PJ force was not a part of it.

Challenged in that regard, Chief Inspector Bédard said, 'But Hugues was getting nowhere and don't let him tell you different. Us, we know Vincent, we know Nabi, the same as we knew poor Pierre and poor Menaud. You do what you want with that. A serial killer is obviously a very serious matter, and right or wrong, Vincent was in the frame. To our mind, a cop killer is worse. We intercepted Vincent, and we believed we had a chance to clear it up. If Julien and I leaned on Vincent a little, it was because Vincent was not being helpful. Like I say, we know this man.' He added, 'I regret the loss of Julien. But we were only concerned with looking after our own. Things like this affect us all.' Chief Inspector Fratticelli confirmed Bédard's sentiments.

Chief Inspector Zidane could refute, but not disprove. Nor could Chief Inspector Nouvelle.

Chief Inspector Zidane noted that Vincent Spanghero's actions were in self defence. On behalf of the police, he regretted Ex-Inspector Spanghero's duress as a private citizen. Spanghero only requested that the gold-plated monogram be removed from the handle of his assigned gun and returned to him. He repeated, 'One last thing to connect me to my former life?'

Spanghero's wife was brought into it. She said her husband was not the man she married, she hardly recognized him, physically or emotionally. 'He talks nonsense.' She was not sure she wanted her children to see him. She was considering bringing an action against Gabrielle Gravel.

Gabrielle Gravel confirmed, 'Vincent Spanghero is a different man now, I assure you.'

But, cleared of all gun-related charges, Spanghero's personal status was not relevant.

The official story: One Judicial Police officer wounded, one killed in the dramatic end to a killing spree fuelled by domestic breakdown. Unofficially it was a mess, but it was a police mess and it was sorted out behind closed doors, as is usually the case when police are pitted against each other. What matters is that the status quo held, such as it was.

Without a clear target within the police, the media turned its focus on dysfunctional families, societal breakdown, the rise in weapons consciousness. The Petitpas family became another object lesson, eventually a clinical reference point, ultimately a political trope exploited on both left and right.

EPILOGUE

The status quo is all we have until it changes. The police can't change it, only reflect it. And live with it. The status quo meant Nabi Zidane regained control of his Béziers unit, if not universal respect amongst the ranks of the regional Police Judiciaire. It meant Mario Bédard would remain an ugly fact of life. There were administrative changes, but those won't change your soul. While Montpellier looked into Julien Lesouple's operational efficiencies and pondered more structural adjustments, Chief Inspectors Fratticelli and Nouvelle were charged with divvying up responsibility for Lesouple's patch... No, if not for the status quo, irony would not exist. But Liza was the realistic sort and and they worked it out with a minimum of fuss. Though one could not help note she was sounding a bit subdued. On the outs with Mario? Who would be surprised?

In exchange for all files attached to a case leading to a certain ambiguously charted hillside, Aliette willingly gave sad Liza poor Julien's four inspectors. There was a major job that needed doing without delay and she wanted no more inter-jurisdictional disputes getting in the way.

With the enlargement of the Saint-Brin territory, Chief Inspector Nouvelle received a memo. Two junior inspectors were being assigned and would report within the month. The request to have Mathilde Lahi's secretarial services exclusively for her needs was approved. Sorting out space issues on the second floor at the Mairie would be her responsibility, but an increased budget for a larger unit would certainly help in that regard. Aliette put Mathilde in charge.

As for ongoing business:

The murder of the cheese producer's wife ended in a first-degree conviction—*assassinat*, with recognition that it was her first offence.

Justine Péraud would spend the next fifteen years in prison, where she would use her acquired skills to develop and produce a tasty Cantal-style cheese. The Ladies (*Les Dames*), as the cheese was called, got written up in a weekend edition of *Midi-Libre*.

Fabien Fleury, the *vigneron* who hated foreigners, was turned in by his in-laws and escorted back from Spain. His daughter described a horrible old man who did not respect her Spanish husband and made awful, surely traumatizing remarks to their two 'half-breed' kids. He was convicted on the strength of the forensics on the round taken from the gypsy's skull. More irony here, in that pathologist Annelise Duflot did not like foreigners much herself... Monsieur Fleury would die in his prison cell—of a massive stroke after a night spent screaming at the Algerian inmates next door.

Coached by Inspector Henri Dardé, the three adolescent girls met with Children's Judge Claire Houde. In an environment free of parents and social workers, they collectively admitted they'd conspired to push their slutty friend into the gorge. They pleaded to be punished equally, and were. The Children's Judge commended Henri on his handling of the matter.

As for Aliette and her new gun...

Lost in the flood of grim reportage and expert opinion concerning the tragic Emma Petitpas and her dysfunctional family was a brief item on the loss of another youth to misadventure with carelessly engineered designer drugs. The good doctor Duflot quickly determined that the bad drugs that killed the street kid called Elf were the same bad drugs that killed the two kids in love being investigated at Saint-Brin. The division of Julien Lesouple's territory left the lab in the barn on the hillside unequivocally to Chief Inspector Nouvelle. Magistrate Martine Rogge immediately approved her request for an intervention. The inspector led the interventon personally, gun drawn, safety off.

'*Messieurs*... we are waiting, if you please.' No doubt the voice of Aliette Nouvelle rang different in the open hills of the Midi than it had in the cramped alleys of a mid-sized city on the Rhine. And wasn't she a little older now? But there were echoes resounding from an earlier time.

This time, when two men came out, guns blazing, she shot at both of them, with no qualms at all. One dead. The other, spitting blood, gave the police a name. Forensics revealed that neither of the hits had come from Chief Inspector Nouvelle's gun; but the obligatory inventory of rounds expended in the operation left no doubt that the inspector had participated with extreme prejudice. Forensics on the gun taken from the one who didn't die brought a match with the round taken from the dealer killed the previous autumn at the lookout on Passage Canterellettes, whence a girl named Virginie eventually secured an unregistered American pistol—and which solved that one for Hugues.

The Divisionnaire called to congratulate her on a job well done. She took that to Gabrielle Gravel. They knew each other well now. Though they would never know what each had said about the other at the enquiry, they shared the status quo like closely bonded friends. Gravel obliged Nouvelle with a good report and Nouvelle was released from the order to attend at PsychoDynamo with a promise of regular practice at the range. After signing off, Gabrielle extended her hand and smiled a certain smile. Virginal mind or otherwise, they both knew the inspector's problematic relationship with her gun would not be resolved anytime soon. When they shook hands, Gabrielle smiled again. But differently. 'You have a gorgeous man, Chief Inspector. I wish you luck with him.' Which was a lovely thing for her to say, and Aliette would have returned the compliment, but honesty had been stretched in too many different directions during their brief time together, and (in truth) her view of Gabrielle's man was probably forever skewed. Suffice to say, when Aliette left Gabrielle there were still many issues up in the air.

That's the status quo for you. No?

Passing through the waiting room, Madame Nouvelle smiled at the new girl answering Gabrielle's phone. She was young and trying hard to establish a new tone. She smiled back and waved, but she was in the middle of a call with a client and taking a note. '… *bon*, Madame Fratticelli, we'll look forward to seeing you Tuesday. But tell me. Fratticelli. Does that mean you're Italian? My great-grandfather was—' Aliette gently closed the door behind her.

Ah, well… One in, one out. She walked away from PsychoDynamo.

It stayed warm and the sun came out. Saturday, she and Sergio walked up into the hills behind Berlou. The mimosa was in bloom. No sand worth playing in between here and the beach (about a thirty-minute ride). Aliette hadn't worn her gun. From where they walked you could see the sea and it was beautiful too. When they got to their spot, she put the bag down and undid her boots. She had finished telling everything she had to tell.

'No dissociation then?' said Sergio, a smile playing on his lips.

She smiled back and laid a ready hand on the phantom space above her hip. 'Are you talking to me, *monsieur*?'

'You're saying you are essentially the same woman you always were. Still Aliette, well and true?'

'Of course.' How else could you expect the centre of the universe to be?

'It's good to know,' said Sergio, and set about preparing the blanket.

While she unpacked the lunch.

— *fin* —

NOTES

French police services operate under the auspices of the Ministry of the Interior.

The National Police provide policing services to cities and larger regional towns. They have both a corps of 'uniforms' and plain-clothes investigators.

The *Gendarmerie* is mainly represented by uniformed cops. It provides basic policing services to smaller centres and rural areas. In 1950, the *Gendarmerie* was placed under the direct authority of the Ministry of Defence, and their ranks flowed from the military. In 2009, management of the *Gendarmerie* was transferred to the Ministry of Interior. In terms of organizational 'culture' the *gendarmes* are still a breed apart from the uniforms in the big cities.

The Judicial Police (*Police Judiciaire*) are brought into either jurisdiction to investigate so-called 'serious crimes.' PJ investigators are trained specifically. They are all plain-clothed.

The Municipal Police serve mayors and town councils, carrying out duties required for crime prevention, public order, security, and public safety. This includes traffic tickets, crowd control, disaster measures coordination, etc.

The *Procureur* ('Proc') is the Public Prosecutor. Operating under the Ministry of Justice, the Proc oversees and controls judicial inquiries:
- supervising investigations (either directly or through assigned instructing magistrates);
- being in charge in the co-ordination of the services involved; and
- deciding which service will be responsible for inquiries. (If not PJ, it might be Customs, etc.)

Without being police officers themselves, the prosecutors and their deputies (substitutes) have all the powers of a judicial police officers. Even if they do not use these powers frequently, they can decide to personally take part in investigation.

Instructing Judge and Magistrate are interchangeable terms. Representing the court (the *Proc*), they act as first-line instruction (think 'refereeing') for police officers conducting investigations. They also can and do go into the field and conduct investigations.

The *Légiste* is the Medical Examiner at a crime scene, also doubling (here) as the pathologist.

A psychologist is a *psychologue*; the abbreviation is *psy*. For either, say psy as 'see' and pronounce the p in front of it (as in: psst! there's a bug in your beer!) *comme ça*: p-see.

As with some place names and geographical configuration, I have taken some liberties with the administrative structure outlined above.

—JB

OTHER BOOKS IN THIS SERIES

Jacques Normand, France's Public Enemy Number One, escaped from prison over ten years ago. But the Commissaire is convinced that the outlaw is alive. Find him, he commands Inspector Aliette Nouvelle.

"This book dropped into my lap and I was smitten: interesting premise, fascinating central character and good writing. Poetic images, film stills and literary writing, none out of place." — *The Globe and Mail*

Inspector Nouvelle returns to solve the case of the murder of a Marilyn Monroe look-alike in a French brothel.

"*All Pure Souls* is definitely not a dimestore detective novel. The writing is good and the dialogue is sharp ... " — *Montreal Review of Books*

When the ex-lovers of a former schoolteacher start dying at an alarming rate, Inspector Aliette Nouvelle is drawn into the investigation, not least because her boss is also in jeopardy.

"The writing may feel impressionistic but the climax is as threatening as they come." — *Hamilton Spectator*

Inspector Nouvelle's investigation into the murder of a Basel art gallery security guard and an unknown masterpiece uncovers a cross-border art fraud conspiracy. She throws herself into the case, using work as an excuse to get some distance from her faltering relationship with Commissaire Claude Néon.

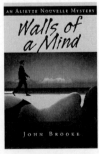

After a difficult breakup with Claude Neon, Inspector Aliette Nouvelle has received a transfer to Saint-Brin, a sleepy wine-producing town in the south of France. When the scion of an old wine-producing family is shot dead on the beach, it appears to be a politically motivated murder. It turns out to be anything but.

About the Author

John Brooke became fascinated by criminality and police work listening to the courtroom stories and observations of his father, a long-serving judge. Although he lives in Montreal, John makes frequent trips to France for both pleasure and research. He earns a living as a freelance writer and translator, has also worked as a film and video editor as well as directed four films on modern dance. His poetry and short stories have been widely published, and in 1998 his story "The Finer Points of Apples" won him the Journey Prize. Brooke's first Inspector Aliette Nouvelle mystery, *The Voice of Aliette Nouvelle*, was published in 1999, followed by *All Pure Souls* in 2001. He took a break from Aliette with the publication of his novel *Last Days of Montreal* in 2004, but returned with her in 2011 with *Stifling Folds of Love*, *The Unknown Masterpiece* in 2012, and *Walls of a Mind* in 2013.